THE
EMERALD DIAMOND

TONY DONAGHER

authorHOUSE®

This book is dedicated to the two most important people in my life, my wife Cheryl and son Ryan. Without their support and love nothing I have done would be possible.

AuthorHouse™ UK
1663 Liberty Drive
Bloomington, IN 47403 USA
www.authorhouse.co.uk
Phone: 0800.197.4150

Published by AuthorHouse 05/04/2018

ISBN: 978-1-5462-8827-5 (sc)
ISBN: 978-1-5462-8828-2 (hc)
ISBN: 978-1-5462-8826-8 (e)

CHAPTER ONE

Dublin 2018

The Criminal Courts of Justice occupy a new, modern building at the southern end of the Phoenix Park. A lasting monument to the funds available in the Celtic Tiger years, the complex houses the Courts, which service the criminal justice needs of the Dublin Metropolitan area as well as the Central Criminal Court and the Circuit Courts for the Dublin area. The criminal courts had, until the opening of the new complex, been spread over several buildings of various states of repair throughout Dublin. The District Courts occupied some of the worst buildings, and this did nothing for the humour of those who had to work in them day after day.

The new complex was a very different story. Consisting of a five-storey, circular, glass-encased building, the impression on entering was one of space and a relaxed, unhurried environment. The courtrooms were spread on odd-numbered floors, with the lower levels reserved for the lower courts and the higher levels reserved for the Circuit courts and the Central Criminal Court. On each of the higher levels, a retaining perimeter wall separated the court entrances from the well of the building in such a way that as one looked up into the building from the ground floor, all one could see would be the occasional head looking over into the void below.

Noise levels were usually at a very modest level. On occasion, there would be some disruption, usually from the District court ground floor level but even that seemed infrequent.

Although the standard of the building had improved dramatically, there was little change in the clientele the building served.

The usual number of petty criminals, drug users and dealers, and traffic offenders occupied the ground floor. The upper floors saw a mix of

1

customers. In the recent past, an increasing number of well-dressed former bankers and property developers were regular visitors.

The lawyers servicing these customers had also seen some change with the harried, tired-looking District court practitioners seen running around, trying to make a living from legal aid work, and mixing with smartly dressed, bespoke suited solicitors from the big five firms who arrived at Court every day in a fleet of taxis bringing them from their plush offices in the IFSC or the better parts of the Dublin business area to work in what, for them, had to be a very unnatural environment.

The Barristers who plied their trade in this building varied from the freshly qualified, brimming with enthusiasm, and eager to make their mark to the seasoned veterans who looked and behaved as though they had seen and done it all, and nothing new would faze them.

The entrance to the complex was through large glass doors with airport-style security, where bags were checked in a rudimentary manner by independent contractors. On occasions, these would be supplemented by Gardaí depending on who was in the complex on the day.

This was one of those days, and as Richard Jennings made his way towards the complex, he noted the very heavy presence of armed emergency response unit Gardaí and a significantly higher number of traffic cops on duty in the area leading to the complex.

On entering the building, Jennings also noticed that the usual security personnel were in fact taking a back seat, and that uniformed Gardaí were manning the security desks and were being overly thorough in searching each bag that went through the system.

The heightened security brought inevitable delays, and as Jennings stood in line for one of the checkpoints, he was joined by a fellow solicitor who had been working the criminal courts for so long that he was considered part of it.

Cathal Flanagan had done nothing but criminal work for the whole of his career. He proudly boasted he would not know a deed of transfer if he saw one, and he certainly could not tell you what a divorce application looked like. However, his knowledge of all matters criminal was encyclopaedic. He had started at the bottom and over his career had represented every type of criminal, from the unfortunate, one-off miscreant who was in the wrong place at the wrong time to hard-headed gangland drug dealers and killers.

You would have thought such a life's work would leave a person cynical and hardened to what life could throw up. Although that was surely a part of his make-up overall, he was one of the most cheerful individuals Jennings had ever known, and he was always available to help anyone who asked.

Given this was his domain, Jennings decided to enquire as to what was the reason for the heightened security.

'Morning, Cathal. What is all this security about?'

Cathal leaned in closer and spoke in a low voice to avoid being overheard. He always enjoyed a sense of mystery. 'There is a new matter coming in this morning for first appearance which has got the whole lot of them in a terrible state. Haven't seen this much activity since the troubles back in the day in the old Bridewell.'

'Who is it, then? Who is coming in?'

'You may find this hard to believe, but even I don't know. I asked some of the lads on the way in who would normally tell me what was going on, and they all ignored me as though I had the plague. They are all in a very tense state, I must say. No doubt we will find out soon enough.'

With the security check over, the two solicitors moved towards Court One, which was the primary remand court for the Dublin area.

'What brings you here?' Flanagan enquired. 'I thought you had given up on the criminal side.'

'I have,' Jennings replied. 'Stephen Jones is off on leave, and so I agreed to cover for him today. Who is sitting, by the way?'

'You have chosen a good day to come down, then. It is your old friend O'Donovan.'

That was not the news Jennings wanted. He and O'Donovan had had a few run-ins over the years, and on occasion these had resulted in judicial reviews of the Judge's increasingly erratic decisions. The number of reviews had reached almost epidemic proportions, and it was only when he was told the State would no longer foot his legal bills on judicial reviews that the penny dropped, and some form of reason prevailed in his dealings with both suspects and the lawyers who represented them.

'I hope you have nothing contentious today, Richard. We have had a very peaceful few weeks with him, and we don't want you upsetting the apple cart.'

'Don't worry, Cathal. A few adjournments and a return for trial, and I will be gone. Even I can't annoy him over that.'

As they entered the court, they were immediately aware of the number of armed Gardaí strategically situated around the courtroom. To see armed Gardai in such large numbers was unheard of in Dublin, where the Gardaí were still unarmed in their day-to-day work. Having armed Gards in a courtroom was extremely unusual and would have required the prior consent of the President of the District court.

Whoever was warranting this level of attention was in serious trouble.

The court was full of the usual Monday crowd, and the addition of the extra Gards did nothing to ease the congestion. The first and second benches reserved for lawyers were already filled with a mix of solicitors and barristers, and that meant standing room only for Jennings and Flanagan on the side of the front benches.

The general noise in the court stopped abruptly as the court clerk rose and announced the arrival of the Judge with usual 'Silence in court' command.

O'Donovan was in his late fifties but looked a lot older. He had been a country solicitor for many years, practicing on his own in a general practice with little or no criminal work. It was ironic that after that career, on appointment to the bench, he was left to languish in the Remand Court in Dublin for the last seven years. He made no secret of the fact that he loathed the job and those who appeared before him in equal measure. It was said he had always aspired to the Circuit bench, and when it became clear that was never going to happen, he decided to make everyone else's life a misery.

His one saving grace was that he started on time and could never be accused of delaying matters. He ran his court in his own way, and if people did it not like it, their remedy lay elsewhere. The Judge greeted the assembled gathering with a cursory 'Good morning' and took his seat.

The court clerk sitting in front of him commenced proceedings with a somewhat unusual announcement.

'Judge, there is a new application not on the list. It is the matter of the DPP and Stephen Moyo.'

That name immediately caught Jennings's attention because it was not an unfamiliar name to him. He looked in the direction of the holding cell entrance and saw a coloured man being brought in. He was in handcuffs, flanked by two Garda, and preceded by an armed Gard. This was definitely out of the ordinary for a Monday morning.

O'Donovan had clearly been informed of what was coming because the appearance of any suspect in his court in handcuffs, let alone under armed guard, would normally have resulted in a shower of abuse on the head of the prosecuting guard. Today, he said nothing other than to make a formal request of the prosecuting Inspector.

'Well, Inspector, what is the nature of the application?'

'Judge, the accused man before you was arrested last night and was charged this morning at the Bridewell Garda Station. Evidence of arrest charge and caution will be given by Detective Sergeant O'Doherty.'

As the Sergeant made his way to the witness stand, another coloured gentleman rose from the well of the court and moved towards the accused in the dock. The Gardaí surrounding the accused moved in close to him but were put at their ease on the sergeant advising that this was an interpreter called to attend court.

The Judge was not expecting this and was clearly annoyed at having extra issues to deal with so early in the morning. 'What language does the accused use?'

'The accused is a Zimbabwe national, and I am advised the language is known as Shona. Mr Marange, who is present in court, is a resident of the State and fluent in this language, and he has acted as an interpreter before the courts on previous occasions.'

'Very well. Have him sworn in, and we will proceed.'

The court clerk rose from her chair and directed the interpreter to come forward.

Having confirmed the interpreter was Christian, he was duly sworn in and took up his position next to the accused.

'Inspector, call your witness.'

The inspector nodded to the detective sergeant, who took the Bible in his hand and took the oath without the need for any prompting by the court clerk. O'Doherty was well known in the criminal court and was one of the most experienced officers in the National Crime Squad. He only ever dealt with high-profile and serious crime, so his very presence in the court room was notice of a serious matter to be dealt with.

He cleared his throat and began in a steady tone. 'Judge, yesterday evening at 9.15 p.m., the accused, Stephen Moyo, was arrested in connection with the recent murder of Father Patrick O'Meara.'

Those words brought complete silence to the courtroom. Father Patrick O'Meara had been murdered two nights earlier in a cottage on the grounds of the Archbishop of Dublin's palace. There had been an outcry in the national press that a retired priest living in the grounds of the archbishop could meet his death in such a way, and that any person accused of his killing would certainly attract adverse attention from the whole country.

On hearing the priest's name, Jennings looked more carefully at the accused. He was clearly not a young man, but he stood very tall and seemed detached from events around him. There was something about him that Jennings felt was familiar, but he could not quite pin down what it was.

The sergeant continued. 'After acting on information received, the accused was placed under arrest and was taken to the Bridewell for further investigation. At 8.30 this morning, he was charged with the crime of murder contrary to common law and cautioned as follows: 'You are not obliged to say anything, but if you do say anything, it will be taken down and may be given in evidence.' The accused made no reply.'

The interpreter had been quietly speaking with the accused, and when he finished, he indicated to the Judge he had translated what was said.

O'Donovan sensed the tension in the room and was clearly eager to move matters on. He looked at the accused man, who had barely blinked in his time in court, and addressed him in what was for him even louder terms than one was used to.

'This is a serious offence, and one which will be dealt with in the Central Criminal Court should it go to trial. As a Judge of the District court, I have no jurisdiction to grant bail, but I can enquire as to your circumstances and appoint a solicitor to represent you should that be required. Mr Interpreter, please explain that to the accused.'

The interpreter spoke in a low voice so that even if one could understand the language, no one else in the court would have heard what he said. Normally that would irritate O'Donovan, but today he said nothing until he was told the accused understood, and he awaited the Judge's next instruction.

'If you cannot afford a solicitor, I can appoint one at your request. If you do not know of any solicitor, either present or in the city, to act for you,

I will appoint one of the solicitors present here today who are on the legal aid panel. Do you have a solicitor in mind?'

'No, Judge,' was the reply through the interpreter.

'Very well. Perhaps you would care to look at the array of talent before you and choose.'

Normally when this sort of event occurred, there was no shortage of faces turned to the accused as a legal aid brief. A high-profile murder was certainly not to be easily dismissed in any criminal lawyer's practice. Today, however, most present were studying papers in front of them with great intensity because the appointment in this type of case could well be a burden not worth the enhanced fee it would certainly bring.

Moyo looked round the room, and his gaze fell on Jennings and stopped. Jennings and Cathal Flanagan were amongst the few solicitors present who had not turned away from the accused, but it was apparent that it was Jennings who had attracted his attention.

As the two men looked at each other, Jennings realised who this man was.

The accused inclined his head towards the interpreter and said something to him. When the interpreter pointed to Jennings, he nodded his head in agreement.

The interpreter said, 'The accused has asked if that gentleman could act for him,' indicating Jennings to the Judge.

O'Donovan looked to see who was being chosen, and when he saw it was Jennings, a smile crossed his face. 'Well this is an interesting choice. Why would you ask for Mr Jennings?'

A further brief exchange occurred, and the interpreter's next words brought complete silence to the courtroom.

'He says he knows this man, because he was one of the prosecutors of the deceased man in Zimbabwe.'

O'Donovan could hardly believe what he heard. 'Is that so? And please tell me what was the deceased accused of in Zimbabwe'?

A further exchange and pause whilst the interpreter sought to clarify what he was being told. The reply was brief and to the point.

'Assisting terrorism.'

CHAPTER TWO

Salisbury Rhodesia, 1977

The High Court of Rhodesia and the offices of the Attorney General and the Director of Public Prosecutions were in Vincent Buildings on Jameson Avenue. This was the main thoroughfare through the capital city of Rhodesia, and Vincent Building sat opposite the near twin Milton Buildings, which housed the Ministry of Defence and other security ministries.

The country had been going through five years of civil war. History would show that at that time, the endgame of the military conflict was not that far away, but times were, to say the least, turbulent. The two opposing buildings were amongst the busiest of all government departments in the capital.

Richard Jennings was one of the youngest members of staff in the office of Director of Public Prosecutions. The war had taken its toll one way or another with people leaving the country and being away on military call ups and it was by no means unusual to find young recently qualified persons undertaking tasks which in years gone by would have taken years of service to reach. At 24 years of age, Jennings had been prosecuting criminal matters in the lower courts for two years. He was in his second year of High Court prosecutions, dealing primarily with murders and terrorist-related offences.

The then Director of Public Prosecutions was a very large, gruff man who had a formidable reputation both as a lawyer and as a boss. He demanded the very best of his staff and would support them to the hilt, provided they were doing their job as they should. Although they were all civil servants, the Director was firmly of the view that the officers under his control were officers of the court first, and it was to the courts and the law of the land that they owed their allegiance. He was often heard to say if it were otherwise, there was no point in the war being fought at all. In his view, it was only the protection of the law through the courts that offered any real hope for peace and development in his adopted homeland.

George Humphreys had come to Rhodesia after the Second World War as a recently demobbed army captain, having been called to the Bar two months before the outbreak of the war.

His career as a Barrister had only really started in Rhodesia as a Prosecutor but he very quickly achieved recognition as a highly skilled and thorough Advocate. His only failings lay outside the court, where he was prone to occasional extensive drinking sessions with members of his favourite sports club, which would in turn sometimes result in visits to police stations on the other side of the fence on which he should have been. However, he had never been prosecuted himself for any offence, and perhaps he wisely saw the error of his ways and calmed down in his activities when he was promoted to what was then the new office of the Director of Public Prosecution.

A call from the Director first thing on a Monday morning was always going to get your attention. He was known to spend hours at his desk after normal finishing time but being in the office at 8:30 was unusual. His secretary, a woman of indeterminate age, however never seemed to leave the building because she was always in before everyone else and apparently never left until her boss did.

Mrs Steyn was an Afrikaner by birth, but she spoke in a peculiar, clipped English accent. No one knew anything about her past, and no one would dare ask, but she was without question one of the more formidable people in the office. She was theoretically just a secretary, but in effect she ruled the administrative side of the office. If she called, you paid attention.

There was no formal welcome or introduction when Jennings answered his phone.

'The Director wishes to see you now, please,' was all that was required. No response or chit-chat was required in return.

Jennings immediately got up from his desk and began the walk round the open corridor to the Director's rooms. The concept of an open corridor had the desired effect of keeping the building cool in the summer months, but someone overlooked the fact that rain water and linoleum flooring did not mix. The result was a smooth and sometimes hazardous surface that had to be managed carefully until you reached the fully enclosed inner corridors. The trustee prisoners or "bandits" as they were called, were already at work, sweeping and cleaning the corridors, and they stood to one side as any staff member walked past on their business.

It was ironic that one of the most prized jobs a convict could secure would be the work detail in Vincent Building cleaning the courtrooms and the offices of those people responsible for putting them into prison. Such was the dysfunctional nature of the prison service that there was often heated dispute between prisoners as to who was entitled to such a perk.

In any event, the benefit of cheap labour meant the corridors were at least kept spotless, and the smell of beeswax polish was never far away.

As Jennings turned into the final corridor leading to the Director's office, he noticed two men in suits sitting outside the reception area. That was also unusual for so early on a Monday morning. It was unheard of for the Director to see anyone from outside the office until at least eleven in the morning, when he had had a chance to clear his desk of any pressing matters and ensure all his prosecutors were in court doing what they were paid to do.

He presented himself in front of Mrs Steyn's desk. She looked up with neither greeting nor comment and indicated he should sit next to the other two gentlemen whilst she rose and went into the Director's office. Jennings did as he was instructed and simply nodded in greeting to the two, who reciprocated the greeting but who also seemed in no need of conversation.

After barely a minute, Mrs Steyn returned and announced, 'The Director will see Mr Jennings and Mr Jones now' One of the two men, the older one, rose. The other stayed where he was, staring ahead of him without a comment.

Jennings indicated for Mr Jones, whoever he was, to proceed ahead, and then he followed him and Mrs Steyn into the office.

The Director remained seated behind his desk. His was by far the largest desk in the building, and it remained a mystery to any who visited how he could possibly know what was on it because it was always covered in correspondence, law reports, and other material beloved of barristers.

'Good morning, Richard. Take a seat. Do you know Mr Jones?'

'Good morning, sir. No, we haven't met.'

Mr Jones extended his hand, and the Director completed the introductions.

'James Jones, Special Branch'

This was becoming more interesting. When they were both seated, the Director looked at a set of papers clipped together in front of him and then spoke to Jennings.

'You would know Father Patrick O'Meara, I believe?'

Another unexpected question. 'Yes, sir, I know him.'

'How well?'

'Not very well. I met him socially a few times, when he was in from the mission visiting his brother and their family. John O'Meara was a good friend of mine from when we were at school.'

'You are of course aware of the fact that the good father is in custody pending trial for aiding and abetting terrorism.'

'I am, sir.'

'And you also know that the charges arise out of the incident in which his nephew, your friend, died at the hands of the terrorists he is alleged to be aiding and abetting?'

'Yes, sir, I am aware of that. I hope he gets what he deserves. John was not only a good friend, but he was an exceptional officer. He would still be with us if it were not for his uncle.'

'You have strong feelings about the trial, do you? You realise the offence carries the potential of the death penalty?'

'I do, and as I say, I hope he gets what he deserves.'

'And you say you only met him socially at John's parent's home?'

'That's correct. I would say we met maybe six times in the last ten years.'

'Very well. Have you any idea why he has made a specific request to see you in Chikurubi, then?'

That was not a question that was expected.

'No, sir, I do not. I am aware from talking to colleagues that he has refused legal representation at his trial. I have no idea why he would want to see me.'

'Well, he does. Mr Jones here has been assisting the investigating officer with the preparation for the trial. He has useful background information on the priest, and he and his officer will be taking you out to Chikurubi now to meet the priest. Talk to him and see what he wants. Then you come

11

back here with Jones and tell us what he has to say. You will not talk to Mr Jones about anything he has to say before you both come back here, and he will not ask you to do so. Is that understood?'

Jennings replied, 'Yes, sir.' Mr Jones, who still had not said a word, simply nodded his head in agreement.

'Very well, off you go. And when you are leaving Chikurubi, phone in to let Mrs Steyn know so that I will be available.'

The Director turned his attention back to his papers, and it was apparent the meeting was over. As the two rose, the door to the office was opened on cue by Mrs Steyn, who was either standing and listening to the conversation through the door or had an uncanny sixth sense insofar as her boss was concerned. The general consensus was it was the latter.

CHAPTER THREE

The journey out to Chikurubi Prison Complex was in total silence. It was apparent that Mr Jones, if that was in fact his name, was not for casual conversation, and that the young man with him clearly would not speak unless instructed. Jennings had noticed the service-issue revolver in the holster beneath the man's jacket as they got into the unmarked but clearly government-issued car, which had been parked in a reserved bay outside the building.

Chikurubi Prison Complex took up some one hundred hectares of ground on the western outskirts of the capital. The complex held in effect three prisons, a prison farm, and the training camp of the Prison Service. On arrival at the complex, you first went through an innocuous gate set in ordinary fencing and then drove through manicured fields of vegetables tended by a large number of convicts, all dressed in white shirts and shorts.

The prison farm provided not only vegetables but also dairy produce and meat in the form of pigs, beef, and chickens to the complex and the Prison Service as a whole. Given there was no shortage of labour, the standard of produce was always sufficient to meet the needs of the prisoners and even leave some surplus for sale. To get to work on the farm was considered a good deal by any of the long-term inmates, and the temptation to escape whilst there was seldom acted on—hence the low level of security on entering the complex.

After travelling through the fields for perhaps a mile or so, you came to another gate and fencing that was somewhat more severe and clearly of a higher security level. This was the entry to the prison training ground, and squads of recruits could be seen being put through their paces in parade ground drills. There was the regular sound of gunfire from a rifle range. Since the war had taken a grip, the prison service had had to become more militarised in its operations, and all staff had to undergo weapons training on par with that given to the police and defence forces. Outlying prisons were regular targets for attacks, and the prison warders were now more soldier than warden for most of their time.

After passing through the training grounds, you came to yet another level of fencing and security, and again the level of security was increased. This was the entry to the medium-security prison. This consisted of a double parallel fence with guard posts at regular intervals, manned by armed wardens, and regularly patrolled by dog units between the fences. The prison buildings consisted of rows of single-storey blocks, each of which held up to a hundred or more prisoners in dormitory-style conditions. The prisoners were those convicted of anything from having no registration card to attempted murder, and for these inmates, there was nothing to do day after day except sit in the dormitories or outside in the yards between them, waiting for meals and head counts.

There were regular attempts at escape from this part of the complex. After looking at it, Jennings could understand why. It must have been soul destroying, having to sit day after day and do nothing, yet that was what these convicts were facing until either their release or transfer to a farm.

They finally made their way to another checkpoint in the fence on the other side of the complex, and they proceeded into the maximum-security part of the prison. Their identities were thoroughly checked, and the reason for their visit was sought. A call was made from an office adjacent to the gate, and after a short discussion, they were permitted to carry on. They were advised Chief Superintendent van Tonder was expecting them.

Whatever depression took hold of someone on seeing the medium-security setup, the entry to the inner sanctum would break most people's spirits.

The prison had been built to house the most serious and violent of criminals, including those facing the ultimate penalty. It was rumoured to be modelled on an American design, and it consisted of a large, concrete, hexagonal building that rose five floors from an area of ground cleared of vegetation for five hundred yards in any direction.

On five of the six sides of the building, on each alternate level were openings with steel bars across them, but one side of the building was solid concrete from top to bottom with no openings of any kind.

Jennings knew from previous visits that this was the execution block, which housed the cells and the gallows room where the ultimate penalty was meted out. Once a prisoner went into this block, he would never again see the light of day unless an appeal against the sentence was successful or a pardon was granted by the President. Either scenario was unlikely, and the very sight of the sheer concrete was enough to send a chill through people, even if they were visitors.

The young driver pulled the car into a marked space set back from the large double doors of the complex, and Jennings was sent on his way by Mr Jones.

'Off you go, then, Jennings. Try not to stay too long,' he said with a smirk. Clearly it was his attempt at humour.

To the side of the main double doors was a service entry door with an armed warden on duty.

Jennings advised him who he was and told him whom he was coming to see, but before he could even produce his ID card, the door opened, and another warden invited him to enter.

On going through the service door, which was immediately locked and bolted, Jennings found himself in the inner reception of the prison. This was where trucks bringing convicts from court or transfers from other prisons would arrive and be processed before entry to the prison itself. Several offices, all with glass windows and heavily barred by steel bars, looked out onto the open parking area where the trucks would offload their occupants. A doorway marked 'Administration' was set to one side of the windows.

On the opposite side was a doorway leading to what was described as the visitor's area, and next to that door was an office with a similar glass window with steel bars and a steel chute system, used to exchange items belonging to visitors that were not to be taken into the visiting area.

It had been some time since Jennings had last been in this reception area, and the first thing he noticed and remembered was the smell. The smell was a mix of carbolic soap, boiled cabbage, and floor polish, and it was one of the most unpleasant odours he had experienced. He commented on it to one of the warders, who said he was not aware of any smell at all. Obviously being subjected to it day after day dulled the senses, but the smell would stay with visitors for days after and even seemed to stick to the clothes they were wearing.

Jennings assumed he would be going to the visitor's area and was making his way across to the doorway when the door on the administration side opened, and one of the largest men he had ever seen emerged.

Chief Superintendent Marius van Tonder was a giant of man. At six foot five and over two hundred pounds, none of which was fat, he took up most of the doorway as he emerged. His uniform had clearly been made to measure and was immaculate. His belt was polished to the extent you could see your reflection in them, as were his boots.

He extended his hand to Jennings, and the hand that took Jennings nearly swallowed it. Whilst firm, the grip was clearly not intended to be intimidating in any way.

'Mr Jennings? Chief Superintendent van Tonder. I was told to expect you. Perhaps you could come with me to my office.'

He turned on his heel, and Jennings followed him though into the administrative section. They went down a long corridor with various doors leading off it, each marked with some description about its purpose or inhabitant. At the end of the corridor, there was a door which bore no title or description, and van Tonder entered through this door into a large, sparsely furnished office. He took a seat behind a large desk and invited Jennings to sit in one of the two chairs in front of the desk. When both were seated, he picked up a file and pushed it towards Jennings.

'I understand the padre has asked to see you?'

'That is so, but I do not know why. Do you?'

'I don't. He keeps to himself, and I suppose whilst we share a common belief, our respective denominations would be somewhat opposed. I have asked for him to be brought up to let you talk to him in my office. You will be more comfortable here.'

'Isn't that against standing orders?'

'It is, but in this prison, I make the rules. It is one of the perks of being in charge of a place like this. How well do you know the padre?'

'I used to be friend of his nephew—the one who was killed. I would have met him from time to time at family get-togethers and such, but no more than that.'

'Interesting. Since his coming here, he has asked to see no one at all. You know he has declined legal representation? He has even declined visits from his own bishop. And yet he wants to see you. If I am not mistaken, you may be on the prosecution team?'

'I am as mystified as you. I am not directly involved in his prosecution. May I ask why he is in maximum security already, when he is still just a remand prisoner? Surely he should be in the remand centre in town?'

'He would be normally, but we do not have the facilities to cater for such a high-profile inmate in the remand prison. We are better able to look after him here, and to be honest, his being here has been very useful to us.'

'In what way?'

'How familiar are you with the gospel of Matthew?'

That was not a question Jennings was expecting, and he truthfully answered, 'Not at all.'

'Matthew 25:36 is the parable in which Jesus speaks of people caring for the sick and visiting those in need in prison. The padre is a caring man. He has a built-in supply of those in need of his care and help right here. To be honest, he has had a calming and beneficial impact on most of the prisoners since it was known he was here. This is not a happy place, Mr Jennings. No one wants to be in a prison. Even the warders are mostly here because they could not get any other job. There are some people here who are genuinely evil and deserve what they get, but the majority are here for reasons beyond their control.

'The padre holds daily prayer sessions in the prison courtyard, and if anyone one wants to see him individually, he provides a level of pastoral care of which I have never seen the like.'

Jennings was confused at what he was hearing. 'You almost sound as though you admire the man.'

'In many ways, I think I do. He has made an impression on me, which is not any easy achievement.'

'You are aware of the charges he is facing?'

'Of course, but as I say, people come to this place for many reasons. It is for others to Judge. My duty is to provide for their care and safety, both from others and from themselves. You clearly harbour some animosity towards the padre, and that is your right. Perhaps after you have spoken to him, you will see him in a different light.'

Before Jennings could reply, there was a knock on the door, and a warder came in leading Father O'Meara, who was dressed in prison-issue khaki shorts, a shirt, and sandals, which were made locally by prisoners out of discarded tyres. Nothing went to waste in this place.

van Tonder rose, shook O'Meara's hand, and said to Jennings, 'I will leave the two of you now. You have as long as you need. When you are finished, knock on the door, and a warder will see you out, Mr Jennings. Padre, that will not apply to you, I am afraid.'

This last comment was said with a not unkindly smile, which was reciprocated by O'Meara. A private joke between two diametrically opposed personalities.

As the prison officers left the room, O'Meara came forward and extended his hand to Jennings, who hesitated in reciprocating the gesture. O'Meara sensed Jennings hesitation, dropped his hand, and enquired if he could be seated.

'Of course, Father. You will forgive me for not greeting you, but after what you did to John, I have no desire to be here, and I have no idea why you should want to see me.'

O'Meara paused before taking a deep breath and replying. 'I can understand your reluctance to spend any time with me, but I remember you as being a good friend of John's. He often spoke well of you when he was visiting me on the mission.'

'John was an exceptional man and a good friend. It makes it even more of a tragedy that you could not see your way to doing anything to give him shelter when he needed it most, particularly because he was your nephew. You almost certainly sent him to his death when you refused to let him, and his men take shelter in the mission.'

O'Meara paused before he spoke. It seemed almost as though he were unsure whether he should be saying anything at all. 'What you are saying of John is entirely correct. That is why I need to speak to you, as someone who I know will honour and protect his memory.'

CHAPTER FOUR

Jennings was not at all sure where this conversation was going. 'I would be grateful, Father, if you could say directly what it is you want to tell me. Your motives are not really of concern to me, and I do not believe anything you say or do can damage John's memory.'

'That is probably true, but in my experience, when people are put on trial, matters not entirely relevant to the case in hand arise that can do damage to unintended targets. Please bear with me, because I know you don't want to be here, but there is really no one else I can talk to whom I would trust.'

'Very well. What is it you have to say?'

'When I came to Rhodesia as a newly ordained priest, I was sent to the mission with no real clue as to what I was to do or how I was going to achieve anything. My training in Maynooth provided no practical training in dealing with the realities of mission life. For the first ten years I was in the mission, it was a constant struggle to keep things going with what little resources were made available. I could see so many things could be achieved, but money was always an issue, and there was never enough to do what I wanted.

'All that changed when John's father, Sean, arrived in the country. Sean was the eldest son and I was the youngest. In those days, it was inevitable that any large family from a middle-class background would see one son off to the church, and I was always going to be the one to go. My father had been a fairly successful farmer and had also opened a general dealer's business, which Sean took over and turned into one of the more successful businesses in the county. He was always a good man with figures, and he had a good business sense, or so my father said. I would later come to see it as a ruthless side, where he would only do what was best for himself; he could care nothing for anyone else.

Before continuing O'Meara stood up and turned to look out of the window. It seemed to Jennings he was going back to what should have been a happier time in his life as a young priest on a mission. Turning back to Jennings he continued.

'Anyway, about five years after I arrived in the country, Sean turned up out of the blue. I later found out he had gotten into some sort of trouble in Ireland, and it was felt prudent he leave the country for a while and keep out of the way.

'Rhodesia seemed far enough away, and in any event, I was already out here. He arrived and immediately set up a construction business, which laid the groundwork for the business he now controls. Whatever faults he may have, Sean is an extremely hard-working man and has a knack of making money from projects other people would stay clear of. He used to visit me every few months, and he soon saw that I was going nowhere with my ideas for the mission with no financial support. He came up with what I thought was a good idea.

O'Meara returned to his seat and took out a handkerchief to mop his brow before continuing.

'The Church in Ireland was always very keen on supporting the missions, but any money taken at masses ended up in the Church's control. Only a very small portion of what was donated would ever get to me or any other mission. Sean's idea was to cut the Church out of the loop and allow for donations to come directly through a trust he set up in Ireland. I thought this was brilliant, particularly when the money started coming in to allow me to extend the school, build a clinic, and get a proper dairy herd in place.

'What I didn't know at the time was that the bulk of the moneys being donated to the trust came from criminal activities of so-called Republicans in both Northern Ireland and Ireland. Cash that they raised through their activities was 'donated' to the trust though collections at masses, and that money was then used to purchase goods and materials for the mission, as well as provide some cash. All the goods purchased were bought from businesses Sean had set up and were sold to the mission at a significantly higher price than would have been the case if they had been sourced legitimately. It was a simple but very effective money-laundering activity.

'When UDI came in 1965, the sanctions that followed really played into Sean's hands. Things which we could have bought directly from outside the country now had to be paid for from the trust and make their way to Rhodesia through all sorts of devious routes. Medical supplies were the best example. Money donated to the trust would be used to purchase medicines from companies set up by Sean in other countries in Europe, and at a very considerable mark-up. The medical supply company would show legitimate profit and on the face of it was a well-run legitimate business. I never really took any interest in the workings of the trust and relied on Sean to run everything. He had complete control.

'I began to suspect that things were not right in the last few years, since the war began to really take hold. Where other missions were unable to source funds or medical supplies, there was never a problem for Sean and my mission. Over the years, the clinic had been extended, and we had two doctors working almost full time with us. They were the ones who finally picked up that things weren't right. There was one supply of antibiotics that arrived which would have been enough to keep a fully operational city hospital running for a year. It was only when they opened the consignment that the extent of what was going on became apparent. Half the boxes contained nothing but crumpled-up paper. Not only had we paid for medicines we did not ask for, but we never even received what was supposed to arrive. When I confronted Sean, he tried to say we had made a mistake in the order, and when I told him about the boxes filled with paper, he shrugged it off and said it was something he would have to look into.

'Just after that consignment I was in Ireland on leave and made my own enquiries and found out precisely what had been going on when I came across records in Sean's room in our family home and worked out what he had been doing.'

'When I came back to the country, I confronted him. He laughed at me and called me a fool for ever thinking the never-ending supply of money was legitimate in the first place. He said that there was nothing I could do about it because my signature was on all the documents setting up the trust and on various documents over the years. If I tried to put a stop to what was going on, the only people who would suffer were the people I was supposed to be looking after. He suggested in strong terms that I shut up and leave things alone.'

Jennings had been listening to this with some interest. Since the introduction of exchange control legislation, as the war progressed, it was almost a national pastime for people to try to get access to money outside the country through false invoicing and other devices, some of which were very hard to detect. As part of his caseload, he had had to prosecute several well-known businessmen who had made significant sums of money through such devices.

'This is all very interesting, Father, and it doesn't say much for Sean—or you, for that matter. Given your circumstances right now, a possible exchange control prosecution doesn't really rate very highly. In any event, what has it got to do with John?'

'That is what I am coming to. Sean is a very devious man and would always cover his own tracks. He very seldom would put his own name or signature to any documents, and he used his family to protect him from any direct involvement. Unknown to John for the lasts few years, virtually all transactions through the trust had apparently been sanctioned by John as a trustee.'

Jennings indicated to O'Meara to pause as what he was being told did not make any sense to him. 'Hold on for a moment Father Even if that is so, how can that affect anything now that he is dead? He died a hero. No one is going to go digging into shady business deals to which he may or may not have been a party.'

'I am afraid that that has already happened. If you look at the papers served on me for the trial, you will see a reference to a detective sergeant from the Fraud and Gold Squad. There can be no reason he should be giving evidence, if not to reveal Sean's activities.'

Jennings had not been part of the team preparing for the trial and knew nothing of the proposed evidence to be led. 'I still cannot see what the relevance of this is to your position.'

O'Meara took in a deep breath and said in a voice that betrayed his emotions, 'The relevance is that three weeks before John's death, I had written to Sean telling him that I was going to expose what he was doing, adding that it would bring an end to his and his family's illegal profiteering. By family I meant Sean and his son Cian. I wasn't talking about John, who I am sure knew nothing of what had been going on. You can see how it would look, though. I was confronting a family profiteering from the war—and then a son of the family arrives at my doorstep looking for help, and I turn him away. It makes my position even more serious in that I was not only assisting the guerrillas but was also settling scores with my brother.'

Jennings paused for a moment as he realised the potential seriousness of this material coming out at a trial. 'But I thought you were offering no contest to the charges.'

'That is so. I do not intend to challenge any of the evidence to be led as to events on the day in question. But I am not going to be entering a guilty plea either.'

'You realise the offence you are charged with has a potential death sentence. Even if you say nothing, a not-guilty plea will be entered.'

'That is precisely the point. The issues about Sean are there to muddy the waters. They have no relevance to the charges against me, and all it will do is show up John's family in a bad light. I do not want that to happen because John does not deserve that.'

Jennings could sense the reason for his visit was about to be made known. 'You know I am not on the prosecution team. What do you expect me to do?'

'I want you to talk to the Director and see if there is some way the trial can be kept to the events at the mission and no more. As I said, I will not be contesting the evidence, and the Judge will decide my fate.'

'Even assuming I could do something for you, what is the benefit to the prosecution? If you are asking for favours, you have to be able to give something in return.'

Father O'Meara paused to consider what Jennings had put to him. 'The one thing an Irishman can't stand is an informer. It goes against the national psyche to assist the authorities in any investigation into crimes. That said, if you can achieve what I am asking of you, I have a list of names and bank accounts that your friends in Special Branch will find very interesting. It would certainly be detrimental to Sean and a number of other businessmen involved with him.'

Jennings was immediately aware of the significance of what O'Meara was offering. Getting details of people trying to get money out of the country would be of enormous value to the State 'And where is this list? When will you hand it over?'

'The list is in a safe place, and it will be given over as soon as I have your word that none of what I have told you will be raised at my trial. If you can do that, I will accept it and let you know where the list is to be found.'

'Very well. I will take what you have told me back to the Director and let you know what his views are.'

O'Meara stood up and once again extended his hand. 'Thank you. I know I ask a lot of you, but I do so for John's benefit, not my own. I know you will do the same'

Jennings also stood and paused briefly before taking the extended hand. 'Very well, Father. But I am shaking your hand to close the deal, not out of any respect for you or what you have done. Were it not for you, John would probably still be alive, and this whole sorry mess would have been avoided. You bear responsibility for all this.'

'Responsibility is a very difficult word. It can mean so many things. But, yes, I agree that I am responsible for my own actions, as we all are.'

Jennings moved to the door, opened it, and called to the warden, who was standing a discreet distance down the corridor. 'We are finished here. You can take Father O'Meara back to the cells.'

The priest stepped into the corridor and walked away from Jennings as the chief superintendent emerged from an adjoining office. 'You are done then?' he asked

'Yes, for now. I may have to return, though.'

'No problem there. Nobody here is going anywhere soon. Out of interest, have your views of the padre changed?'

Jennings had to think before replying. 'Well, what he has told me is not what I was expecting, but I don't know if that makes any difference to the way I feel for the man.'

'But at least now you have doubts. That is a good sign. If working in a place like this has taught me one thing, it is that there is never a true black-and-white position in life. Rather, all of us live somewhere in the grey area in between. Good day, Mr Jennings.'

van Tonder turned and entered his office, closing the door behind him. That left leaving Jennings alone in the corridor to make his way back to the admin office.

After processing his release in the daybook, he was escorted to the main gate and let out into the bright sunshine and fresh air, which hit him almost like a slap in the face.

He returned to the car in which Jones and his young driver were waiting and got in with not a word spoken between them. Jones was clearly taking the Director's orders to heart, and the drive back to Vincent Buildings was in complete silence.

CHAPTER FIVE

On their return, Jennings and Jones went straight to the Director's office, where Mrs Steyn was waiting at her desk. She indicated to them to be seated, attended to some paperwork on her desk, and went into the Director's office. After a few minutes, she returned and asked them to go in.

George Humphreys did not stand to greet them but looked up over his glasses and spoke to them when they were both seated.

'Right. What is it the priest had to say for himself?'

Jennings repeated what he had been told as succinctly as he could. Both men were clearly interested in what he had to say, and when he finished, Humphreys looked out of the only window in the room for a short while before he spoke.

'It is very interesting to hear that the priest holds his nephew in such high regard that he is willing to turn informant on his own brother. Maybe there is some decency in the man after all. The only problem for him is that what he has told you is nothing new to us at all.'

Jennings was not expecting that. 'You mean you knew about Sean's illegal dealings?'

For the first time, Jones spoke up. 'Oh, yes. We have known about Sean O'Meara and his activities for years. I was interested to hear it was the antibiotic lark that really triggered his suspicions.'

'How did you know about that?'

'For the simple reason that we did the swap on the consignment for scrap paper.'

Humphreys raised his hand to stop Jones from saying anything further.

'Jennings, you have done enough exchange control work to know that most businessmen are up to all sorts of games to try to not only keep their businesses going but also make themselves a profit. O'Meara is just one of

26

several men who have proved to be very good at it. His plan of using the church Trust was a very clever move when he first started out, and as the years have gone by—and particularly since sanctions have taken a grip—he has used it to great effect.'

'But why have you not put a stop to him?'

Humphreys looked at Jones and said, 'You tell him.'

Jones explained, 'We haven't put a stop to him for the simple reason we have been using him ourselves for the last five years. His contacts with the criminal and nationalist elements in Ireland have given us introductions we need to source things we need to keep the war going. You have to understand that in our situation, you cannot be choosy about who you do business with. O'Meara had been a very useful middle man, and together with half a dozen other similarly minded businessmen, he has been keeping this country afloat.'

As the Director has pointed out Jennings was no stranger to the many devices being used to get money out of the country and necessary materials in but was still not clear what relevance all this had to do with his friend's murder. 'But if that is so, why raise the issue in the priest's trial at this stage. Why not keep a lid on what Sean has been up to and just deal with the events at the mission?'

Jones provided the answer. 'Because unfortunately, Sean has succumbed to the basics of human frailty: greed. In the past year, he has been secretly adding an extra few percentage points profit on the deals he was supposed to be putting through for us. That's in addition to the already good mark-up he was paying himself for his troubles. We can't let that continue, and so it is time to rein him in. We knew there was no love lost between the brothers, and we took a gamble that if we threatened to bring out his dealings through this trial, one of them would crack. Personally, I did not think it would be the priest. If this list he says he has is as good as it sounds, it will certainly help clip Sean's wings. It might even give us some more people to look at talking to.'

Jennings could not contain his surprise at what he was being told 'So this was all a game to flush out Sean O'Meara? It has nothing to do with John's death all?'

For the first time in a very long time, Humphreys showed his volatile nature. He slammed the desk with the palm of his hand and glared at

Jennings. 'How dare you sit in my office and suggest I am party to playing games. This country is at war, if you hadn't noticed. To survive, we must make a deal with the devil, if that is what it takes. There are no games being played here, Mr Jennings. The material O'Meara has brought in over the years has saved lives. He and others like him are a necessary evil we have to put up with.'

The outburst was not only unexpected, but it was also the first time Jennings had ever seen his Director show any emotion at all.

The Director seemed to collect his thoughts before continuing. 'What we do not have to put up with, however, is his arrogance and belief he can steal from the hand that feeds him with impunity. He was on the point of being arrested when this whole unfortunate business with his son blew up. Arresting him then would have been impossible, but now if the information his brother is going to provide is solid, we will move against him as soon as the trial of his brother is over.

'Jennings, with immediate effect, you will be joining me as junior Counsel in the prosecution of Father O'Meara. You will liaise with your colleagues and clear your prosecution list until after his trial is complete. Mrs Steyn will circulate a directive to confirm all of this. You will speak to no one regarding what you have learned today, and you will report only to me regarding any further dealings you may have with O'Meara. Is that all understood?'

'Yes, sir, it is.'

'Very well. We will leave the good priest to his own devices for a few days, and you can speak to him next week and make the deal he is looking for. There will be no mention of any of his family's dealings, provided he pleads guilty and allows the trial to proceed with no stunts being pulled.'

Notwithstanding the Director's earlier outburst, Jennings felt he had to express his views on the issue of a guilty plea. 'Sir, even with the deal done, I do not expect him to enter a guilty plea.'

'No, I suppose not. Very well. Let him go down his own road. The court will enter the appropriate plea, and all he must do is keep quiet and let the evidence tell its own tale. I can't believe he will dispute anything said in that regard, anyway. Mr Jones here will be our liaison officer for the trial, so make sure you get a copy of the docket from him—and make sure it never leaves this office. This trial will attract a lot of attention from outside the country, and I will not have anything leaked from this office that could be used to embarrass us.'

The meeting was clearly at an end. Jennings and Jones stood up to leave, and the door opened as if on cue by Mrs Steyn to see them away.

As they walked down the corridor, Jones took hold of Jennings' arm and indicated they should move into an empty office. 'I will have a docket to you this afternoon. The material relating to Sean will be in it, but of course now that may not be relevant to the trial. Are we all right on that?'

'Fine by me. Just out of interest, what if anything is the plan for Sean O'Meara?'

'You don't need to know that just yet. In due course, another docket will be on your desk that will answer that question. Unfortunately, this war has forced us to deal with people we would rather not have anything to do with, and so nobody's hands are as clean as we would like. But needs must, I'm afraid. What happened to John O'Meara is a tragedy, but if it helps us close some doors and tighten up our control on those we need to survive, maybe it will not all be pointless.'

With that, Jones turned and left Jennings to his own thoughts. Jennings' overriding thought was that he was a very small player in a much larger game, and although the courts and his job demanded the truth be told, he very much doubted if that would happen in this particular trial.

CHAPTER SIX

Jones was true to his word, and by 4.30 a docket marked 'Top Secret—Authorised Access Only' had been delivered by the same young man who had driven them out to Chikurubi. Jennings had to sign for the docket personally at reception, and still not a word was spoken between the two men.

As soon as he got to his office, he opened the docket and began to go through the familiar routine of checking the sub files of witness statements, forensic reports, medical reports, and all the other material that went into a criminal docket. He noted that there were statements from the surviving members of John's patrol, or "stick" as it was called, and that the most detailed account had been given by then Sergeant Stephen Moyo. This ran to over four pages of closely typed print, and it set out in detail the events of the patrol prior to and after they had arrived at the mission. Moyo was clearly going to be the principle State witness.

The rest of the staff had left the office by the time Jennings had gone through the docket. As he prepared to start on it for a second time, he looked up to see the Director standing at his doorway.

'I see you have the docket?'

'Yes, sir. I have just been through it briefly but should be up to speed in the next few days.'

'Good. I have decided to bring the trial date forward. The indict papers were served three weeks ago, and originally, I was going to list the trial for three months' time. Given the latest developments, that is no longer necessary. I will have the case listed for two weeks from now in the A Court, in front of Mr Justice Gardner. I suggest you spend some time on any procedural issues that might arise. You know what he is like on rules, and

I don't want to find out once the trial has started that there are any pretrial issues we haven't dealt with.'

'Certainly I can do that. Is O'Meara going to have Counsel assigned given the risk of the death penalty?'

'He will. I have asked the registrar to appoint Counsel, and that will be done in the next forty-eight hours. You will be told who it is, and you can liaise with him should any issues arise.'

The allocation of Counsel was a matter for the discretion of the criminal Registrar who was an eccentric former policeman, Bill Johnson. One of his eccentricities was to keep some of the more bizarre exhibits from trials in his office on public display. His favourite was a human skull that had been an exhibit in a witchcraft trial and had a very precise hole drilled in the top of the cranium.

Johnson always said that having the skull on the shelf behind his desk guaranteed very short visits by constables who were notoriously superstitious about such matters. His allocation of Counsel was on a strict roster basis regardless of the nature of the trial or the accused. This often meant that a very inexperienced advocate would end up defending matters which they were clearly ill equipped to handle. Jennings was intrigued to see whose name was on the list because this would certainly be a trial which attracted a lot of media attention from both inside and outside the country.

After the Director left him, Jennings set to work on the docket once again.

The offices were empty at this time of night, and it was always a good time to get work done without interruption. Jennings turned his attention to the statements of the Special Branch, who had investigated the activities of Father O'Meara's brother.

It was soon apparent that Sean O'Meara's contacts extended to some very serious criminal elements in Ireland and beyond. It was obvious though that he was the sort of person needed to get material on sanctions lists into the country. They even had copies of bank accounts in the name of the trust, as well as other corporate entities that showed the extent to which Sean had been able to feather his own nest ever since the war and sanctions had built up. The details the brother could provide would be enough to put Sean in serious trouble.

After Jennings had been through the docket for a second time, he closed his office and left for home and an early night. The pretrial indictment papers would need to be redrafted if O'Meara accepted the deal, and Jennings wanted a clear head to get on with that exercise.

The next morning after the regular briefing with his colleagues, Jennings decided to go down to the Registrar and see who was to be appointed as O'Meara's Counsel.

Johnson's office was on the ground floor of the building. On entering it, one was faced with a solid wooden counter behind, which was a desk covered in court files, correspondence, and paperwork with no discernible system evident as to where things were supposed to be. There were no filing cabinets in the room; instead, files were on shelves from the floor to the ceiling, and a cursory glance would show that they were not even in any form of date order. However, Johnson would be able to pick out any file asked for without a moment's hesitation, and no one ever understood how he did it.

He was never a particularly cheerful man, and the skull behind his desk occasionally seemed more cheerful than he appeared to be. From the look on his face as Jennings entered, today was one of his better days.

He greeted Jennings with a broad smile, which was in itself disconcerting. 'Mr Jennings, how good to see you on such a lovely day. Here for word on the O'Meara defence, I assume?'

'I am, in fact. How did you know I was on the prosecution?'

'I always keep my ear to the ground, Mr Jennings. Mrs Steyn told me your current files were to be reallocated, and the Director spoke with me yesterday to advise he wants the O'Meara trial listed in short order. Seemed likely the two were connected.'

Johnson was clearly pleased with his detective work when Jennings confirmed he was to be junior Counsel, and then Jennings asked if defence Counsel had been assigned.

'Well, as you know, I usually work to a very strict roster. But on this occasion, I have been approached by an advocate who tells me none of those on my list will touch this case, but he is ready and able to do so.'

That was a most unusual scenario. Pro Deo work was the bread and butter for most junior members of the bar. No one at their end of the scale would willingly turn down a trial that could possibly run to a week or more at hearing. 'So who is it, then?' Jennings asked.

'Advocate Chirenje will be appointed, although as I understand what he was saying, he will be appearing almost as *amicus curiae* because O'Meara refused to furnish him with instructions, and he is therefore unable to act as Counsel in the normal manner.'

Advocate Amos Chirenje was one of the more colourful advocates in practice at the time. He had been an outstanding student at school and had secured a scholarship to Fort Hare University in South Africa at a time when university education for Africans was not easy to come by. He had graduated with honours and somehow gotten to England, where he completed his training and was called to the bar at Lincoln's Inn.

Chirenje was an extremely competent advocate, and there were a number of young inexperienced prosecutors and police officers who underestimated his skill in court. He had succeeded in many high-profile cases where others would have been completely out of their depth, and it was surprising that he should even want to be involved in this type of case.

Jennings would need to be serving Chirenje with various documents pretrial, and so he enquired whether he had been formally appointed.

'He will get his letter tomorrow, so whatever you need to send can go to him from tomorrow. You have his details, I assume?'

'I do. There is going to be a fresh State Summary to file and serve, and I should have it for you later in the week.'

'Very well, Mr Jennings. You know Justice Gardner's form. Make sure we don't have to deal with any technical misdemeanours at the hearing.'

Having been suitably warned, Jennings left the Registrar to his work and returned to his rooms to rewrite the State Summary. Although there was a general typist pool shared by all the office, it was obvious to him that any work on this docket was to be done by him and no one else.

On his return to the office, he found a note from the Director advising that Father O'Meara was to be brought in to the High Court for service of an amended State Summary the following Monday and to ensure the papers were all in order. That did not give him a lot of time, and so he got to work without delay.

The laws on criminal procedure in Rhodesia had seen major changes since the war had intensified, and the availability of witnesses, particularly policemen and technical witnesses, was ever stretched. In respect of virtually all forensic and technical issues, the law allowed the prosecutor to prove matters through the submission of signed certificates by the relevant witness. These certificates were not even on affidavit, and the system was open to abuse by any investigating office seeking to take shortcuts in their evidential chain of evidence.

It was this area that the Director was concerned about, given the matter was to appear before Mr Justice Gardner. The Judge had once established that a certificate purporting to be a ballistics report for a murder being tried before him did not in fact relate to the matter at all and was meant to be produced in respect of a totally different matter. Ever since then, Gardner examined all documentary and certified evidence put in front of him in minute detail, and he had already thrown out several trials which in his view did not come up to scratch.

Jennings was tasked with ensuring that did not happen here, and that required a careful examination of all the technical evidence and statements of witnesses to ensure they linked up.

One other development in the law was the confirmation of statements recorded by the police before a remand magistrate at the first available hearing after an arrest. The object of this exercise was to avoid a situation where an accused may have made a confession under questioning, only to recant on the confession on seeking the advice of fellow convicts on remand or on legal advice.

The procedure before the magistrate called for the accused to be dealt with *in camera*, without the police or other agency present to ensure the accused person was not under pressure to make admissions that were not freely and voluntarily made. If a statement was confirmed by the magistrate, that statement would be produced at trial with no evidence necessary from the recording officer, and the onus of proving it was either made under duress (or was not the statement of the accused at all) fell on the accused. That there was an onus almost impossible to shift soon became apparent, and many trials were dealt with by handing in a series of certificates and a confirmed statement admitting the offence in all its elements. Trials that would have otherwise taken days of evidence being led were dealt with in hours, and there was almost a conveyor belt system of trials going through the criminal system from petty offences up to and including capital offences.

Jennings looked through the docket for the subfile dealing with recording of statements from the accused. The only document in the file dealing with that issue was a single-page statement duly stamped by a local magistrate with the endorsement following a formal caution: 'The accused declines to make any statement.' Jennings was not used to seeing that sort of response on a file, and he thought it self-defeating to have gone to the bother of confirming the fact that no statement had been made. It was hardly likely that O'Meara would complain at trial that he had wanted to give a statement and been precluded from doing so. It was something he needed to clarify with either O'Meara or his advocate before the trial commenced.

By the end of the week, Jennings had an amended State Summary ready for service, and copies of all reports and certificates from ballistics reports to autopsy reports and other issues were neatly compiled and copied for service on O'Meara.

CHAPTER SEVEN

The following Monday, Jennings found the prison truck already parked in the lane at the back of the High Court when he arrived for work. The prison transport was notoriously unreliable in getting prisoners to and from the various centres to the High Court. For them to be early was almost unheard of.

He decided to make an immediate enquiry to see whether O'Meara had been brought in, and he made his way down through the corridors of the building to the courtyard outside of Court A, which was the main criminal court in the complex. The prisoners were detained in holding cells which were marginally below ground level and were serviced by a reception office in which the warders would sit and wait until called to their respective courts. The smell of Chikurubi was present even in this small holding area, and Jennings never enjoyed his visits to the cells.

On entering the reception office, the warders all stood, and Jennings enquired as to whether O'Meara was in the cells. He was told he was, and he asked for him to be taken up to the court at 9.30 before the day's trial commenced, to serve additional papers on him. This was acknowledged by the senior warder, and Jennings left to get his paperwork together. By 9.30 he was waiting in the court for O'Meara to be brought up.

Courtroom A was the most impressive of all the courtrooms in the building and was reserved solely for criminal trials. The court had a particularly high ceiling to accommodate the public gallery, which was effectively at second-floor level, with seating stepped back from the edge of the front row of seats to provide as good a view as possible to spectators who would watch the trials unfold below them. The walls were panelled with dark teak hardwood, and the windows were at a higher level, which ensured there was never direct sunlight in the court.

The Judge's bench was set a good five feet above the floor of the court, and on either side of the Judge's chair were two slightly smaller chairs for the assessors.

Jury trials had been done away with years before Jennings started work. All criminal trials in the High Court were heard by a Judge and two lay assessors, who were inevitably retired senior civil servants or on occasion even retired senior police officers. Issues of fact were determined by a majority, and in theory it was open to the assessors to outvote the Judge on any factual issues. The reality was that no one had ever known that to happen. Issues of law were for the Judge alone, but since the introduction of the confirmation of statement procedure, 'trials within trials' to consider the admissibility of statements made to the police, which were heard by the Judge alone, had virtually disappeared.

Counsel for the prosecution and defence were accommodated on the same long, extended table immediately below the Registrar's desk. Behind them was another table for police investigators and defence attorneys.

To one side of the court was the former jury box. This had fallen into some disrepair over the years and was used by the press, who regularly complained about the uncomfortable seating. The springs in the cushioned benches had long ago become detached, and money was certainly not to be had to make a reporter's life more comfortable.

In the well of the courtroom was the prisoner's dock. This stood raised from the floor of the court so that the accused, when seated in the dock, would be at almost the same level as the Judge seated on his bench. Jennings never understood why it was necessary to have the dock in such an elevated position, but it certainly gave prominence to the position of the accused in the court whilst at hearing.

Behind the dock were rows of benches for the public, and in any major trial, it was usual for these to rapidly fill with interested onlookers.

The stairs leading up to the dock from the holding cells were so narrow that only one person could go either up or down at any one time. They were also particularly steep, and this, coupled with the fact that most accused brought into the court were in leg irons, made it a very difficult job to get prisoners in and out of the dock. It had been recommended by one Judge that leg irons should not be used because of the difficulty created by the steep stairs. The prison officers had to accept the direction of the Judge, but within the week, an accused, unfettered by leg irons, saw an opportunity. On reaching the top of the stairs into the dock, he vaulted over the wall of the dock and ran out of the court before the trailing warders could do anything to stop him. His attempt at escape was short lived given the only exit was into the courtyard, where several warders were sunning themselves and enjoying a morning cup of tea. Because of his efforts, leg irons were immediately reintroduced without any further interference from the bench.

Jennings was seated at one of the benches in front of the dock when he heard the bolts being drawn below; that signalled the arrival of the warders and O'Meara. He noted he could not hear the familiar jangle of leg irons, and when O'Meara appeared at the top of the stairs, he did so without a warder in attendance.

'Good morning, Father,' Jennings said. 'I see you are still getting preferential treatment.'

'That may be so, Mr Jennings, but not at my request. You have to give me some papers, I believe.'

Jennings drew a bundle of papers from the docket and handed them over to O'Meara, who simply put them to one side on the edge of the dock without giving them a cursory look.

'A copy will be given to Advocate Chirenje, who will be appearing on your behalf. Have you met with him yet?'

'I explained to him that I do not require representation. He tells me that as with a lot of things in the system, that is not a matter of my choosing.'

This was not the time for a legal tutorial, but Jennings felt the man deserved some explanation of what was unfolding.

'You must realise by now that the offence you are charged with carries a range of sentences on conviction, up to and including the death penalty. In any such case, the law requires the accused have Counsel to represent his interests. I assume you have no problem with that.'

O'Meara shrugged his shoulders. 'It is just that I have made it clear from the outset that I do not dispute any of the events on that day. If those events give rise to consequences, so be it.'

'There comes a time, Father, when even a priest must look for help from someone other than the Almighty. Advocate Chirenje is a good advocate. It would do you no harm to accept whatever help he can give you.'

O'Meara stared ahead of him towards the bench and then looked down to where Jennings was standing. 'I appreciate everything you are saying, Mr Jennings. I am not a complete fool. All I am trying to explain is that my principle concern is for the memory of my nephew. Provided you have the approval of the Director for what we discussed, there is no need for this trial to be any more complicated than it needs to be.'

Jennings indicated the papers in front of O'Meara. 'When you read the papers I have given to you, you will see that there is no mention of any commercial activities of John's father or his family. The letter you wrote is not mentioned, nor will it be. All that remains is for you to fulfil your part of the bargain and give us the list you say you have.'

O'Meara smiled for the first time. 'Indeed, but I am afraid that will require mutual trust from both sides. I am not giving anything until the trial is over and done with. At that time, you will be told where to go to get all the information I have.'

Jennings was now becoming frustrated with the priest, and he waved his arm around the courtroom. 'Where the hell do you think you are? This is not a game. In a few days' time, you could well be sentenced to death while standing right where you are now, and yet you still think you can dictate terms?'

'That is where you are wrong, Mr Jennings. This is a game, and one that you are but a part of, as am I. You have a role to play, and so do I. I am simply asking you to make sure that the game is played to the rules we have agreed, and that will be the end of it.'

Jennings was getting increasingly frustrated with O'Meara and decided to leave him. 'Very well, Father. I will speak with the Director. I just hope he will not have any problems with your terms.'

Jennings called down for a warder, and when one arrived at the top of the stairs, he told him they were finished. O'Meara and the warder made their way back down to the cells. Jennings was left to his own thoughts, and after a short while he collected his docket and headed back to his office.

As he walked along the corridor leading from the court to the stairs leading to the first floor, he was met by Advocate Chirenje, who was in his regular pinstriped suit and stiff wing-collared shirt. Even when he was not scheduled for court, he always dressed in the same way. It was one of his affectations which reflected his training in the English tradition.

As they came together, he extended his hand in greeting.

'Jennings, old chap. Good morning.' Another of his affectations, but one Jennings was used to.

'Good morning, Amos. Off to see the priest, I assume?'

'I am, although to what end, I am not sure. I am told he refused representation in the normal sense, and so my function is somewhat limited. I understand from Mr Johnson that there is to be a new set of indict papers served.'

'That is so. In fact, I can give you your set now, if you like.'

As Jennings extracted a second set of papers from his docket, Chirenje extended his hand and said, 'Most kind. At least I can go through these with him now, for what good that is.'

'Thanks, Amos. If you need anything more, let me know.'

With that exchange, the two parted company, and Jennings returned to his office. Given the expedited date for the hearing, Jennings had a lot of work to do in a short space of time. Notwithstanding the changes in the law to facilitate the prosecution in a high-profile trial such as this, it always paid to make sure that all the witnesses were available to give evidence in the event some flaw was detected in their certificate evidence. With the country at war, that was never an easy task if most of witnesses were away from the capital on operations. Normally, requests to have service personnel on standby for a criminal trial were met with a simple refusal. In this case, however, and with the assistance of Mr Jones, not one witness was unavailable.

One exercise that did take some time was going through the large-scale map Jones and his team had prepared for the trial. They had managed to obtain the latest scale ordnance survey maps of the mission and its surroundings, and they had put these together to create a map measuring twelve feet by six feet, on which were marked all the various places of relevance to the prosecution.

Even though the country was at war and the mission was in one of the more dangerous parts of the country, a full and detailed survey of the various scenes of contact with the terrorists had been mapped and marked by various colour-coded pins. It would be Jennings's job to take the Director through this pretrial so that the Director could decide how best he was going to present the evidence to the court.

The map had been set up on two large easels in Courtroom A, next to the witness stand and at an angle which would allow the Judge, assessors, and lawyers a clear view. The public would not have such a view, and it would be up to Jennings to deal with the press at the end of the relevant day's hearing to let them see the map and make what use of it they would.

Any high-profile trial attracted media attention, but this particular case was unprecedented.

The relationship between the deceased and the accused, the involvement of the Catholic Church, and the nature of the charge to be faced by the accused were unique, to say the least.

Within the white community, there was no sympathy whatsoever for the priest, and there was no shortage of articles condemning the man before the trial had even started. This was made an even easier task through the comments of John's brother Cian, who was seemingly giving interviews to anyone who would listen, castigating his uncle and demanding justice for his brother.

John's father was noticeable not only for his silence but also for his absence from the country. The official reason given by the family was that he was too distraught to be in the country for the trial, and he was seeking comfort from his family in Ireland. From what he had been told, Jennings suspected the real reason was one of simple survival. He probably knew it was only a matter of time before he himself would be in a dock in the very building where his brother was to stand trial.

It was well-known that the Director would never give any interview or even discuss a case with the media, but the same did not hold true for a lot of his staff. Jennings was inundated with calls from reporters, both local and foreign, who were anxious for a story that would top their competitors' offerings. They were to be disappointed, though, because Jennings knew if he were to speak to any reporter and was found out, he would be fired without a moment's hesitation.

CHAPTER EIGHT

The Trial

The Director convened a meeting with Jennings and Mr Jones on the Wednesday before the trial was due to commence.

It was soon apparent that the Director knew the docket backwards, and there was little for Jennings to do other than take him through the map set up in the court and go through various locations highlighted by pins of varying colours. Even though the country was at war and the area in question was subject to ongoing terrorist activity, the police had conducted an extensive forensics examination of the areas where contact had been made with terrorists before and up to the fatal shooting of John.

Having gone through the map, the Director decided that Jennings would lead the witness who compiled it through his evidence. Delegation of functions at trial to his junior Counsel was not something the Director was known for, and Jennings was grateful for the demonstration of confidence in him.

They knew who the Judge was, but the identity of the assessors was seldom known until the week before the trial commenced. It would be normal for assessors to be assigned to a particular Judge for anything up to a month at a time, but in respect of a high-profile trial, they were usually appointed for that trial only.

Jennings enquired of the Director if he knew who they were.

'Mr Johnson tells me Mr Cunningham and Mr Richardson will be sitting.'

That was hardly surprising news. George Cunningham was a retired former deputy commissioner in the police, and John Richardson was a retired former Secretary from the Ministry of Internal Affairs. Both would have sat as assessors on many trials and would be considered conscientious and reliable. Of all the panel of assessors available, these two were probably the best, and unlike some who never seemed to take much interest in the proceedings, these two were known to take an active part in trials.

On the Monday morning of the week of the trial, Jennings was at his desk by 8.00 a.m. Court commenced promptly at 11.00, and there was no way that this trial would not start on time. Jennings had his papers collected and had set up in the court by 9.30 a.m. and could hear the activity in the cells below as the prisoners were brought through the courtyard from the adjacent laneway.

The arrival of the prisoners was never a particularly silent affair, and there would usually be a fair amount of shouting and cursing by warders trying to move along their charges. Today, however, there was almost no noise at all, save for the banging of the gates against the walls, bolts being opened and closed, and cell doors being secured. The normal general buzz of conversation was particularly muted, which was also unusual.

Jennings heard the retaining bolts on the door leading up from the cells to the court being drawn, and he looked up from his desk to see who was coming into the court. He saw Superintendent van Tonder arrive at the head of the stars into the dock. As ever, his uniform was immaculate, and today he was in full first dress uniform.

'Good morning, Superintendent,' Jennings said as he stood and moved towards the dock. 'We don't see you here very often.'

van Tonder smiled and opened the hatch doorway at the back of the dock to come down to Jennings' level 'Yes, good morning, Mr Jennings. It is not a place I need to be in very often, but needs must on occasion.'

After this brief exchange, Jennings inquired after O'Meara's well-being.

'He seems in good enough form for a man on trial for his life. He is a very self-assured man, and his faith is obviously a comfort to him. Do you want to speak to him at all?'

It would not be considered proper for a member of the Prosecution to be talking to an accused person on the morning of the trial, and even though O'Meara had elected not to have formal representation, the fact that an Advocate had been appointed to protect his interests made it even more important that Jennings keep his distance at this stage.

'No, thanks, but if he needs anything, Mr Chirenje will be along shortly and will look after him.'

'Very well,' van Tonder replied. 'I have some administrative issues to deal with, with the Registrar. I will leave you to your work.' With that, van Tonder moved through the court and exited through the doorway usually reserved for Counsel. He was clearly familiar with the layout of the building, and no one was going to challenge his right to use whatever was the easiest route through the complex.

Over the course of the next hour, the courtroom slowly began to fill up with the personnel needed to run a criminal trial. The stenographer was in early setting up her machine, and the Judge's Registrar was in soon after preparing the bench with pads, pens and other necessary bits and pieces.

The Director came in just before 10.30a.m. and set about preparing himself with no discussion between himself and Jennings, or anyone else for that matter. Before any trial in which he appeared, the Director was known to be totally absorbed in his own thoughts. It was a very foolish man who would interfere with that through idle discussion. The only comment made to Jennings was a simple 'Everything in order?' That required an equally simple 'Yes, sir' in reply.

Advocate Chirenje had been in his seat for some time prior to the arrival of the Director, and he too had little need of discussion with anyone present. Whilst the prosecution teams were supported by Counsel, police, and technical witnesses, the defence Advocate had a lonely seat to occupy on a pro deo Brief. He would not even have the luxury of an instructing attorney to assist him.

The public gallery and the press box were filling up, and by 10.45 a.m. the courtroom was full. There was the usual level of tension in the room that went with any high-profile criminal trial. The Registrar looked around to see that all personnel were where they were supposed to be, and he enquired of both Counsel if they were ready to proceed. When they confirmed that was the position, he then nodded to a senior warder who was in the dock, and he descended from the dock to collect the prisoner.

The door up to the dock could only be unlocked from the cell side and the knock on the door rang out through the stairwell and brought silence to the courtroom. The sound of the bolt being released could be clearly heard, and the sound of footsteps coming up the stairs echoed through the court, which was now completely silent.

Jennings turned in his chair to see O'Meara emerge in the dock behind a senior warden, and he moved into the dock where another warden took up his position next to him. When they were all in a row, they sat down. O'Meara was in his own clerical day attire. Most accused who found themselves in this position usually showed some signs of apprehension or concern, but O'Meara showed neither.

Advocate Chirenje had also turned to witness his client's arrival in the dock, and he too noted the apparent lack of concern. He caught Jennings' eye and raised an eyebrow before turning to face the bench and await the arrival of the Judge and his assessors.

Meanwhile, the Director had not moved a muscle and simply sat with his hands crossed in his lap, looking at the charge sheet before him, which he would shortly be reading out to the accused.

On being satisfied all personnel were present and correct, the Registrar checked his watch and moved to the doorway at the side and to the rear of the Judge's bench, through which the Judge and the assessors would enter the court. He gave one final glance around the courtroom and then made his way through the door to the anteroom in which the Judge and assessors were waiting.

Precisely at 11.00 a.m., as the sound of the bells from the Anglican Cathedral could be heard, there was a loud knock on the door. The Registrar came in and called out, 'Silence in court,' in a loud and somewhat unnecessary tone, given the room was already completely silent.

The Judge entered first followed by the assessors. Mr Cunningham moved behind the Judge's chair to take up his position to the Judge's right, and Mr Richardson stood to the Judge's left in front of his seat. When all three were positioned, the Judge gave a perfunctory bow, which was reciprocated by Counsel and Registrar. As the Judge took his seat, so too did the rest of the court.

Justice Gardner was coming to the end of his career on the bench. He had been a competent advocate in his day and had proven to be a competent Judge over the years. His attention to detail ensured that his court ran smoothly, and very few of his Judgements were ever successfully appealed against. Notwithstanding the dice were heavily loaded in favour of the prosecution, he would always ensure that the defence was given every opportunity to present its case as effectively as possible.

Having made himself comfortable, he adjusted his glasses and said, 'Call over the list, please, Registrar.'

The Registrar rose from his seat and said. 'May it please Your Lordship and the court to hear the matter of the State and Patrick O'Meara.'

The Registrar took his seat, and the Director and Advocate Jennings rose.

The Director spoke first. 'May it please Your Lordship and gentlemen assessors. I appear for the State with Mr Jennings.'

Advocate Chirenje then said, 'May it please the court, I appear for the accused at the direction of the Honourable Court.'

With the initial formalities completed, the Judge directed the charge be put to the accused.

Jennings resisted the temptation to turn to see O'Meara, and he waited whilst the Director read the charge sheet before him and said, 'Patrick O'Meara, you are charged with contravening Section 45 of the Law and Order Maintenance Act 1963 as amended, in that on or about the fifteenth day of March 1977, you did at or near St Mary's Mission, Inyanga, wrongfully and unlawfully aid, assist, or abet terrorism in that by your conduct and deeds, you furthered the aims of a terrorist organisation. Further, by your actions you caused the death of one John O'Meara through aiding and abetting terrorists aforesaid. How do you plead, guilty or not guilty?'

Instead of the simple answer required of the question put to him, O'Meara put his own question to the court. 'Is it permissible for me to ask a question?'

This was not what was expected in a criminal trial, and Jennings could feel the Director bristle at the nerve of the accused seeking to digress from what should have been a simple opening of the trial.

Justice Gardner was equally unimpressed. Given the relative height of the bench and the dock, the Judge was able to look directly at O'Meara, and his reply was brief and to the point.

'You may not. The charge put to you is clear and unequivocal. You have the benefit of Counsel, who I am sure has explained the details and import of the charge, and there is only one answer to be given at this time: either guilty or not guilty. Statements, questions, and any other issues will be dealt with in due course. Do you understand that?'

'I do,' replied O'Meara. 'But I am not able to either admit or deny the charge as framed. I do admit to some elements of what has been put to me, but I cannot admit to all the elements of the charge. Perhaps I could explain that to the court.'

Before he could say anything further, the Judge said in a voice markedly louder than before, 'This is a criminal trial, and you may not and will not use this as an opportunity to make any statements at this time. You will be given every opportunity to give evidence on your own behalf later in the proceedings. For the moment, you must enter a plea, and if you refuse to do so, a plea of not guilty will be entered on your behalf.'

The Judge turned his attention to Advocate Chirenje as he continued. 'Mr Chirenje, I assume you have explained the basic procedures to the accused. Do you have instructions from him as to his plea?'

Chirenje had risen from his seat while the Judge was addressing him, and he was clearly uncomfortable at the opening of the trial, which should have been the least troubled part of the proceedings. 'I have endeavoured so to do, My Lord, but it would appear my efforts have not been successful. Would you permit me to address the accused?'

This sort of behaviour was not something the Judge was used to in his court, and he was going to have none of it now. 'You may not, Mr Chirenje. If the accused has not taken heed of your advice, which I am sure is sound advice, matters will proceed based on a not guilty plea entered by the court. You may explain that to the accused during the lunch recess, but for now we will proceed.'

Chirenje acknowledged this with a brief nod of the head and said, 'As Your Lordship pleases.' He resumed his seat.

The Judge then addressed O'Meara. 'A not guilty plea having been entered by the direction of the court, the matter will now proceed. Mr Humphreys, do you have an opening statement?'

The Director rose from his seat and moved to a lectern which was to his left side on the bench in front of him. He placed a sheaf of papers on it and addressed the court.

'My Lord and gentlemen assessors, this is a matter in which the State alleges the accused, through his conduct, aided and abetted terrorists. It is a most serious charge and carries serious penalties. In this case, there is an added element which makes it even more serious, in that it will be the State's case that through his actions and support for a terrorist organisation a member of the BSAP Support Unit, John O'Meara, lost his life. The State will seek to prove to the standard required of a criminal prosecution that the accused was able to provide assistance to the deceased and his men, and that he deliberately chose to refrain from doing so. As a consequence, John O'Meara paid the ultimate price in losing his life.

'My Lord and gentlemen, I propose opening the State case with the evidence of Section Officer Stephen Moyo.'

The silence in the courtroom was relieved for a moment as people moved in their seats to look at the first witness to be called. Moyo came into the courtroom from the adjourning waiting room.

Section Officer Moyo was an imposing figure in full first dress uniform. It had only recently been the case that African police officers could be promoted to the ranks formerly reserved for whites, and Moyo would have been one of the first to have been promoted. That he was promoted to the rank of Section Officer was proof of the fact that such a promotion was well deserved because he had not had to start at the first rank of Patrol Officer.

The sound of his boots on the floor drew attention to the Black Boots of the Support Unit, which gave them their nom de guerre. Although they were all member of the police force, the Support Unit was primarily a paramilitary unit, and they were now soldiers first and policemen second. In recent years, they had established themselves as a force to be reckoned with and were held in high regard by the other military units in the country.

Moyo stepped up into the witness box and was addressed by the Registrar. He was sworn in, and the Registrar took his seat.

The Director rose and commenced his examination by establishing Moyo's identity rank in the support unit and other background facts relevant to the hearing. Moyo answered all questions directly to the Judge in the traditional manner, directly and firmly, and he immediately impressed those in the court with his demeanour.

The Director then continued. 'Section Officer, you were at the time a sergeant in the Support Unit. Is that so?'

'That is correct, My Lord.'

'And I understand you knew the deceased, Patrol Officer O'Meara. Is that correct?'

'That is so, My Lord. Patrol Officer O'Meara had been in command of my stick for eighteen months before the incident at the mission.'

'How would you describe the late Patrol Officer?'

Moyo paused for the first time before giving his answer. 'My Lord, he was the best officer I have served under.'

Humphreys paused himself before continuing to let that answer register with the court.

'Section Officer, perhaps you could elaborate on that for the benefit of the court. What was it about Patrol Officer O'Meara that you found so admirable?'

'My Lord, he was one of the people. He could speak our language, and he knew and respected our culture and traditions. He was a true leader of men, and we would have done anything he asked of us. We know that in turn, he would do whatever was required to look after us.'

Humphreys again paused before asking, 'Perhaps you could expand on that aspect. In the time he oversaw your stick, how many times had you seen action with terrorist groups?'

'Many times, My Lord. We had a very successful unit and had killed many terrorists on operation in the Eastern Highlands area.'

'And how many members of your stick were killed in that time?'

'None, My Lord. Patrol Officer O'Meara never put us in a position where we could not defend ourselves properly, and he had a good sense of the bush and how to use it to best look after us. That was not always the case with other officers.'

'Very well,' Humphreys continued. 'Could you tell the court about terrorists captured by your unit?'

'Yes, My Lord. We captured many terrorists, and we were also able to rescue a large number of villagers who had been abducted and were being forced to go to Mozambique for terrorist training. If it were not for Patrol Officer O'Meara, all those people could be dead by now.'

Having established the deceased's credentials, Humphreys turned his attention to the large map positioned to Moyo's side.

'Section Officer, I would like you now to look at the map on your right and take us through what is shown on the map by the various coloured pins.'

Moyo was handed a metre-long pointer and adjusted his position so that he could point to the map and still address the court. The members of the press in the old jury box probably had the best view in the court. Even the Judge and assessors had to lean forward to see the map clearly, and once all persons were paying attention, Moyo continued with his evidence.

'My Lord, we had been on patrol in the area for four weeks before the incident at the mission. We had initially been told we were to be on patrol for a two-week term, but that was extended due to operational reasons and commitment of reinforcements to areas outside this area. We had a number of contacts with terrorists in the first days of our deployment, and these are marked here and here.' As he was saying this, he indicated points to the west and south of the mission station.

'What was the result of these contacts?' he was asked.

'My Lord, we killed four terrorists and captured two. We then engaged in pursuit of the remainder of the group, which we estimated to be about seven in total.'

'And in which direction were these remaining terrorists going?'

Moyo again pointed to the map. 'Towards the mission station, my Lord. I should say that it is also the direction they would go if they were retreating back to Mozambique, and that is what we thought they were doing.'

Humphreys waited whilst the Judge and assessors finished taking their own notes of what was being said, and when the Judge looked up to indicate Humphreys should continue, he asked his next question.

'Were you correct in your thoughts, or did something happen to make you change your views?'

'My Lord, we later learnt that in fact, this group was an advance group of a very large number of terrorists who had crossed over from Mozambique. At that time, our intelligence was that there was to be a large incursion in the Burma Valley south of Umtali, and the majority of the resources available was deployed in that area to deal with that. It was seen afterwards that this information was wrong, and the main incursion was in fact in our area, where we were operating with limited resources and back up.'

'And what was the result of the position in which you found yourself?'

'We had been on patrol for longer than we had planned and had used up more of our ammunition and supplies than was intended. We were not able to receive resupplies due to the other operations, and that put us under pressure. Patrol Officer O'Meara decided we should withdraw to a position closer to the main road and await resupply and reinforcements.'

'And is that what you did?' asked Humphreys.

'It is, my Lord, but in the process of withdrawing, we were ambushed by another group of terrorists, here.' He pointed to an area about six miles south of the mission.

Whilst Justice Gardner usually relied on his own notes in trials, he had stopped taking notes and was now paying careful attention to the witness to let him give his evidence at his own pace. The assessors to either side picked up on this and also stopped their own note taking.

Humphreys indicated to Moyo to continue.

'My Lord, in this contact we suffered casualties. Two of the men received serious gunshot wounds and required immediate casevac. We radioed in our position and called for casevac, but we were told there was no air support available. We were told we had to seek a secure location and try to hold a position until choppers would be available.'

Moyo had not until that moment looked at O'Meara in the dock, but he did so now for the first time. O'Meara did not return his gaze and remained facing forward, staring at some point above the head of the Judge.

'Section Officer Moyo, please continue and tell the court what happened thereafter,' said Humphreys.

'My Lord, because of the injured men, Patrol Officer O'Meara decided we should make our way to St Mary's Mission to seek assistance. He knew the area, and he knew that there was a hospital there that would be able to provide medicine. There may even have been a doctor present. He said we could set up a defensive position there if we were being chased by the terrorists. He also knew the priest in charge of the mission.'

'And who was that priest?' Humphreys asked.

Moyo turned in the witness stand and raised his arm to point at the dock. 'It was the accused, Father O'Meara.'

'Please carry on. What happened then?'

'When we arrived at the mission, I went with the Patrol Officer to speak to the priest. We had to leave the men in a secure position away from the mission, in case the terrorists had already got there and were waiting to ambush us.' Moyo pointed to the map again and continued. 'My Lord, in this area there was very little cover for us. The grounds had been prepared for crops, and anyone approaching the mission would have been seen from a long way. With men who were injured, we could only make slow progress, and if we had all proceeded and come under attack, we would have been exposed.

'When we got to the mission, the accused came out to meet us, and Patrol Officer O'Meara explained our position. He told the accused that we had wounded men and were in need of shelter and medical supplies. I should also say, My Lord, that the mission itself had a very solid perimeter fence and would have been a secure place to defend if we came under attack while waiting for casevac or reinforcements.'

'And what was the response to this request from the accused?' asked Humphreys.

Moyo paused before turning to O'Meara and said, 'My Lord, he refused to help us.'

Throughout Moyo's evidence, the court room had been almost entirely silent. This last answer generated a general murmur of discontent, which caused Justice Gardner to look away from the witness and glare at the courtroom. This had the desired effect, and silence ensued.

For the first time, the Judge asked a question. 'Section Officer, when you say he refused, what do you mean by that? What exactly did he say to you?'

'My Lord, he said that he could not help us, because if he did, the terrorists would kill us all. He said that we were not able to protect him and the people at the mission, and the only way he had been able to survive in the war was to make it clear he did not support government forces.'

There was a general murmur through the courtroom at this, which was again silenced by a glare from the Judge. Gardner looked down towards the witness and indicated he should pause by holding up his hand. He lowered his hand and turned his attention to the courtroom.

'I will not tolerate interruption in this case through noise from the gallery. It is essential the witness give his evidence, and the court should hear the evidence without background interference. If this happens again, I will not hesitate in clearing the court.' He turned back to the witness and said, 'Please go on. What did you understand he was saying when he said this?'

Moyo again looked to O'Meara before continuing. 'My Lord, most mission stations have either closed or agreed to have security forces based with them. This mission was different. To the best of my knowledge, no terrorist attacks had ever been made on the mission. There must be a reason for this.'

The Director had been listening to the evidence and the exchange between the Judge and the witness, and he was clearly annoyed at the interruption. He needed to get the witness back on track to deal with the relevant facts and not get involved in speculation. There would be plenty of that later.

Before the Judge could say anything further, he addressed the witness. 'Section Officer, if you could please relate solely what you saw and heard on the day in question. Any thoughts or conclusions will be for the court to draw at a later stage. Please tell us what happened after the accused refused to assist.'

Moyo looked back to the court and continued. 'Patrol Officer O'Meara told the accused we had wounded men and we were low on medical supplies. He asked if he could at least help us with that.'

'And what was the response to that request?'

'The accused said that even as we were speaking, we were almost certainly being watched by Mujhibas. If he was seen to be giving us anything, the terrorists would be told.'

Once again, the Judge raised his hand to pause the witness. 'Section Officer, for the record, please explain what a Mujhiba is.'

'My Lord, a Mujhiba is an informer. They could be anyone who gives information to the terrorists, but they are usually children and women who have been threatened by the terrorists, and so they give them information, food, and support.'

Humphreys was anxious to move the evidence on, and so he asked the witness to continue before the Judge could intervene again.

'My Lord, we could see there were people in the mission who were watching us and could hear what was being said. Patrol Officer O'Meara then spoke to the accused in a loud voice, so they could hear exactly what he was saying. He told the accused that if he did not give us what we required, he would take it, and those in the mission who resisted would be dealt with. He told the accused what was needed and told him to get one of his orderlies from the clinic to bring us the supplies. Then we would leave.'

'And did that happen?' asked Humphreys.

'Not immediately, My Lord,' replied Moyo. 'The accused had to be persuaded to assist.'

'And how was that done?'

'Patrol Officer O'Meara struck him with his open hand and aimed his rifle at him.'

Despite the earlier warning from the Judge, this evidence again gave rise to general murmuring from the court which was again ended with a glare from the bench.

Humphrey asked, 'And what then happened?'

'The accused called one of his staff and told him to give us whatever we needed.'

'Was there any further discussion with the accused?'

Moyo paused before he answered. 'Yes, My Lord. He apologised for hitting the accused and said he had done that for the benefit of the Mujhibas, so it would seem the accused was not voluntarily helping us. He said this quietly so that no one could hear except the three of us standing together.

'When the medical supplies and water were brought out, we left the mission, returned to the men, and decided what to do.'

Jennings could imagine the dilemma that faced O'Meara and his men. In the past year, as the terrorists' numbers increased and the resources of the security forces were stretched further and further, the terrorists had changed their tactics. For many years they had done what they could to avoid contact with security forces, but now they were not averse to setting their own ambushes and following up any units they felt had been weakened enough to provide an easy target. With two men seriously wounded, the patrol was vulnerable if they were in fact being pursued. O'Meara would have been acutely aware of the danger.

Humphreys resumed his examination. 'Section Officer, please tell the court what happened next.'

'My Lord, when we reached the men, it was obvious that they would not be able to travel very far. Patrol Officer O'Meara decided that the best thing to do would be to split up and lay a false trail for any terrorists following upon us. We had done this before when we were at full strength, and it had always worked. These men were not properly trained, and they would always follow the easiest and most obvious trail without thinking.

Patrol Officer O'Meara decided to lay the trail with myself and one other constable, and he let the others find as secure a position as possible and await reinforcements.'

'What time of day are we talking about?' asked Humphreys. He already knew the answer from Moyo's statement, but it was important the court understood what was to unfold.

'My Lord, it was late afternoon when we set off. We knew we had to lay the trail as quickly as we could before dark, because the terrorists would never try to follow us at night. If we could get ahead of any terrorists following, the rest of the patrol would have more time to find a secure position.'

'And did you in fact carry on in the night?'

'We did, My Lord. We trained for this type of patrol often and were good at it.'

'Could you indicate on the map where you were going?'

Moyo picked up his pointer again and looked at the map to get his bearings. He marked a route with the pointer leading away from the mission and towards what appeared to be an area of hills and rocky outcrops. 'We went in this direction, My Lord, to try to get to the hills, where we could set up a defensive position.'

'And where did the rest of the patrol go?' asked Humphreys.

'They went in this direction,' Moyo replied, indicating away from the mission in the opposite direction.

'Section Officer Moyo, please tell the court what happened that night.'

Jennings knew that Moyo was approaching the end of his evidence because it was early the next morning that O'Meara would die. Although he had read Moyo's statement a dozen or more times, hearing him tell the story in person was difficult. Humphreys was also aware that this would be the most important part of the evidence, and he was anxious to let Moyo finish his testimony.

Moyo had paused for a while as he looked at the map with its different coloured pins standing out from the coloured relief. It was obvious that he was not looking forward to reliving the events of the night, but he knew it had to be done. After a deep breath, he continued with his evidence.

'My Lord, we had gone approximately two kilometres from the mission when the Patrol Officer decided to use two of our claymore mines to set up an ambush in this area'. As he said this he pointed to a cluster of red pins. 'After we had set up the mines he then ordered myself and the Constable to leave him alone and for us to return to the men. He would continue on his own and make sure any who survived the ambush would continue to follow him. My Lord we argued with him that it was madness, but he was in charge and said that it was the only way he would feel the rest of the patrol would be secure. He said that on his own, he could move quickly. He knew the area well from having been there as a child. He knew where he was going. He would not listen to me and ordered me to return to the men.'

'The constable and I left and made our way back to the men by going around these kopjes.' He indicated a series of kopjes as he spoke. 'We got back to the men just before dawn. About an hour after sunrise, we heard the claymores, and so we knew the terrorists had followed the trail we had laid.'

Humphreys interrupted at that point. 'Please, could you indicate how far away you would have been from the deceased at that time?'

Moyo pointed to the map and replied, 'It would have been about five kilometres on a straight line, but we were in a valley, and the sound of the claymores could be heard very clearly at that time.'

'And did you hear anything further?' asked Humphreys

'We did, My Lord. We could hear the sound of gunfire and knew that the terrorists had made contact with Patrol Officer O'Meara.'

'And how long did this last?'

'My Lord, it is hard to be accurate, but I believe the contact continued for half an hour.'

Humphreys turned for the first time and looked at the accused in the dock before asking his next question. 'If you could hear the contact from your location, do you think the accused would have heard it from the mission?'

Moyo also turned and looked at Father O'Meara as he replied, 'He would have heard everything.'

'Please carry on, Section Officer. What happened next?'

'My Lord, we were finally relieved by a fire force stick, and the injured men were casevaced to Umtali. We were resupplied and joined fire force to search for Patrol Officer O'Meara. We were not going to leave that place without him.'

'And did you find him?'

'We found him, My Lord.' Moyo stopped at that point, and for the first time, his voice faltered. 'We found his body at the top of a small kopje overlooking the valley and the mission station.' As he said this, Moyo dropped his shoulders and head. He was clearly struggling with the memory of the events.

Justice Gardner was obviously aware of the distress of the witness and enquired if he wanted to continue. After a moment, Moyo raised his head, straightened his shoulders, and said, 'I apologise, My Lord. I wish to continue.'

The Judge made an uncharacteristic comment for him. 'There is nothing to apologise for, Section Officer. This was clearly a most distressing incident, and it is understandable you are upset at having to repeat what happened, but it is necessary for us to hear everything to determine whether or not the accused is guilty of assisting these terrorists who killed your officer.'

Before he replied, Moyo turned again to look at the accused, who for the first time returned his look. While staring directly at him, Moyo said in a clear and strong voice, 'My Lord, if the accused had allowed us to stay in the mission, we could have defended our position, and we would all have lived. Of that I am certain. The terrorists killed Patrol Officer O'Meara, but it was that man'—he pointed at the accused—'who made it possible for them to do so.'

Despite the previous warnings given by the Judge, there was a general outburst from the gallery.

Advocate Chirenje, who had been steadily taking notes throughout the evidence, leapt to his feet at this last statement. 'My Lord, I must object to that statement. This is a matter for the court to determine, not for the witness to give his opinion on.'

The Judge was clearly annoyed at the public outburst but was even more annoyed at the interjection of Advocate Chirenje. The gallery was silenced by his now usual glare, and he turned his attention to Chirenje, who was still on his feet. 'Mr Chirenje if I am not mistaken, you are here at the request of the court and not on behalf of the accused. Is that not so?'

Chirenje had been in practice long enough to know what was coming. 'That is so, My Lord. The accused has not retained me and has not provided me with instructions, but as an officer of the court, I feel I must do what is necessary in the interest of justice to ensure a fair trial for the accused.'

When Chirenje had got to his feet, Humphreys had sat down, and Jennings could sense that he was almost enjoying what was about to happen.

Justice Gardner glared at Chirenje and spoke in a louder voice than was probably necessary. 'How dare you suggest that the accused needs the assistance of Counsel to have a fair trial in my court! Your function is simple. It is to assist the court in respect to any technical matters that may be relevant in the highly unlikely event this court should not itself deal with such matters. You have no instructions from the accused, and you may not interrupt the witness. Neither will you have the right to cross-examine him, as you well know. I will not tolerate any interruption from you during the evidence of any witness unless and until you can advise the court that you have instructions from the accused in that regard. Is that clear?'

Chirenje had appeared before Justice Gardner on more than enough occasions to realise when he was sailing close to the wind. In his best Kings Inn style, he bowed his head as he said, 'I do apologise to the court if my efforts at assisting in securing a fair trial are outside my remit. It will not happen again.'

This brief exchange got the press writing more furiously than ever, and it was apparent to Jennings that it had all been stage-managed by Chirenje for the benefit of the press and in particular the foreign press. They would have a field day with being able to report on a defence Counsel being silenced by the Judge. Jennings could almost see the headlines: 'Defence Barrister Silenced in Effort to Achieve Fair Trial for Priest.'

It was obvious the Director was also annoyed at this outburst from Chirenje. He wanted this trial to proceed with minimum fuss because the last thing he wanted was for suggestions to be made in the international press that this was some form of kangaroo court. The Director knew full well that the changes in the law in Rhodesia meant it was very difficult for defence Counsel to defend their clients, but he was also satisfied in his own mind that the changes in the law were necessary to protect the country during a civil war.

The Judge regained his composure and turned his attention to the accused in the dock. 'Father O'Meara, lest there be any misunderstanding, have you at any time retained Advocate Chirenje as defence Counsel?'

O'Meara rose from his seat and replied, 'I have not.' Then he sat down.

The Judge turned to Chirenje and said, 'Mr Chirenje, I trust you understand the position and are prepared to continue?'

Chirenje slowly rose to his feet. Before replying, he turned to the dock and looked at O'Meara, who did not return his gaze. He turned back to the court and with a shrug of his shoulders said, 'May it please the court. I apologise if I in any way acted improperly, but as Your Lordship will hopefully appreciate, I have always acted in what I believed to be the best interests of my client. I accept that in this rather unusual situation, I do not in fact have a client and will continue to appear on the basis as set out by Your Lordship.'

Having established beyond any doubt that he was effectively being muzzled by the court, Chirenje took his seat to the obvious consternation of the Judge. However, Gardner was sufficiently astute to realise that if he carried on with this sideshow, no useful purpose would be served, and he indicated to the Director that he should continue.

The Director rose once again and addressed Moyo, who had been watching this legal spat with little sign of interest.

'Section Officer, could you tell the court what happened to the men in your patrol who were injured.'

Moyo cleared his throat and replied, 'Both men survived and will soon return to operational duties, My Lord.'

The Director looked to Jennings to inquire if there was anything else he needed to deal with at that stage with the witness. Jennings would never presume to make any suggestion, and so he simply shook his head. The Director turned to Moyo and said, 'Thank you, Section Officer. If you would answer any questions of the court, please.'

Before he turned to the assessors, the Judge indicated to O'Meara he should stand, which he did. The Judge then addressed him. 'You are entitled to cross-examine the witness on anything he has said. Do you have any questions for him?'

O'Meara looked at Moyo, who did not turn to look at him, and he replied, 'I have no questions for the officer.'

The Judge turned to each assessor in turn and asked them in a low voice if they had any questions of the witness. Neither did, and the Judge then said, 'Thank you, Section Officer, for your evidence in this matter. I would like to commend you and your men for your conduct, and for the manner in which you gave your evidence today. I am sure Patrol Officer O'Meara would be very proud of both you and your men.'

Moyo looked impassively at the Judge and simply said, 'Thank you, My Lord.' He stepped down from the witness box and left the court without a glance at any of the participants—and most important without looking at O'Meara in the dock.

The Director then stood and addressed the court.

'My Lord, the next witness will be Detective Inspector Brookbank of CID Umtali, and his evidence will be led by Mr Jennings.'

Jennings rose from his seat, turned to the court orderly, and indicated the inspector should be brought into the court.

Brookbank was a young man for his rank, as was the case with many officers in the force. The war had at least ensured speedy promotion through the ranks

Having sworn him in and laid out his credentials as a criminal forensic investigator and ballistic expert, Jennings took him step by step through the map and the pins inserted on it. He relayed in detail what was depicted by each pin and drew the court's attention to the fact that each location was numbered or identified by some letter. He had a sheet, which was present in the court, with an index showing what had been found at each location.

Jennings then asked him to sum up his findings.

'My Lord, it was apparent from what I found that the terrorist group consisted of at least ten men who were heavily armed. Against that, Patrol Officer O'Meara was armed with only his FN rifle, and he used two claymore mines most effectively in that we found four terrorists dead at this point.' As he was saying this, he indicated a spot on the map that had a large black pin.

'At the point where we found the body of the deceased Patrol Officer O'Meara, we found evidence that he had been killed using a Tokarev semi-automatic pistol through several close-range shots to the head. We were able to establish this from bullet casings found at the scene and the final autopsy report carried out on the deceased.'

Jennings paused to let the court take in what they had been told. He then asked, 'Given what you found, was there any realistic opportunity for the deceased to have survived this contact?'

Brookbank looked back to the accused before turning to the court and replying, 'My Lord, there was little chance of one man on his own surviving the numbers he had to fight against. Had he been in a more secure position with the support of his patrol members, he may well have survived, but in the position, he found himself, there was going to be only one outcome.'

Jennings looked to the Director to see if there was anything else he needed to deal with. On seeing a shake of the head, Jennings advised the court that he had finished his examination. He asked the witness to answer any questions from the court.

As with Moyo, the Judge first asked if O'Meara had any questions, and then he inquired of his assessors. No one had anything to ask, and so the Judge thanked the witness, who stood down.

The Director then rose and addressed the court.

'My Lord and gentlemen assessors, at this time I propose to submit certificate evidence pursuant to the provisions of Section 265 of the Criminal Procedure and Evidence Act. This relates to the post-mortem report, chain of evidence affidavits in respect of the recovery of the body, and its preservation pending the post-mortem, ballistics, and other reports. Finally, I tender in evidence the confirmed statement of the accused.'

As he said this, Jennings handed to the Registrar the various reports and certificates in turn, which were passed up to the Judge.

The Director then took his seat, and the Judge turned to the assessors and spoke with each in a low voice so as not to be overheard. Having spoken to each in turn, he said, 'Mr Humphreys, the court will adjourn to enable the reports to be considered by myself and the assessors. I propose resuming the hearing tomorrow at eleven o'clock, if that is in order.'

The Director indicated that he had no problem with that, and the Judge then rose. The court fell silent as he and the assessors left the courtroom.

As soon as the door closed, there was an immediate outburst of noise as those present began to discuss what they had heard and seen during the morning's evidence. The Director turned to Jennings and asked him to collect his papers and return them to his office. Then the Director left without anything further being said.

As the Director was leaving, Jennings turned to speak with Mr Jones, who had been sitting behind them throughout the morning. Jennings was surprised to see Cian O'Meara standing at the back of the courtroom. He indicated to Jones to look behind him.

'I thought he was not going to be attending,' said Jennings.

'That was my understanding,' replied Jones. 'Although after all he has been saying in the press, it is hardly surprising to see him here. If his uncle's list is as good as he promises, I doubt he will be too keen to return to a courtroom anytime soon.'

Jennings returned to his work of packing up the papers and made his way out of the court and back to the Director's offices. As he emerged from the barrister's corridor, he saw Cian, who was obviously waiting for him.

Jennings had met Cian through John and had never taken to him. He always felt he had the mark of a bully about him and was far too much of a loudmouth for Jennings' liking. The two sons could not have been more dissimilar, and Jennings was in no mood to have to talk to him but that was not going to be possible to avoid.

'Hello, Cian. I thought you were going to stay away from the trial,' Jennings said.

'I was,' Cian replied. 'My father insisted I come so that he would hear exactly what was going on. He did not want to rely on the press. How do you think the trial is going?'

Jennings knew he had to be careful with what he said to this man. 'Well, it is early days, and it is unusual in that there is no actual defence being mounted. There is not too much I can say, really.'

'I understand that,' O'Meara said. 'I have been there for most of the day, and it is obvious the man is going to be convicted. What I want to know is, is he going to hang?'

Jennings could not comprehend the level of hatred apparent from Cian's tone. He was apparently hoping for his own uncle to be put to death. Even for Cian, this was a new low.

'I really can't comment on that,' Jennings said, moving away as he spoke. 'It is far too early to speculate on sentence. In any event, even with what has happened, surely you can't want your own uncle sent to the gallows?'

O'Meara grabbed Jennings' arm to prevent him from moving away. He said in a low, menacing tone, 'All I am telling you is that the man was the cause of my son dying like a cornered dog. He has betrayed his own flesh and blood, and if your court can't get us justice, we will see he gets what he deserves in our own way.'

Jennings shook off Cian's grip and was angered at this outburst. 'Cian, I know what has happened is upsetting for you and your family, but don't think for one minute you can come in here and make threats about a man who is on trial for his life. This is a matter for the court and the law. It has nothing to do with you and your family. I suggest you try to calm down before you do or say something really stupid.' With that, Jennings turned and walked away, leaving Cian alone in the middle of the corridor.

Jennings was of two minds regarding whether to report the incident to the Director, but he thought better of it and decided not to say anything. It was probably Cian's blowing off steam, and in any event, he was hardly in any position to affect his uncle now. Having returned the Director's papers to the safe custody of Mrs Steyn, he left his own papers in his office.

He had his desk cleared of all other dockets and so was at something of a loose end. Jennings was not too sure what he should be doing when he looked up to see the Director come into his office.

The Director closed the door behind him and said, 'I want you to speak to our accused and get the list he has promised before we go any further. I saw his nephew in the courtroom today, and I don't want him getting cold feet over our arrangement through any delayed sense of loyalty to his family.'

Jennings was a bit concerned at his request that he speak to the accused now that the trial had started. That would be a highly unusual, if not unprofessional, thing to do. Even though strictly speaking he had not instructed defence Counsel, any communication with an accused at this stage should be through Counsel and not directly. However, he was not going to refuse what was a clear instruction.

Jennings said, 'I will go down to the cells and see if I can speak to him now. The prison transport should not be here yet.'

The Director replied, 'The transport is here, but I have asked Superintendent van Tonder to hold back to allow you to speak to him. They are waiting for you.' Without any further comment, the Director turned and left.

Jennings followed him out and made his way back down to the holding cell below the court. After entering the court and heading through the narrow public entrance, he noticed the warders were milling around, waiting to go. They were clearly not impressed at being kept back.

van Tonder emerged from the reception room and indicated to Jennings to follow him. He showed him into a cell where O'Meara was sitting on the cement bench.

As he walked in, O'Meara stood. Jennings said, 'Please sit down, Father. I won't keep you long. I wonder if you saw Cian in the courtroom today?'

O'Meara replied, 'I did, but he did not speak to me.'

'I am aware of that.' Jennings said, I spoke to him outside the court. He is a very angry man.'

O'Meara said, 'He has been an angry man all his life. Recent events have simply brought it to the fore.'

Jennings wasted no time in getting to the reasons for his being there.

'The Director wants your list of names now. He is concerned that having seen Cian in the court, you may feel that you have done enough damage to the O'Meara family and go back on our agreement. Is he right to be concerned?'

O'Meara smiled briefly before replying. 'Richard, you could not begin to understand the hatred my brother and the rest of my family feel towards me already. There is nothing I can do about that. But I am a man of my word and will give you what I have promised. How long will it take to close the State case so that matters can be finalised?'

'I think we should be done early tomorrow, given you are not raising any defence,' Jennings replied. 'It will be up to you whether you give evidence in your defence, but even if you choose not to, you can still be questioned by the Director and the court. That may take some time. The evidence should be all over by the end of tomorrow, and then it depends how long the court needs to reach a verdict.'

O'Meara seemed to be considering this for a moment and then said, 'Very well. I will have the list for you tomorrow morning. There is no point in delaying matters, and you have kept your side of the bargain. Tell the Director he need have no concern about me.'

The two men stood up from the bench. 'I will see you tomorrow then, Father,' Jennings said, and with that he left the cell. He advised van Tonder on the way out that he was finished with the priest, and they could leave for the prison.

CHAPTER NINE

On arrival in the office in the morning, Jennings went to the Director's office. As usual, Mrs Steyn was already at her desk, typing away. On being advised he wished to see the Director, she indicated to a chair in the room and carried on typing without saying a word to him.

When she was finished what she was doing, she stood up and went into the Director's office, closing the door behind her. A few moments later, she re-emerged and advised the Director would see him. Jennings entered the office as she closed the door on her exit.

The Director did not invite him to be seated, and so Jennings knew all that was required was a simple report, which he gave. He told the Director of the meeting with O'Meara the night before. The Director said, 'Very well. Make sure you get to him as soon as the prison transport arrives. Have the list in your pocket before we resume. I will deal with it later, when the trial is over.'

Jennings decided to collect his papers and await the arrival of the prison transport in the courtroom. As he went through the narrow pedestrian entrance to the courtyard adjoining the court, he saw the transport had already arrived, and the prisoners were being escorted into the holding cells.

He saw van Tonder standing to one side and approached him to enquire as to Father O'Meara's whereabouts. Jennings had not seen him in the group of prisoners. 'Good morning, Superintendent,' he said. 'I don't see Father O'Meara. No problems there, I hope?'

van Tonder smiled and gave a nod towards the courtroom 'No problem at all. He is in the court, waiting for you. He told me you would want to see him first thing before any crowd developed, and so I arranged early transport. He says you think the evidence will be done with today. Is that right?'

'I should think so,' Jennings replied. 'He has chosen not to enter a defence, and as I understand him, he proposes to not give evidence. He may or may not be questioned by the Director and court, but that shouldn't take too long. Then the court can retire to consider its verdict.'

'I assume you believe a guilty verdict will follow. What is the State's position on sentence?' van Tonder asked.

'I haven't even discussed that with the Director yet,' Jennings replied. 'To be honest, I doubt whether there will be any submissions on this case. From all previous cases under the section of the Act, as you well know, the State believes the maximum penalty is appropriate and then leaves it up to the court to decide what to do on any given set of facts.'

'And do you feel this man should go to the gallows?' van Tonder asked.

'The laws are there for a reason, Superintendent. You of all people know the situation the country is in. If we don't have the ultimate penalty for assisting terrorism, there would hardly be any point in prosecuting those who do assist them.'

'I suppose so,' Van Tonder replied. 'It just seems to me that in this case, O'Meara was in a no-win situation whatever he did. You know rightly that if he had provided shelter, the chances are the mission would have been burned to the ground within the month, and all those there killed or worse. What was he supposed to do?'

'If things have got to that stage, maybe he should not have continued in the mission. Most other missions operate on a restricted basis now. Why does he have to be different?' Jennings countered.

'He obviously felt he had a duty to his flock, and that could not be served by trying to run the mission by proxy. It seems unfortunate that a man who is trying to do good is likely going to pay for that with his life. Does that not seem wrong to you, Mr Jennings?'

'I don't have any view on that, Superintendent. My job is to prosecute breaches of the law, not to debate the rights and wrongs of the law.'

This discussion was clearly going nowhere, and van Tonder shrugged his shoulders. 'Very well, Mr Jennings. We all have our roles to play. Perhaps one day you will spend some time with me in the H wing, and we can discuss the matter further.' With that, he turned and went off towards the entrance to the court with Jennings in tow.

When they went into the courtroom, Jennings saw O'Meara sitting outside the dock on one of the front benches, reading a copy of the day's *Herald* newspaper. Not only was that totally against regulations, but there was also no sign of any warder in the court. Having heard the two of them come into the room, O'Meara stood up, folded the paper, and handed it to van Tonder. 'Thank you, Superintendent. It was good to catch up on the news,' he said. 'Good morning, Mr Jennings. An early start for us all. I have what you asked for.'

After taking the paper from O'Meara, van Tonder made his way through the dock and down to the cells below. When the door was closed, and the bolts were thrown, O'Meara took a sheet of paper out of his inner breast pocket.

As he handed it over, he said, 'That is a list of names of people Sean has been dealing with here and in Ireland. The Special Branch will have an interest in them. I also have given you certain account details of banks in this country which may prove of interest.'

Jennings looked at the list, which had several names and details written neatly in longhand. 'How do we know these details are correct?' he asked. 'Have you no supporting documents we can get?'

'One of the skills we were taught at the seminary, Mr Jennings, was to memorise large tracts of the liturgy for various services. I am more fortunate than most and have what some people refer to as a photographic memory. I can assure you the details are correct. Your Mr Jones will be able to verify most of the details for you before the day is over.' As he said this, he took another piece of paper from his pocket and handed that to Jennings. 'This is something you should also have.'

Jennings opened the folded piece of paper and saw that a series of numbers were written on it, with a hyphen between each number. 'And this is what?' he asked.

'That is the combination to Sean's safe at his home. If you gain access to that, you will find that the details I have given you are correct. There will also be other information which should enable the authorities to put a stop to what he is doing.'

'Father, it is one thing to provide the list you have given, but if there is the level of information in the safe you say there is, you could end up having Sean in prison with you for a very long time. How can you do that to your own brother after what you did to John? None of this makes sense to me.'

O'Meara paused and then spoke without looking at Jennings. 'What Sean has been doing over the last few years has been wrong. He has abused my trust and has used the Church for his own benefit and gain. I am not a total fool. I know he has been playing a double game and working for the government as well. They will not put him in jail, but at least they might be able to rein him in and stop him from doing any more harm to the people he is supposedly trying to help. As I said to you at the beginning, my only loyalty here is to the memory of John. If the price of that is to cause Sean some hardship, it is a small price to pay.'

'Very well,' Jennings said. 'I will pass this on. As I said, we should be done with the State case today. You still have time to reconsider your position and give evidence in your own defence. You must realise by now the foolishness of staying silent.'

O'Meara shrugged his shoulders. 'I have reconciled myself to accepting whatever the result is here. My true Judgement will come at another time, so what happens here is not really that important.' He stood and made his way down to the cells, leaving Jennings alone in the courtroom.

CHAPTER TEN

When O'Meara left, Jennings was alone in the court and was tempted to go through the list he had been given. It was a small country, and there was a good chance he would recognise a number of the names listed. As he was about to open the list, he looked up and saw Jones come in through the advocates' entrance.

'Good morning, Mr Jennings. The Director told me you would be here. Have you got anything from our friend?'

Jennings stood and extended his hand with the sheet of paper O'Meara had given him. 'This is what he gave me. It is a list of names. He also gave me this.' He handed over the combination details. 'You will need a warrant to search the house, but that may well be what you are really after.'

Jones took both pieces of paper and smiled. 'Well, the priest has come up trumps. Don't worry about the arrest warrant; I have had that ready for days. I will be off, then, and see you later. Have a good day in court.' With that, he turned and left.

Jennings returned to his room, collected his papers, and made his way back to the court, avoiding as best he could the increased number of reporters milling about in the courtyard adjoining the court.

By 10.15, the courtroom was full and ready for the arrival of the Judge and his assessors.

The Director had come in to the court at ten o'clock, and apart from a 'Good morning' to Jennings, he said nothing and simply prepared his papers for the day.

At precisely 10.30, the Registrar knocked on the door and announced the arrival of the court. After the usual preliminaries, Justice Gardner looked up from his papers and indicated to Humphreys that he should continue.

The Director rose from his seat and stood at the lectern. 'May it please the court, that is the State's case.' He returned to his seat.

The Judge made a note in his court notebook and then addressed the accused in the dock. 'I understand that you have indicated you do not wish to give evidence in your own defence. That is of course your right, but I must advise you that in terms of the provisions of the criminal code, should you not elect to give evidence, you may nevertheless be questioned by the representative of the State and by this court. Should you fail to answer any questions put to you, that may result in adverse inferences being drawn against you by the court in coming to its verdict regarding the charges you face. Do you understand what I have said to you?'

O'Meara stood in the dock and said, 'I do understand, and Mr Chirenje has very kindly explained the law to me as well. I will not be giving any evidence.'

This was by no means the normal run of a criminal trial, and the Judge was clearly not happy with what he heard. He cleared his throat and said, 'Lest there be any misunderstanding, you are facing charges which, if proven against you, carry severe penalties. This is your only opportunity to defend yourself against a conviction in respect of these charges with the consequences that may follow. I must ask you to reconsider your position, and if necessary, I am happy to adjourn the trial for a short while to enable you to take advice from Mr Chirenje. Do you wish me to do that?'

O'Meara replied without hesitation. 'I do not, but thank you for the consideration shown to me.'

The Judge stared at O'Meara for a short while and then turned to each assessor for a discussion to which no one else in the courtroom was privy. After he spoke to each man, he looked to the Director, who rose from his seat. 'Mr Humphreys, do you wish to question the accused?' he asked.

Humphreys paused before he replied. 'My Lord, given there had been no attempt to rebut the evidence presented for the State in the matter, I do not propose questioning the accused.'

It was not unusual for an accused to elect to not give evidence, but it was almost unheard of for a prosecutor to not question an accused, if only to try to copper-fasten whatever evidence had been led from the State. Even if the accused said nothing in response to questions, that invariably led to the prosecutor asking the court to draw adverse inferences against the accused. In fact, Humphreys had issued a directive several years ago when the laws were changed to advise that a failure to question an accused in the type of situation now before a court would be viewed with displeasure, to say the least.

Advocate Chirenje was also clearly taken aback because he had set himself ready to take detailed notes of the questioning of the accused.

After a moment, the Judge turned to Chirenje and said, 'Mr Chirenje, with the State having elected not to question the accused, and with the accused having indicated he does not wish to give evidence, there is no need for the State to address the Court on matters of fact. I invite you to address the court on any issue of law you feel may have arisen which requires the consideration of the court.'

Chirenje remained seated for a moment as he collected his thoughts. Then he rose and moved in front of the lectern to his right to address the court. 'My Lord and gentlemen assessors, the facts on which the State seeks a conviction of the accused has not in any way been disputed by the accused. Despite that, I would respectfully submit that in law, the accused cannot be convicted of the offence charged and should be acquitted.'

The Judge looked up from his notes and said, 'Please continue, Mr Chirenje. On what basis do you make such a submission?'

'My Lord, the criminal law requires two elements for any offence. They are the criminal act and the intention to commit a crime. In this case, the State has shown very clearly that the accused did nothing on the day in question, and they have also failed to lead any evidence to establish the intention of the accused. If the accused were to be convicted of this offence on the facts presented to the court, it would be open to the State to prosecute any citizen of the country who failed to take an active role on the side of the State against those alleged to be terrorists, based solely on their inaction rather than their action. I submit, My Lord, that that cannot be the law.'

The Judge took a moment to consider what he had heard and then asked, 'On the night in question, the Section officer, then Sergeant Moyo told the Court that had they been given shelter they would have been better able to defend themselves and there is a chance that Patrol Officer O'Meara would not have been killed. The action you say is missing is in his refusal to provide that assistance."

Chirenje responded immediately "Precisely My Lord. One is accused of not doing something whilst the section he is alleged to have contravened require he be guilty of doing something and to, and I quote "aid and abet terrorism. That must require action in my submission, not inaction.'

The Judge turned to the Director and said, 'Mr Humphreys, any reply?'

Humphreys rose and said. 'My Lord, this argument has been raised by my friend on more than one occasion. If I am not mistaken, he has addressed your Lordship in similar terms before. The law, as has been determined by the court, makes it clear that the failure to assist members of the defence force when called upon to do so constitutes acts that aid and abet terrorism. Although Mr Chirenje is entitled to make the argument on each occasion he appears in the court defending such matters, I would submit the door he is seeking to open for the accused to escape conviction has been closed some time ago.'

'I agree, Mr Humphreys,' the Judge said. 'I have indeed had these submissions from Mr Chirenje before.' He turned to Advocate Chirenje. 'Unless there is anything new you wish to address the court on, Mr Chirenje, am I correct in assuming you have no further submissions?'

Chirenje rose slowly from his seat, gave a theatrical bow for the benefit of the gallery, and said, 'I have no further submissions, My Lord.' He resumed his seat.

The Judge turned to his assessors and had a brief discussion with each. He then turned to the court. 'This court will now adjourn to consider its verdict. I propose adjourning the court to tomorrow at 11.00 a.m., if that is convenient to all parties.' Despite the enquiry, this was not an invitation for discussion. With no further comment from any of the Counsel before him, Justice Gardner rose, bowed perfunctorily, and made his way from the court followed by the assessors.

When the Judge left, Humphreys turned to Jennings and said, 'I want you to speak to Mr Chirenje when you have a chance. Find out if there is anything we need to know about in the event of a conviction, for sentencing purposes. If possible, I don't want a media circus.'

Jennings nodded. Whilst Humphreys was collecting his papers. Jennings moved behind him towards Advocate Chirenje, who was still sitting and staring up towards the bench. 'Well, Amos, I am afraid the Judge was not for listening to you today.'

Chirenje looked up and smiled at Jennings. 'Not today, and indeed not on any day soon, I am afraid. Perhaps in years to come, such submissions will receive a better reception, but until the war is over, the task of the defence will always be difficult.'

Jennings pulled up a chair and sat next to Chirenje as Humphreys walked past them and gave each a cursory nod of the head.

'The Director is not one for small talk, is he?' said Chirenje. 'I assume your visit is not a social one. What does the good Director want?'

Jennings smiled at Chirenje's astute sarcasm. 'You are right on all counts, Amos. He wants to know what you have planned, if anything, for mitigation in the event of a conviction.'

Chirenje smiled. 'A conviction is guaranteed, Mr Jennings. But as for mitigation, my hands are tied. Not only will the court give me little room for any input, but the good priest has told me in direct terms that I am to say nothing on his behalf.'

'But surely you have told him of the possible sentence he is looking at. He has to have something to say in mitigation.'

'Whether he does or not, I cannot say. I have been given specific instructions on this issue. In fact, they are the only real instructions I have been given at all. The good priest is a very difficult man to deal with.'

'Very well. We will simply have to wait and see what the Judge does in the morning.'

Both men collected their papers and left the courtroom to the warders and prisoners who were waiting to come in and do the daily clean-up. The court had emptied very quickly as soon as the Judge had left, and mundane activities resumed, oblivious to the day's events.

CHAPTER ELEVEN

The next morning, Jennings was in the office early. Despite his early start, he found Mr Jones sitting in the reception area.

'Good morning, Mr Jennings,' he said. 'An early start for you as well, I see.'

'Mr Jones. Any luck with your search? I assume that is why you are here?'

'Quite right, Mr Jennings. Our search proved very productive. The list provided will keep us busy for weeks, but the real jewel in the crown was what we found in the safe. The information there will cause Sean and his son an enormous amount of bother. It will also give you plenty to do for the next few months, I imagine.'

Before he could elaborate, Mrs Steyn came in the reception area and said, 'The Director will see you now, Mr Jones.' She turned on her heel, and Jones followed her out.

Jennings did not waste any time thinking about what Jones had said. He was more concerned with what was to come later in the day. A conviction was almost guaranteed, but the real concern would be the sentence imposed. The death penalty had been imposed in several similar cases, although seldom carried out because after the obligatory appeal to the Appellate Division, some sentences were set aside. Of those that were not, presidential pardons were often quietly entered on petitions of clemency. That still did not mean that in certain cases, the appeal and petitions failed to spare the convicted person from the gallows. That reality always focused the mind on days such as this.

The court was already full and waiting for the Judge and assessors fifteen minutes before the scheduled commencement time at 11.00 a.m. There was very little chat in the room, and it was almost unnaturally quiet.

At 10.55 a.m., there was a very loud noise from the cells as the bolts were drawn from the door heading up into the court. Jennings turned in his seat to see O'Meara arrive with his warders.

O'Meara caught his eye as he took his seat and almost had the hint of a smile on his face. For someone possibly facing the death penalty, he seemed incredibly composed.

At eleven o'clock precisely, the Registrar called out, 'Silence in court,' which was superfluous. The Judge and his assessors came in and took their seats after the usual bow to the courtroom.

The Registrar waited until he was sure the Judge was ready and then announced, 'May it please the court to resume the matter of the State versus O'Meara.'

Justice Gardiner adjusted his glasses and looked up towards O'Meara in the dock. 'The prisoner will please rise for the Judgement of the court.'

There was a brief pause while O'Meara stood flanked by his warders.

When the Judge was satisfied they were ready, he began his ruling. 'This is an unusual case in many respects. Sadly, given the current events in the country, the facts are not uncommon. What is most unusual is the approach of the accused to the matter. He has chosen, despite having the benefit of an experienced and able Counsel, to not attempt to refute any of the evidence led by the State. Neither has he chosen to give evidence in his defence. The only avenue open to the accused was advanced on his behalf by Mr Chirenje, who appears at the request of the court and who has done what he can with no assistance from the accused. The submission made by Mr Chirenje cannot be accepted by the court. In any other case, it would be necessary for the court to go through the evidence and provide its reasons for its findings, be they for or against the accused. In this case, that will not be necessary, and the court must accordingly find the accused guilty of the offence charged and does so accordingly.'

There was an audible release of tension in the courtroom. Everyone had expected a far longer ruling than that given, but, what the Judge had said was all anyone could have said. What had seemed inevitable had come to pass, and the only issue now was the sentence to be imposed.

The Judge made an entry in his court book and then turned to Mr Chirenje. 'Mr Chirenje, whilst not strictly within your brief, have you any instructions regarding mitigation?'

Chirenje rose from his seat and turned to look at O'Meara, who was still standing in the dock. O'Meara simply gave him a barely noticeable shake of the head, and Chirenje turned slowly to the court.

'My Lord, I have no instructions from the accused in respect of mitigation.' He paused briefly and then said, 'Given the seriousness of the offence, however, and the range of sentence options open to the court, if I do not advance some mitigation, I would not be fulfilling my duty to the court or the accused. I have here several letters and testimonials from both clergy and laypersons who speak of the good character of the accused and his work for the people of this country in the mission over many years. I would ask the court to accept these and give them such weight as the court considers appropriate.'

This was another departure from what would normally happen in a trial, and Jennings was ready for an explosion from the bench at the suggestion made by Chirenje. Never before had a court simply accepted documents in mitigation, unsupported by direct evidence of witnesses. On this occasion, however, he simply took the documents and said without hesitation, 'Thank you, Mr Chirenje. The court will accept the material you have and take time to consider it before passing sentence.'

Chirenje had his papers ready and handed then to the registrar who in turn passed them to the Judge. The Judge was clearly of a mind to leave to consider sentence and said, 'Very well. If there is nothing further …?' when he was interrupted by a firm and loud voice from the dock.

'My Lord, may I speak on behalf of the accused?'

Jennings, Humphreys, and Chirenje turned in their seats to see who on earth had the temerity to be speaking up at this junction.

The answer was even more surprising when they saw Superintendent van Tonder standing next to one of the warders flanking O'Meara. He had obviously come up from the cells during the Judge's ruling, and none of the advocates had noticed his arrival.

Justice Gardner was not known for his patience, and this type of intervention would normally provoke a furious outburst. Instead, he simply said, 'Superintendent, this is a most unusual request. I have to assume that this does not come from the accused, given what I have been told so far.'

van Tonder looked at O'Meara before replying to the Judge, 'My Lord, the accused had no idea of my intention, and had I advised him, he probably would have told me to not address the court. That is why I have spoken to no one of the matters on which I wish to address the court.'

Gardner was clearly perplexed at what was happening in his court. He normally ran matters according to the book and without having to deal with unusual requests. In any other trial, he would almost certainly have dismissed the request without a thought. But in this case, with over a dozen foreign reporters furiously writing down every word, he was clearly being cautious in what he was doing. The issue of sentencing was entirely for the Judge alone, and so he turned to his two assessors. He could not be heard but was apparently seeking their advice as to what he should do.

After his discussions with the assessors, he addressed the two Counsel. 'This is most unusual, but in the absence of any strong opposition from either side, I would accede to the Superintendent's request to speak on behalf of the accused. I assume you have no objection, Mr Chirenje. Mr Humphreys, what is the State's position?'

Before replying, Humphreys turned to Jennings and asked in a whisper, 'Have you any idea what is going on here?'

Jennings replied, 'None at all, apart from the fact that when I was in Chikurubi, it seemed to me the Superintendent held the priest in high regard. I have no idea what he is going to say.'

Humphreys rose and said to the Judge, 'This is most unusual, My Lord, but in the interest of fairness to the accused, if the Superintendent is of the view that he has information that would be of assistance to the court, the State will have no objection to his giving evidence.' He resumed his seat.

The Judge said to van Tonder, 'Superintendent, this is a most unusual request, but as the State has no objection, the court will hear your evidence. Please take the stand.'

Van Tonder made his way from the dock to the witness stand and was sworn in by the registrar. In his first dress uniform, he was an even more imposing figure than he was in his normal work uniform. He had the full attention of the courtroom as he cleared his throat and began his evidence.

'My Lord, I am the officer in charge of Chikurubi Prison, and I have been for the past several years. I have overall responsibility for the Chikurubi complex jn particular of the maximum-security prison. This is the prison in which the accused, Father O'Meara, has been held pending trial.'

At this, the Judge interrupted and asked the same question Jennings had asked. 'Why was he not held in the remand prison? Surely it was not appropriate for him to be held in the maximum-security prison pending trial?'

'My Lord, it was an administrative decision of the prison service, and special provisions were made for the accused. He was kept separate from the general population except when carrying out his function as a chaplain. He carried out this work at his own request, and in my view, it was a useful service for the prisoners under my care.

'My Lord, the maximum-security prison holds a very large number of prisoners, and it is fair to day that we are at full capacity. We hold a large number of prisoners who would have been convicted of offences relating to the current terrorist operation in the country from both factions involved, ZIPRA and ZANLA. As best we can, we try to keep these groups separated because there has been a number of incidents when there have been serious outbreaks of violence between the two sides.'

The Judge held up his hand to pause van Tonder in his evidence whilst he took a note. 'Superintendent, I thought these people were all supposed to be working together with a common purpose of overthrowing the lawful government of the country. Are you telling me that they fight amongst themselves?'

'That is precisely what I am saying, My Lord. There is a very marked difference between the two sides in their training and political orientation, and this has led to the trouble to which I have referred.'

The Judge nodded and said, 'Very well. Carry on.'

'My Lord, approximately four months ago, the accused was in the C wing attending to a prisoner who was terminally ill when there was a breach in security and an outbreak of violence. Several officers who were working in the wing were isolated and were assaulted with weapons made by the prisoners, including sharpened objects used to stab and cut. It was an extremely serious situation, and the officers were at risk of their lives.

'It was then that the accused intervened. He put himself between the prisoners and the officers and was able to prevent further violence. He also provided medical assistance to one of the officers, who had been stabbed and was seriously injured.'

The Judge stopped taking his notes and inquired, 'How precisely did he achieve this?'

'My Lord, he physically put himself between the prisoners and the officers and told them that if they were to try to kill any officers, they would have to kill him first because he could not allow them to make their own position worse by continuing with their actions. He said that they were the lucky ones who would one day complete their sentences and leave the prison to return to their families, but if they continued, they would achieve nothing but their own deaths. After some time, the prisoners stood back and allowed other officers to regain control of the situation.

'My Lord I can say without a shadow of doubt that had the accused not acted as he had, there would have been at least one fatality amongst the officers concerned, if not more. In my view, he was prepared to sacrifice his own life for those who were under threat. In all my years in the prison service, I have never seen such a courageous act on the part of a prisoner.'

Gardner paused for a moment before saying, 'Tell me, Superintendent. Has the officer who was stabbed made a full recovery?'

'I was that officer, My Lord, and yes, I have made a full recovery.'

Despite previous warnings, this revelation caused an immediate murmur amongst the gallery as they looked from van Tonder to O'Meara, who had not shown any emotion at all during the evidence.

Justice Gardner was apparently lost for words and needed a few moments to compose his thoughts before he asked a further question of the witness.

'Superintendent, I hear what you have said, and it clearly goes to the credit of the accused that he acted in the way he did. However, I fail to see how this can affect the position regarding sentence. Given the unusual circumstances that follow this case, I will ask you for your views as to what I should do.'

van Tonder was clearly not expecting this question, and he looked to O'Meara before he turned to the Judge. 'My Lord, the accused had been prepared to give up his own life to protect and to save those who were his warders. In my view, that shows this is a man of strong character and courage, and for that reason and in recognition of what he has done, I would urge the court to consider a sentence which reflects what he has done in saving the lives of other people.'

Despite sentencing being a matter for the Judge alone, Gardner often sought the views of his assessors and turned to them to ask if they had any questions of the witness. Neither assessor had, and the Judge enquired of Humphreys and Chirenje if they had any questions of the witness. Similarly, they had no question, and so the Judge thanked van Tonder and asked him to leave the witness stand.

Gardner considered his notes for a short while and was clearly undecided as to how he was to sentence O'Meara. He closed his notebook and said to the advocates, 'Once again, this case has had an unusual turn, and I am not going to rush to sentence. I will now adjourn the court until half past ten tomorrow, when the court will pass sentence. I must say, however, that whilst the evidence of Superintendent van Tonder has been compelling, I am not sure to what extent it has any relevance in my approach to sentence. This court will now stand adjourned.'

As all present rose and awaited the departure of the Judge and assessors, the Director collected his papers and said in a quiet voice to Jennings, 'In all my years, I have never heard the like of what has been going on in this trial. God knows what Gardner is going to make of this last intervention. I will need to see you in my office later. Mr Jones has some news about our Mr O'Meara Junior. You will be working on that matter with him, and so you need to be in on developments from the start.'

Humphreys left without any further comment, and Jennings collected his papers as Advocate Chirenje came over to him.

'Well, Jennings, where do you think we are going now? The gallows or prison?'

Jennings had learnt from previous experience to never engage with defence Counsel on issues that were still to be decided, but in Chirenje's case, he felt comfortable enough to venture his honest opinion, which was that he felt after van Tonder's intervention, the death sentence was unlikely.

'You are probably right in that, but I must say that at the end of the day, I do not think that what we have been through here will really have much impact on the good priest's future at all.'

'Why on earth do you say that, Amos?' asked Jennings.

'Come now, Mr Jennings. None of us live in a total vacuum in this room, even though we often pretend to do so. You know as well as I do that with the political manoeuvring going on now, it is a matter of when, not if, there is going to be a major change on the political front. I cannot see any more executions under your law and order legislation in the face of that. None of the current political players will want to take responsibility for executions at the end of hostilities, and certainly not of a priest. I could see a general amnesty as having to be part of any political settlement, and whatever we have been doing here will be a mere footnote in the history of the struggle.'

Jennings had always felt that events outside the court may well overturn whatever was done in the court, but this was the first time anyone had openly articulated the view before him.

'I suppose you may well be proven right, Amos, but as the saying goes, "Ours is not to reason why ..."'

Chirenje burst out laughing before Jennings could finish. 'Please do not continue, Mr Jennings. Neither you nor I have any desire to fulfil that particular prophecy. Good day to you.' With that, he turned and left, chuckling as he went.

After Jennings had returned to his office and deposited his papers, he made his way to the Director's office and saw Jones waiting outside the office, reading the day's edition of the *Herald* newspaper.

Mrs Steyn indicated to Jennings to sit, and she went in to the Director's office. Jennings had barely had time to take his seat when she came out and invited them into the office.

The meeting with the Director was brief. Jones advised that Cian had been arrested at his father's house following the search and their initial enquiries, and he was being held under police custody pending direction from the office as the charges to be preferred. On the information obtained, preliminary charges could be brought under either the exchange control legislation or the law and order legislation, and the decision as to which route to follow would determine whether Cian would remain in custody or be released on bail pending further enquiries.

The Director turned to Jennings and said, 'What is your view? Do you think he will stay and face the music if we let him out on exchange control, or will his father try to get him out of the country?'

Jennings paused before answering. 'I think his father is more likely to let him face the music here and look after his own interests, rather than run the risk of losing everything he has built up over the years. Money is his main concern, and he will see Cian's prosecution as simply a bad business deal that has to be put to bed. I don't see Cian going against his father's instructions.'

Humphreys looked from Jennings to Jones, and there was a hint of a smile as he said, 'You may know this family better than you think. Mr Jones has told me that the father has already been offering a deal if we keep his son out of jail. As you say, it is all about money with him.' He turned to Jones. 'Charge him with what you have under exchange control and get the docket to Jennings as soon as it is complete. He will put together the final charges he is to face, and I am sure he will derive maximum benefit for the State in the charges to be preferred.'

With the conversation clearly ended, both men left the office. Jones and Jennings discussed when they would next meet to consider what to do with Cian. 'I would like to bring him before the Magistrate's court today for preliminary remand and bail, if that is okay with you. The main event should be over soon enough in the morning.'

'That is fine with me,' said Jennings. 'Have him booked into the cells before lunch, and we will do the remand court at 2.30 this afternoon.'

Jones left, and once again Jennings was left with his own thoughts as to what had been an extraordinary few weeks.

A man was on trial for his life, having been in part to blame for his own nephew's death. He in turn had not sought to defend his actions but had instead thrown his own brother and surviving nephew to the wolves to ensure the dead nephew's memory was not blemished by the wrongdoing of the father and son. By the time Cian came answer his charges, the trial of his uncle would be largely forgotten, and it would not be unheard of for a hearing under the exchange control legislation to be dealt with under the D Notice regime, which would effectively mean there could be no notice or publication of any of the details of Cian's prosecution put into the public domain.

The evidence of van Tonder had struck Jennings as showing O'Meara in a different light altogether. This was not a man who was afraid of death or personal injury. He was a man prepared to risk his own life for another but faced with the choice to defend his own nephew against the others at the mission, he chose the mission. This was man who clearly has a deep conscience to wrestle with, and Jennings felt he would never understand what it was that made him do what he had done.

CHAPTER TWELVE

By 10.15 a.m. the following morning, Court A was packed. Even members of the Director's office had moved their lists to enable them to be present at the final hearing in the matter. There was a discernible tension in the air as O'Meara was escorted up from the cells by Superintendent van Tonder, and it was noticed immediately that he was the only prison officer with O'Meara. The usual warden had been left outside the dock, and it was only van Tonder who sat impassively by his side as the arrival of the Judge was awaited.

At precisely 10.30 a.m., the Registrar, having already been out of the court to advise the Judge that all was ready, emerged and gave the usual command for silence. The Judge and the assessors took their seats, and after a moment the Registrar called on the case before the court for sentence, indicating as he finished that the prisoner in the dock should stand for sentence.

Jennings could not resist turning slightly to look at O'Meara, who as usual impassively stared ahead at a point above the Judge's seat.

Gardner cleared his throat and began.

'This is a matter which from the outset has been conducted in a most extraordinary fashion. The offence with which the accused was charged and convicted carries the most serious of penalties, including the possibility of the ultimate penalty. For his part, and for reasons not apparent to the court, the accused has chosen not to defend his actions in any way throughout these proceedings. It may be that this conduct could be construed as indicating remorse. If that were so, he would be deserving of credit from the court regarding sentence. However, it could also be that the way the accused has dealt with the trial is indicative of a contempt for the law of the land and this court. Had he any genuine remorse for his actions in failing to assist the deceased at his hour of need, and thereby aiding the forces intent on the overthrow of the lawful government of the day, he has had the opportunity on many occasions to express such remorse. The fact that he has chosen not to do so is, in my mind, an aggravating feature of this case. The accused is an educated and intelligent man, and he must appreciate the significance of his actions in this trial.'

Jennings was concerned for O'Meara at the tone of the Judge's opening remarks. It seemed Gardner was heading in only one direction, which was not going to be in O'Meara's favour.

Justice Gardner paused whilst reading from his notes, and he turned to the next page of his notebook as he continued. 'However, I must also consider the evidence given in this court by Superintendent van Tonder. The Superintendent is well-known to the court as a man of exceptional integrity, and his evidence as to the conduct of the accused whilst in custody was indicative of a side of the accused's character, which he himself was not prepared to disclose to the court in his own defence. I have some difficulty in my own mind in deciding what weight, if any, to give to the evidence of the Superintendent. It relates to events after those giving rise to the charges of which the accused has been convicted, and in very unusual circumstances.'

If there was to be any lenience shown at all, it could only arise from van Tonder's evidence. The next words of the Judge would virtually determine the type of sentence to be imposed. The silence in the court room was complete. Whether Justice Gardner was aware of the drama of the moment, no one could tell, but he proceeded after taking a sip of water with his reasons for sentence.

'In my view, it would be wrong to disregard the evidence of Superintendent van Tonder.' As he said this, there was a murmur in the court that caused the Judge to pause whilst not resorting to his usual admonishment to the court.

'I feel that the evidence of the Superintendent was compelling to the extent that it has shown the accused is a man of some courage in a situation where he could have chosen to do nothing and witness a person being killed. He chose to put his own life at risk, and for that he is entitled to the consideration of this court in coming to an appropriate sentence.

'The accused has no previous convictions, which is hardly surprising. It goes without saying that a man who has dedicated his life to work on a mission has proved a valuable service to the community in which he has chosen to live. Having said all that, at the most critical of times, when his own nephew and other members of the security forces needed his help, he chose to do nothing and is accordingly to be sentenced for that.

'The sentence to be imposed is fifteen years' imprisonment with labour. Considering previous rulings on the matter, there is no room for the suspension of any part of the sentence, and the accused will therefore serve the entire of the sentence subject to whatever administrative decisions as may be brought to bear.'

The Judge indicated to O'Meara that he should be seated, and he addressed Advocate Chirenje.

'Mr Chirenje, do you have any final application to the court?' This was an invitation to formally apply for bail pending appeal, but such applications, although always made, were seldom if ever granted.

Chirenje rose and turned briefly to look to O'Meara, who simply shook his head. He turned back to the court and said, 'There are no applications, My Lord.'

The Judge nodded and said, 'Very well. That concludes matters before the court. This court will now adjourn.' With that, he stood and left the courtroom, which erupted in conversation before he had departed.

van Tonder wasted no time in moving O'Meara down the stairs, and the advocates put together their papers and left the room with the usual farewells offered and accepted.

On the way up the stairs to their office, Humphreys said to Jennings, 'A good result, I feel. Thank you for your assistance. You can get back to the mundane work now. Please keep me advised of developments on O'Meara Junior.' This was hardly a request, but Jennings confirmed he would do so, and they parted company as they went through the reception area of the offices.

* * *

It was only a short drive from Vincent Building to Rotten Row Magistrates Court, but Jennings decided to leave almost immediately. He made his way to his car once he had collected the few notes that had been left earlier by Jones in relation to the exchange control offence for which O'Meara Junior was to be placed on remand. There was always activity in the Magistrates Court. Jennings had spent the beginning of his career there and still had several good friends working there.

As he pulled into the public car park, he looked in his rear-view mirror and saw Jones arriving in an unmarked police car with a uniformed officer beside him and someone in the back whom Jennings could not identify but assumed was Cian O'Meara.

Having parked his car under a row of jacaranda trees, which provided good relief from the midday sun, he walked towards the hexagonal complex and saw that Jones had parked in the reserved police bays and was taking O'Meara down to the vehicle access and directly into the holding cell area. Unusually, O'Meara was not in handcuffs and was walking beside the uniformed officer, engaged in what appeared to be light-hearted conversation with Jones.

As Jennings came up behind them on his way to the main entrance to the complex, Jones turned whilst waiting for the access gate to be opened, and he nodded in that direction. This brought O'Meara's attention to Jennings, and there was a marked change in his demeanour as their eyes met.

Before O'Meara could say anything, Jones grabbed his arm and turned him towards the access gate, which was being opened by a warder. He pushed him forward and indicated to the uniformed officer to go on with him as he turned to come up the ramp to meet Jennings.

'I wasn't expecting you down so early. Just as well you are here, though. Our friend has said he wants a word with you before we start.'

'Really? Any indication what he has to say?'

'None at all, but he seemed to think it was necessary to talk to you before he was put on remand.'

Jennings was unsure what O'Meara could possibly want to speak to him about, but he had no concern in talking to him. It was not as though he was any position to cause any problems at this stage. If he misbehaved, any question of bail could go out the window. Once they were in the court, those issues were for Jennings to deal with, not Jones or any other policeman. He thought it unlikely that O'Meara was up for polite conversation, though, upon having seen the look on his face.

After going through the security check at the entrance, Jennings and Jones parted company. Jennings went to say hello to his former colleagues in the staff room, and Jones went in the direction of the cells' access to do whatever was needed to process O'Meara.

As usual there was no shortage of activity in the complex. Court 6, as the initial remand court, was always a hive of activity. Today was no different. In addition to remands, the court took up any short matters that could be dealt with by way of a simple plea, and the court was usually run by a uniformed Section Officer who, whilst having no formal legal training, knew enough about the law relating to bail and remand to put most qualified practitioners to shame.

Section Officer George Andrews had been at the court for over ten years. Virtually every new prosecutor starting out would be assigned to Court 6, and if they had any sense, they paid careful attention to how the policeman ran his court and how he conducted the basic proceedings that were disposed of in their hundreds every week. Jennings had spent three weeks with Andrews in the court and had admired his ability to run what was an exceptionally busy court with apparent ease. This was his turf, and if you had any sense, for the time you were allocated to the court, you accepted you were there as an observer and nothing more.

It was very seldom nowadays for anyone from the Director's office to appear in the remand court, and far from being upset about the disturbing presence of a law officer, the Section Officer seemed delighted to see Jennings.

'Mr Jennings,' he said by way of formal greeting. 'To what do we owe the pleasure of such exalted company in such humble surrounds?'

Jennings knew Andrews well enough to know he was being ribbed, and he took it in the vein intended. 'Just here to see the wheels of justice are still being kept well-oiled, Mr Andrews,' he said. 'I can assure you I will not be here any longer than I have to be, and will then leave you alone to your own devices.'

Andrews laughed and indicated to Jennings to take a seat beside him.

'I assume you know why I am here?' Jennings asked, to which Andrews simply nodded. 'I understand O'Meara wants to speak to me before the remand hearing. Any problem with that?'

'None at all, but you will have to talk to him in the holding cell. I don't care who he is—he is not getting special treatment in my court once he is booked in.'

'No argument there, George. Can I go through now?'

'Be my guest,' said Andrews, and he called one of the prison warders over to instruct him to let Jennings in through the dock entrance to the holding cell behind the court.

It was a particularly hot day, but the courtrooms were well ventilated and generally cool, even at the height of the summer. The holding cell was a different matter altogether. The only ventilation came from a single barred opening high up on the wall to the outside of the complex, and because there were usually over sixty persons crammed in waiting their turn, the cell stank with the odour of unwashed inhabitants, and the temperature was through the roof. It was so hot that Jennings immediately broke out in a sweat and almost gagged at the smell in the cell. To add to the uncomfortable nature of the cell, the lighting was provided by a few single bulbs encased in steel mesh, which gave barely enough light to see past the first rows of prisoners.

Jennings had told the warder whom he was looking for, and O'Meara's name was called out. Bodies moved as O'Meara made his way through the crowd and towards Jennings.

Jennings had seen the effect this cell had on people. Whatever their attitude before being booked in, a short time spent in this cell had a marked effect on people who were not used to the indignity of being in cramped and inhospitable surrounds. O'Meara was no exception. From the way his eyes darted back and forth, he was clearly in a distressed state.

As he arrived in front of Jennings, he grabbed the bars and indicated to Jennings to come forward, so they could speak with as much privacy as was possible.

'Well, Cian, what do you want?'

O'Meara stopped looking from side to side and fixed his eyes on Jennings. 'I suppose you think you are smart, having me on this side of the fence, don't you, Jennings? You couldn't get a decent result out of my uncle, and so now you go for the rest of the family. Is that it?'

Jennings was taken aback at his tone and the strength of feeling O'Meara expressed. 'I really don't know what you are on about. I am doing my job and nothing more. The only reason you are here is because of your own actions and those of your father.'

O'Meara snorted. 'That is bullshit, and you know it. The only reason I am here is because my bastard of an uncle turned us in. Only three people knew the combination to my father's safe, let alone where it was in the house. Yet your Mr Jones was able to go straight to the safe and open it without even having to look at his notes. He got that information from somewhere, and the only person who could have given it to him was my uncle. You are the only person he had spoken to outside the prison since his arrest, and so it was to you he gave the combination, wasn't it?'

'I am not here to tell you anything,' said Jennings. 'You wanted to see me. If that is all you have to say, I will leave you alone, and you can wait your turn to be dealt with.'

'Fair enough. You have answered my question, anyway. There is something I wanted to say to you, and only to you. For whatever reason, my sainted uncle seems to feel he can confide in you. Well, you can tell him something for me and my father. He should have got the rope for what he did to John, and we will never forgive him. He might think he has escaped the death penalty now, but you tell him from me that someday we will get justice for our family, and he will pay for what he has done. Even if he gets out of prison, you tell him that someday somewhere we will get to him, and when that day comes, he will answer for what he was done to us.'

Jennings was shocked at the level of hatred in O'Meara's voice. 'Cian, look at where you are. You are in no position to threaten anyone. What you have just done would justify me in refusing consent to bail, and you can sit in the remand prison for as long as it takes for me to decide to deal with you. That could be months down the road, as far as I am concerned. Making threats is not the way to help yourself. Maybe a couple of hours in here will give you time to reflect and cool down—although cooling down hardly seems an appropriate suggestion, does it?'

'You can be as smart-arsed as you like, Jennings, but I will be getting out of here. Whenever that is, the day will come when Patrick O'Meara will stand before his God and answer for what he has done.'

There was clearly no purpose in continuing the discussion, and Jennings turned on his heel and left the cell. The cool air in the courtroom was truly welcome relief, and he mopped his forehead as he made his way through the gathering crowd in the court to seek out Mr Jones.

Jones was standing outside the court with his uniformed colleague. Jennings took him to one side and told him of his meeting with O'Meara.

'Obviously not a happy man, our Mr O'Meara,' said Jones. 'Look, it is understandable he will be mouthing off, but so long as his uncle is in Chikurubi and he is on the outside, there is nothing he can do to hurt his uncle. In fact, it is a good thing we are letting him out on bail. Let's just get this hearing over with. and we can get his prosecution done and dusted. Then we can actually get some money out of the family. That is all I am interested in. This Irish family is driving me crazy.'

'I was thinking of dealing with him at the end of the list,' said Jennings. 'Maybe that will put some manners on him.'

Jones sighed at that comment and said, 'Mr Jennings, let's just take the steam out of this, shall we? I want out of here as much as you do. Let's just get in there, do what we have to do, and get out of here.'

What Jones was saying made sense to Jennings, and he asked Andrews if his matter could be called first when the remand magistrate came in. Andrews had no problem with that. As soon as the magistrate arrived and was ready to commence the afternoon's work, Jennings introduced himself, and O'Meara was called from the cell.

The hearing itself was a formality. The basis of the charges were explained to the magistrate, and he was advised there was no objection to bail on terms set out. The entire process took no more than ten minutes, and for his part, O'Meara said nothing other than to accept the conditions of the bail and confirm his name and address.

Jennings and Jones left the court together, and Jones said he would go to the cells and see to the release of O'Meara. He then suggested Jennings make his departure. 'I don't think seeing you any more than is necessary will be good for anyone today,' he said. He left Jennings as he went down the stairway to the holding cells.

*   *   *

The docket on O'Meara and his associates was prepared by Jones and the Fraud Squad over the next six months. In that time, the political situation in the country had seen dramatic and fast-moving changes. There was no doubt now that the war was not going to be won by either side on the field. It would be up to the politicians to resolve matters. Attempts at an internal settlement were falling apart, but pressure on both sides from their respective supporters meant that an end to the war was now certainly in sight, albeit some way off.

Given the scale of what Cian O'Meara and his father had been involved in, it was decided to prosecute him before the High Court. In addition, charges were brought against several of the family businesses, and on a basic arithmetic calculation, if all charges were successful, it could mean the end of the O'Meara family business.

CHAPTER THIRTEEN

Jennings had had little to do with Jones leading up to the O'Meara hearing, but he met with him on the morning of the hearing, which was scheduled before Mr Justice Cohen. Justice Cohen was also reaching the end of his judicial career, which had been marked by his compassion and civility to all who appeared before him. He was primarily a commercial Judge, and it was seldom he would have been seen in the criminal courts. Jennings assumed it was because of his commercial background that he had been allocated the matter.

As O'Meara had indicated through his attorney at an early stage, there would be a plea. The proceedings were always going to be brief, although given the levels of fines that could be imposed, the stakes were undeniably high.

Having heard the outline of the State case, the Judge considered his papers for a while before turning to Jennings.

'Mr Jennings, I see from the indictment that you have the charge framed as against the accused personally and a number of companies that I assume are in the control of the accused. Is that the position in a nutshell?'

'It is, My Lord,' Jennings replied.

'Well then, Mr Jennings, I need your help. You see, although you are entitled to do what you have done, I am the man to impose the penalties. It seems to me that if you want me to bring the hammer down on someone, I can do that, but I am not going to do it twice. Do you follow me?'

Jennings knew immediately what was coming. In his career as a Judge, Cohen had very seldom sent anyone to prison. Given the choice, he would impose penalties on the companies and let O'Meara off the hook with a slap on the wrist.

Jennings stood and addressed the Judge. 'My Lord, the State would have no difficulty in the court imposing penalties as against the corporate bodies, provided the charges as against the accused personally stand adjourned until all penalties are paid to the State in full.

Justice Cohen was delighted to hear such a sensible decision and made the order as required to give effect to the deal. With the business of the court concluded, the Judge adjourned and left the court.

O'Meara left the dock and was talking to his legal team as Jennings made his way past them. On his way past, however, O'Meara caught him by the arm and moved in close to him.

Jennings was taken aback at O'Meara's conduct and said, 'Get your hands off me.' The altercation had caught the attention of O'Meara's legal team, who seemed at a loss as to what to do.

O'Meara held on to Jennings for a moment before releasing him and smirking. 'Never forget what I told you in Rotten Row, Jennings. You think this is over, but it is far from over. There is an Irish saying my father taught me years ago that applies. I will give you the English version and make sure you remember it: "Our day will come."'

Jennings was about to make a reply when Jones appeared at his side from nowhere and moved him on by a gentle push on the shoulders.

'What the hell was that all about?' asked Jennings.

'Never mind O'Meara. He is just blowing off steam. Your work is done here. The money has mostly been repatriated already, and all in all, this has been a good day's work. Let it go at that.'

Once they got out into the corridors, they said their goodbyes, and Jennings went to report to the Director.

The balance of the moneys to be repatriated duly came in to the country, and O'Meara was released to go on with his life. The Director had allocated other work to Jennings so that when the matter came before the court again, he was not in the court. In fact, he was not to see O'Meara for many years to come.

However, the trial of the priest and subsequent events would always remain fixed in his memory.

CHAPTER FOURTEEN

Dublin 2018

The answer given by the interpreter was clearly not what O'Donovan was anticipating.

'Well, that is a strange reason for seeking the assistance of a solicitor. Mr Jennings, what do you have to say to the accused's request?'

It had been a while since Jennings had actively appeared in any criminal court, and despite his curiosity as to what was developing, he had no desire to return now.

'Judge I do not believe I am on the legal aid panel anymore. Perhaps another appointment would be more appropriate.'

'Mr Jennings, in case you had not noticed, this is a criminal court, and you stand before me. As far as I am concerned, you are still practising in the criminal court, and a specific request has been made of me to appoint you to represent a man on most serious charges. Surely as an officer of the court, you will appreciate the position I am in.' This last comment was made with a knowing smile, and Jennings knew he was being punished for earlier perceived wrongdoings by the Judge.

Several years earlier, Jennings had taken this very Judge on judicial review when he refused to appoint him as solicitor to a well-known but minor-league criminal whom he had represented for the better part of a decade. For whatever reason, the Judge had decided that a newly qualified solicitor should have a crack at the whip, and he had appointed him to act even though the accused had made it known very clearly in court that he'd wanted Jennings. The following High Court review had given rise to a very critical Judgement of Judge O'Donovan, and he had clearly not forgotten the case.

'Mr Jennings, a specific request having been made of this court, I will appoint you and any administrative matters that need to be dealt with to ensure you are able to act can be dealt with later. I trust that is in order.'

Jennings knew that this was a lost battle and replied, 'Would the court permit me to take initial instructions from the accused in case there are any further applications to be made?'

O'Donovan was having none of it. 'No, Mr Jennings. You may take your client's instructions in the normal way in Cloverhill Prison, which is where I must remand him in custody, as you well know. Any further applications you may have to make—and I am sure there will be several—can be done later in some other forum. Now, Inspector, is there anything else to be dealt with in relation to this accused?'

The inspector advised there was not, and the Judge remanded the accused in custody for the maximum two-week period, to appear in the Cloverhill Court. Before the accused and his escorts left the court, Jennings enquired of the inspector if he could interview Moyo in the court cells. He was advised he could do so.

Jennings turned to Cathal Flanagan, who had been watching the proceedings with interest, and asked if he would take care of the other matters on his list while he went to see his new client.

'Happy to assist as ever, Richard. I must say, you have a knack of attracting trouble. Defending this man is certainly going to be the poisoned chalice of the year, if you will excuse the metaphor given the deceased. God rest him.' Despite the obvious seriousness of the situation, Flanagan said this with a smile. He was not known for his love of the Church, having represented many adults who had been abused in church orphanages and institutions in years gone by.

Jennings thanked him and then made his way out of the court and down through the stairway to the holding cells below, where there were interview rooms available for practitioners to meet with their clients.

He advised the prison warder whom he wanted to see and was asked to wait in a room pending the arrival of the accused from the courtroom above. Given the size of the complex and the small number of prison staff available, it would take some time for Moyo to get to him. As he sat in the interview room, Jennings's memories of the trial of Father O'Meara came flooding back.

His thoughts were interrupted by the door being opened and Moyo in handcuffs being led in by a prison warder. Without having to ask, the cuffs were removed, and Moyo took a seat opposite Jennings. The warder left the room, closing the door behind him but remaining in view through the mesh-enclosed observation panel in the door.

Jennings reached across the table and extended his hand, which Moyo took and responded with a firm grip. 'Well, Stephen, it seems you have found yourself in a bit of bother,' he said.

Moyo simply replied, 'That is true, Mr Jennings. I hope I have not caused you any problems, but when I saw you in the courtroom I knew fate had put us together.'

'Please call me Richard. It was a long time ago, but I believe you are the same Stephen Moyo who was with John O'Meara in the Support Unit. Am I right?'

Moyo smiled as he replied. 'I am the same man, but as you say, it was a long time ago, and we have both got older. The years have gone by too quickly.'

'That is so, but I was just thinking of your evidence at the trial of Father O'Meara. It came back to me as though it were yesterday. You made an impression on everyone who heard your testimony. You clearly had a lot of respect for John.'

'John was a good man, and he always spoke well of you. He always said you were a man to be trusted if ever we needed an attorney.'

'I often wondered what happened to serving officers like you after independence came. I know it was not only the white man who was forced out of government jobs once ZANU PF came to power.'

'That is correct. Initially there was some pretence that things would progress on merit, but that soon changed. I left the force in 1982. I was lucky in having a sponsor to set me up in my first business. In fact, you know the man I am talking about because you prosecuted him as well.'

This last comment certainly caught Jennings attention. 'Really? Who was that?' he asked.

'My sponsor was Cian O'Meara.'

This was another name Jennings was surprised to hear that day 'Cian O'Meara. How did that come about?'

'I never really found out how he knew I was leaving the force, but before my notice period was up, Mr O'Meara arrived at my home and offered to assist me in setting up any business I might be interested in. He said it was to repay me for what I had done for his son.'

'Well, that sounds fair enough,' said Jennings. 'What business did you get into?'

Moyo smiled again. 'What all good black businessman at the time wanted: bottle stores, and buses. I was lucky, was very successful, and expanded my interests into a lot of things—in farming and commercial enterprises. I have been able to give my family a good life, and despite what has been happening in Zimbabwe, from a financial point of view, I want for nothing.'

'And what of Cian's involvement in all of that? He never struck me as being motivated purely by a sense of decency.'

Moyo sighed before continuing. 'Indeed not. Cian was involved in every aspect of my businesses over the years, to an extent that in many ways, he controlled what I was doing. But it was a price I was prepared to pay to see my family prosper.'

'And what of your family?' asked Jennings.

'My wife sadly died many years ago. We only had one son, John. John is a member of the MDC and was taken out of his house six months ago in Harare. No one knows where he is now. We have tried to find him but have come up with nothing so far. People often disappear in Zimbabwe now, and unless the person is a high-profile politician, no one ever hears anything about it.'

'I know the country was falling apart, but if you had succeeded in your business ventures, you had to have your own contacts to help you.'

'You would have hoped so, but there were two things working against us. The first was that about a year ago, Cian O'Meara's support disappeared. I never knew how much he had been protecting me from Mugabe's cronies, who were always looking at me as a soft target for their own ends. The second problem is it was not only John who was an MDC member. We all became supporters of the MDC. That was really the end of the road for us.'

Jennings had followed developments in Zimbabwe from the late 1900s and had taken a interest in the formation and rise of the Movement for Democratic Change. What had started as a trade union activist group had developed into a cohesive and well-supported opposition party. He was surprised at the level of support the party had, and at the price many of its supporters paid in seeking to get rid of the ruling Mugabe party through lawful means. Many of their supporters had been killed by thugs loyal to Mugabe, and it was very seldom any of these killers appeared before any court to answer for their crimes. It amazed Jennings that they continued the fight because it seemed every election could only result in more deaths and little if any change in the country.

'So, is that what brought you to Ireland?' asked Jennings. 'Did you have to leave?'

'It would have been the sensible thing to do, but no, I did not have to leave. I chose to stay in Zimbabwe and continue the struggle. I only came to Ireland because Father O'Meara insisted I do so. He said there were things that needed to be dealt with, and they could only be resolved here in Ireland. He said he could only share the details with me in person when the time was right.'

Jennings considered the man before him, who dropped his head as he spoke the final words. For the first time, he had shown some emotion. From the movement of his shoulders, Jennings could tell he was struggling to express himself.

'They say that I killed Father O'Meara. I swear on the life of John O'Meara that I did not. I would never have thought of harming him. Whatever I may have thought of him at the time, and whatever the courts may have found him guilty of, John always said he was a decent and good man. After he left Zimbabwe, we remained in contact through letters, and I would never have dreamed of hurting him. He asked me to come to Ireland. Why would I harm him when he was calling me to help him? It makes no sense.'

Jennings gave him a moment to compose himself before he said, 'Stephen, at this stage, I do not need to hear anything from you about what did or did not happen to Father O'Meara, and whether or not you were involved. All of that will be dealt with in time. For the moment, I simply wanted to meet you to see if I was the right man to look after you. From what I have seen and heard, I would be very happy to try to help you, if you still want me to do so.'

Moyo looked at Jennings and smiled. 'Thank you, Richard. I do want you to represent me, and together we will prove I had nothing to do with the killing of Father O'Meara.'

'Okay, let's move on to immediate issues, then. You heard what the Judge said about bail. The District Court cannot grant bail to an accused charged with murder, but I can make an application for bail in the High Court, if you want me to do so. Given you are a foreign national and the nature of the charge, that will be a difficult battle to win at this early stage. My advice would be to bide our time for the moment and let me find out what the basics of the prosecution case are against you. Unfortunately, that will mean you will be in custody in Cloverhill for a while, but if I can get enough information, hopefully I can apply for bail in a few weeks' time.'

Moyo replied, 'One of the consequences of being an MDC supporter is to spend time in a Zimbabwe remand prison. I have served my apprenticeship, and any prison in this country is more likely to be a holiday camp compared to Harare Remand Prison.'

The fact that Moyo could find humour in his current predicament confirmed what Jennings knew of the man from his evidence all those years before. He was dealing with a man of courage and strength.

'Very well. I am going to leave you now, and I will be out to see you in the next few days, when I have some more information. If there is anything you need or want to tell me, you will be allowed to phone me at any time on any of these numbers.' He passed over his business card.

Jennings and Moyo stood, and the warder who had been standing outside realised their initial meeting was over and opened the door to let out Jennings. Jennings left the room and made his way back up to the circular hall, looking for Cathal Flanagan to ascertain what had happened to his other matters in his absence.

As he approached the remand court he saw Flanagan talking to a man he immediately recognised.

Kenneth McGeough was a Garda detective whom Jennings had come across on several cases in the past. He was an unusual man in many respects, not least of all because of his background before joining the Garda Siochana.

McGeough was born and raised in Ballymun, North Dublin. His father had died when he'd been a toddler, and his mother had raised him and his brothers and sister on a basic cleaner's wage and what little social support was available. He could easily have gone the way of many of his contemporaries and fallen into petty crime and other antisocial activities as a youngster. Instead, he found he not only enjoyed school, but he thrived on it. The better he did, the more proud his mother became.

He also developed a talent as a boxer at a local club, and because he was big for his age, he soon got a reputation amongst his peers as a person not to mess with. Not that that happened often, because he had a gentle side, which meant he felt no affinity for those who felt the only way to impress was to pretend to be the hard men of the neighbourhood.

McGeough was to complete his leaving cert with one of the top scores in the country, and it seemed inevitable that he would go on to university. All of that changed, however, when one of his best friends was set upon by a gang of local teenagers and died because of a merciless kicking given to him purely because they did not like the look of him. The young McGeough was distraught with grief and was heard to say he would not rest until those responsible paid in kind for what they had done.

Fortunately for him, a local councillor saw in him the talent and ability he knew could be put to good use, and in typically Irish fashion, he managed to persuade those with influence to recommend to McGeough that if he applied to join the Gardaí, he would be accepted. For a young man from Ballymun with no previous family connection of any kind with the Gardaí to be accepted into the force was unheard of, and McGeough himself saw that as a challenge to be embraced.

Not surprisingly, he passed out of his training as one of the top students and was soon back in Ballymun as a probationary guard. Within three weeks of his arrival, he brought in those responsible for his friend's death to the local barracks, and all were only too keen to admit their roles. They ultimately received sentences ranging from ten years to life.

One aspect of the case that was never resolved, however, was that the then ringleader of the gang disappeared at about the same time McGeough reported for duty. From that time, the ringleader had never been seen or heard of. Although no one ever said it out loud, the local folklore was that Garda McGeough had dealt with this man in his own way, and given the man was a known scumbag with no one left to grieve his departure, his disappearance was soon dismissed and never followed up. The confessions of the rest of the gang, combined with the disappearance of the gang leader, created a legend for McGeough that he had carried throughout his career: if he was on your case, you had better be very careful about what you did.

As his career progressed, some of his colleagues did question his ability to do as well as he did in Ballymun. Some were foolish enough to suggest that perhaps the reason for his success was his proximity to known criminals. The reality, however, was that McGeough had the respect of the clear majority of Ballymun residents who knew that if they turned to him with information or asked for help, they would be dealt with fairly and honestly. He would never betray a source and would always deal with any issue put on his plate, no matter how seemingly trivial.

In recent years, McGeough had been assigned to the Store Street Detective Unit. Even though he was no longer in his own area, he still managed to bring in results while investigating crimes in Dublin's inner city.

Cathal Flanagan saw Jennings approach and held up Jennings' list of files as he approached. 'All dealt with, Richard. Garda McGeough and I were just discussing your latest client.'

'Really? And why would that be of interest to you, Detective'? Jennings asked.

'No real reason, Richard. You will see from the book of evidence in due course that I was the first detective on the scene when Father O'Meara was found. I have been taken off the enquiry, though, so it will be interesting to hear what you make of things in due course. Maybe we can have a pint sometime, and you can tell me about the priest's previous activities. It sounds as though he had an interesting time back in the day. Anyway, as I say, maybe a pint sometime in the future.' Before Jennings could reply, McGeough turned and left.

Cathal and Jennings watched him go, and when he was out of earshot, Flanagan said what Jennings was thinking.

'What an odd conversation. Why on earth would they take a man like McGeough off such a high-profile case? And what was he on about having a pint? Everyone knows he has never touched a drop of the stuff in his life. Most peculiar. Anyway, good luck, Richard. I think you may need it this time.'

As Flanagan left, Jennings stood watching McGeough, who was making his way through the security exit at the main doorway. As McGeough reached the door, he stopped and turned, and his eyes met Jennings. McGeough gave an almost imperceptible nod of the head and went on his way, leaving Jennings even more confused than he had been.

CHAPTER FIFTEEN

The practice Jennings worked for had originally been based out of offices on Lower Abbey Street. He had been with the firm for fifteen years, and whilst offers of partnerships had been made on a regular basis, he had refused them as diplomatically as he could. He simply was not willing to get involved in the politics of what was essentially a family practice.

Over the years, the style of the practice had changed. it had developed from what had originally been a small general practice to a middle-size commercial practice in which the conveyancers and commercial solicitors ruled the roost. Litigation, particularly the criminal side of the practice, was considered an unfortunate but necessary part of the practice mainly because the senior partner and founder of the firm, Gerard Hughes, would not consider any discussion regarding ceasing practice in those areas. With the recent economic crash in Ireland and particularly in the property market, it was just as well that Hughes had stuck to his guns. Without the litigation income, the past few years would have been very difficult for all involved.

Although the practice bore Hughes's name, his influence in the running of the firm over the years had changed. To some extent, this was of his own design because he was generally happy to take a back seat and leave the main work of the practice to his partners. However, that did not preclude him from exerting influence at partners meetings, and invariably matters that were potentially contentious were resolved after his input at the end of any debate.

On returning to his office, Jennings wondered what Hughes would make of his latest client. He had never interfered with any legal aid appointment on the basis that if the practice was to accept the money paid by the State, it was to take the work assigned. Having said that, on numerous occasions he had also made it clear that some of the more notorious clients that had been represented by the practice were not what he would like to see as private clients, and so it was very seldom that any made the transition. Hughes was not afraid of controversy, but by the same token he did not look for it.

The new office of Hughes and Co took up four floors of a newly built office block just off Church Street. It was more convenient than the original office to the Four Courts, and Hughes had made a sizeable profit on the sale of the original building which had housed the practice just before the economic crash. The new offices lacked any of the charm of the old building, but one of its major advantages was that employees could access any of the floors through the elevator with a pass card, which meant they did not necessarily have to go through reception when coming and going.

Jennings had decided to avail of this facility and took the lift to the fifth floor, where he had his office. He managed to get to this office without seeing any of the other staff at all. He had had the same secretary, Grainne Kellet, for ten years. She was invaluable in keeping his work schedule under control and, more important, shielding him from anyone he did not want to see.

It was unusual for Grainne to not be at her desk when he arrived, and he assumed she was down at the main reception or otherwise engaged. He took his seat behind his desk and opened his computer to check e-mails and messages.

In the process of doing this. Grainne appeared at the door to his office. 'Hello. Richard.' she said. 'An interesting morning at the CCJ, I hear.'

Jennings smiled as he looked up and replied, 'You could say that. How did you hear what has been going on?'

'You made the RTE at midday, and so the whole firm is buzzing at the news. I can't see Mr Hughes being so happy, though.'

'Why do you say that? Has he said anything to you?'

'Not directly, no. I was just called down to his office, and he said that he would like to see you as soon as you arrived. It did not seem to me to be an invitation.'

Jennings realised that this was her polite way of telling him to get down to Hughes office immediately. As he stood to leave, she said, 'And just one other thing. There is a Father Murray waiting in reception who will be joining you and Mr Hughes.'

Grainne stood to one side to ensure Jennings did leave, and she saw him off to the stairwell to get down to Hughes' floor. On reaching the main reception, he advised the receptionist on duty that he wanted to see Mr Hughes. He was asked to wait while she rang through to his office. Whilst at reception, he noticed a man who he assumed from his clerical garb was Father Murray sitting in the waiting area, reading one of the papers left for the benefit of waiting clients.

The receptionist had barely put the phone down when Hughes's office door opened, and he emerged.

Gerard Hughes was in his early seventies, although he looked younger than that. As usual, he was brisk in his manner. People who did not know him took it to be a sign of being agitated and short-tempered, but in reality, he was neither.

He indicated to Jennings to go through to his office and went into the waiting area to call in Father Murray, whom he greeted with a handshake before leading him into the office.

On entering the office, Hughes introduced Jennings to the priest and invited them to sit on the visitor's chairs opposite him as he took his seat behind his desk. As usual, not a scrap of spare paper was on his desk. Jennings could never understand how he managed to keep his desk as clear as he did. That was certainly not the same in his own office.

'Richard, I hear you have been appointed to represent the man accused of the murder of Father O'Meara. Father Murray here is from the Archdiocese of Dublin and would have known Father O'Meara well. He has asked to see you. He has also asked me to attend this meeting, although I do not know why. Father, perhaps you can enlighten us as to the reason for your visit.'

Father Murray put his hand into his inside coat pocket and took two envelopes out before he spoke. 'I should just say that events in the courts this morning really have nothing to do with my being here. I intended to come see you, Mr Jennings, today in any event following Father O'Meara's death. I am afraid that events this morning, however, may have made my task somewhat difficult.'

'In what way, Father?' asked Hughes.

Murray proffered one of the envelopes to Hughes and said, 'This is the original will of Father O'Meara. Sometime before he died, he asked me to keep it safe and to bring it in to your firm on his death. I have read a copy of the will, and he has appointed Mr Jennings—or should he not be in a position to act, the senior partner of this practice—as executor and trustee of his estate.'

Hughes took the envelope proffered to him by the priest. Before opening it, he asked Jennings if he was aware of the will and its apparent provisions.

'I most certainly was not. I have not seen Father O'Meara since the trial in Zimbabwe in the seventies. He tried to contact me when I was first in Ireland, but I did not see the point in meeting him, and we never met. I had no idea about his will and cannot think why he would have appointed me as an executor of his estate. As a priest, he would not have had much to administer anyway.'

Father Murray replied, 'Our order does not mandate vows of poverty, Mr Jennings. Most of us have acquired savings and such over years. Father O'Meara was somewhat different because not only did he have his own personal property but he also inherited a substantial estate from his father and was the principal trustee of a trust set up for the benefit of the mission in Zimbabwe with which I believe you may be familiar. That trust has seen significant growth in income in the past years since Father O'Meara has been in Ireland, and the total assets both here and in Zimbabwe now run to several million euro. Father O'Meara had specifically told me that if it was at all possible, he wanted you to take over the management of the trust and assist it in continuing its work in Zimbabwe.'

Hughes had been listening to this with careful attention and had not yet opened the envelope he was holding. 'And the other document, Father what is that?' he asked.

Father Murray turned to Jennings and passed the envelope to him. 'This is a personal letter from Father O'Meara to you, Mr Jennings. I was told by Father O'Meara that in the event of his death other than by natural causes, I was to give this to you. I have no idea as to its contents, and I was given very strict instructions to directly place it in your hands. Father O'Meara made it very clear to me that in the event you were unable or unwilling to accept this, I was to destroy it without opening the envelope and ensure it was seen by no one other than yourself. Will you accept this on that basis?'

Jennings was at a complete loss as to what was being given to him, and he paused before he accepted the envelope.

He turned to Hughes and said, 'Gerard, I have no idea what this is all about, but in view of my being appointed to act for the man accused of O'Meara's murder, surely there is a conflict of interest here? How can I act as executor and represent the man accused of killing the testator?'

Hughes paused before replying, and he directed his question to Father Murray. 'Father, you say that Mr Jennings is nominated as executor, but in the event, he does not accept that appointment, is there provision for an alternative appointment?'

'That is my understanding of the will,' Murray replied.

Hughes then turned to Jennings and said, 'Richard, this is certainly a most unusual situation, but I suggest before any decisions are made, it is necessary for you to take the letter from the late Father O'Meara and see what he has to say to you. That of course is a suggestion, not an instruction, but it seems to me that given your history with Father O'Meara, he must have had his reason for the apparent appointment. The contents of the letter may well help us in understanding his wishes and come to a decision. If you do not want to take up your appointment, I see no difficulty at this time in the alternative provisions being given effect, but that is something we may have to consider again.'

'Very well,' Jennings replied as he took the envelope from the priest. 'I will read the letter, and we can decide where we are going to go from there'

'Thank you, Mr Jennings,' said the priest as he stood up, obviously keen to leave after making his delivery. 'From the way Father O'Meara spoke of you, I am sure you will make the right decision. If you need to speak to me on any issues, please contact me through the diocesan offices.'

Hughes and Jennings shook the priest's hand as he made his way out of the office, and Hughes indicated to Jennings to remain and close the door behind the departing priest.

'Well this is a strange turn of events, is it not?' he said. 'You say you never had any dealings with O'Meara since you came to the country?'

'That's right. I simply did not see the point in meeting him. After his conviction, he was one of the first group of prisoners to be released on amnesty, and he left the country soon afterwards. Apart from the trial and the fact that his nephew and I were friends, we certainly had nothing in common. I never saw the point in meeting him.'

Hughes looked out of the window whilst Jennings talked. He stood for a while before he turned. 'Do you recall when you were interviewed for a position here, and I told you that you had come with a very good recommendation?'

Jennings was confused by the question. 'I do recall that, and it struck me as odd at the time because I did not know anyone in the country then.'

'Well, that is not entirely correct, is it, Richard? You knew Father O'Meara. He was my parish priest then, and when I said to him that I had a man from Zimbabwe who was coming in to see me about a job and mentioned your name, he spoke very highly of you. He said if I gave you a job, I would not be disappointed.'

'But why did you never tell me of that?' asked Jennings

'Because O'Meara asked me not to. It was not for me to challenge his wishes. Why don't you take that letter and read it in your own time? We can talk again in the morning.'

CHAPTER SIXTEEN

Jennings left the office holding the envelope in his hand, and he made his way back to his own floor. He went into his office to find Grainne going through his correspondence and arranging files in the order with which they needed to be dealt.

Grainne turned to him and asked, 'Are you going to be taking on the defence, then?'

He had to pause before he replied. 'I am not entirely sure. There have been a few more twists in the tale today that I need to think about. If I do, it will mean reorganising our schedules. You know what happened the last time we got involved in a major criminal defence.'

Grainne smiled at that. 'I remember it only too well. I spent most of my time keeping the press out of reception. We hardly ever got any work done for the duration of the trial.'

The case she was referring to had been something of a cause celebre at the time because not only was their client acquitted but the actual perpetrator was brought to justice through evidence Jennings had discovered.

'Grainne, I have been given something I need to consider, and I can't do it here in the office. Cover for me for the rest of the day, and I will see you tomorrow.'

'Fair enough,' she said. 'Anything that needs to be done won't be hurt by another day's delay.'

Jennings turned on his heel, left the office, and made his way out of the building. It was still early afternoon, and Abbey Street was busy enough but not so crowded as to be unpleasant. He decided that a visit to his local pub was in order, and he knew that he would be undisturbed there for as long as he needed.

The Red Lantern was not what one could call a trendy bar. Very little had changed in the building in over sixty years. The only concession to the change in times was the installation of a colour TV to allow regulars to follow the racing, and that was only allowed after a local Paddy Power opened its doors nearby.

This was not a pub that would attract any tourist traffic. Not only was it slightly off the main street but it had not succumbed to the need to provide food and exotic drinks such as cappuccinos. If you wanted food it was the owner's suggestion you one went elsewhere, although in the winter months he did provide a daily soup and roll.

Today would have seen the usual regular punters and possibly a lost tourist, but Jennings knew he would be able to find a table to himself out of the way of the regulars. Sure enough, on entering the pub, he found just such a table towards the back of the pub.

Being a regular had its advantages in that a simple nod to the barman on the way past would result in a pint of Guinness arriving on his table without the need for ordering it. Jennings took the time waiting for the Guinness to reflect on the day's events. It was certainly one of the more bizarre days he had experienced, and as he turned the letter over in his hands, he wondered what else the late Father O'Meara would provide.

John, the barman, left the pint on the table. As Jennings let it settle, he opened the envelope and took out the document it held. On unfolding it, it was clearly a handwritten letter addressed to him.

Dear Mr Jennings,

As you are now reading this letter, it will be the case that I have passed on, and not through natural causes. You will also be aware, I am sure, that I have nominated you as the executor and trustee of my estate. I hope that you will be able to see your way to acting as such.

I apologise for what must seem to be a somewhat dramatic gesture, but regrettably there have been developments over the years since we last met that have given rise to certain issues which you will, in time, come to realise make this letter necessary.

Having read this letter, if it is your view that you do not want to act as my executor, I will understand and simply ask that this letter be destroyed. You can allow Mr Hughes to act in your stead. I have known him for many years, and he will do what is best for my estate and the trust that will survive me.

It seems like it was only yesterday that we were in the courtroom in Harare, but of course many years have gone by, and a lot has happened in the intervening years. My brother Sean passed away five years ago, and his son Cian has taken over from where he left off.

I am sure you will recall that Sean and his son were not averse to making money out of a bad situation, and it would seem the son had been able to outdo the father in recent years.

Cian has been one of the few white men in Zimbabwe to not only retain his wealth but thrive under Mr Mugabe's rule. It says something of the man that when legitimate farmers were being dispossessed of their land, Cian was able to acquire a dairy farm just outside Harare although he had never been a farmer in his life. To say that his business dealings are irregular would be putting things too mildly, and unfortunately for me, I have not been left immune to his activities.

You will remember the trust that was set up by Cian's father and was used to over invoice supplies of medicines for the mission. After my trial and the prosecution of Cian, I assumed that the trust would be dissolved. Just before I left, Sean put a raft of papers in front of me to sign, which he said were intended to do just that.

In fact, what I subsequently learnt I had signed was a power of attorney in Cian's favour, allowing him to continue the trust and operate as sole trustee in my place. If I had thought Sean was devious in his dealings, Cian was to prove even more so. He has also shown a ruthless streak that Sean never displayed.

In the recent past, I have been able to undo the power of attorney and resume control of the trust. The reality is that even though the trust was a vehicle for Cian to launder money, a very large sum of money was in the trust and had been used over the years for the benefit of the mission. I suppose I should have some concerns as to the providence of the money, but *without the money from the trust, the mission and the people it serves would be in an even worse state than they are now. I am sure what I have done will be seen as condoning criminality, but that is something I have had to live with. Cian has not had anything to do with the trust and its activities since I revoked the power of attorney, and I believe all transactions since then have been within the bounds of the law. Should you accept my nomination, I know that you will ensure the trust is run legitimately and for the benefit of the people of Nyanga.*

To say that Cian was not pleased with what I have done would be an understatement. He feels the money in the trust is his to do with as he pleases, and I have no doubt you will have to deal with him if you take on the role of my executor. I also have no doubt you will be well able to deal with him. Given our past shared history, that is one of the main reasons I am asking you to act.

Cian has also been involved in activities outside the trust, and I have tried to put an end to them. At the time of writing this letter, there remains one issue which is particularly difficult, and I had hoped to have had that resolved before I died. As you are reading this letter, that has not come to pass, and it is unfortunately something that you will have to deal with if you decide to act as executor.

Before you make up your mind as to whether to take up the appointment, there is a man in Ireland who will be able to explain to you precisely what Cian has been doing these last few years. Cian's activities in recent years have escalated even by his standards, and I fear that the people he has got involved with are more ruthless than even he can contemplate.

Once you hear what this man has to say, you may decide not to get involved at all in my affairs, and that is a decision I would of course respect. However, I would ask you to meet this man before making any final decision. Consider what he has to say. When you do meet, you will remember him from my trial. I am sure you will have no hesitation in accepting him as being a genuine and truthful person. His name is Stephen Moyo.

The last two words brought Jennings to an abrupt halt in his reading. He read the words over to make sure he was correctly reading what had been written. The man whom he was now representing and who was accused of murdering the author of the letter in his hands was the same man the deceased was recommending to him as a go-to to resolve issues relating to his death. He put the letter on the table before him without reading further. The pint of Guinness before him had remained untouched, and Jennings absently picked it up and drank from it without thinking. He was immune to the low buzz of conversation in the background.

He slowly turned the letter over to the last page and read what was there, which consisted of details as to how to contact Moyo. A residential address and a mobile number were neatly written down. It was truly ironic that none of these details were required given the latest turn of events.

Jennings mind was in turmoil, and he suddenly had no desire for any further drink or even the disconnected company of the regulars in the pub. He needed to be on his own to clear his mind and try to make sense of what was happening.

On leaving the pub, he made his way to the quays and walked along the Liffey in the direction of the Customs House. It was a walk he had always enjoyed regardless of the weather. On a good day, when the tide was in and the river was at its height, this was one of the more pleasant walks to be had. On a bad day, with the tide out and the shopping trolleys and detritus clearly visible on the riverbed, it reminded him how quickly things could change and to never take for granted what was often only seen on the surface.

He lost track of time and found he had in fact walked past his intended destination. He was almost at the end of the quays opposite the 3Arena. The realisation as to how far he had gone brought him back to the real world, and he decided rather than retracing his footsteps, he would take the Luas back to town and get home.

The journey home was uneventful, and after a basic ready meal prepared in the microwave and a few minutes in front of the television, he decided to try to get some sleep. That attempt proved fruitless, and after an hour or so of staring at the ceiling, he turned on his side light and picked up the letter from the priest, which he had left on the table. He read it again and was left no clearer as to what to make of it.

Sleep was clearly not going to come easily, and so he decided to get out a scrapbook that he had not looked at in over twenty years from the attic.

From his early days as a prosecutor, he had kept every newspaper article in which a trial he was involved in had been reported. He did not see this as a vanity, but for some reason he felt it may one day be useful to be able to remind himself of cases he had won and lost.

By far the largest amount of material related to Father O'Meara's trial, and he slowly turned the pages, looking at the photographs and reading the reports from another time and space. There were several photographs of the priest both before and after his arrest, photos of the police in their investigations, and more photos of the witnesses coming and going at the trial.

His attention fell on the photograph of Section Officer Moyo. The photo did not really do the man justice, but as soon as he looked at it, he knew the man he was now representing was someone he could trust.

He went through the balance of the photos, and there was one other that caught his eye. Cian O'Meara was being interviewed by a reporter and was clearly in an animated state. The date on the article was the day of the sentence hearing, and Cian was clearly not slow to vent his anger at what he felt was a lenient sentence. The anger in his eyes had been captured and was clear to anyone who looked at the photo, even if one knew nothing of the story behind the photo.

Jennings closed the scrapbook, and his mind was brought back to the present.

The three principle characters from the photos and articles who had played such a prominent part in his life all those years ago were now back in his life, either in person in the form of Cian and Moyo or by proxy in the case of the priest.

Jennings had deliberately stopped taking instructions in criminal matters some time ago after a series of particularly nasty trials that took their toll on both himself and his staff, particularly his secretary, Grainne. In the last high-profile trial, he had acted in, she had been subject to abusive calls and threats. Jennings had decided when that trial was over, he would never get involved in anything similar. Now he was on the brink of getting involved in something that would again bring unwanted attention and pressure. For a moment, he has unsure about what he should do.

He threw the scrapbook onto the table in front of him. As it landed, it fell open on a page in which the image of the priest and John O'Meara had been placed side by side. With all that had gone on, the one person Jennings had not thought of was John. On seeing his face staring out from under his BSAP cap with the look of determination and optimism that had always marked him in his short life, Jennings suddenly realised what he had to do.

Jennings knew that had John lived and were he sitting next to him now, he would expect him to represent Moyo to the best of his ability. He had died in making sure Moyo had lived. If Jennings did not act now, John would have seen that as cowardly and dishonourable. In that moment, Jennings knew what he had to do. Having made up his mind, he returned to bed and was asleep in minutes.

CHAPTER SEVENTEEN

Jennings was always an early riser, even in the middle of winter, when the sun only came up after 8.00 a.m. He would always wake without the need of an alarm by no later than 6.00 a.m.

On waking, he lay in bed for a while to remind himself of the previous day's events. He could barely believe all that had gone on in the space of a day, but at least his mind was now made up as to what he was going to do.

He was going to act for Moyo in the criminal trial, and he was going to accept the nomination as executor and trustee of the late Father O'Meara's estate. In respect to the latter, he knew he would be able to rely on the input and experience of Gerard Hughes, and his own input would be minimal in real terms.

Having dressed and left without his usual coffee, he was sitting at his desk by 7.30 a.m., long before even the most enthusiastic of fellow employees would arrive. In fact, the only people in the building at that time of the morning were the two ladies who cleaned the offices.

Jennings was treated to their usual early morning welcome and discussion of the day's weather before he was able to politely make his way to his office. His first task of the day was to contact Cloverhill and get an appointment to see his new client. In the normal course, he would have waited until he had got some information from the Gardaí before going to take instructions for a bail hearing, but after the events of the previous day, he wanted to see Moyo without delay.

Given the number of prisoners held on remand and the demand for consultation rooms by solicitors, Cloverhill reception was not an easy place to get through to. Jennings knew that by phoning early, he had at least some chance of the phone being answered without too much delay.

He thought his luck was in when the phone was answered on the second ring. He identified who he was and what he wanted. There was a pause before the officer who'd answered the phone replied. In fact, it sounded almost as though he had put his hand over the receiver whilst Jennings was talking to him.

'Mr Jennings, sorry to keep you waiting. I need to transfer this call to Governor Halligan. Please hold on.' Before Jennings could even reply, he was subjected to the music so loved by telephone companies.

Jennings knew Governor Halligan from previous cases and was intrigued as to why a simple request to interview a client needed his attention. Halligan was a somewhat eccentric individual, and although Jennings had met him on a few occasions, he had never really had any dealings with him.

After a few minutes, Halligan came on the line. He sounded as though he had just run up a flight of stairs when he first spoke. 'Mr Jennings, lovely to speak with you again. An early start to the day, I see. I understand you wish to see Mr Moyo?'

'That's right, Governor. Is there a problem with that?'

'Oh, no, not at all. It's just that Mr Moyo is not with us now. I am afraid he was involved in an incident last night and is in Tallaght Hospital receiving treatment. Nothing too serious, I hope. I was just coming back from the hospital when your call came in.'

The Tallaght Hospital would have been the closest hospital to Cloverhill, and from Jennings's own experience, prisoners were only ever referred there when there was an issue that the prison's own medical staff could not address. By definition, a referral to the hospital for a prisoner could never be described as 'nothing too serious.'

Jennings immediately felt his pulse quickening. This was not good news. His tone when he spoke to the Governor reflected his concern. 'Governor don't dare suggest a referral is not serious. What the hell happened to him? He was only admitted yesterday.'

'I am afraid I can't go into the details, Mr Jennings. There is a Garda investigation and an internal inquiry to deal with that. The Inspector of Prisons has also been notified. All I can tell you is that Mr Moyo is receiving the best possible treatment, and the injuries sustained are not life-threatening.'

'Injuries?' Jennings enquired in almost a roar. 'What injuries?'

'Mr Jennings, please try to understand I am as concerned as you are about your client's condition. Raising your voice to me will not help matters. All I can tell you is that he is in good hands now. If you wish to see him at the hospital, I will of course make sure the officers on duty there will do all they can to assist.'

'Thank you, Governor. I will be leaving now. Please make sure I am expected.' He put the phone down before Halligan could say anything else.

Jennings quickly wrote a note to Grainne explaining what had happened, and he made his way down to Abbey Street, where he knew he would get a taxi. At that time of the morning, it would be easier to use a taxi than his own car. As anticipated, there was a queue of taxis awaiting the start of the day's rush. Fortunately, as he was going out of the town and the start of the rush hour was predominantly in the other direction, they made quick time in getting out of the centre of the city and on to the M50. As usual, this was busy in both directions, but traffic was moving well for a change, and he managed to get to the hospital in fairly good time.

On entering the hospital, he enquired at the main reception as to the whereabouts of Stephen Moyo. He was immediately referred to a ward on the second floor. Normally he would have expected to find anyone admitted to A&E during the night to still be there the next day. To be admitted directly to a ward was unusual, to say the least.

On reaching the ward he was directed to, he saw Detective McGeough standing in the corridor and talking to a prison officer. They were both outside a door that was obviously a private ward, and they looked up as they heard Jennings approach.

McGeough was the first to speak as he moved away from the warder and approached Jennings.

'Richard, good morning. Sorry to have to find you here at this time and in these circumstances, but your client is going to be fine. He has been fairly badly beaten, but thankfully there are no life-threatening injuries.'

'Kenneth, what the hell happened here? He was only admitted to Cloverhill yesterday. How could they have been so incompetent as to let him be beaten on the first night he was in the place? Surely given the charges he is facing, they were aware he was a high-profile prisoner who would be at risk of just this sort of thing. He should have been under careful watch from the outset. Unless of course it was prison staff who administered the beating?'

This last statement was said loud enough for the prison officer to hear. Just as he was about to speak, McGeough raised his hand to him and took Jennings by the arm.

'No need for that, Richard. Whoever was responsible will answer for what they have done, but one thing I can tell you is it was not prison staff. Why don't you come with me, and we can have a coffee and a little talk about things?'

Jennings stood his ground. 'I would like to see my client first, if you don't mind.'

'Richard, if you want to see him, you can, but he is under sedation and will be for a while. Have a look in the room, but he is under medical care now. Let's have a coffee. Perhaps after that, the medics can tell us how he is doing.'

Jennings saw the sense in what was being suggested, and the two turned away to make his way to the public canteen on the first floor.

McGeough offered to get the coffee, and Jennings went in search of a table where they could have some privacy. When McGeough sat down, Jennings made an enquiry as to something that had been on his mind since he'd first seen him in the ward.

'I thought you had been taken off this case. How do you get to be the first detective on the scene?'

McGeough smiled. 'You are right and wrong on that. You are right that I was taken off the O'Meara murder investigation, but this is a separate matter altogether. I had been sent to Blanchardstown on loan when this call came in, and so here I am. Strictly speaking, I am not on the O'Meara, job but this latest incident is clearly linked to it, so at least I will have access to the main investigation file.'

'I could not make sense of why they took you off the case in the first place. You must have annoyed someone to be taken off such a high-profile inquiry.'

McGeough smiled again as he said, 'Not so much annoyed as not being the right face to fit this inquiry. I thought something was odd when I heard an arrest had been made within the day of the killing, and it was even more surprising when I found out that the arrest was allegedly down to information given to my colleague Sergeant McLaughlin. You know him, and how he ever got to be a sergeant, no one knows. To think he has an informant who would provide the information as to the identity of a killer in a high-profile case like this is a joke.'

'So, what are you saying? Has Moyo been set up?'

'I am not saying anything at all just yet, Richard. Don't try to put words in my mouth. I have been at this game for long enough to know that things very seldom fall in your lap. From what I have seen of your client—and again this is just gut instinct—I don't see him as being a murderer. From what little I could establish, the priest and your man had known each other for a long time, had been seeing each other regularly, and got on well. It makes no sense for him to suddenly turn on him and kill him.'

Jennings gave what he had been saying some thought, and as he sipped his coffee, McGeough asked him a question.

'From what went on in the court yesterday, it seems Moyo and you have some common ground to share.'

'He was in the police back in the day in Rhodesia. He was a witness in the trial of the priest when he was prosecuted for assisting terrorism. You would have got on well with him as a policeman. He was, and I am sure still is, as decent and honest a man as you can find. He was very loyal to the deceased in that case, who was a good friend of mine. That is the only link though. I never knew that he was in the country before yesterday.'

McGeough considered this. 'You would not have had a chance to interview him fully yet. When you do, if you find anything that would help me in this latest inquiry, will you pass it on?'

'Provided it does not conflict with my defence of him on the main charges, of course I will be happy to assist. You feel that it was not the prison staff involved. How can you be so sure of that?'

'Richard, you know as well as I do that a prison is a completely different subculture to normal life. Prisoners and inmates do not live and work to the same rules as applies to you and me outside the walls of the prison. This incident happened too quickly to have had anything to do with the staff. Your man was clearly targeted before he'd even arrived.'

'But even given the killing of a priest is unusual, why would he be targeted so quickly, and by who?'

'Those are precisely the questions that need to be answered. You mark my words: although his injuries are serious, you will find they are not life-threatening. This beating was done for one of two reasons, either to let him know he is in for a hard time in prison, or to try to get him to a place where he can be more easily got at. I think it is more likely the case that he was given a beating to get him out of the prison. My job is to find out why he needs to be out of the prison, and who wants that.'

'But if that is true, what can you do to protect him in the hospital?'

'I will have an armed Garda on his door from here on, and you can be rest assured he will be safe as long as he is in here. In the meantime, I will find out who did the beating in the prison. Hopefully from there, we can find out who we really need to be talking to.'

'You are unlikely to get any help from the prison officers,' Jennings said. 'In my experience, when things like this happen, they close up tighter than a Carlingford oyster.'

McGeough laughed at that. 'I agree, but then, I will not be relying on the staff to find out who is to blame. As I said, a prison is a different culture to the outside. It is also impossible to keep things hidden in a prison for long. You simply have to know the right people to talk to and provide the right incentive to get what you need to know.'

Jennings finished his coffee and rose as he said, 'Right. I will leave you to your inquiries, and if you don't mind, I would like to see how my client is doing.'

'No problem,' replied McGeough. 'I will come up with you to check on my end of things, and I'll leave you with him.'

The two men walked back to the ward in silence. On arrival at the ward, Jennings saw that McGeough was true to his word. An armed Garda was sitting outside Moyo's ward.

McGeough indicated to the Gard that Jennings was to be allowed entry, and he opened the door to let him in. On entering the room, he saw that Moyo was propped up in bed, had a drip inserted, and had bandages around his head. His face was badly swollen, and his left eye was puffed up and closed to a slit. His remaining eye was unaffected, and he clearly recognised Jennings as he came in. When Moyo tried to speak, the nurse at the side of the bed put a restraining arm on his shoulder.

'Mr Moyo, please do not try to talk just yet. We have not seen your x-rays, but there is a chance you have a jaw fracture. Speaking now will not help you.'

As Moyo relaxed back into the pillows, he indicated with his head toward the door where Jennings was standing, and the nurse turned and spoke to him.

'You are Moyo's lawyer?' she asked, and without waiting for a reply, she continued. 'I am afraid Mr Moyo cannot talk to you just now. He has suffered a rather serious beating, although fortunately there are no life-threatening injuries. I can assure you he is in good hands now, and if you leave your details at the nurse's station, we will call you as soon as he is able to speak to you.'

Jennings knew better than to argue with the nurse. As he approached the bed, he said, 'I am not here to cause any discomfort to Mr Moyo. I can assure you I am here solely out of concern, and to see if there is anything I can do for him.'

'I am sure you will be able to do a lot for him in due course,' the nurse replied. 'But for the moment, your services are not required. I ask that you to allow Mr Moyo to rest and recover.'

Jennings looked to Moyo, who seemed to be taking in this exchange with some humour. The man smiled as best he could at Jennings and closed his remaining good eye.

Jennings realised there was nothing he could do, and he left the ward to find McGeough and the Gard in conversation.

As they paused in their discussion, Jennings bade farewell and left the hospital campus to find a taxi to get him back to town.

CHAPTER EIGHTEEN

The traffic had increased substantially, and the return journey was longer than the outward journey, which gave Jennings some time to reflect on the latest developments.

If McGeough was right, and the beating Moyo had received was for some ulterior motive, who would be behind that, and for what purpose? Who could have given Sergeant McLaughlin enough information to warrant Moyo's arrest so soon after the murder of O'Meara?

The more he thought about it, the more the words of the departed priest's final letter came back to Jennings. If what he had to say was correct, it would seem more like as not that Cian O'Meara would be a prominent player in the events to unfold.

On his return to the office, Jennings was advised by his secretary that Mr Hughes wanted to see him as soon as he arrived.

Without taking off his overcoat, he made his way down to Hughes' floor and was directed to go straight in by his secretary.

Hughes was seated behind his desk but was turned away from the door and was looking out over the view from his window. He heard Jennings come in and turned to him. 'Hello Richard. I hear you have had another interesting start to the day. How is Mr Moyo?'

'As well as can be expected, I suppose. At least he is under decent protection for the moment. Ken McGeough is the investigating officer for the assault, and so I am fairly sure no further harm will come to him.'

Hughes smiled at the mention of McGeough's name. Even though he had been out of criminal practice for some time, he seemed to keep abreast of what was going on. He would have known precisely who McGeough was and what he was capable of. 'Well, that is at least something. Have you decided what you are going to do about the late Father O'Meara's wishes?'

'I have made a decision. I read the letter Father Murray brought me from Father O'Meara. What he had to say in that, and what has happened to Moyo, leaves me in no doubt that I must accept the nomination as executor. I am going to represent Moyo as well.'

Hughes did not respond immediately. Jennings knew from years of working with him that it was usual for him to respond when he was ready. There was no room for idle chatter to break what some may have considered an awkward silence.

After a while, Hughes brought his hands together on his desk and said, 'I am sure you have come to the right decision. I knew the late Father O'Meara. He must have had very good reasons to want you to act as executor. Some may say it is bizarre for a man to represent the person accused of the murder of the deceased, but in this case, it seems to me that nothing much will be as it appears on the surface.'

Jennings replied, 'I feel that will prove to be the case, and I need to tell you that from the letter he sent me, there may well prove to be difficult times ahead in dealing with the estate. I am going to have my hands full with the trial and will really need your help with the estate work.'

'You know you only need to ask, Richard. Have you heard where the funeral is likely to be? I assume you will be attending.'

Jennings had not even thought about that given the speed with which things had developed. He suddenly realised that O'Meara had only died less than a week ago, and Jennings had no idea what arrangements had been made for his funeral. He assumed that the post-mortem would have been carried out by now, and the body released for burial. He realised he needed to determine what the funeral arrangements were.

'I need to find that out,' he said. 'I assume that Father Murray will probably be the best person to ask. I will let you know as soon as I find out.'

Jennings left Hughes in his office and went back to his own, where Grainne was just going through the morning's post. Although Jennings's life may be about to turn upside down, the mundane daily work still had to be dealt with, and Grainne was not going to let that slip.

Jennings told her of his decision to act as executor and to represent Moyo, and she accepted the information without comment. He then asked her to get Father Murray on the phone because he needed to find out what the funeral arrangements were. Then he turned to deal with the work she had left on his desk. In many ways, it was a relief to get back to matters less complex.

By mid-morning, Grainne had tracked down Father Murray, and Jennings learnt from him that the funeral was scheduled in three days' time, in the Dublin Pro Cathedral. He learnt that apart from Cian O'Meara, there were very few family members who would be attending. All the priest's siblings had died, and only a few nephews and nieces would be in attendance.

Jennings advised Hughes of the arrangements and made a call to the hospital to enquire after Moyo. He was told that he was still under mild sedation, but his condition had improved, and he would be able to talk to Jennings the following day.

CHAPTER NINETEEN

The next morning, Jennings arrived at the hospital by 9.00 a.m. He had ascertained that Moyo was allowed visitors outside normal visiting hours, and he wanted to spend some time with him to find out what had been going on in the last few days of the priest's life, as well as how Moyo had come to be arrested for the murder so soon after the priest's death.

As Jennings made his way down the corridor to the room he had been directed, he noticed there was an armed Gard sitting outside a door and that another unarmed Gard was making his way towards them with a coffee in each hand.

As he approached, the Gard who was seated stood and made a conscious movement into the centre of the corridor, facing Jennings. The Gard with coffees stopped in his tracks and was looking for somewhere to put his containers when Jennings realised they didn't know who he was and were carrying out their duties of protecting Moyo to the letter.

Jennings stopped where he was and identified himself. He offered to display his solicitor's ID card and was invited to do so by the armed Garda His colleague approached and took the card from him. After a glance at the card and Jennings, it seemed they were satisfied as to who he was.

'Sorry about that, Mr Jennings, but Detective Garda McGeough told us we were to check everyone coming through here,' said the unarmed Garda.

Jennings acknowledged that he understood they were doing their duty, and the armed Garda opened the door he was standing next to, letting Jennings enter.

Moyo was propped up on his pillows and seemed to be asleep. As Jennings walked in, Moyo opened his eyes and immediately sat up straighter in his bed.

'Morning, Stephen. How are you today?' Jennings inquired.

'Much better than yesterday, thanks. It is amazing what a good night's sleep and painkillers on demand can do for you,' he said with a smile.

Jennings pulled up a chair and sat next to him. 'I want to have a general talk with you, Stephen. No notes or anything today. If you feel tired at any time, just tell me, and I will come back later. There have been a few developments in the last few days which leave me rather confused, and only you can clear up what is happening.'

Jennings explained the visit of Father Murray and the nomination of Jennings as executor of the estate. He recounted the letter in which O'Meara had told him to seek out Moyo. Recent events had made that unnecessary, and so Jennings wondered what had caused O'Meara to be worried about his future.

'It is true that we have been brought together in a way that even Father O'Meara would not have anticipated. The fact that he has nominated you to be his executor, and what he said in his letter, means that he had faith in you. If that is so, I will tell you everything I can about recent events. However, you may find some of it hard to believe.'

'Just start wherever you want, Stephen. I have spent a lifetime listening to people telling me things that sound incredible.'

'Very well. But first you can tell me something. You have been away from Zimbabwe for many years now. Have you any idea of what has been going on in the country?'

'I only know what I read in the press and on websites. There are a few that seem to give good coverage, but unfortunately none of it ever seems to be good news.'

'Unfortunately, that is true,' Moyo said. 'For a short time, a few years ago, when we had a government in which the MDC and Zanu PF were forced to work together, it seemed as though things were going to change for the better. Mugabe was too cunning to allow that to continue, and at the elections in 2010 he proved just how ruthless he can be. The situation in the country was worse than it has ever been. Despite Mugabe being forced out, things have not improved yet, and there are a lot of people still wanting to get money out of the country.'

'But what has that got to do with O'Meara's death? He has been out of the country longer than I have.'

'Yes, but his legacy continued in the trust that was set up, and in his nephew's dealings in the county. I know all about the activities of his father, and the son was even worse, using every trick in the book to benefit from the misery of the country. He made sure he had contacts at all levels of government, and he always looked after his people in return for favours. Especially in recent times, those contacts have given him a new avenue to exploit. That's taken him to a new level altogether.'

'And what is that?' Jennings asked.

Moyo paused before he answered in one word. 'Diamonds.'

'Diamonds? Was Cian dealing in diamonds?'

'Dealing would be a simple term,' said Moyo. 'Let me explain what has been happening. About six years ago, there was a discovery of substantial diamond fields in the Marange area of the country. Apparently, they had been lying on the ground for years, and nobody cared anything about them because nobody knew what they were. All that changed when a local mining company confirmed they were indeed diamonds, and they also confirmed the extent of the find. It was the start of a time of madness that has not been seen before. Hundreds of people flooded the area, looking for these little stones that could bring them more money than they had ever dreamt of.

'The buyers initially were local businessmen, but in no time at all, there were buyers of all nationalities making their way to Marange with bundles of cash. Mutare turned into something out of the Wild West, with Russians trying to outbid Lebanese and Pakistanis, and all of them trying to outbid the Chinese. That was never going to work, and the government very quickly moved in to control the area and take over the mining and distribution of the diamonds.

'What should have been a national treasure became the source of huge financial wealth to the top members of the party. They gave the Chinese exclusive rights to prospect and mine in return for their years of support, and the Chinese were not slow in establishing themselves in the area.

'I am sure you have read of reports of miners being beaten and even killed in the area, and all of those reports are true. In fact, what has been going on there is worse than anything that happened in Matabeleland in the eighties, but they have learnt their lessons, and the control by the army and police is so tight that nobody knows what is going on in the area.'

'But if that is the case, how do diamonds feature in our case?' Jennings asked.

Moyo took a drink of water from a plastic cup before continuing. 'The Chinese were only interested in the wholesale exploitation of the fields. There is so much out there that if even 10 per cent made its way out of the government's and the Chinese's hands, there would be a fortune to be made. That is where Cian got involved.

'Over the years, he had become almost a personal banker for a large number of Zanu PF top dogs. He was the man to go to if they wanted money out of the country and hidden from the party or their family. The UN and EU sanctions just created a market for a man with Cian's skills and contacts. He was able to use the trust to get millions of dollars into the hands of his clients, as he called them.

'When the diamond trade got going, Cian was able to corner the market as the middle man between those who got their hands on the diamonds and the end purchasers in Europe. Some of the top politicians had access to the pick of the diamonds, and Cian handled the exporting of them from the country, the sale in Europe, and then the deposit, less his commission, into hidden accounts all over the world.'

'But surely there is a ban on dealing in diamonds from Zimbabwe?' Jennings asked. 'It can't be that easy to dispose of rough diamonds. And how did he get them out of the country in the first place?'

'There is no ban on the trade in diamonds from Zimbabwe,' Moyo said. 'They are not considered to be conflict diamonds because there is no civil war or insurrection in the country. The Kimberley Process has no interest in controlling their trade. Getting them out of Zimbabwe is where Cian was using the trust.

'Ever since independence, the Holy See has an Apostolic Nuncio in Zimbabwe. That has the same status as an embassy, and correspondence and documents that come and go from there are protected in the same way as any diplomatic material.

'From the time the trust was set up, a set of financial reports and documentation would be put together and sent out of the country to Ireland every two months. No one ever considered this unusual because it was fairly normal for anybody associated with the Church to report back to its funders.

'Over the years, however, Cian came to realise the benefit of this as a means of safe communication. He managed to put a civilian employee under his control in the Nuncio in Zimbabwe, and at this end he had a similar civilian employee available to intercept any post in which he had an interest.

'It was not every post that he used, and so on each end the employees concerned had no clue that they were involved in any criminal activity. Cian was generous to each person with cash and gifts, and they both thought he was a genuinely decent man intent on helping the mission and keeping his uncle's good work going.

'Once the diamond trade got going, the post system was perfect to get out small-volume but very high value parcels of gem-quality diamonds. They were the pick of the crop and were sold for the benefit of the very elite in the party. Cian got his commission as middle man, and everyone was very happy.

'It is difficult to say how much he has got out of the country and how much he has made for himself, but Father O'Meara and I believed it runs to millions of euros.'

Moyo reached for his plastic cup to take another drink while Jennings took in what he was hearing. He had always known Cian would prove to outdo his father in criminal activities. If what Moyo was saying was true, Cian had certainly achieved that.

Before Moyo continued, Jennings asked, 'But where did it all go wrong? It must have brought us to this. Father O'Meara would never have been a knowing party to this, even if his trust was a beneficiary of what Cian was doing.'

Moyo put down his cup and continued. 'You are right that he would never have accepted this behaviour. He only found out about it by accident when the employee at this end came in to work late for some reason. Instead of the post being intercepted and the parcel of diamonds being given to Cian, the post was put on Father O'Meara's desk. When he opened it, he found the parcel of diamonds amongst the other documents. That is how it all fell apart.'

'But if that is so, Cian would have simply closed that door and found another way to get the diamonds out of the country. What has any of this to do with Father O'Meara's death and your arrest?'

'Richard, you know that Father O'Meara was a clever man. When he found the diamonds in that post, he did not immediately confront Cian. He wanted to find out more about what was going on, and so he put the diamonds back in the post and followed the trail to where it led. Of course, Cian featured very quickly, but Father O'Meara also found out that Cian had had to engage the help of several other high-level criminals in the country to help him get rid of the diamonds to best advantage.

'Unfortunately, there was a development Father O'Meara could not have anticipated that brought things to a head. About eight months ago, rumours started to circulate in the country that a very large diamond had been found. Its exact size has been the subject of wild speculation, but if the stories about it were even half correct, it would rate as one of the largest diamonds found anywhere in the world in the last one hundred years. By all accounts, it is also supposedly of extremely high quality. It is said to be worth tens of millions of euro. Of course, the government denied all the rumours and has effectively shut down any story relating to the fields, but I now know these "rumours" were not that at all. They were the truth. The diamond does exist, and it is as large as they said.'

'And how do you know that?' Jennings asked, although in the back of his mind, he felt he knew the answer already.

'I know it is true because it was in the last post that arrived in Dublin before Father O'Meara was killed.'

'How do you know that?' Jennings asked.

'Because Father O'Meara told me, and he also showed it to me. It is a stone the size of a golf ball. It was the only stone in the last packet that came to Father O'Meara before he was killed. I believe Cian knew that O'Meara had the stone and that he obviously wanted it. That is why he was killed.'

Jennings allowed Moyo to take another drink whilst he considered what he had been told. He knew Cian was a ruthless man who would use every dishonest trick in the book to make money for himself, and Cian certainly had no respect for the law. But to kill a man—and not only a man but his own flesh and blood—seemed to go too far even for Cian. Jennings needed to voice his doubts with Moyo.

'Stephen, you will come to know I have no respect for Cian as a man, but even for him, I find it hard to believe he would go so far as to kill his own uncle.'

Moyo put down his cup and adjusted himself on his bed before continuing. 'It is not really relevant what Cian would or would not do. You cannot move in the world he does without engaging other and even more ruthless people. Cian had sourced a buyer for the diamond, and it was the buyer who would have carried out the killing, either through his own people or with local criminals. We are talking about very wealthy people from outside the country who would not hesitate to take a man's life for what they believe to be their own.'

Jennings had heard and read about the trade in diamonds from Zimbabwe over the years, but as with many things, the tighter the control exerted by Mugabe over the fields, the less news there was that leaked out, and other more important issues made the headlines. The exportation and marketing of diamonds was still subject to strict controls in the legitimate market, but the illegal trade was reputed to far exceed the legal trade in gems and high-end diamonds. The Russians seemed to have a more than keen interest in the trade.

As Jennings looked at Moyo, he noticed that the man seemed to be in some discomfort, which was hardly surprising given what Moyo had been through. He decided that he had heard enough for one day and would take up the story again later. He still had not officially received anything from the Gardai on the murder charge, and he would need to spend time with Moyo to discuss that soon. For the moment, Stephen needed to recover to face what lay ahead.

'Stephen, I am going to leave you now. You have given me a lot to digest, and you need your rest now. I will speak to Mr McGeough, who is heading up the investigation into your assault. I'll see what we can do to look after you from here on.'

Moyo smiled at that. 'I am not really concerned for my welfare, Richard. Nothing good will come of this matter, and anyone touched by these diamonds will be affected in some way or another. It is something Father O'Meara was concerned about and look what happened to him. I doubt either you or your Garda friend will be able to protect me. What was done to O'Meara was really a warning to you, if you decide to take on Father O'Meara's wishes to act as his executor. You need to be careful in what you say and do as much as I do.'

Jennings stood from his chair and shook Moyo's hand before leaving the room and stepping into the corridor. The armed Garda was standing to one side of the door; the other Gard was farther down the corridor talking to another man. Jennings saw that it was McGeough, who dismissed the Gard as he approached.

'How is your client?' McGeough asked.

'As well as can be expected, I suppose. How are your enquiries going at the prison? Found out anything useful yet?'

McGeough smiled and took Jennings by the arm as he guided him away from the room and down the corridor. 'Richard, I told you that things work differently in prisons. I have found out who was responsible, and I have also found out that a Cian O'Meara is in the frame as someone who has an unhealthy interest in Mr Moyo. Can you shed any light on that for me?'

'Ken, I said I would help you in any way I can, and I will. But for the moment, what I have been told has to stay with me. I need to check on a few issues, and if there is anything I can give you, you know I will do so.'

McGeough stopped walking and looked back and forth along the corridor to make sure no one was in earshot. He moved closer to Jennings and said very quietly, 'You know I do not expect you to breach any confidences. You need to know that what I have established so far is that apart from Cian, there are some other very dangerous people interested in your client. These are not people who will respect the law or the police. I would suggest, you stay away from O'Meara if you can. He is trouble, and you need to leave him to me.'

'All right, Ken. I hear what you are saying, but for the moment my concern is for my client. How are you going to keep him safe?'

'That is not going to be a problem for the immediate future. I am owed a few favours in the hospital, and so I can make sure he stays here for the next few weeks, if necessary. That will give me time to make the necessary arrangements inside to make sure he is protected.'

'I assume I should not ask what you mean by arrangements,' Jennings asked

McGeough simply replied, 'All you need to know is that when he gets back to Cloverhill, he will be in the safest place possible. We will speak again soon, so for now, look out for yourself and remember what I said about O'Meara.'

McGeough left Jennings and made his way back down the corridor to Moyo's room. Jennings returned to his office.

CHAPTER TWENTY

On his return to the office, Jennings dealt with the messages neatly left for him on his desk by Grainne. He then told her he was not to be interrupted for the next hour. Despite the reassignment of a large amount of his current workload, clients tended to view their solicitors as their personal property and were seldom happy when redirected to another member of the firm. After dealing with the most pressing of matters, Jennings called for the O'Meara probate file, which held the will of the late Father O'Meara.

The envelope brought in by Father Murray was a standard A4 brown envelope, but it was apparent it held more than a few pieces of paper. On opening the envelope, Jennings found that in addition to the will, there were copies of bank statements and financial statements relating to the trust. In addition, there was a letter apparently signed by the deceased with a list of wishes in respect of his funeral arrangements.

The first thing that Jennings noted was that the will was handwritten. That struck him as odd given he had found out that the priest and Gerard Hughes had known each other for some time. He had assumed the father would at least have had the will drafted and prepared in the normal way, if not by Hughes then at least by a solicitor. In any event, on the face of it, it appeared to have been properly executed and signed by both O'Meara and two witnesses who appeared to be fellow priests.

The will was direct and to the point. The priest had left his entire estate to the trustees of his trust and given them total and unfettered discretion as to the administration of the trust. The only condition was that the trust was to be used to primarily benefit the mission in Zimbabwe, but after that, the choice of beneficiaries and the use of funds was left to the trustees.

Provision was also made that if for whatever reason the trustees were of the view that the trust had to be dissolved, then after all expenses and debts were discharged, the net proceeds were to be divided. One-half of the proceeds were to be shared equally between the surviving family members of Stephen Moyo, and the balance went to any organisation the trustees felt would work for the benefit of the people of Zimbabwe.

Jennings had a cursory glance at the other documents and was amazed by the size of the funds amassed in the trust over the years. It appeared the vast bulk of the cash reserves were held in local Irish banks, but in addition there were properties owned in both Zimbabwe and Ireland, and the trust had clearly been used to fund not only the activities of the mission but also Zimbabwe students studying in Ireland.

Jennings also saw that Stephen Moyo could potentially be a major beneficiary of the trust in the event it was ever dissolved. At the moment that seemed unlikely, but that information in the hands of the Gardaí could certainly add to their case in giving him some motive for the priest's demise. The Gardaí would have no knowledge of the terms of the will, and for the moment Jennings had no reason to contemplate sharing it with them. It was something he would raise with Moyo to see if he knew anything about the will.

There was no mention of any bequest to any member of the O'Meara family, and Jennings decided he would use one of his local investigators to make enquiries as to who, apart from Cian, may have been left behind who might seek to challenge the will in any way. With no direct family members to provide for, that was probably an unlikely scenario, and it was more out of curiosity than anything else that he wanted to find out a bit more about the priest's family.

The man he decided to use was Colm Murphy, a former sergeant who had been retired for several years but who took on private work from time to time. Not only had he Murphy his contacts on the force but he had also always had a good working supply of informants whom he had looked after over the years and who were still prepared to repay in kind for what he had done for them.

One thing that did strike him was the request that after his funeral, his remains would be cremated, and the ashes interred at a site reserved on the hill above the mission. Jennings knew from experience that the Catholic Church's position on cremation had changed over the years, but for a priest to seek cremation was unusual.

There were more than enough funds to have made provisions for his body to be sent back to Zimbabwe for burial, but that was clearly not his wish. He advised in the letter that he had sought and obtained the local Bishop's permission in respect of this request. This again showed the careful nature of the man who had apparently planned for virtually all eventualities. How strange it was that he should then die a violent and unexpected death.

Over the next few days, Jennings gave instructions to his local investigator and sent initial letters to the various banks and institutions, advising of the death of the priest and of Jennings' nomination as executor. There was no final death certificate until after the post-mortem result and inquest into the death had been finalised, and so there was no immediate rush to apply for probate.

The funeral service of Father O'Meara was a straightforward if somewhat dull affair. There were no grieving family members, and although the church was filled with local parishioners and clergy, the general mood was not one of sorrow but of quiet respect for a man who had devoted his life to the Church and the service of others. Jennings noted that Cian was nowhere to be seen, but he did notice that McGeough was at the back of the congregation. That struck him as odd given that he was not directly involved in the murder inquiry.

Jennings tried to get to McGeough after the mass but was unable to do so, and he resolved to meet up with him soon to see what he could tell him of his investigations on the assault, as well as what he was planning for Moyo's future in custody.

As for Moyo, Jennings had a daily call to him either by phone or in person, and he was pleased to see how quickly the man was recovering from the assault. Each day Jennings saw him, he was visibly stronger. That was good news, but Jennings was concerned that Moyo's recovery would mean a return to Cloverhill.

Jennings had not yet received any disclosure from the State as to the case against Moyo, and so he deliberately chose not to discuss the case with him at all. Their discussions were restricted to general topics relating to affairs in Zimbabwe. It was apparent that Moyo was a very well read man. In any normal society, he would have been able to command a position of importance in any organisation in the commercial or public sector. In a dysfunctional society such as Zimbabwe, however, his talents were unlikely to have ever been put to good use.

The initial remand following Moyo's appearance in the Criminal Courts of Justice was for one month. Strictly speaking, this should have only been for two weeks, but Jennings had agreed to a longer period in circumstances where it was obvious nothing much would have happened in two weeks and given there was no prospect of a bail application succeeding, the longer remand made sense.

CHAPTER TWENTY-ONE

The month went by very quickly, and Jennings was in court at Cloverhill for the remand hearing when he was approached by Cathal Murphy, a solicitor from the Chief Prosecution Solicitor's office. That office was the solicitor's office of the DPP, and solicitors from there had the task of getting matters prepared for hearing before the Circuit and High Courts in Dublin.

They also prosecuted cases in the District Courts, and so it was by no means unusual to see a member of their staff at Cloverhill. From previous dealings with the CPS office, Jennings knew that Murphy only dealt with cases before the Central Criminal Court. His appearance at Cloverhill was unusual.

As Murphy came across to Jennings, they exchanged the usual pleasantries. Murphy explained that Moyo's trial had been assigned to him and asked if they could step out of the courtroom.

Jennings had had a number of dealings with Murphy in the past, and he had always found him to be a conscientious and decent man with whom to work. He took his job seriously and was meticulous in what he did, particularly with making sure there was full disclosure to the defence in accordance with the law. Too many trials had gone wrong with lapses in disclosure, but none had slipped by on Murphy's watch. Jennings at least took comfort in that.

When they were in the corridor and removed from any eavesdroppers, Murphy said, 'I have been asked to tell you that we will be looking for an expedited hearing of the Moyo matter. The book of evidence has been finalised, and I will be looking for a return for trial today with a trial date a month from today.' As he said this, he was passing what was clearly a book of evidence to Jennings.

Jennings was completely taken aback at this development. 'What's the rush, Cathal? It might be a high-profile case because of the deceased, but there are dozens of other cases pending that should surely take priority.'

Murphy glanced from side to side and was clearly uncomfortable at having this discussion with Jennings. 'Richard, I am simply telling you what I have been told to do. I have no idea why this is being pushed on. I am simply the messenger. However, I will make sure you get everything you need to prepare for the trial. Have you decided on which Counsel you will brief yet?'

'Well, I had decided on Gerry Grant as junior Counsel, but I was not expecting to hear what you have told me. I will need to have a look around and see which senior is available at short notice. If you succeed in your application for an expedited hearing, that may narrow the field, but I am sure I can deal with that. I assume you will give me full disclosure so at least I can then see what the case is that we must meet. As it is, I have not tried to take instructions, particularly because my man has been in hospital for the last few weeks.'

'I am aware of the assault, and that should never have happened. I have arranged for disclosure of everything I have now to be sent to you, and it should be in your office later today. From what I have seen, there will be very little that is not included in the book. For all the urgency in pushing this case on, as you can see, the book is one of the shortest I have seen.'

Jennings knew he could take Murphy at his word and replied, 'Okay. Do what you must, and I will get Counsel briefed. We will see where we go from there. Whatever happens, though, you can tell those instructing you that I am not going to be pushed into a trial without being properly prepared.'

Murphy smiled at that. 'It will be good working with you again, Richard. I will pass on your message.'

Murphy turned away and went back in to the courtroom. Jennings followed him after digesting what was the latest in a series of unusual developments. It made no real sense for the DPP to expedite this case above others. There were enough recent gangland killings and banking trials to clog up the system for years. Apart from the identity of the deceased, when it came down to it, this was a straightforward murder.

The return for trial of his client was done in Moyo's absence when the court was told of his recent assault. There was no objection from Jennings, and so the case was duly returned for trial to the Central Criminal Court one month from the date of the return. Jennings returned to his office to try to contact his proposed junior Counsel, Gerry Grant.

Gerry Grant was of a similar age to Jennings, and the two had been working together almost from the day Jennings had started work in Ireland. Grant had always impressed Jennings as being a thorough barrister, and he was particularly good on his feet. He had saved the day on several trials with a carefully thought out and executed line of questioning.

Jennings knew his mobile number by heart and phoned him as soon as he was behind his desk. In front of him was an envelope marked 'Private and Confidential' bearing the stamp of the DPP. Jennings assumed this was the disclosure of which Murphy had spoken.

Grant answered the phone on the second ring.

'Hello, Gerry. Would you be interested in a new murder? Deceased was a priest, and the accused is a former country man of mine. The DPP have served a book on me this morning with a return for a month from now, so if you are interested, it might need a bit of juggling on your schedule.'

'Well, Richard, nice to hear from you again,' Grant replied. 'I assume this is the case that has been in the press, and I was hoping to get a call from you. Of course, I would be happy to take the brief. But what is the rush all about?'

'No idea, I am afraid, but I will send a copy of the book and the disclosure I have just got from the DPP to you tonight. My man has been in hospital for a while, and I have not tried to take instructions from him until the disclosure was in. I will get on with that now.'

'Very good. I have heard in the library that the DPP will be briefing Sean O'Halloran as senior.'

This was interesting news to Jennings. O'Halloran was considered one of the top prosecution Counsel at the bar. He had made a name for himself as a junior and had taken Silk comparatively early in his career. He had almost exclusively acted for the prosecution for the past fifteen years. He would be a formidable opponent and he was known to fight his cases with enthusiasm.

'Right, that is interesting. Do you have any suggestions for a senior?' Jennings asked.

Without hesitation Grant replied, 'Donal Gilmartin. This case would be right up his street, and he would be well able to deal with O'Halloran.'

Jennings smiled at the reply. 'Just the man I was thinking of, Gerry. I will give him a call later today, but if you see him in the library perhaps you could sound him out as to availability?'

'Will do. Speak again soon.' Then Grant was gone.

Jennings picked up the Directory from his desk and looked up Gilmartin's number. Just as O'Halloran had made a name for himself as a prosecution Counsel, Gilmartin had an equal reputation as defence Counsel. The two men were known for having an intense dislike of each other, although no one really knew why. It was unusual for members of the bar to display open hostility to one another. Their world was one in which conflicts in court seldom continued outside the courtroom, but it was an open secret that O'Halloran and Gilmartin would not even share a table at a bar dinner, let alone have a social conversation.

Jennings got Gilmartin's number and reached his voicemail. He explained why he was phoning and asked if he could reply and let him know whether he was interested in taking on the brief. He warned him of the expedited hearing date.

He had barely hung up when his phoned pinged for a text message. It was Gilmartin, and his message was all Jennings needed to hear. It said, 'Thanks. Will be available. In court now. Speak later. Donal.'

CHAPTER TWENTY-TWO

Having resolved the issue of Counsel, Jennings opened the envelope in front of him and started to go through the paperwork it contained. The documents had been sorted out into sub files, which would have been typical of Murphy's input and not necessarily that of other members of the prosecution staff.

The sub files consisted of witness statements, Garda statements, forensic reports, and post-mortem reports. With respect to the technical sub files, each held its own statement relative to the chain of evidence necessary to show that there was no technical interference with any samples or substances. This would prove turgid reading for anyone, but it was necessary to examine it in detail. Fortunately, Jennings knew this was something Gerry Grant enjoyed doing because he would be only too delighted to find some fault with a technical issue to be exploited to the full in front of a jury.

Jennings was immediately struck by the fact that apart from the technical sub files, the witness statements were particularly thin. He scanned through them, and it was apparent that somehow the Gardai had received a very early tip-off to look for Moyo and were able to find two items of sufficient importance in his possession to warrant his immediate arrest.

The first was a hunting knife with an eight-inch blade which had traces of blood on the handle The second was a hold-all bag containing ten thousand euros in cash. The hold-all was identified as belonging to the priest by a member of staff from the archdiocese.

A further statement from a bank official at the bank where the trust's account was held confirmed that the day before the priest's demise, a withdrawal of ten thousand euros in cash was made. There was nothing in the statement to indicate who had sought the withdrawal or who had collected the cash from the bank, and that was an obvious omission.

Jennings was concerned at the lack of detail, which from previous experience he would not have expected. Either this case was being rushed and mistakes were being made, or there were glaring gaps in the chain of evidence that had been ignored.

Moyo had said nothing under interview, and it was apparent that the State was relying on this case being portrayed as a straightforward robbery and murder.

With what Jennings knew of the relationship between the priest and Moyo, that made no sense. Moyo was not a poor man, and apart from that, he had a very clear endorsement from the priest.

Whilst Jennings had been proven wrong about some people before, he simply did not see Moyo as a killer.

Jennings turned to the sub files of technical issues, and the first thing he looked at was the custody record, which dealt with Moyo's detention following his arrest. His attention was drawn to the observation made by the Gard in charge that the prisoner appeared 'intoxicated and disorientated'. That should have led to at least a medical examination by a doctor and hopefully a blood sample, but there was nothing of the sort reflected in the documents provided. Jennings made a note to follow that up with Murphy.

It was also interesting to note that the search warrant for Moyo's apartment had been applied for and issued within six hours of the alleged time of death of the priest. That was fast work by any standards. Jennings noted that McGeough's statements confirmed what he had told him in the CCJ: that he was the senior Gard present when the body was found. However, the warrant had been applied for by Detective Sergeant John McLaughlin, and it appeared he was in effect the investigating Gard from there on.

Jennings had respect for McGeough, but McLaughlin was at the other end of the scale. Jennings had had several run-ins with him over the years. McLaughlin's track record was, to say the least, not impressive. He had faced a few disciplinary hearings over the years in respect of trials that had gone wrong.

To have been able to get a warrant so quickly, McLaughlin had to have had solid information. It was something that Jennings knew he would have to investigate later, to see if he could find out the source of the information.

The last thing Jennings looked for before he decided to take a break from the papers was any sign of CCTV footage that would have put Moyo anywhere near the priest at the material time. There was nothing, and that was also something which struck Jennings as odd. Apart from the fact that the Archbishop's residence was bound to have had its own CCTV coverage, as he knew from previous cases, that was a part of Dublin which had a large number of CCTV cameras in operation on commercial premises. It would have been an obvious line of inquiry to find footage which put the accused in the area at the relevant time.

Jennings put the papers back in their folders and asked Grainne to take copies and get them off to Counsel with the usual covering letters. Then he decided that he had done enough for the day.

Now that he had something to work with, he would need to speak to Moyo and get his version of events. He decided that would wait till the following morning, and he left the office with a brief farewell to Grainne on the way out.

CHAPTER TWENTY-THREE

The following morning, Jennings was in his office with the cleaners and before the rest of the staff. He was intent on going to see Moyo in the prison to begin the process of getting proper instruction to prepare for trial, and he wanted to go over the papers he had been given before he'd left.

Grainne Kellet was meticulous as to arriving on time for work, and Jennings thought it odd that by 9.15 a.m, he had heard nothing from her in the outer office. She would always pop her head around the corner to say hello, but there was no sign of her this morning.

His curiosity was interrupted when he took a call from reception and was told that there was a gentleman waiting to see him in reception—and he was not prepared to wait for an appointment later in the day. It was apparent from the tone of the receptionist that whoever it was, he was probably standing in front of her and was not going to go away.

'Who is it?' Jennings asked.

Her reply immediately got his attention. 'A Mister Cian O'Meara.'

Jennings paused for a moment before asking her to bring him up to him.

A few minutes later, there was a knock on his door, and the receptionist led O'Meara into the office.

It had been many years since Jennings had seen O'Meara, and the years had apparently treated him well. He had not put on much weight and looked in good health. He carried himself as a man in charge of his own affairs—and one used to getting what he wanted.

Jennings did not offer his hand but invited Cian to sit. The invitation was refused.

'I am not going to be here long enough for pleasantries, Jennings. I understand you are to be the executor of my uncle's estate. Is that right?'

'That is right. I would have been contacting you in due course as one of his few remaining relatives to advise you of that.'

'I have no interest in the priest's estate, Jennings. What I am concerned about is the fact that he stole something of mine, and I want it back.'

Jennings could see that O'Meara was in an agitated state, and he decided he would do what he could to make his discomfort worse. 'And what is it you say has been stolen, Cian? That is a very serious allegation to make of a deceased relative, let alone a priest.'

'Don't try to be smart, Jennings. You have been speaking to your client Mr Moyo enough to know want I am talking about. I want what is mine returned to me without any delay or fuss. Maybe then, people can get on with their lives without any unpleasantness.'

'Cian, in the first place, I do not know what you are talking about. In any event, what you are saying sounds to me like a threat. You should know I don't take kindly to threats.'

'Jennings, you have never struck me as being stupid, so I will allow you your little game of professing ignorance but what I will tell you is that games you play may have an impact on other people who really should not be involved. I would never threaten you because that would be a waste of my time. All I am saying is that your actions may influence other people that could have been avoided.'

O'Meara took a card from his inner pocket and threw it on Jennings' desk. 'That has my contact details. I expect to hear from you shortly.' As he was reaching the door, he stopped and turned to him again. 'I see Grainne is not in yet, Richard. I hope she is not unwell. There seems to be a lot of contagious illness around these days. People have to be careful who they mix with, you know.' And with that, he was gone.

This last statement caused immediate concern. How did O'Meara know his secretary was called Grainne? More important, how did he know she was not in the office? He immediately got his mobile phone and dialled Grainne's number. He let it ring for a while, and when the call was obviously cut off, he was even more concerned. Grainne would never not answer her phone if she saw he was calling her.

He called down to reception to inquire if there had been any word from her and was told there was not. Jennings decided that he would immediately go to her house to find out what was going on.

CHAPTER TWENTY-FOUR

After telling Hughes what had happened, Jennings left the office and took a taxi out to Terenure, where Grainne lived on her own in a row of converted terraced houses. He had only ever been there once or twice, and it was in a very quiet area, which was well suited for a person like Grainne.

His previous concerns were heightened as the taxi turned onto the street. He could see a Garda patrol car and an ambulance parked outside Grainne's house.

He told the taxi driver to wait from him and ran towards the entrance of the house to be met by a Gard coming out of the house carrying a Garda evidence bag.

'Gard, I am Richard Jennings. Grainne works for me. What is going on here?'

The Gard paused and looked over his shoulder into the hallway of the house. 'Detective Garda McGeough is inside, Mr Jennings. He said he thought you would be along, so you'd better go in and speak to him.'

Jennings hurried into the house and met McGeough in the hallway. 'What is going on here, Ken?' he asked, trying to look over his shoulder into the living room where there were several Gards and, slightly hidden from view, the paramedics from the ambulance.

'It's okay, Richard. Grainne is fine. You can talk to her in a minute. Let me tell you what we know.' He indicated a side room for the two to have some privacy. 'Apparently Grainne was getting ready for work this morning when there was a knock at the front door. When she asked who it was, she was told it was Bord Gais inquiring about a gas leak. Grainne had no reason to be concerned and opened the door. Two men then came in, grabbed her, and took her into the living room. They told her to be quiet and do as she was told, and no harm would come to her. Grainne was obviously terrified,

146

but she kept calm by all accounts. She asked what they wanted and was told to shut up.'

'But what did they want, Ken? And who were they?' asked Jennings.

'I can't answer either of those at the minute, but fortunately for Grainne—and very unfortunately for the two of them—Grainne's nephew was upstairs and heard the commotion.'

Mention of Grainne's nephew caught Jennings' attention. 'You mean the army ranger nephew?'

McGeough smiled as he replied. 'None other. Apparently, he came in late last night, unknown to Grainne, on a week's leave. He has his own key, let himself in, and went straight up to his room. Unluckily for our two friends, he is a very light sleeper. When he heard what was going on, he took what you could call decisive action.'

As McGeough was saying this, Jennings saw the paramedics and two Gards working their way down the hall with a man on a stretcher who was clearly in some discomfort.

'That is one of them,' McGeough said. 'Afraid it looks as though he has a shattered collar bone and probably a couple of fractured ribs. The other one got away but lost a fair amount of blood from a good smack in the mouth. There was a good deal of blood on items of furniture, which we are taking away to see if we can get any DNA traces to identify him. The one on the stretcher has nothing on him at all to identify him, and he has not said a word since he was put out of action by the nephew.'

'This is Cian O'Meara's doing,' Jennings said, and he felt the anger rise in him. He told McGeough of O'Meara's visit earlier in the morning and what he had said about people associated with Jennings being hurt.

McGeough took a moment to take in what he had been told.

'It would seem to be the case, Richard. This little exploit certainly escalates matters. I had told you Cian was taking an unhealthy interest in your client, and this is obviously another step in the game. Are you sure you don't have anything to tell me now?'

Jennings was torn between telling him everything he had been told by Moyo and the diamond and adhering to his duty to his client. As much as he trusted McGeough, he was a Gard, and Jennings' only source of information as to what may be going on had come from his client. To divulge any of the information he had at that time would be a basic breach of client confidentiality and was not something he was prepared to do.

'Ken, I have told you before. When I can talk to you, I will. In the meantime, I would like to see Grainne, if that is all right with you.'

'Of course. She is in the kitchen having a cup of tea. Quite a tough lady. Annoyed she is going to be late for work, apparently.' McGeough stepped aside, and Jennings made his way through to the kitchen.

For the first time in their working lives, Grainne got to her feet as he came in the room and embraced him in a fierce hug.

Once he managed to disengage himself, he noticed that despite what McGeough had said, she had obviously shed a tear or two and was clearly traumatised over recent events.

'Grainne, are you all right?' he asked.

'I am now that it's all over, Richard. God knows what could have happened if Padraig was not here.' As she said this, she motioned towards a well-built young man sitting on the other side of the kitchen table. He rose and took Richard's outstretched hand.

'Hello, Richard. Padraig Carey. Good to meet you.'

'Padraig, I can't thank you enough,' Jennings said.

'No problem. I don't know what is going on here, but I think I may hang round for a while. I have a lot of leave due to me, and it's been a while since I've spent any time with Aunt Grainne. She has told me a little about your new client, and this seems to be too much of a coincidence to be unrelated.'

Jennings could tell this was a man who would not be messed about, and he was only too delighted to hear Padraig would be able to keep an eye on Grainne until this case was resolved. The attack on Grainne was out of line even for the local Dublin gangsters whom Jennings had dealt with in the past. An attack on him would make sense, but this was brutal intimidation on a new scale.

Jennings turned to Grainne, who had resumed her seat and was nursing her cup of tea. 'Grainne, this is all down to me representing Stephen Moyo. Cian O'Meara was in the office this morning, and from what he said, I know he was behind this. I can't put you at risk again, and so from hereon I will work this case on my own. You take a few days off, and when you are ready, come back. I will arrange for you to work on other matters, away from me.'

Grainne looked at him for a while before putting her cup down and firmly saying, 'Richard, if I did as you ask, these thugs would have achieved their purpose. I am not going to be intimidated by O'Meara or anyone else, and you should know me better than to suggest I stop working for you. I will be in later today, and there will be no more discussion about this. Padraig has very kindly offered to look after me for as long as this takes to get sorted, and so I suggest you get on with it.'

Jennings looked from Grainne to Padraig, who simply smiled and shrugged his shoulders in resignation.

'All right. I suppose that puts me in my place, then. I will see you later, when you are ready to come in.'

As he left Grainne's house, Jennings' anger increased at an exponential level. He knew that this was down to Cian. For him to resort to an attack on Jennings' staff was beyond the pale, even for Cian.

Before he got back to the taxi, he pulled Cian's card from his shirt pocket and punched in the numbers on his mobile. The call was answered on the second ring.

'Hello, Jennings, I was not expecting a call from you so quickly.'

'How did you know it was me?' Jennings enquired. 'I don't recall giving you my number.'

'You did not have to. I have kept this phone solely for your calls to me, so no one else but you has the number. Do you have something to tell me?'

Jennings was so furious at the smug tone that he could feel his face redden. 'I do, Cian. First, you need to know that one of your thugs is in Garda custody, and the other is probably on his way to hospital as we speak. You will be pleased to hear that Grainne is absolutely fine and looking forward to coming back to work.'

The pause on the other end of the line told Jennings that this was not what O'Meara was expecting to hear. The hesitation in his voice was further proof of that. 'I don't know what you are talking about, Jennings. I assumed you wanted to talk to me about my stolen property. I know nothing about any thugs and certainly know nothing about your secretary's welfare.'

'Cian, you have never been a good liar, but as soon as your man starts to talk, I am sure the Gardai will have an interesting conversation with you. Insofar as what we were talking about earlier, I am telling you this once and for all. Even if I did know anything about supposedly stolen property, I would not talk to you about it. This little exercise of yours has proved to me how desperate you must be, and desperate men make mistakes. You are obviously starting down that road.'

O'Meara had regained some composure, and his voice was more self-assured and forceful as he replied. 'You are not good at taking suggestions to heart, Jennings. There is more at stake here than just you and your staff, and you need to understand that.'

'Don't worry, Cian. I understand all right. But here is something for you to understand. You will never get anything from me, so go fuck yourself.' With that, he ended the call before O'Meara could reply.

His exchange with O'Meara had helped calm him down as he got into the taxi and gathered his thoughts.

Upon returning to the office, Jennings went over the papers he had been given by Murphy once more. He decided it was time for him to have a detailed discussion with his client as to precisely what had happened on the day of the priest's murder. He knew it was too late in the day to get to see him in Cloverhill, and so instead he phoned through to arrange a meeting first thing in the morning.

CHAPTER TWENTY-FIVE

Jennings arrived at Cloverhill reception at 9.00 a.m. sharp. After going through the usual formalities, his client was brought down to the consultation rooms with very little delay. Perhaps this was a sign of enhanced treatment after the beating Moyo had received.

In any event, as Moyo came into the room, Jennings noted he seemed to have made a remarkable recovery and greeted him with a warm smile and firm handshake.

'Good to see you, Stephen. Seems you have made a good recovery.'

'Thank you, Richard. I am feeling much better now. Your friend McGeough said I would be properly looked after. Please thank him for me when you next see him.'

'I will indeed. Stephen, the DPP has directed that your trial is to start in a month from now. I can also tell you that Cian O'Meara tried to have my secretary kidnapped yesterday, so we need to get serious about this matter. I need to get proper instructions as to what was going on around and including the time Father O'Meara was killed. Are you up for that now?'

'I am,' Moyo replied. 'But there are parts of the days of which I have no recollection, no matter how hard I try to recall what happened. Can I ask you, Richard, whether you've found the diamond yet?'

This was not what Jennings thought would be Moyo's main concern. For a man on a murder charge who had been told his trial was due to commence soon, Jennings would have thought the whereabouts of a diamond, even one of significant value, would be the least of his worries.

'No, I have not. To be honest, I don't think that is the most important issue to be dealt with right now. You are going to be put on trial for murder. That is far more important than any diamond.'

'But that is where you are wrong, Richard. If the diamond is found, all

151

my problems will go away. Father O'Meara's murder and everything since then is all related to the diamond. If you find the diamond, the real killers will be found. That is the best way I can be found not guilty.'

'That may or may not be the case, Stephen. But for the moment, let's go through what the State has. Then you can give me your version. I have a dictaphone with me, so I will record what we are discussing, if that is all right?' As he took the machine out of his jacket pocket, he could sense that his client was not too keen on the idea of their discussion being recorded. To allay his fears, he said, 'And I can assure you this recording is only for my benefit. No one else will ever get to hear it, except my secretary.'

'Very well, Richard,' Moyo replied. 'It's just that from experience, when conversations are recorded, they sometimes fall into the wrong hands and cause problems that no one intended.'

Jennings was confused at his client's apparent reluctance but pressed on. 'All right, let's get started,' he said. 'The Gardai say that on searching your apartment, they found a knife hidden which had traces of the deceased's blood on the handle. How did that come to be in your room?'

Moyo looked him square in the eyes and replied, 'I have no idea. I have never owned such a knife, and I have no idea how it came to be in my room. It is not mine—I swear it.'

'That is all very well, Stephen, but it must have got there somehow. Is there anyone else who has access to your room and would have known the priest? Did you have many visitors at all?'

Moyo hesitated before he said, 'I have hardly any visitors. Whoever put that knife in my room was able to do it after Father O'Meara was killed and before my arrest.'

'But that is precisely the problem, Stephen. We are talking about a six-hour period, and you will have to be able to come up with something better than "It's not my knife".'

For a moment, Moyo showed signs of hostility as he replied, 'I thought people in this country were innocent until proved guilty. Why do I have to prove anything? That is what you expect in Zimbabwe, not Ireland.'

'All right, Stephen, calm down. You are presumed innocent, and you don't have to prove anything at all. But if you can't provide something to cast doubt on the State's version of events, you are not going to get any sympathy from a Dublin jury in a case where the murder weapon is found in your room, and all you can say is, "It's not mine." Anyway, let's move on to the next issue.

'The prosecution has a record of a sum of ten thousand euros in cash being withdrawn from one of the trust accounts the day before the priest was killed. They say that that money was found in your room when you were arrested. How did it get there?'

Moyo once again showed some irritation in his reply. 'I don't know, Richard. I never received any cash from Father O'Meara. Can the bank not tell us who made the withdrawal?'

'A valid question, and one that will be asked, I assure you. But for now, your answer is the same as in respect to the knife. You have no knowledge how the money got into your room?'

'That is correct, Richard. I have no idea at all.'

'Stephen, the room you occupy is in shared accommodation, is it not? How would a stranger get access to the premises if you were not there?'

'Theoretically, you must know the key code to the main entrance and the key to your room, but very often other tenants leave the main door open with a block of wood or some such to let in friends. It is hardly a secure place, and we have had trouble with people coming and going who should not be there.'

'Any CCTV that you know of?'

'I don't know about that, Richard, but the manager of the building should be able to tell you that.'

Jennings paused for a moment before moving on to the next issue that concerned him. 'There is a suggestion in the custody record that when you were taken in to the charge office, you seemed disorientated or under the influence of drink or drugs. What do you say about that?'

'I do not drink, Richard, and I certainly do not take drugs. It is right to say I was disorientated, though. When the police broke into my room, I was asleep on the bed, but as far as I remember, I was fully clothed. I could not understand what they were saying to me, but there was a lot of shouting and questions being fired at me. I was disorientated and confused and said nothing. I really didn't know what was going on.'

'Were you seen by a doctor at the Garda barracks, or at any time after your arrest, to give a blood or urine sample?'

'There was a doctor called, and I gave a blood sample. After some time, when they had given me some food and something to drink, they took me to a room for questioning. I did what I would have done in Zimbabwe and said nothing.'

'And how did that go down?' Jennings asked.

'They were not happy with me, but at least in this country, you don't get beaten for failing to answer questions. They told me that the interview was being recorded, so I assume you can see what was being said.'

Jennings had not been given that footage yet, but it was something he would be asking for. The issue of the doctor's visit was of concern because there was nothing in the book of evidence about that, and that was something that should have been there.

He was going nowhere with the obvious issues to be addressed, and so Jennings decided to approach things from a different route.

'Stephen, you say the knife is not yours, and you know nothing about the money. You have had no visitors to your room, and you say that when you were arrested by the Gardai in your room, you were asleep. But when they woke you, you were by all accounts disorientated and later it appeared to a custody officer that you were under the influence. Take me through events as you remember them from the time you were last with Father O'Meara.'

'Richard, that is part of the problem I have. I have a vague recollection of meeting Father O'Meara and having a general discussion about Cian O'Meara and the diamonds. After that, I remember leaving him and saying we would be in touch. That is all I remember until the police came to my room.'

'So, playing devil's advocate, what you are saying is that in the absence of some natural medical reason for your memory loss, your inability to remember anything at the critical time has to be down to some external cause. Having said that, you have no suggestion as to what that might be. Can you not see that that is going to be very difficult for us to present to a jury?'

Jennings could sense Moyo's tension as he listened to what he was saying, and he replied in a forceful tone, 'Richard, you ask me questions which I answer truthfully. I cannot lie to you, and I cannot explain the knife, the money, or the fact that I can't remember anything after I left

Father O'Meara. Maybe I was drugged somehow. The blood test result would show that, surely?'

'They would normally be very useful, but for some reason the test results are not even mentioned in the book of evidence. There will have to a be a good reason for that. But even if they do come to light and show you were under the influence of a drug, how did that get into your system?'

Moyo sighed and slumped back in his chair. 'Richard, you are my lawyer. That is for you to establish. I can do nothing from here. I will tell you again that if you find the diamond, these problems will go away. Cian O'Meara is responsible for all of this, and all he wants is the diamond. Find that, and we can use that to get me out of here.'

Jennings had noticed a change in Moyo's tone and attitude as their discussion progressed. He seemed almost belligerent and was not the same calm, measured man Jennings had met on previous occasions.

'Stephen, accepting what you say is true, say I find this mysterious diamond for which Cian is so desperate. What are you saying I need to do, then? Negotiate with him and barter the diamond for your release? How much influence do you think Cian has here? This is a Garda investigation into the murder of a prominent and well-respected priest. You are the prime suspect, and in my view, there is enough evidence to put you in front of a jury with a serious risk of a conviction. Cian O'Meara is not going to make that disappear in exchange for a diamond. In any event, the diamond is apparently not his to own.'

Moyo said nothing for a moment, and when he replied, he did so in a tone that showed the pressure he was under. 'Richard, I am telling you that Cian O'Meara is responsible for everything that has happened. I do not know how he will do it, but if you find the diamond and he knows you have it, he will do everything it takes to get it back. If that means he will provide the evidence to convict the real killers of Father O'Meara, he will do that. That is my only hope of avoiding being found guilty. Please, if you want to help me, find the diamond.'

'Stephen, don't misunderstand me. I will do everything I can to help you, and if it means finding this diamond, I will do what I can to do that. There is one thing you must understand, though.'

'And what is that?' Moyo asked.

'Even if I find this diamond, I am not going to be a party to any illegal deals with O'Meara. Others may be prepared to deal with the devil, but I will not. If what you are saying is true—and it may well be that the diamond is the key to finding Father O'Meara's killers—there will have to be a legal way of proving that, or else I will not be involved. I am not concerned about myself here, but someone close to me has already been put at risk because of my representing you. I will not let that happen again. Do you understand what I am saying?'

Moyo had had his head down whilst Jennings was talking, and he very slowly raised it to reply. 'Richard, all I ask is that you do what you can to help me. I do not want you or anyone else to get into trouble because of me, but if you find the diamond, I just know things will get better for me.'

It was clear to Jennings that no purpose would be served in continuing their discussion, and he decided to call it a day. 'All right, Stephen, that's enough for now. I will do everything I can for you, but you must help me as well. If anything at all comes back to you about events immediately before the priest was killed and you were arrested, get the prison authorities to call me. In the meantime, I will do what I can and get back to you in a few days time.'

Moyo stood, and just as Jennings was about to open the door of the consultation room, he said, 'There is one thing I remember, Richard.'

Jennings paused and turned. 'And that is?'

'I had asked Father O'Meara if the diamond was in a safe place, and he said the best place to hide something was in plain sight. He said I was not to worry about the diamond because he had it in view every day. I did not know what he meant by that, but maybe that is why the people who killed him were in his room. Maybe they thought he had the diamond in his rooms.'

Jennings considered this but made no reply, simply nodding his head and leaving the room. As he walked away, he did think it was a strange thing for the priest to have said, and it must have some significance. What was even more strange was that there was no indication that the rooms occupied by the priest had been searched by anyone. That was odd if the reason for the killer or killers of the priest being in the room was to search for the diamond.

CHAPTER TWENTY-SIX

On his return to the office, Jennings decided to call his barristers to arrange a meeting with them. Whilst he had a need to discuss what he had, or perhaps more importantly did not have, to prepare the defence, he was worried about the whole issue of the diamond and the apparent significance Moyo attached to it being found.

He had his own views on the matter, but it was important in his mind to sound out his Counsel for their view. When they met, he would decide whether he'd tell them everything. A meeting was arranged for the following morning in the Four Courts building. Both Grant and Gilmartin were in the Four Courts on civil work that day and were not going to be in the criminal courts, where Jennings would normally meet his barristers.

They were meeting early, and so the meeting was held in the public cafeteria, which was almost empty. Jennings and Grant got themselves a full breakfast, but Gilmartin had a cup of coffee, black with no sugar. His diet reflected his personality: robust and no extras. Physically, he was an imposing man of over six feet and with no unnecessary weight. He had a full head of hair and was always meticulously turned out.

Gerry Grant was completely the opposite. Whilst similar in height, he carried too much weight and could never be described as well turned out. His gown had several rents and tears in it, which he always took great pride in saying showed he was a man of experience in the rough and tumble of the courts.

Upon seeing the two of them sitting side by side, Jennings was almost tempted to smile, but he knew such frivolity would not go down well with Gilmartin and kept his thoughts to himself.

Gilmartin opened the discussion, expressing the same thoughts Jennings had shown in his meeting with Moyo. 'Well, Richard, unless there is something up your sleeve you have not disclosed, you don't give us much to work with for Mr Moyo. Is there anything positive we can use?'

'I wish there was,' Jennings replied. 'There is an issue with a missing blood sample, and I need to find out whether there is any CCTV at Moyo's apartments. But for the moment, we have virtually nothing except a man who says he is innocent and thinks that will suffice.'

Gilmartin replied, 'That clearly is not enough, and the first thing we need is to find out what the position is on the blood issue. We'd better get a formal letter seeking discovery of any blood test carried out and see where that takes us. Given their haste in bringing the matter on, we must hope that the omission from the book is not an oversight.'

Gerry Grant nodded in agreement and said, 'I also thought it odd there was no reference to any blood test. It is such an obvious matter for disclosure that I can't see it was omitted by accident. I hope there is not going be any funny stuff over the samples taken.'

Gilmartin took a sip from his coffee and stared at Jennings for a moment. 'Richard, I have known you long enough to know there must be something more going on than a simple issue of discovery. You would not have called this meeting if that was all you wanted to discuss. What is it you are not telling us?'

Jennings decided it was time to take someone into his confidence, and with the two men sitting in front of him, he knew he could have absolute faith in the information provided being kept confidential.

'Very well,' he said. 'I will tell you what is not in your brief, but even for you gentlemen with your experience, what I have to tell you will sound bizarre.'

Jennings then told them the history of his dealings with the priest in Zimbabwe and how that came to lead to Moyo choosing him as a solicitor. Then he told them about the diamond issue and Moyo's belief that if the diamond was found and returned to O'Meara, that would resolve his problems. He also told them of Grainne's narrow escape and his subsequent discussion with O'Meara.

When he had finished, Jennings had to wait for some time before he got any response. It was Gerry Grant who spoke first.

'Of all of this, what do you believe is true? Is there a missing diamond that would be valuable enough to kill for?'

'I cannot see why it is not true,' Jennings replied. 'It is a known fact that diamond smuggling has been going on in Zimbabwe for the past few years, and Cian O'Meara is just the sort of man who would have got involved in that. Added to that, the history of Cian and his father in Rhodesia lends some credibility to the idea that Cian would be involved in this sort of thing. Then there is Cian's own admission that he believes I have what he wants. All in all, I think what he is saying is very probably true.'

The two men turned to Gilmartin for his thoughts, and he looked from one to the other before saying, 'This may all be very interesting if we were writing a novel or a script for a film. We are not. We are dealing with a man standing trial for murder. All you have told me so far is that our man has links, albeit indirectly, with a possible gangster who would engage in serious criminal activity for very serious monetary rewards. Nothing you have told me is of any help in defending the man. If the Gardai get wind of any of this, it gives your man the motive for murder—which now seems to be missing on the State papers. It would be foolish in the extreme to raise any of this in front of a jury. In any event, in the absence of any real proof of what our man has to say, I cannot see a Judge allowing any of it before a jury anyway. If that is the best you have, Richard, Mr Moyo is in serious trouble.'

'I agree,' Jennings said. 'I will try to find out some more about the missing evidence and see where that takes us. But for the moment, I don't see any reason for optimism as to a happy ending.'

The barristers rose, said their farewells, and left the cafeteria. Jennings was left on his own to consider his next move. He decided he would have to get on to Colm Murphy to find out if he had unearthed anything of use.

CHAPTER TWENTY-SEVEN

On his return to the office, the letter seeking further disclosure was waiting in his e-mail inbox from Gerry Grant. He immediately dispatched it to the CPS office.

In the normal course, it could take weeks for a reply to come back, but in this case, Jennings was confident he would not have to wait long. In that he was correct, because a reply was forthcoming three days later.

In respect of the blood sample, he was told that 'unfortunately' there had been a break-in at the State forensic laboratory, and several samples had gone missing, including the one taken from the accused. There was nothing that could be provided to the defence.

The fact was there had been a break-in at the laboratory had made the national headlines at the time, and although that may have been coincidental, there was certainly nothing to suggest it was in any way linked to Moyo's trial.

As to CCTV, he was advised that the system at the archbishop's residence was not operative at the material time, and a statement from a security firm confirmed that to be the case. He was told no other CCTV footage had been found despite Garda enquiries in that regard.

Another dead-end.

The last thing Grant had included in his letter was for details relating to the withdrawal of the money from the bank. He had asked for copies of any withdrawal documents or signed acknowledgements of receipt, and at least in that respect, a statement was provided by a teller as to handing over the cash to a black gentleman who had presented a letter at the counter from Father O'Meara, a copy of which was attached, asking for the money to be given to the bearer of the letter, who was identified as Stephen Moyo.

The teller had been asked to try to identify the person who had collected the money by photograph, but he was unable to identify Moyo from several photographs presented. All he could say was that it was a black man who had collected the money.

A copy of the letter of introduction was provided, and as Jennings looked at the letter, he felt there was something not quite right about it but was unable to define what it was that troubled him. He would show the letter to Moyo on his next visit, and perhaps that would help.

Before he could give the matter any further thought, Grainne came into this office to tell him that Colm Murphy was on the phone for him and needed to speak to him. Colm Murphy was not known for small talk, and this conversation was no exception.

'Well, Richard,' he said. 'I have some things to show you that you may find of interest regarding Mr Moyo. When can we meet up?'

Jennings' focus was immediately transferred from the paperwork to his conversation with Murphy.

'I can meet anytime you like, Colm. Do you want to come in here or meet elsewhere?'

'We won't meet in the office. I am in the Red Lantern at the minute. Could you come down to me now?'

Murphy had to have something of interest to be looking for a meeting straight away, and Jennings was not going to put him off. 'I could be with you in ten to fifteen minutes, if that is okay.'

'That's fine. I will be in the snug at the back when you come in.' He paused briefly before adding, 'And Richard, it would be as well for you to keep an eye out to make sure no one follows you. No real cause for alarm, but just to say keep your eyes open for anyone who might be watching you.'

Before Jennings could reply, Murphy hung up, and Jennings was left even more puzzled.

On his way out of the office, Jennings was conscious of the warning that he may be followed, and he did what he could to avoid this by stopping to look at shop windows on occasion and even doubling back once, as though something of interest in one of the windows was worth a second look.

He was satisfied he was not being followed when he arrived at the Red Lantern. After making his way in, he went to the rear of the pub, where he found Murphy sitting alone with a newspaper raised in front of him.

As Jennings approached and sat on a stool opposite him, Murphy lowered the paper. It was apparent Murphy was looking over Jennings' shoulders to see if anyone else was coming into the pub. At that time of day, there would be very few visitors, and from where he was seated, Murphy could see any new arrivals as they entered.

'What is all the cloak and dagger stuff about, Colm?' Jennings asked.

'Only taking precautions, Richard. After what I must tell you, you will understand.' Murphy indicated with a wave for the barman to organise a fresh cup of coffee for Jennings and then opened a well-used briefcase that had been sitting on the table beside him. He took out a folder, and from that he pulled out a sheaf of papers and what appeared to be a group of photographs.

'Richard, when you asked me to do a bit of background work on your client, I started off by making inquiries at his digs. Fortunately for me, I know the manager. Anyway, from what he told me and indeed gave me, I was able to progress inquiries in a certain direction. During those inquiries, it became apparent to me that your office was being watched. I specifically did a bit of surveillance on your office to confirm my suspicions, and sure enough, you have been followed regularly for the past few days, especially when you have been out to Cloverhill and the immediate time after that.'

'Any idea who is organising it?' Jennings asked.

'We'll hopefully get to that later, but for now I want to show you a few photos.'

Murphy took a paperclip off some of the photographs and spread them out in front of Jennings. He could tell straight away that these were stills taken from CCTV footage.

'These are stills from CCTV taken outside of Moyo's digs and from inside the reception hallway. This set were taken four days before the priest was killed.'

Jennings could see the photos followed in sequence, and they showed three men, two white and one coloured, approaching the building and entering the reception area. They were not particularly easy to identify on the street, but when they were in the hallway, they could be clearly identified. The pictures were so good that Jennings could immediately identify one of the white men.

'I know that man,' he said 'This is one of the bastards who broke in to Grainne's home. The guards have him in custody now.'

'They do,' Murphy said. 'I don't know for sure, but I would think it is more like as not that the other white man is the one who got away.'

'Who is the coloured fellow?' Jennings asked.

'That I don't know. Perhaps your client could enlighten us. Anyway, on the day this visit occurred, your man was not too happy to see these people. My contact tells me that despite them claiming they were friends of Moyo, when he came down to see them, they were clearly not on friendly terms. There were raised voices and a bit of pushing and shoving, but then the visitors left and Moyo went up to his room.'

Murphy then unclipped another set of photos and replaced the first set with these. 'These were taken from footage on the day of the priest's killing. You see your man arriving at the digs, and the time he comes in.' He pointed to another set of photos. 'Here are our two friends arriving sometime later. Tell me if you see anything of interest.'

As Murphy sat back, Jennings leaned forward and studied the photos. 'This fellow here.' He pointed at the man he had earlier recognised. 'He is carrying a briefcase that looks familiar.'

'I agree, Richard. I would be confident that it must be the very briefcase our friend Sergeant McLaughlin says he found in Moyo's room with the cash in it. So what do you make of this?'

This was material that should have been taken up by the Gardai. If Murphy could come by it so easily, why had they not taken it up, and why did they say there was no CCTV footage?

Jennings put these questions to Murphy.

'You have to ask the right questions of the right people to get information, Richard. When McLaughlin arrived at the digs to pick up Moyo, he never asked about CCTV. He had his man, a weapon, and what he assumed was incriminating evidence in the form of the cash. That was all he wanted. You should know as well as I that he would never bother his arse doing anything he did not have to.'

'But surely your man would have told him about the CCTV footage?' Jennings said.

Murphy smiled as he replied. 'I know the manager for the same reason McLaughlin does. As they say in the papers, he is a man "known to the Gardai". Let's just say that he would not voluntarily give McLaughlin the time of day. He has had a good few run-ins with him, and McLaughlin treats him like dirt every time he sees him. He's not the sort of fellow you would take home to meet the family, but he is certainly not the worst. I have always looked after him, so he was very happy to share this with me.' Murphy paused and put down a set of what appeared to be statements in front of Jennings.

'These are statements from the manager and from the man who services the CCTV system. He confirms the system was working properly and that the dates and times reflected would be accurate. Not bad for a few days' work, even if I say so myself.'

Jennings was certainly impressed with what Murphy had found, but the material in front of him raised serious questions that only Moyo could answer. Why had he not mentioned any of these visits, and who was the coloured man in the picture? He would need to get out to Cloverhill sooner rather than later to confront Moyo with this. He was still worried though about why the material he had now had not been found by the State. This type of evidence should have been sought by the DPP on reviewing the file. Someone had to have thought to look for this.

He expressed his concerns to Murphy.

'The DPP would rely on what McLaughlin put in his file, and if he said there was no CCTV, that would be the end of that. What I can say, though, is that our man has since handed over this same footage to a Gard we both know.'

'And who was that?' Jennings asked.

'Ken McGeough,' he replied.

'Ken McGeough?' Jennings repeated. 'He is not even on this investigation. What was he doing looking for this?'

Murphy replied as he put his papers together and back into his folder. 'That is for you to ask him. I have some other leads to follow, but I suggest you and Mr McGeough get together and find out what his interest is. It would not be unusual for him to be sticking his nose in where it is not wanted, particularly if there was a bad smell to upset the old nostrils. I will leave these with you.' He handed over the folder. 'The originals will be delivered to your office later today. And for god's sake, be careful where you go and who you talk to. Something is not right about this whole case.'

CHAPTER TWENTY-EIGHT

Jennings left the pub before Murphy and returned to his office. He kept the warning about being followed in mind and made numerous checks and deviations on his return to make sure he was not in fact being followed.

On his return to the office, he advised Grainne to expect documents and photos from Murphy. He gave specific instructions as to having copies made of everything, and for the copies to be stored separately from each other. This was a precaution he had taken on other sensitive cases.

However, he did give her one instruction that was unusual.

'Grainne, I want you to look though the photographs that will be coming in. If you see anyone you recognise, I want you to take the photos to Mr Hughes and get him to record a statement from you.'

'But why can't I just do the statement with you?' she asked.

'Because it may be necessary for you to give evidence in the case in due course. Having already seen the photos myself, if I take a statement from you, it could be suggested I prompted your memory or influenced you in some way. Putting Mr Hughes in between us will stop any such allegation in its tracks.'

'Very well. Anything else I need to do for you?'

'Yes, please. Can you get Cloverhill on the phone for me? I need to speak to Mr Moyo.'

'Will do,' she said. Before he could say anything more, she added, 'And please check your messages before you leave. There are some that are urgent.'

'All right, Grainne. As soon as I get back, I will follow up on all this, but they will have to wait until I get back. What I must do is more important.' With that, he left Grainne with the folder from Murphy in her hand.

A short while later, Jennings retraced his steps back to the Red Lantern. It was approaching lunch time, and so anyone who had been following him on regular basis would have assumed he was going for an early lunch because the Lantern was a regular lunchtime venue for him.

On entering the pub, however, he did not intend to stay and spoke briefly to the barman to request an exit through the rear of the premises. Again, this was not an unusual request because over the years, Jennings had often left by the back of the pub through the rear entrance, which led to an alleyway and then came out on a street immediately in front of a taxi rank. Through his subterfuge, he hoped he could further avoid any followers. He got into the first available taxi and asked for Cloverhill Prison.

Despite the driver's best efforts to engage in conversation, Jennings was not in the mood. The driver soon tired of monosyllabic replies and left him to his own thoughts. Jennings peered through the window at the street he had come to know so well.

His mind began to wander, and he thought back to the days of the trial of the priest in what was then Rhodesia and the only home he had ever known. Now, he was in a new homeland, but the events of the recent past were drawing him back to the new Zimbabwe in a way he would never have imagined—and if truth be told, he would never have wanted.

On arrival at the prison, he asked the driver to wait for him and made his way through reception, filling out the usual paperwork for visiting solicitors. As had previously occurred, he was not kept waiting long before he was ushered through to a consultation room. Moyo was brought in shortly after.

Moyo seemed cheerful in seeing Jennings again so soon after their previous meeting. That was to change as Jennings said, 'I want you to look at some photos, Stephen, and explain to me who the people are that you see.'

As Jennings was putting the two sets of photos down in order in front of Moyo, he could see the alarm appear on the man's face.

'Where did you get these from?' he asked.

'Don't worry about that,' Jennings replied. 'Just tell me who these people are and tell me why I have never heard about them from you and only found out about them from my own investigator.'

Moyo dropped his head and looked away from the photos before looking up again to face Jennings. The man was on the brink of tears as he spoke.

'I do not know the names of these men,' he said, pointing to the two white men. 'But this man I do know.' He pointed to the black man.

'Who is he, then?' Jennings asked.

'His name is Jonathan Kaseke. He is a CIO operative from Zimbabwe.'

The mention of the CIO immediately got Jennings attention.

The original Central Intelligence Organisation had been established in the latter part of the war in Rhodesia. It was neither police nor military, but its original members were drawn from both sectors to establish what was in effect a covert intelligence gathering and enforcement agency. Its operatives were answerable to only their own Director, and he in turn was answerable only to the Prime Minister. As with similar organisations all over the world, no one really knew what they were doing or indeed who was working for them, and so their activities took on a mystique all of their own.

Unfortunately, as the war progressed, their involvement in economic crimes and the activities of people who would never had been considered criminals widened. They relied on an ever-increasing network of informers and people they could coerce into betraying their own friends to achieve their own objectives. Because of their activities, although they may have provided services to the State, they certainly made no friends in the regular services, be they police or military.

After the war in the period of so-called integration, when the respective military wings of the former foes were merged into a new Zimbabwe Defence Force and the former British South Africa Police became the Zimbabwe Republic Police, the CIO saw an influx of operatives who had been trained in this type of work by both Russians and Chinese. In a very short space of time, the CIO became the most feared organisation in the country, and in the more recent past their activities were known to result in people disappearing or, if they were lucky, languishing in prison for years on spurious charges. The growth of the opposition in Zimbabwe had led to an exponential growth in their own levels of savagery and tactics against the people they were supposed to protect. The reality was that from the early days of its inception, the CIO was answerable to only one master: Robert Mugabe.

Jennings' tone showed Moyo the strength of his concerns over what he was just told. 'Stephen, what the hell is a CIO man doing in Dublin, and why did you not tell me this before? How am I supposed to help you if you keep serious information from me?'

Moyo had not lifted his eyes from the photographs as Jennings fired his questions at him, but as he did reply, Jennings could see tears forming in his eyes. 'I did not tell you because this man'—he pointed at Kaseke—'has my son John. If I do not get the diamond back to him, he has promised me my son will die.' Moyo was clearly disturbed and Jennings gave him a few moments to compose himself.

'Stephen, it is time for you to tell me everything that has been going on—and when I say everything, I mean it. I cannot help you if you continue to keep things from me.'

'Very well, but you must understand I have not told you everything because of my concern for my son. If he dies because of me, I could not live with myself.' Moyo took a deep breath and began.

'You will remember that I told you my son disappeared in Zimbabwe? Well, that was not entirely true. We knew he had been detained by the CIO, but we did not know where he was being kept. He had been in the opposition movement for some time, and it is not unusual for people like him to be picked up for no reason. We simply hoped he would be released after some time.

'When Father O'Meara told Cian that he had the big diamond, Cian obviously passed that on to the CIO, and they decided they could use John to get back the diamond. This man Kaseke is known to my family, and he arrived in Dublin and told me that they had John in Dublin. He said if I did not get back their diamond from the priest, I would never see John alive again. That is what they told me when they came to me the first time. I told them I would speak to Father O'Meara and do what I could, and they gave me a week to get the diamond back. I went to Father O'Meara, and he said that he would not give in to these people, that he would speak to Cian, and that I was not to worry.'

'Two days later, Father O'Meara was dead, and I was arrested. I have no idea where John is, or even if he is still alive. But if you can find the diamond and tell Cian you have it, I am praying John is still alive, and we can save him.'

Jennings took a few moments to digest what he had heard. 'What about the other visit to your apartment?' he asked, pointing to the second set of photos. 'This happened some hours after Father O'Meara died. Why have you nothing to say about that?'

'Because I do not remember them even being in my apartment. I swear to you that the last thing I remember is leaving the Archbishop's grounds and making my way back to my apartment. I cannot remember anything after that until the police came in and arrested me.'

'How can you be sure that your son is even in Ireland, Stephen? Maybe they were just saying that they had him here to trick you into handing over the diamond.'

'I know he is here because they told me where to go on the day to see Father O'Meara, and I could see him with Kaseke and the other two men in a car outside the Archbishop's palace entrance. He was no more than fifteen feet from me, and I could see he looked terrified.'

'And you told all this to Father O'Meara on that last visit to him?'

'I did, and he said he would speak to Cian and do whatever he had to do to get my son released. That was the last conversation we had.'

Jennings was not sure whether he felt anger or pity for the man in front of him. He had thought he had left the corruption and violence that was commonplace in Zimbabwe behind him when he'd left that country. Now he was finding out that one of the members of the organisation that was used to terrorise its own people was in his adopted home town and engaging in the same type of activities.

'Stephen, with what you have just told me I cannot leave here and not report what you have told me to the authorities. You are telling me of kidnapping, extortion, and murder. My secretary is being attacked in her own home, and god knows what else is coming down the line because of diamonds and some thugs from Zimbabwe. Things have gotten out of control. There is only one way to put a stop to it. I am going to go to Ken McGeough and tell him everything you have told me. I know I can trust him, and you will have to rely on my judgment on that.'

Moyo's shoulders dropped as Jennings spoke, and after a short while of silence, he looked up and said, 'I have to trust what you are going to do, Richard. One man is already dead because of this. I hope my son or someone else is not going to die as well.'

Jennings could sense that after having finally told him what was really going on, Moyo was resigned to leaving matters in his hands. It was almost as though Moyo was relieved to finally have told the truth of what had been going on.

'Stephen, with what I have now and with what you have told me, there is every chance I can get the charges against you dismissed, possibly even without going to a hearing. When the DPP sees what I have, they are going to have to question what McLaughlin has put together. They will not want to risk prosecution in such a high-profile case that will fall apart in public. Try to stay confident, and hopefully we can get you out of here and get you back together with your son, and you can both go home.'

Moyo smiled. 'I can but hope, Richard. Even if you succeed, I cannot see us returning to Zimbabwe, at least not until things there change for the better. Ireland is not a bad place to live. Maybe I can apply for refugee status here until things change back home.'

'If what you tell me is true—and I am sure it is—and if we can secure John's release, I have no doubt asylum will not be an issue. I can tell you there will not be a day that goes by that you will not think of Zimbabwe. The wide-open spaces, the smell of the first rain, the setting sun, even the drought in the bad years and all the people you have left behind. You will never forget that.'

'I hear what you are saying, Richard, but if that is the price to be paid to stay free until we can go back and try to rebuild the country, it is a price I will willingly pay. Maybe we can go back together sometime?'

Jennings was pleased to hear Moyo speaking with a view to the future. He hoped he would be able to deliver on what he had promised as he bid farewell and returned to his waiting taxi. Now that he had something to work with, he felt a bit more positive for the future of his client.

As he got into the taxi and asked to be taken back to Church Street, the driver held up a paper and said to him, 'I have a copy of the Evening Herald, if you want to have a read on the way back.'

Jennings thanked him and took the paper. His newfound optimism vanished when he looked at the front page and saw Cian O'Meara staring out at him. The banner headline in large lettering read, 'Businessman Killed in Brutal Attack.'

CHAPTER TWENTY-NINE

Jennings could not believe what he was looking at. His hopes of establishing who had killed the priest and getting Stephen Moyo out of custody and reunited with his son were not going to be easily realised if his only link between them all was now dead.

He quickly read what little was in the body of the article. All it said was that a body had been found in an apartment in the northern inner city, and that the man had been identified as Cian O'Meara, a businessman who had worked abroad for many years but who had recently been living in Ireland.

It was reported he was the nephew of Father O'Meara, who had recently been killed. The Gardaspokesman had confirmed the death was being investigated given the clear indications that he had sustained serious injuries prior to his death.

O'Meara must have been killed by Kaseke and those with whom he was working. There was no other possible explanation of his being killed in such a fashion.

Thoughts of returning to the office immediately went out of his mind as he took out his mobile phone and looked up the number for Ken McGeough.

McGeough answered on the second ring. 'Ken, Richard Jennings. I need to see you urgently.'

'As I do you, Richard. Where are you now?'

'In a taxi heading back to town from Cloverhill.'

'All right. Do you know where the Crown and Anchor is in Dun Laoghaire? If not, just tell your driver to get you there, and I will meet you in about thirty minutes. Is that okay?'

Jennings confirmed he would be there and advised the driver of the change in destination. He then phoned the office to advise Grainne he would probably not be back that day.

When Grainne answered her phone, he could tell she was upset about something.

'Grainne, what is the matter?' he asked.

'We have just seen the *Evening Herald*. Cian O'Meara has been killed.'

'Yes, I know. I have just seen the same paper. He was not a very nice man, but all the same, no one deserves to die like he apparently did. But why are you upset about that? He was hardly decent towards you.'

'The reason I am upset, Richard, is because I told you to check your messages. If you had, you would have seen three from him yesterday. In each one he was getting more and more irate. In his last message, he said it was imperative you contact him immediately. You never did, though, did you?'

Jennings recalled her specific instructions to check his messages, but he had been too busy. What if he had been able to contact O'Meara and get to him before his killers? Was that what O'Meara was trying to get him for? Jennings' mind raced, and he could not think of anything to say to Grainne to alleviate her upset.

'Grainne, I can't talk now, but I will when I get back. What happened to O'Meara was not my fault or yours, so don't think it was. He was a man who mixed in bad company. His death is not down to us.' Before she could say anything further, he hung up.

The Crown and Anchor was on the main promenade that fronted the shoreline in Dun Laoghaire. It was clearly a high-end establishment. Large hanging baskets overflowing with multicoloured arrangements of flowers were on the outside walls, and elaborate menus were enclosed in glass cases on either side of the entrance.

On entering, Jennings noted the subdued lighting and recessed tables, each of which were enclosed by high-sided and well-padded partitions. An ideal place for a quiet lunch or other assignation with no chance of any prying eyes or eavesdroppers.

Jennings chose a table towards the back of the premises, from where he could see anyone coming in. He ordered a large Jameson and water. He was not one for drinking in what was still office time, but the latest news about O'Meara and what he had earlier learnt from Moyo had unsettled him. Grainne's not unsubtle observation about his tardiness in returning calls also played on his mind more than he cared to admit.

McGeough arrived as promised within thirty minutes and ordered himself a coffee before taking a seat opposite Jennings. 'Well, Richard,' he said, 'you called to see me. What is so urgent? I assume it may have something to do with Mr O'Meara's unfortunate demise?'

Jennings hesitated before he began. 'It may or may not have anything to do with his killing, but there are things I have ascertained from my client that go outside of client privilege and suggest to me a serious crime has been committed—and there is a real risk of things getting worse. O'Meara's death has confirmed my fears, so bear with me, and I will tell you what I know.'

Jennings then took McGeough through what he had learnt from Moyo, including the details regarding the diamond dealing, the priest's involvement in trying to shut that down, and the hiding of the large diamond on which O'Meara was apparently desperate to get his hands. Jennings told McGeough what he had learnt from his investigator and added that he had been able to identify one of the men on the CCTV footage. Moyo had identified Kaseke.

Jennings told him he knew McGeough had the same footage, and finally he told him of the apparent kidnapping of Moyo's son and the threat to have him killed.

McGeough listened without interruption. When Jennings was finished he took out an envelope from his inner jacket pocket. From that, he took out a sheaf of paperwork, which he held out in front of Jennings.

'What you have told me is very interesting, Richard, and it certainly explains a lot. I have been doing my own investigations into the late Cian O'Meara, and what I have found is not very pleasant.'

McGeough took a photograph from out of the papers and placed it in front of Jennings. It was a photo of the man in custody and the man from the CCTV footage.

'Our friend here has been particularly unhelpful with our enquiries and has not even been kind enough to give us a proper ID. Luckily, with our European connections, I have been able to get a name and some information on him. It seems he is a Latvian who has been working for a major Russian gangster as an enforcer for the past five or six years. There are warrants out for his arrest in Germany and France for assaults and worse, but he has proven highly elusive. What has been particularly annoying is that whenever his boss is seen in public in countries where there is no extradition, he almost makes a point of having this thug around him. It is almost as though he takes pride in displaying him.

'Anyway, he is still not being very helpful, but as you know, I have the CCTV from Moyo's apartment. That may help persuade him to tell us something, but I doubt it.'

McGeough then took another photo from his papers and put that down in front of Jennings. 'This man is the other fellow who was at Grainne's house, and the one we think her nephew gave a good hiding to. He is also Latvian and an altogether more interesting person. He has no record for crimes of violence but is a known forger, and he has convictions in respect of hacking bank accounts and other similar activities. I am sure that he is probably long gone from our jurisdiction, and we are unlikely to see him again.

'I had not been able to identify our black friend, but with what you have told me, I can certainly follow that up and see if I can track his whereabouts. A Zimbabwean would need a visa to come into the country legitimately, but I very much doubt he did that. Probably came in through the North from the UK, so it is not going to be easy to trace him unless he sticks his head up where he shouldn't. What worries me is that having been with these two Latvians, he may be a lone agent now. If that is so, he may be feeling a bit isolated. People who get themselves in that position are often more dangerous than they would otherwise be. That of course makes Moyo's son's position very worrying.'

'Surely it will not be too hard for you to track down Kaseke if he is still in Dublin. It is obvious he is here for the diamond, and knowing the way the CIO operates, I doubt he would be put off by a little hiccup in being left alone.'

'If this organisation he works for is like others in the world, he will prove very elusive to find, Richard. These people are used to working in the dark, and even in a strange country, he will not be easy to find. I think we are going to have to hope he will make contact to try to force matters on the diamond.'

'Well, I am the only person who could possibly help him on that front,' Jennings said. 'I can't see him simply turning up in the office and asking for a cup of tea and a diamond in exchange for John Moyo.'

McGeough began putting his paperwork back together. 'I do believe he will contact you in some form or another. You are his only link with Moyo, and that puts you in the frame as a possible target. With what has been done to O'Meara, that must be a worry. I can organise some protection cover for you, but you are going to have to be very careful from now on as to your movements, until we get this man in custody.'

Jennings was taking this into consideration when a thought that had been troubling him for some time came to the fore. 'Ken, you were first on the scene at the priest's killing, and then you were on the job for the assault on Moyo. We both know you were following up on matters McLaughlin should have taken care of and which strictly speaking you have nothing to do with. Perhaps there is something you need to tell me?'

'All right, Richard. I suppose it is time we were both up front with each other. From the moment I arrived at the Archbishop's palace and saw the priest on his bed, I had a feeling this was no ordinary killing. The priest had suffered several stab injuries that suggested a personal attack rather than a random intruder. The room was also not right. It was too orderly and tidy. I became suspicious when I was taken off the case as soon as I started asking after Cian O'Meara.

'You know me well enough by now that that would not sit well, and so I started my own discreet enquiries about our friend. It seems he had been a very bold boy for years. He had been both informer and criminal and had been trying to play one side against another for the last fifteen or so years, ever since he took control of his father's operations. In the more recent past, he had got involved with the Russians and has been providing very useful information on people trafficking—and more important, drug deals that have been going down through Europe. For that, he has been given a very high level of protection by our own Gardai and other agencies in the UK and Europe.

'The problem with people like O'Meara is they start to think they are invincible. He had told his handlers he was on the verge of making it into a very closed circle of the top Russian mafia, and he was doing it with a major deal which involved contacts in Zimbabwe. No one on this side knew precisely what he was up to, but now that you have told me about the diamond, it all makes sense. He was obviously involved in getting the diamond to his Russian paymaster. Then when Father O'Meara got involved, it all went pear-shaped on him.'

Jennings thought about that for a moment and then said, 'But why kill him now? He has not got the diamond, and I don't know where it is. Without him, what chance do Kaseke and his friends have at finding it?'

'The sort of people O'Meara was dealing with do not take failure easily,' McGeough said. 'I have had a bit of experience of Eastern European gangs operating here, and if they feel they have been taken for fools, they retaliate in as brutal a manner as they can. Rational thinking goes out the window with those people. The fact that this man Kaseke is still involved suggests to me that maybe payment had been made for the diamond, and the failure to deliver was put down to O'Meara's incompetence. They would kill for a lot less, so that is probably what has happened.'

'So, what do I do about Stephen Moyo in the middle of all this?' Jennings asked 'He is still sitting in remand prison for a murder he almost certainly did not commit. Should the CCTV footage and information I have given you not be put to the DPP? They would have to think twice about continuing with the prosecution.'

'Richard, that would be the worst possible thing we could do right now. Just think about what you are suggesting,' McGeough said as he leaned across the table to emphasise what he was saying. 'If we put this information in front of the DPP, I agree they will probably pull the prosecution against Moyo. That means he would be released and on the street. Think what that means.

'First, they would know that we have information to prove Moyo was innocent, and so the investigation would be back on. They would not want that. Second, whereas Moyo in prison is comparatively safe, on the street he would be a target for these thugs to get at, even with Garda protection. If they do have his son, it would be too easy to use that as leverage against him, whereas if he is locked up in Cloverhill, there is nothing he can do for them. You are already going to be a focus for their attention. We don't want to give them a choice of targets.'

'Well, thanks for that,' Jennings said dryly. 'So, it's all right for me to be bait, but not Moyo? That makes me feel a lot better.'

McGeough smiled. 'I would rather have you as the target, where I can now work with you. If I must look after two of you when one is an unknown quantity, I could end up losing both. I don't intend on doing that, so try to relax.'

'Okay, so what do I do about preparing for the trial? It is listed to start soon enough, and right now I have nothing to give Gilmartin to work with.'

McGeough did not make any immediate reply, and Jennings could tell there was something he had not disclosed despite their very recent agreement to be honest with each other. He decided to press him. 'Well, Ken, what have you not told me yet?'

'All right, Richard, but don't repeat it to anyone, and especially not to your Counsel unless and until I give the go-ahead. Do you agree?'

'I don't really have a choice, but what is the concern about Counsel? They are on the same side as I am.'

McGeough smiled as he said, 'The difference is Donal Gilmartin is too honest. If you tell him what I am going to tell you, he will insist on going to the DPP or bringing some motion before the court, and that will put an end to any chance we have of flushing out Kaseke and finding Moyo's son. You know him better than I do, and you have to see what I am saying is right.'

Jennings had not in fact thought of that as being a problem, but as McGeough spoke, he could see the sense in what he was saying. The very qualities that prompted Jennings in briefing Gilmartin could, in these peculiar circumstances, work against them.

'Okay, I agree. So, what can you tell me?'

'You have been told that Moyo gave a blood sample at the station when he was initially detained, right?'

'Yes, and that is recorded in the custody record. Unfortunately, it appears the sample was taken in the break-in at the forensic laboratory before it was analysed, so that is the end of that. Or is it?'

'The custody sergeant on duty that night was Eammon Hughes. I don't know if you know him.'

'The name is not familiar,' Jennings replied.

'Eammon was one of the first sergeants I worked under when I started out as a Gard. I think he may also be related in some way to your own Mr Hughes. But in any event, he was coming up to retirement and he had been custody sergeant for the past few months, pending going on leave pre-retirement. After the sample was taken, he was responsible for keeping it in his locker and then getting it off to the lab the next day.' McGeough paused before providing the best news Jennings had had all day.

'Fortunately for us, Eammon was in a bit of a panic with his leave coming up, and when he went to get the samples to send up, he got Moyo's mixed up with another from a suspected drunk driver. He sent the wrong one into the lab. He only realised his mistake after the break-in had taken place. He did though tell our friend McLaughlin about this mistake.

'McLaughlin, being the man he is, told him not to worry and to get rid of the sample because there was more than enough evidence against Moyo, and so they did not need it. He told Eammon that if it was found out that he had made such a cock-up with a prime exhibit in a case like this, it would not look good on his record, especially with his retirement coming up. He told him that it was all for luck that there had been a break-in, and if he kept his mouth shut and got rid of the sample, that would be the end of it.'

Jennings could see where this was going. 'He didn't get rid of the sample, did he?'

'He did not,' McGeough said with a smile. 'And what was even better is because McLaughlin is such a smarmy git, Eammon not only told me about this, but he gave the sample to me. I called in some favours and had it analysed, and there was more than enough Rohypnol in the sample to wipe out Moyo's memory of the events the previous night. That explains his lack of memory and even his disorientation on his arrest.'

It was very seldom in the criminal defence world that any defence would be provided with such a clear dereliction of duty on the part of an investigating officer. If that was made known, it would inevitably lead to the dismissal of any charges against the accused. In this case, and coupled with the CCTV footage, Jennings was certain no court would allow a prosecution to continue against Moyo.

'That certainly is good news, Ken, but how do we get that in front of the court at the right time? I will have to tell Gilmartin what we have at some stage.'

McGeough replied, 'I have sworn statements from Hughes and a declaration from the lab to verify the results. The lab technician owes me a favour or two, and so she will say nothing until necessary. All we must do is wait until McLaughlin is on the stand, and then we put all of this to him. Gilmartin will crucify him, and whoever the Judge is will have no option but to declare a mistrial and let Moyo away.'

Jennings tried to take in all he had heard. This was certainly not the way any normal criminal case would have progressed, and for a moment, as he savoured the prospect of securing the acquittal of his client, he forgot that he himself could now be a target.

'So where do go now?' he asked McGeough. 'You try to find Kaseke, and I just sit tight and wait?'

'For the moment, that is exactly what you need to do. If I am right in what I think is going on, you may not have to wait too long before you hear from Kaseke. He will probably know the trial is coming up soon, and he will want to bring as much pressure to bear on Moyo as he can before then.'

The two men were preparing to leave when a final thought occurred to Jennings. 'Sorry, Ken. You did say that the other Latvian who got away was a forger?'

'That's right. Why?'

It was Jennings' turn to smile now. 'Because I think I have just found one way to knock a hole in the State's case that could give them a headache without having to rely on you and the good Sergeant Hughes.'

'Do what you have to, Richard, but remember that there is more than one person at risk in this now. Watch yourself.' With that, they left the pub.

CHAPTER THIRTY

The next morning, Jennings spoke with Grainne, who seemed to have calmed down regarding his not returning O'Meara's calls. She seemed reconciled to the fact that his killing was in no way attributable to any action—or more important, inaction—on their part.

Jennings had no time to appease her any further because he wanted to compare the handwritten note provided in the book of evidence that was supposedly a note from Father O'Meara authorising the release of money to Moyo with the handwritten letter from the priest that had accompanied his will. Jennings had always had a feeling something was not quite right with the bank letter, and now that he put the two together and studied them, his suspicions were confirmed.

Father O'Meara had been a meticulous person in everything he did in his lifetime. That extended even to his handwriting, which was probably the most precise and neat Jennings had ever seen. In particular, the downstroke on the letters 'a' and 'd' could barely be seen. On the letter to the bank, however, there was a clear loop in the downstroke. The more Jennings looked at it, the more obvious it became to him that he was looking at documents written by two different people.

Being satisfied himself would not be enough, however. He was about to call through to Grainne when she came in the office, and he asked her to get the details of a handwriting expert they had used in a trial a few years previously.

He could barely remember his name, but he knew Grainne would not only remember his name but would probably remember his contact details. In that he was not mistaken, and within ten minutes, she was on the phone to Harry McGonigle, one of the country's top handwriting experts, to arrange for the two documents to be sent to him by courier for examination.

After seeing the documents on their way with the courier, Jennings found he was suddenly very weary and needed time to reflect on what had unfolded during the day. He was tempted to head back to the Red Lantern, where the day had effectively started, but he knew if he did, the temptation to consume more than he should may prove insurmountable. Instead, he decided to make his way home to reflect on the day's events.

Despite everything that had been brought out, the single question that still had no answer was where the diamond was. After the events of the day, Jennings was beginning to share his client's view that matters would only finally resolve themselves if the diamond could be found. All Jennings had to go on was the observation apparently made by the late priest that he had had it in sight daily, but that sole cryptic clue meant nothing to him. As he left the office, he tried to put all the day's events out of his mind to start afresh on another day.

CHAPTER THIRTY-ONE

Over the course of the next few days, Jennings had to attend to a number of other matters that only he could deal with. That fact allowed him the time to mull over what he had been told by his client and McGeough.

With less than three weeks to go before the start of the trial, he decided to contact Donal Gilmartin and advise him of the apparently forged document presented to the bank. He was anxious to see what his views on that were and to at least show that there was perhaps something with which they could work.

After explaining what he had seen and stating that he had sent the documents on to an expert, he hoped for a positive response from Gilmartin. Unfortunately, the opposite was the case.

'Richard, that is interesting, all right, but it really does not help us much on its own. Have you had a sample of Moyo's writing sent to your expert?'

Jennings immediately realised that in his own excitement and armed with the knowledge McGeough had given him that one of the men involved in the attack on Grainne was a forger—which he could not yet share with Gilmartin—the fact that the letter to the bank was not written by the priest was of no real use.

'I have not yet sent a sample of Moyo's writing, but I will do so as soon as I can. Surely, though, this gives us something to work with?'

'It may or may not. On its own, it could be argued this was done by Moyo himself, and that just makes things worse for us. I am afraid we will need something better than that, Richard,' Gilmartin said not unkindly. 'I know you always put in a lot of effort in your cases, but sometimes you need to step back a bit and look at the evidence objectively. Not all clients are innocent, you know.'

What Gilmartin was saying was obviously true, but it was on the tip of Jennings tongue to tell him what he had learnt from McGeough. He knew he could trust Gilmartin completely, but if he did tell him, perhaps McGeough would be proven correct, and that could have dire consequences for both Moyo and his son. There was too much at stake to make any further disclosures at this stage.

Jennings had no real sample of Moyo's writing, and so he decided to set off for Cloverhill as soon as Grainne was in. After recent events, he had resolved to be more careful about working with her to keep up with any messages and other events in the office, and he was conscious of her still feeling they were somehow to blame for Cian's demise.

Grainne came in early as usual. After having satisfied themselves there was nothing he needed to attend to, she put a call through to Cloverhill to arrange a meeting with Moyo. Jennings hoped to give him some good news, but he felt it best not to share anything McGeough had told him just yet. He knew Moyo's real concern was for the safety of his son and that his own problems were not at the forefront of his thinking,

On arrival at Cloverhill, Jennings found Moyo already waiting in a consultation room, and he explained the reason for his visit. He told Moyo of his comparison between the letter sent to the bank and the letter from the priest to him accompanying the will. He did not tell him what it was that got his attention, but then he asked Moyo to provide samples of his own signature. He asked him to write out a passage from a textbook he had brought with him, and then he asked him to copy the letter that was in the book of evidence.

All of this was done with little discussion between the two. Jennings felt that whilst Moyo was happy to be doing something positive, he was clearly a worried man. The fact that the trial was due to start in a few days' time was obviously a factor, but his concern for his son was also ever-present.

As they finished the handwriting exercise, Jennings decided to question him about the priest's daily routine.

Moyo said, 'Father O'Meara was a man of very regular habits, Richard. He was an early riser and would always go for a walk before saying mass at eight o'clock in St Francis in Drumcondra. He never missed a mass in all the time I knew him, and he always said it was the one thing he looked forward to every day. It gave him a chance to reflect on life and what he was to do with the rest of the day. He worked with local community groups and would have meetings most days. Then he would spend the afternoon reading or resting in his rooms.'

'These meetings you refer to—were they always in the same place?' Jennings asked.

'No, they could be anywhere,' Moyo replied. 'The only venue that was constant was St Francis for mass.'

Jennings did not immediately reply, and Moyo realised where he was going with the question. 'You think the diamond may have been hidden in St Francis? He said it was hidden in plain sight and that he could keep an eye on it every day to see it was safely hidden. The church is the only place he went to every day.'

Jennings agreed with him that that was a place to concentrate his search, and he said he would contact Father Murray to see whether there were any personal belongings or places the priest may have used to keep anything belonging to him in the church.

Jennings left Moyo in the room, made his way back to the office, and decided on his schedule for the remainder of the day.

CHAPTER THIRTY-TWO

First on Jennings' list would be getting Moyo's sample to his expert. Then he would look for Father Murray and perhaps make a visit out to the church himself, to see if he could find anything.

Because he was already out of the office, Jennings decided that it would save time if he were to go to St Francis directly and try to contact Father Murray whilst there. In any event, he often found being away from the office gave him time to think without interruption.

His resolution to keep up to speed with Grainne prompted him to call her first and let her know what he was doing. What she said to him brought an immediate change to his plans.

'Richard, there has been a call from a Jonathan Kaseke. He has left a number for you to call and said it is urgent. He mentioned a John Moyo. I thought he meant Stephen, and when I asked if that was right, he was insistent that it was John, not Stephen, whom he wanted to talk to you about.'

After his discussions with McGeough, Jennings was expecting some contact from Kaseke, but not as soon as this. 'Give me the number, please, Grainne. I will phone him straight away,' he said.

'There is no point in giving it to you now, Richard. He specifically said he would not be at the number until later in the day, and you were to call at precisely one o'clock this afternoon. He would be there to take your call. The number he gave is a Northern number, and I phoned it straight back. It is a hotel in Newry. They confirmed he was staying there and said specifically that he had told them he would be back at midday and would be expecting calls then.'

'Okay, Grainne. I will be back in the office in about half an hour. I was going to try to see Father Murray at St Francis, but you might just track him down for me and arrange a time for me to meet with him at St Francis.'

'Richard, you also need to give Mr McGeough a call. He said it was urgent as well, so you might try him on your way in.'

Jennings immediately called McGeough, who by the sound of the call was in a car on hands-free.

'Richard, I have some news for you which might please you. You know that there were two men involved in Grainne's incident, and we have one in custody. Well, I have a lead on the other one now, and with a bit of luck, I might be able to confirm it's him later today.'

'That is good news,' Jennings replied. 'Where are you now? You sound as though you are in a car.'

'I am,' he replied. 'I am on my way to Newry. Obviously just for personal shopping, but you never know what bargains you find up there.'

'That is good news, Ken, especially because I have just got a call from Mr Kaseke, and guess where he is?'

'I would guess Newry as well. Am I right?'

'You are. I must phone him at midday, and the number he gave is for a hotel in Newry. Maybe you could call in and have a quiet word?'

'I would love to, but I am already over my limit on favours up here, so just for the moment, I will stay away. There is always a chance I have been seen by him, and so I don't want to scare him off. Just as well we spoke. Record your call if you can. We are running out of time, and the fact that he has called you so soon after Cian being killed is not a good sign. I sense pressure may be building on more than just you and your client.'

By the time Jennings made it back to the office, he was just in time for the call to be made to Kaseke. He dialled the number Grainne had given him, and the call was answered by the receptionist at the Canal Court Hotel. Jennings was familiar with the place from previous visits to Newry. He was put through to Kaseke's room, and the call was answered after the fourth ring.

'Mr Jennings,' Kaseke said. 'So kind of you to call me promptly, as requested. I trust you are well.'

The civil tone of his voice belied everything Jennings knew of the type of man with which he was dealing. He was immediately on his guard in his reply to him. 'Mr Kaseke, I am sure neither of us needs to pretend this is a friendly call. What is it you want from me, and more important, where is John Moyo?'

'Mr Jennings, you have been away from Zimbabwe for too long. You know we Shona never get to the point in any conversation without exchanging pleasantries. To do otherwise is to show disrespect, and I think we should each show the other some respect given the current position.'

'And what is that position, Mr Kaseke? I have no interest in dealing with the CIO, and I know of nothing that may be of interest to you at all. What I do believe is that you are engaged in kidnapping, extortion, and most probably murder, so please do not insult me by engaging in small talk.'

Jennings could sense Kaseke bristle on the other end of the line. The CIO in Zimbabwe was universally feared, and no one in his right mind would talk to them in such a manner. Even lawyers representing their clients had to show due humility and 'respect' just to keep a conversation going.

'Mr Jennings, I know nothing of the criminal activities you speak of. What I believe is that the late Father O'Meara came into possession of an item which is the property of my government, and we need it returned. I believe you can assist in that regard, and if you can, it may be that my former department could offer some assistance in respect of your client's son, whom I understand may have been missing for some time.'

'What do you mean, former department?' Jennings asked, 'I suppose you deny you are a CIO operative?'

'Absolutely,' Kaseke replied. 'If you have any doubt on that, by all means call the embassy in London. You will find I am now the commercial attaché to the embassy. A very interesting challenge, as you can imagine, but it's also useful to hold diplomatic status when it is necessary to travel, as I am sure you understand.'

Jennings immediately understood the significance of what he was being told. If true, Kaseke could travel freely in the UK and would have been able to travel to Northern Ireland without any visa or travel restrictions. Coming into the Republic from the North was not an issue, and even if he was found in the South, his diplomatic status would result in a polite return to the UK.

More important, if he held diplomatic status, whatever he got up to in the UK would probably be covered by his status, and he could engage in criminal activity with near impunity.

'Mr Kaseke, what you say is of course very interesting, but when I spoke to Cian O'Meara, he was claiming that Father O'Meara had something that belonged to him. Now you say the priest had something belonging to your government. What is the truth, I wonder? In any event, I told Cian O'Meara, and I will tell you now, that I do not have what you are looking for.

'You, on the other hand, do know where John Moyo is, and I can prove that. Your diplomatic shield may stay intact, but proof of kidnapping and extortion by Zimbabwe diplomats will not look good in the press.'

Kaseke burst out laughing at Jennings retort. 'Mr Jennings, do you really think anyone in my government cares what you people think of them? You have definitely been away from home for too long. If we are not going to be polite, let me then be blunt. You either have what I want, or you can find it. Once you have it, it would be in your client's interest for you to contact me here, and we can arrange an exchange of the item for something of equal value to your client and his family. Do we understand each other?'

'Oh, we understand each other, all right, but how am I supposed to give you something I do not have? My client's trial starts in less than three weeks, and even if I were to agree to look for the item you want, I need time I do not have to do that.'

Kaseke paused before he replied. 'Time is such a precious commodity, Mr Jennings. Let me put it to you this way. If we cannot resolve our issue before the trial of your client concludes, it will be too late for either of us to work together. Please do not misunderstand me when I say that there are other people also involved who may not be as patient as you or I would like. We will all have to work to a very strict timeline if things are to be resolved as we would all hope. You may contact me only through this number, and I hope it will not be too long before we speak again. Goodbye.' He hung up before Jennings could reply.

Whilst Jennings considered what he had just heard from Kaseke, Grainne called him to advise that Father Murray would be available at St Francis during the afternoon, should Jennings wish to see him. He told her that he would do so and asked her to let Murray know. If he was to find the elusive diamond, the only logical place to look would be St Francis.

CHAPTER THIRTY-THREE

The meeting with Father Murray was scheduled for later that afternoon, and Jennings arrived slightly in advance of the scheduled time and took the opportunity to wander through the church.

It was empty at the time, and as with all similar churches, it provided a peaceful haven from the bustle of traffic out on the street. Although not the oldest church in Dublin, it had been there for many years, and the build-up of candle wax, incense, and floor polish gave the church the distinctive odour which seemed to be common to churches the world over.

Father Murray came in from the sacristy carrying a large cardboard box, which he placed on the pew next to Jennings as they exchanged greetings. He sat down beside the box.

In answer to Jennings queries as to the late priest's routine, Murray confirmed that Father O'Meara would attend daily mass every morning and would spend some time after mass in private contemplation and prayer after mass. He advised that there was a locker kept for the use of each priest in the sacristy, and that he had personally emptied the locker and the contents were all in the box between them.

Jennings thanked the priest for his help and took the cardboard box back to the taxi he had kept waiting. He returned to his office.

Father Murray had told Jennings that the box contained Father O'Meara's personal chalice, ciborium, paten and rosary, and a number of books. These were things he would have kept with him over the years. Murray said that he felt the chalice and ciborium may have some intrinsic value, but for the rest, they were personal items which he believed would be of no value or interest to anyone else.

Jennings took the box and placed it on a conference table in the corner of his room. He was intrigued to see the contents of the box, and he carefully used a pair of scissors to slit open the masking tape and open the box.

It was apparent that the books formed the base of the box, and on top of that were other smaller boxes which bore the name of a jeweller who had once occupied premises on what was then Sackville Street, and which were clearly of some vintage.

He carefully lifted out the largest of these. On opening it, he saw it held what he immediately recognised as being a ciborium. It had been years since he had been this close to such an object, but there was no mistaking what it was for anyone who had spent part of his youth as an altar boy every Sunday at family mass.

Although it was recognisable, it also appeared to Jennings to be somewhat unusual. It consisted of two identically sized hemispheres joined together with a stem bearing an intricate woven pattern. If the lid were removed and it was inverted, it would not be possible to tell which side was top or bottom were it not for the fact that one side had a fixed base and the other did not. It was also noticeable that the bottom half was considerably heavier than the top, but that was probably explained by the addition of the base plate.

Jennings opened the smaller box and found that it contained the priest's chalice, which was of a similar design. As opposed to two semi spheres, the top and bottom were in the shape of a tapered mug without any handle. The stem was more slender and had the same pattern as appeared on the ciborium.

Finally, Jennings opened the smallest box and found in it a rosary resting on a small black velvet cushion. On lifting it from the box, it appeared to be made of the same metal as the other two items. What struck him as odd was that the crucifix was attached to the rosary upside down to what would normally be the case so that the arms of the cross were farther away from the attaching clasp, and there was no figure of Christ on the cross.

Jennings had placed the three items on the table in front of him and was going through the books when Grainne came in and stood beside him. She picked up the ciborium and carefully examined the item before placing it on the table and taking the rosary out of its box.

'This is very interesting, Richard,' she said, picking up the ciborium again. 'Do you know what you have here?'

'I know what they are, Grainne, but why are they of interest'?

'I have seen this type of ciborium in a catalogue of religious artefacts from an auction years ago. These three are part of a set, and the engraving dates them back to when priests would have had to travel far and wide to their parishes. If I am not mistaken, the bottom part of the ciborium is actually a compartment for the storage of the communion hosts, and we should be able to open it up using the cross on the rosary as a key.'

Whist speaking, she turned the ciborium on its side, rotated it, and then stopped as she held the cup up and examined the base.

'Do you see how the engraving is slightly off-centre compared with the stem?' she said, pointing to what she was looking at. 'If I am right, we should be able to twist this so that the engraving lines up.' She did so as she spoke. 'When everything is aligned, this should then open out.' It did on a hinge as she pulled it down. 'And there you have the base with the keyhole for the rosary,' she said, pointing to a squared-off opening on the edge of the base.

Jennings watched as she took up the rosary, inserted the cross into the opening, and twisted it. The base fell open on a separate hinge.

Both fell silent as the contents fell onto the table. It was an almost totally transparent, rough stone the size of a golf ball.

Grainne was the first to speak. 'Is that what I think it is?'

Jennings picked up the stone and held it up between them between his thumb and middle finger. The stone was so clear that he could see straight though it. He realised that what he was holding had been responsible for the death of two men already—and may well be responsible for the death of another.

'I am afraid it is, Grainne. The question now is what do I do with it?'

Before either could say anything, Jennings's mobile began to ring. When he took it out of his pocket, he saw it was McGeough.

'Ken,' Jennings said, 'this is a bit of luck. You are just the man who could help me with a problem that has literally fallen into my lap.'

'Always happy to help, Richard, but I need to see you. I need to talk to you about my shopping trip up in Newry. Can you get out to Dun Laoghaire again—same place as last time?'

'I can,' Jennings replied. 'But while I have you on the phone, do you have any contacts in the diamond trade? I think what I have got is very interesting, but it needs an expert to have a look at it.'

'I do know someone, as it happens,' McGeough said. 'I don't know if you remember the Grafton Street jewellery raid from about seven years ago? The owner of the store is Paul Cohen, and he is one of the top diamond merchants in Europe. I still see him from time to time, and if what you have is what I think you have, he will be very interested in meeting us.'

'That would be great. The sooner you can get him along, the better. I feel time is not on our side now.'

'I will give him a call now. If I can, I will bring him out with me. As you say, time is not on our side, but with what I must tell you and with what I think you are going to show me, we might be able to change the odds a bit in our favour. Let's say we meet around eight tonight. Can you manage that?'

'I will see you then,' Jennings said, and McGeough ended the call.

Grainne was still staring at the stone he held. 'Richard, I am not a superstitious woman, but just looking at you holding that stone gives me the shivers. Please be very careful with what you are going to do.'

Jennings could see that she was not exaggerating her concerns, and he was anxious to calm her. 'I can assure you that whatever I do, it will not result in any harm to me, you, or anyone else for that matter. This stone has caused enough misery, and I won't let that continue. Try to put it out of your mind. More important, though, you must tell no one what we have found, not even Mr Hughes or your nephew. The fewer people who know about this, the better.'

'All right, Richard,' she said as she made her way to the door. 'No one will hear about this from me, but please be very careful until this whole mess is sorted.'

With the excitement of finding the stone, Jennings had forgotten about the handwriting sample that he had taken from Moyo in Clover Hill. He called to Grainne as she was leaving and pulled out the paperwork from his inner coat pocket. 'Please get this over to Harry McGonigle with a note to say this is from our client. He needs it for comparison purposes to complete his report. I know he will be doing this as a matter of urgency, and I need something I can give Counsel to work with before the trial starts.'

Just as he was about to leave the room, she turned and said, 'Oh, and I forgot to say that I had been through those photographs and was able to identify both men who attacked me. I have done the statement with Mr Hughes, and that is on the file now. I hope that will help in some way.'

As she left, for the first time Jennings began to feel as though enough material was available to provide the basics of a defence for Moyo. The problem was how to get it across given McGeough's warning to not make any disclosure. He would have to talk to McGeough and at least get some concession from him to give his barristers something to work with, even if all the pieces of the puzzle were still missing.

CHAPTER THIRTY-FOUR

Jennings made it to the Crown and Anchor before McGeough and had a cup of coffee on the table in front of him. He had been conscious since his warning from Murphy to take care that he had not been followed, and he was confident no one had in fact followed him here. In any event, he chose a table to the back of the bar where he could keep an eye on the comings and goings of people from the pavement.

He was just about to give McGeough a call when he saw him coming through the entrance to the bar. He was followed by another man whom Jennings assumed was Cohen.

Jennings had had no idea what to expect of Mr Cohen, but as a diamond dealer, he had at least expected him to be dressed in a suit and tie. This gentleman was instead wearing denim jeans and an open-neck shirt with a loose linen jacket. He was clearly not a young man, but his hair, which was a very distinctive silver grey, was tied back in a ponytail. Were it not for the fact that he was clean-shaven and that the clothes he wore were clearly at the expensive range of casual wear, he would be mistaken for an aging hippie rather than a diamond merchant.

McGeough made the introductions, and Jennings noted that Cohen was so soft-spoken it was almost hard to hear him. Certainly, he would have been difficult to hear if he were in a crowded pub, but by the looks of him, Jennings thought that was a venue in which he would seldom be found.

As was his way, after Cohen's credentials had been given by McGeough, and after Cohen himself explained to Jennings his expertise, McGeough cut to the chase.

'Right, Richard,' he said. 'You have something to show Paul, I believe?'

'I do,' Jennings replied, and he took the diamond, wrapped in tissue paper, from his pocket. He opened the tissue, held the stone on the palm of his hand, and extended his hand towards Cohen.

Cohen's reaction was not what Jennings had expected. Before he even went to touch the stone, he had a sharp intake of breath. That was followed by immediately looking behind him and to either side of him in the bar, to see if there was anyone close to them. Cohen then took Richard's hand in his left hand and placed his right hand over his palm to cover the diamond from view.

Jennings was taken aback by the sudden gesture. This was evident to Cohen, who immediately said in an excited voice, 'I am so sorry, Mr Jennings, but what you have there has given me quite a fright. Mr McGeough did not say precisely what it was you had to show me, but I was not expecting that. Perhaps I could examine the stone more carefully, but if you please, not where other eyes may be watching.'

Jennings also noticed McGeough's reaction to the stone: he was immediately on his guard.

'For Christ's sake, Richard. If that is what I think it is, what the hell are you doing walking around with it in your pocket?'

Jennings could tell McGeough was more than a bit annoyed at what he saw was a clearly stupid thing for Jennings to have done. On reflection, Jennings realised that perhaps it had not been the wisest thing to have taken the diamond out of his office for a trip around Dublin, but given they were together now, he felt any oversight in security on his part was now avoided.

'Gentlemen, calm down. I appreciate this is probably not the best place to be showing this to Paul, but things have been moving rather quickly. To be honest, I thought the safest place to keep this would be on me,' he said. 'Ken, is there anywhere near here that we can use privately?'

In this exchange, Cohen still had hold of Jennings's hand in between his own hands. He must have realised that this would certainly look odd to any casual observer, and so he said in a hushed tone, 'Perhaps you could return the stone to your pocket until Ken can get us somewhere more private.' He released Jennings's hand, and Jennings placed the diamond back in his suit pocket, all the while holding the stone in a firmer grip than he had previously.

McGeough got up from the table and went across to the barman, who was sat at the far end of the bar and out of earshot. A brief discussion with the barman was followed by the barman picking up a telephone on the work surface. After a few words were exchanged with whoever was at the end of the line, he replaced the phone and indicated towards a door at the other end of the bar, behind where Cohen and Jennings were seated.

Within a few moments, the door opened, and a very large rotund gentleman emerged and walked past Cohen and Jennings towards McGeough, who was making his way back towards the man. As they met, the large gentleman flung his arms around McGeough and gave him a huge embrace. This was certainly not anything Jennings had seen with McGeough before.

As the two men disengaged and approached the table, Jennings and Cohen both stood up, and McGeough introduced the man who was clearly pleased to see him.

'Gentlemen, this is Gerry Hunt, the owner of this establishment.'

Jennings recognised the name straight away. Gerry Hunt was a legendary gangster who had a fearsome reputation but who had not been seen in public for years. For some reason, he had never been before a court of law. The obvious affection shown to McGeough given the man's reputation was, to say the least, a cause for some concern.

As Cohen and Jennings introduced themselves, McGeough asked if they could use his office for a short meeting.

'Of course, Ken. Come, gentlemen. I will show you the way.' He set off towards the door through which he'd come.

The three men followed Hunt into a corridor, and at the end of the corridor, they came to a large wooden door which had a keypad fixed to the wall bedside the handle. Hunt entered a code, and after a second there was a loud buzz. A lock could be heard releasing, and Hunt pushed the door open.

The four men went in to what was possibly one of the most opulent working rooms Jennings had ever seen. The carpet was a thick pile and clearly top end, and the furniture was all heavy leather and oak with what were obviously expensive and original paintings on the walls.

'Make yourselves at home, gentlemen. Any friend of Ken's is a friend of mine. Take as long as you want. Ken, if you need anything, just dial zero on the phone, and whatever you want will be sent up. Now, is there anything else I can do for you?'

'There is one thing,' McGeough said. 'I would be concerned that there might be some people watching us who should perhaps mind their own business. You wouldn't be able to get some of your lads to check out the street, could you? If there is anyone there who shouldn't be, perhaps they could be persuaded to go away?'

Hunt smiled as he replied, 'Certainly, Ken. Leave it to me, and I will make sure you are not disturbed.' He left the room, pulling the door closed behind him.

The sounds of the locks engaging were clearly audible, and it was then that Jennings noticed that there were no windows in there. For all intents and purposes, they were locked in a sealed room.

'Is that the Gerry Hunt I think it is?' Jennings asked.

'It is indeed,' McGeough replied. 'Gerry and I go back a long way. I suppose you might be concerned about his reputation, but you don't need to be. Apart from a few minor indiscretions, Gerry has been running legitimate businesses for years now, and he is one of the few men in the town whom I would trust implicitly.'

'Well, I suppose if you are okay with him, I should be too,' Jennings said. 'But being locked in a room with no exits that's owned by one of the country's most notorious gangsters is not my idea of being secure.'

'Relax, Richard. We are safer here than anywhere in Dublin, and although it may look as though we are in a sealed room, I can assure you we are not. If we must leave in a hurry, we can do so safely and without anyone seeing us. Gerry has not got to where he has in life by not being cautious and security conscious.'

Throughout this exchange, Paul Cohen had been pacing up and down the room and trying to distance himself from the conversation by looking at the artwork on the wall. However, he was obviously keen to get back to the real reason they were in this room, and he approached Jennings with his hand extended. 'Mr Jennings, if you would kindly let me examine your stone now that we are in a more private environment?'

Cohen's soft voice and obvious enthusiasm for the task in hand calmed Jennings, and he took out the stone and gave it to Cohen, who held it in an almost reverential manner as he sat in one of the heavily padded guests chairs in front of Hunt's impressive office desk.

Cohen carefully placed the stone on the desk and took out a loupe, a notepad, and a pair of callipers from an inner pocket of his jacket. He then examined the stone from various angles and took measurements of the stone, which he wrote on his pad. This exercise took only a few minutes, but it was another few minutes before he turned and spoke to Jennings.

'Mr Jennings, do you know anything about the diamond trade?' he asked.

'No, I can honestly say I know nothing at all,' Jennings replied.

'Very well. Let me mention a few matters to you. First, without more precise equipment, I can only give you my views on what we have here from my visual inspection. If it were possible to take this stone with me, I can examine it more carefully and provide you with a better report as to the intrinsic merits of the stone. But I think, given Mr McGeough's presence, that this stone may be part of a larger picture I may not wish to be involved in right now.'

Cohen did not wait for a reply and continued.

'Diamonds as a rule are generally valued by weight and colour. The physical size of a stone is not necessarily a good indication of value. In a diamond, big is not always best. Having said that, in the last year, one of the biggest rough diamonds found in the last century went on auction in Sotheby's and failed to sell at a bid of sixty-one million dollars. That stone came from Botswana and is known as the Lesedi la Rona. It was brought to a legitimate auction floor because it was discovered on a legitimate mine in that country, which has some of the more strict and comprehensive laws as to diamond trading.

'This stone is not anywhere near the physical size of the Lesedi stone, but from my initial examination, it is my view that this stone, were it to be placed on auction, would attract bids of between thirty and forty million.'

Despite his quiet tone, Jennings could tell Cohen was in a state of high excitement as he gently placed the stone back on its tissue on the desk.

For his part, Jennings was stunned by what he had heard. He had assumed the stone would be of value, but the figures he had just heard were almost impossible to comprehend. The thought that he had been walking around Dublin with a stone worth tens of millions loose in his pocket nearly made him feel ill.

McGeough was the first to break the silence that followed Cohen's valuation. 'Richard, if Paul is right—and I am sure he knows what he is talking about—that stone certainly explains why people have been doing what they have to get their hands on it. It also confirms my concerns as to the possible people looking for the stone. There are only a few people in this part of the world who would have that sort of money available.'

'Russians?' Jennings guessed.

'Could be. It would explain a lot, but we won't trouble Paul with things he does not need to know. Paul, would it be all right if I left you to get back into town? Richard and I need to discuss a few things in private.'

'Of course, Ken,' Cohen replied as he stood up from the chair. 'I do not want or need to know anything more about this stone now, but I should tell you that if the time comes to sell this particular stone, because it obviously came from a less than legal source, it will be difficult to sell on the open market. However, if a way comes that it can be done, I would only ask that you remember me should you wish to engage an agent to sell it.'

Jennings stood and extended his hand to Cohen. 'To be honest, I don't know what is to come of this stone, but for the moment I can only thank you for your input. Rest assured if it is to be sold, you will certainly hear from me.'

Whilst the two were talking, McGeough had been on the phone. A moment later, Hunt appeared back in the room.

'Gerry, Paul needs a lift back to town. Could you sort that for me?' McGeough asked.

'No problem, Ken. But I have to tell you your concerns about unwanted guests seem to be right. There are two gentlemen outside across the road who have taken a very definite interest in my humble establishment since your arrival.'

McGeough paused for moment before he said, 'That is unfortunate. I don't suppose there is any chance their attention could be diverted while Paul leaves?'

Hunt burst out laughing. 'Diverted' is a lovely word, Ken. I can certainty organise a little diversion, and perhaps during the diversion, these gentlemen might even be persuaded to explain their interest in my establishment. Would that be of any interest to you?'

'It would, Gerry, but I need the men intact, so please be gentle with them.'

'Of course,' he said with a hint of a smile. 'Now, Mr Cohen, you come with me, and once we have established a little diversion, I can get you to wherever you need to be going.'

CHAPTER THIRTY-FIVE

Once they were alone, McGeough turned to Jennings and said, 'Well, that was an interesting meeting. The value of that stone in your pocket explains a lot, but there are a few things I need to tell you about my trip to Newry.'

With the excitement of the meeting with Cohen and the diamond, Jennings had forgotten that McGeough had told him he had news for him.

'I hope that is good news, Ken, because the trial starts soon, and I have very little to give Gilmartin.'

'I am aware of that, Richard, and we need to consider our options here and try to use what we have to help Moyo and his son.'

The two men sat in a pair of the heavy leather chairs, and McGeough took out an envelope from his coat pocket and removed several photographs.

'These are photos of your man Kaseke up in Newry, going into a private house. He would have no reason to be in the area, so there had to be something of interest there for him.' As he was talking, he turned the photos over and stopped at a photograph of a man emerging from the house with what appeared to be a medical bag.

'This man is Padraig Hennessey. He was a doctor in general practice but was struck off years ago after getting involved with dissident republicans and doing things he shouldn't. He claims now to be a salesman for a pharmaceutical company, but he is also known to provide medical services to people who might not want to be seen in a hospital.

'It would appear that the man who was given a bit of a hiding by Grainne's nephew is in fact in that house and is recuperating from his injuries. There are always at least two local thugs in the house with him, and apart from your man Kaseke and our former doctor friend, there have been no other visitors to the house in the last week.'

Jennings looked at the photos, which had clearly been taken from a hidden surveillance point and were clearly taken by someone who knew what he was doing. 'How did you get these, Ken? Are the PSNI involved in this now?'

McGeough collected up the photos. 'No, not yet. Let's just say that I have people who are prepared to help me who would not normally work with police on either side of the border. The people Kaseke seems to be working with have been stepping on a few toes, and there are a number of local people who would be very happy to see them removed from the scene.'

'I don't suppose Mr Hunt would be one of those people?' Jennings asked.

'The less you know the better. What I can tell you is that Gerry is not what he is portrayed as in the media. He does mix in circles you and I would never have access to, and that may well be what gets us a result for Moyo and his son.'

'Richard, there are several things in play here. First, your man Moyo is facing trial for a crime you and I are fairly certain he did not commit. Second, his son is being held captive and is being used to try to recover the diamond in your pocket by people who we know will not hesitate in killing to get what they want. Third, there has been no real attempt to properly investigate the priest's killing, and the prosecution of Moyo is being pushed through at an unusual pace. At best this is incompetence on the part of McLaughlin, but at worst this has the feel of a cover-up. Someone wants this murder off the books quickly, regardless of the outcome of the trial.'

'So where does that leave us?' Jennings asked.

'It means we will have to deal with this in two separate ways. You can deal with the litigation, and I will have to deal with what is going on in the background. Between the two of us, we need to pull the strings together and hopefully get the result we both want.'

Jennings considered what he was being told for a moment and then said, 'But we know that Kaseke is looking for the diamond in exchange for John Moyo. Surely you are not suggesting we negotiate with him? I thought it was the case that you never negotiated with kidnappers or terrorists.'

McGeough paused for a while before replying. 'Richard, there are literally thousands of kidnappings every day around the world. The clear majority are family members who are returned after a process of negotiation and payment of a ransom. The idea that you never negotiate with criminals is good for television and films, but the reality is very different. If we are to have any chance of getting John Moyo back to his father alive, we will have to deal with Kaseke and give him what he wants. But we can't do that and involve either the Gardai or the PSNI. Negotiations will have to be done covertly, and I will tell you what needs to be done. I know you don't like what I am saying, but believe me, it is the only way. If the time comes to involve the PSNI, I will do that.'

Jennings considered what McGeough was saying as he spoke, and he could see that the man was probably correct. Any involvement of official channels would not see any quick or decisive action.

'All right, Ken,' Jennings said. 'But I must give Gilmartin something to work with. Right now, he has nothing.'

'I agree, and things have moved on since we last spoke a few days ago. Let's list what we can and cannot give him, and you can then you go to him and see what he makes of what we can give him. First off, we have the CCTV footage from Moyo's apartment. I have the statement from the manager, and you have the footage. That shows that there are people involved in this apart from our man Moyo.'

Jennings picked up on this thread. 'We also have a statement from Grainne to say that two of the men in the footage attacked her in her own home, and one of them is now in custody. For them to be in her home when I am the solicitor for the accused has to be cause for concern.'

'Okay,' McGeough replied. 'That hangs together. We then have Eammon Hughes's evidence on the blood sample. For the prosecution, that is at best gross incompetence and at worst a deliberate cover up by McLaughlin of critical evidence.'

'I will also hopefully have the evidence from Harry McGonigle,' Jennings said. 'That will show that Moyo did not write the note the prosecution is relying on that was presented to the bank to withdraw the cash. I am waiting on his final report, but that will certainly give any jury something to think about.'

'The main problem is the fact that we do now have the diamond,' McGeough said. 'If we tell Gilmartin about that and of the kidnapping of the son, he will almost certainly insist on that being disclosed to the DPP office. He will not be a party to concealing evidence of the commission of a crime, be it in Dublin or wherever. It could also seriously backfire on us because if we do not get the son free and prove Kaseke's involvement, then if the existence of the diamond is disclosed, the State might be able to argue that your man was part of the operation to recover the diamond and that he did in fact kill the priest.'

'But without the evidence as to the diamond, all the rest is purely peripheral evidence that might raise some doubt in a jury's mind, or perhaps get a Judge to declare a mistrial for suppressing evidence,' Jennings said. 'The bloody diamond is the cause of all of this, and we must tell Gilmartin about it at some stage.'

The two men paused, and both were struck with the difficult position they faced. Make full disclosure of everything they knew, and that could well result in John Moyo being killed. Disclose some but not all of what they knew, and Stephen Moyo could be convicted for a crime he did not commit and be sent to prison for life. If that happened, it was likely John would die in any event.

Both men came to the same conclusion without either having to voice it. They needed to get John Moyo released before the trial was over. Only then could the full evidence they had uncovered be brought into the open. That was going to mean that McGeough would have to take control of when and where an exchange was to be made, and Jennings was going to have to try to feed his barristers what he could to keep the State at bay in the prosecution.

This was not a position either man would have wanted for the other, but both knew what was at stake, and they knew what had to be done.

McGeough stood up and made his way to the phone on Hunt's desk. He dialled a single number and spoke briefly before turning to Jennings.

'Richard, you need to see Gilmartin and give him what we have just discussed, apart from the kidnapping of John Moyo and the fact we now have the diamond. Between you two, you can decide on how best to use what we have. In the meantime, I will have to do what I need to do to secure Moyo's son's release and deal with Kaseke. Once you have spoken to Gilmartin, get in touch with Kaseke and tell him you are in position to deal with him.

'The one thing you must get from him is positive proof that the son is still alive. Speak to John personally, if you can, and it would be good to get some information from Moyo about something only he and the son would know that can confirm you are talking to the right man. That will take a few days to organise, and it will give me the time I need to get organised over the border. One of Gerry's men will get you back to town, but we must decide what to do with the diamond. It makes no sense for you to be carrying it around.'

Jennings had almost forgotten about the stone in his pocket. On being reminded about it, he realised he wanted nothing to do with it. 'What do you suggest we do?' he asked. 'If you want to keep it, I am happy with that.' As he was talking, he took the stone from his pocket.

McGeough took it from him and said, 'Give it to me, and I will keep it safe. Just don't ask me where, because the answer may not be to your liking.'

As he said this, Hunt and one of his men came into the office.

Hunt said, 'Mr Jennings, this is Mick. He does a bit of work for me. From what Ken has told me, it might be useful to have him around as a driver and general gofer. How does that sound to you?'

Jennings had not expected this, and before he could reply, he noticed McGeough standing behind Hunt and nodding his head, indicating an acceptance of the offer was the only correct answer to be given.

'Well, Gerry, that is very good of you. I would welcome your and Mick's help.'

After a brief exchange between McGeough and Hunt, Jennings made his farewells and left the two of them alone.

Once the door was secure, McGeough turned to Hunt and said, 'Gerry, I need your help, but what I want you to get into has already cost two lives, and the people we are going up against will not hesitate in killing again.'

Hunt looked down at McGeough and said with a grin, 'At last, Ken. Something to bring a bit of excitement into my life! Whatever you need from me, you have it—you know that. Now, show me what you have and tell me what you need.'

Jennings and his newly acquired driver went out of the building through a rear entrance. They got into a late model Mercedes parked outside the building.

'Right, then, Mr Jennings. Where to?' Mick asked.

'If you could just get me back to my office for now. But I need to get out to see a client in Cloverhill prison first thing in the morning. Would that be okay?'

'Of course, it is, Mr Jennings. A trip out to Cloverhill is always good for the soul, especially if you don't have to stay there too long, if you know what I mean,' Mick said with a laugh.

Jennings assumed from the fact of who his employer was and his apparent knowledge of Cloverhill that Mick may have strayed from the right side of the law in the past. Before he could make any enquiry, Mick offered him the explanation he sought. 'Cloverhill is a shithole, Mr Jennings, but at least in my case, I copped on. When I got out of there, I sorted myself out and made sure I would never go back. Had Mr McGeough to thank for that.'

'Really?' Jennings said. 'What did he do for you?'

'Sure, he was the man who put me there in the first place, but when my case was over, he introduced me to Mr Hunt. Ever since then, I have been on the straight and narrow.'

'So, what do you do for Mr Hunt Mick?' Jennings asked.

'Just odd jobs, Mr Jennings. Things like I am doing now. Helping out where I can.'

Jennings decided that it was probably advisable not to enquire too deeply into Mick's employment, and the two men lapsed into silence as Mick made his way across town to get Jennings back to his office.

CHAPTER THIRTY-SIX

The next day, Jennings got into his office early, phoned Cloverhill, and advised of his need to see his client. Mick was already waiting outside the office on his arrival, and they made it across town in good time. After going through reception, Jennings found Moyo already waiting for him in one of the consultation rooms.

Jennings updated Moyo on events. For his part, Moyo seemed both anxious and relieved as he heard everything from Jennings. It was only when he had finished that Jennings realised how much had happened in a relatively short space of time.

'So, Richard, this policeman and you have a plan for both my trial and to rescue John. Is that correct?' Moyo asked.

'I am dealing with the trial, and McGeough will do what he can to deal with Kaseke and get John back to us safely. I do not know what he is going to do, and to be honest, I would rather not know. The fact that John is apparently in the North adds another layer of complication, but if anyone can work things out, McGeough can.'

Jennings explained that McGeough had asked him to get some piece of information that only Stephen and his son would know so that he could be sure it was in fact John being held by Kaseke.

Moyo thought for a while and then said, 'There is one thing that only John would know. Just before my wife died, John and I had spent her last night with her. We were the only two in the room, and she said to us that she knew her time was coming, and she was not afraid to go because she knew she had a friend waiting for her.' The memory of what he was saying clearly had an effect of Moyo, and there was the hint of a tear in his eye. 'I had not spoken of John O'Meara in many years, but my wife knew how close we were even though she had never met him. My wife said to us that we did not have to worry about her because John was there on the other side, and he was waiting for her now. She said she knew he would look after her, and then she died. Those were the last words she spoke, and only John and I were there to hear them. Just ask him who was going to look after his mother when she died. If he says John O'Meara, you will know you are talking to the right man.'

Jennings decided he would leave Moyo alone with his thoughts. He left the man in the room and returned to the city with Mick at the wheel. On this occasion, barely a word was shared between them.

Upon his return to the office, Jennings found Grainne arranging papers on his desk. She turned to greet him as he entered his office and handed him a document, which he recognised as a report from Harry McGonigle.

'This just came in from Harry, and he asked if you could speak to him as soon as he came in,' she said.

'Okay, I will speak to him now, if you can get him for me. Anything else to worry about?' he asked.

'If there was, I wouldn't tell you, now would I?' she said 'With Moyo's trial coming up, I have kept everything and everybody away from you as best I can. Concentrate on what you have to do for that poor man.' With that, she was out the door.

Jennings took his seat and was about to start on the report when the phone rang. He was told by Grainne that she had McGonigle on the line. Without waiting for any reply from him, she put the call through. Jennings spoke as he was holding the report out in front of him.

'Harry, I have only just got into the office and have your report, but I have not had a chance to read it yet. Can you give me a summary?'

'Certainly, Richard,' McGonigle replied. 'An interesting case, but one in which I am sure you will be pleased with my opinions. First, the document given to the bank was certainly not written by the priest. There is absolutely no doubt about that. Second, there is no doubt in my mind that your client was not the author of the document.'

'That is good news, Harry. Is there any particular reason why you can be so sure?'

'There are a number of features which I go into in some detail in the report, but there is one thing I need to check with you. Is your client left- or right-handed?'

Jennings had to think about that for a moment. The exercise in taking samples of his writing had taken some time, and Moyo had been sitting directly in front of him for the whole of the time he was writing. 'I am almost certain he is right-handed. In fact, I am sure of it. Why is that important? I thought that it was accepted now that you could not definitively tell whether a person was left or right-handed, especially if they were a competent forger?'

'That is usually the case, but you may recall not too long ago I was a witness for the State in the Murphy trial. A very nasty murder in which the handwriting evidence was of some importance to link the accused to the deceased. In that case, it was my view that the author of the documents in question was right-handed, and the accused was right-handed. I am not saying that that was the deciding factor in the case, but it was certainly a key element of the prosecution case. I would be amazed if they tried to say in this case that I did not know what I was talking about if I give my honest view that the author of the bank document we have was left-handed.'

Jennings tried to recall the case McGonigle was talking about, but it did not come to him immediately. He asked who the prosecuting counsel was. Harry McGonigle had a very good relationship with the DPP office, and with his contacts in that office, he would know who was on the prosecution team for the Moyo trial.

'Funny coincidence, Richard. The senior in the Murphy case was Sean O'Halloran.'

That brought a smile to Jennings face for the first time in a while. The vision of O'Halloran trying to discredit a witness he had used himself to secure a conviction with Gilmartin all over him would be a sight worthy of ticket sales.

McGonigle continued. 'Richard, if you can confirm for me that Moyo is indeed right-handed, I will make a few amendments to my report and you will have the final version within hours. I hope this of value to you.'

'Oh, it certainly is, Harry,' Jennings replied. 'I will speak to Moyo and get back to you as soon as I can.' He hung up and immediately asked Grainne to get Cloverhill on the phone, advising that he needed a telephone conversation with Moyo. Given recent experience in the prison, he did not expect there to be any delay to the request being met. He had Moyo on the phone within half an hour and confirmed that he was indeed right-handed.

Jennings immediately phoned McGonigle and left a voicemail for him.

Then he turned to what he knew would not be a pleasant conversation. He needed to speak with Kaseke.

Jennings dialled the number he had for the Canal Court Hotel. On asking for Mr Kaseke, he was told that he was not available, but Jennings could leave a message. He did so and impressed on the receptionist the urgency of the matter.

Barely a minute or so after he hung up, his mobile rang. He looked at the screen and did not recognise the number. He answered nevertheless and recognised Kaseke's voice.

'I thought you were not available, Kaseke?' he said.

'Mr Jennings, lovely to hear from you. I will always be available for a friend. What can I do for you?' From the tone of his voice and the background noise, Jennings assumed he was not in any place that was conducive to a private conversation.

'We need to talk,' he said. 'I believe I now have what it is you are looking for, and we need to discuss the method of its return.'

'Well, that is good news Mr Jennings. Perhaps I could give you a call in an hour's time. It will be good to be able to discuss matters more privately.'

'Very well,' Jennings replied. 'You can get me on this number when you are free.' And with that he hung up.

CHAPTER THIRTY-SEVEN

Jennings decided to use the time available to contact Gilmartin and Gerry Grant to set up a meeting to discuss their strategy for the trial, given the material he could now disclose to him.

As usual, Gilmartin was not interested in any lengthy discussion on the phone, and their meeting was scheduled for the close of business that day in the Law Library. Gerry was far more amenable to finding out what Jennings had to offer, but Jennings declined because the thought of going through everything twice did not appeal, and he was concerned about the next call he had to make to Kaseke. He could tell Grant was somewhat put out by his apparent reluctance to talk, but he assured him there was enough for the two barristers to get their teeth into and would reveal all at their meeting.

Jennings then called in Grainne to discuss putting together copies of the report of McGonigle and copies of the other material which they had been accumulating for both barristers. At least the basics of a defence were coming together, but Jennings knew that the only way to secure the discharge of Moyo would be to prove he was not the man guilty of the killing of the priest. The presumption of innocence was all well and good, but a man caught in possession of the murder weapon without compelling evidence to prove he was not the party responsible for the killing was always a difficult task in front of any Irish jury.

Kaseke's call came in within the hour, and Jennings could tell from the change in his tone that he was now alone and not in any mood for polite conversation.

'Now, Mr Jennings, we need to discuss the return of my property. I assume you will need something in return from me?' he said.

'I will of course,' Jennings replied. 'First of all, I need proof that John Moyo is safe and well. I need to speak to him personally, and I need some form of additional proof that he is alive. I suggest we arrange a call later this evening, and you can send me a photo of him with today's *Belfast Telegraph* in his hands. Can that be done?'

'Of course,' Kaseke replied. 'But if you excuse me for saying so, this is all a bit melodramatic. You have what I need, and I am not going to do anything to prejudice my recovering the item. It is almost as if you do not trust me.'

Jennings could almost hear the mockery in his voice but would not rise to the bait. 'Kaseke, I have no desire to be dealing with you, but if I have to, we need to be sure that we both have what each of us want. I assume you will want to check the item before proceeding with any exchange?'

'I will, but that can wait until you are satisfied Mr Moyo is alive and well. I will arrange the call for eight tonight, if that is in order?'

Jennings confirmed that would be agreeable and was about to hang up when Kaseke continued.

'I understand the trial of Stephen Moyo is to commence shortly. Is that correct?'

'Yes, why?'

'I would have preferred if you and I dealt with the exchange, but given the circumstances, perhaps it would be best if we were not to be seen anywhere together. It strikes me that the most opportune time for our exchange would be some time in Belfast at a time you will be very obviously engaged in defending Mr Moyo in Dublin. I am sure you can arrange for a trusted intermediary to act in your stead?'

Jennings was not sure where Kaseke was going with this, but he confirmed he could have a third-party act for him and ended the call.

Jennings then called McGeough to advise him of his discussions with Kaseke and McGonigle, and to inform him of the meeting with Gilmartin. There was one issue he had to clear with McGeough that he had not raised thus far.

'Ken, you must know that insofar as the evidence relating to the CCTV footage at the apartment and the blood sample, your name is going to come up. If we must call you as a witness, will that not cause you personal problems in the force?'

McGeough did not hesitate in replying. 'There is more at stake here than any difficulties that might arise for me. With the recent problems the Garda Siochana has had to deal with, they are not going to be pleased with my actions, but that is their problem, not mine. They protected O'Meara for far too long and putting McLaughlin in charge of the case was never going to be their best move. If you need to call me, do so. But hopefully between you and Gilmartin, you can think up some way of limiting my exposure. Eammon Hughes has retired now, and he is not concerned about being called as a witness. They are hardly going to challenge the certificate from the forensic laboratory, so it might not be necessary to mention me at all. That is the least of our problems now.'

'All right, that we can look at,' Jennings replied. 'There is one thing, though, and that is I was assuming you would be the go-between for any exchange with Kaseke. But given the exchange will be in the North, surely as a Gard, that puts you at an unacceptable risk. If you can't do the job, who can?'

McGeough paused before answering. 'Richard, we are getting into muddy waters now. You set up the meeting and let me worry about who will do what. It is better for everyone that you know as little about what is going as possible.'

'I take it that your friend Mr Hunt may be involved? If that is the case, I really do not want to know what is going to happen.'

Jennings could tell from the tone of his voice that McGeough found his concern amusing. 'Sometimes you must work with those on the dark side, Richard. I have already told you Gerry is not as bad as he is made out to be, but in this type of situation, he is the best man we can have on our side. I can assure you of that. Let me know how your meeting goes with Gilmartin, and phone me when you have spoken to Kaseke.' Then he hung up.

CHAPTER THIRTY-EIGHT

Jennings had a room booked in the Law Library for the meeting with the two barristers, and he was waiting in the room for them when they both came in together.

Gilmartin got straight to the point and asked what Jennings had to offer. Jennings spent the next half hour going through the material he had assembled. He provided the updated report that had come from McGonigle with his views as to the documents presented to the bank to permit the withdrawal of the money. He was satisfied the document was written by neither the deceased nor the accused.

He showed them the CCTV footage, and they studied the stills extracted for the footage that showed the man who was in Garda custody for the break-in at Grainne's house as being one of the men at Moyo's apartment. They were also able to identify the briefcase being taken into the apartment as the one found by McLaughlin containing the cash drawn from the priest's account.

Finally, he went through the statement of Sergeant Hughes as to the blood sample and McLaughlin's instructions when he found out that it had not in fact been removed from the Garda laboratory.

Throughout the exercise, Gilmartin had said nothing and Grant had made very few comments, allowing Jennings to reveal what he had without interruption. When he had finished his presentation, he waited for Gilmartin to comment.

He had to wait for some time because Gilmartin went back over the statements he had been given, turned over the stills from the CCTV, and considered each carefully. Eventually he put the papers down in front of him and looked up to Jennings.

'Richard, I have been at this game for a very long time. In all my years, I do not believe I have ever seen a more crude attempt at a stitch-up as you have here. It is almost too good to be true. I assume that the evidence in respect of the blood sample did not come voluntarily from Sergeant Hughes?'

Jennings had deliberately not mentioned McGeough's name during his presentation, but he knew that that could not last. Gilmartin knew full well that he had to have had some inside assistance in obtaining the evidence before them. 'You are right, Donal. I have got a bit of help here from Ken McGeough.'

Gilmartin considered this and looked from Jennings to Grant before he said, 'And I assume the good detective would rather not be mentioned at the trial if possible?'

'I believe that is the case,' Jennings replied.

'Very well,' Gilmartin said. 'McLaughlin as investigating officer should have found all of this is material himself, and the state should have then disclosed it to us. What has happened here is either incompetence of the highest order or a deliberate attempt to have an innocent man convicted. If it is a deliberate cover-up of evidence, that alone should result in the Judge declaring a mistrial. But we need to go further and have our man discharged either on direction of the Judge or, if we get that far, by an acquittal from the jury. Gerry and I will discuss how best to go for that. In the meantime, will you make sure Sergeant Hughes and the apartment manager are both available to give evidence?'

'I will,' Jennings replied. 'Is there anything else?'

'You know there is, Richard,' Grant said. 'What about the missing diamond? Surely the involvement of this Kaseke man proves there is something to that that needs to be considered?'

Before he could reply, Gilmartin interrupted. 'Gerry, I am sure if Richard had anything we needed to know about any allegedly missing diamond, he would have told us. As I recall our latest conversation about the matter, it seemed to me the least said about that issue, the better. I would take it from Richard's silence on the matter he has either taken that advice, or alternatively there may be matters he feels are best not shared with Counsel.'

The latter part of this statement was said looking directly at Jennings, and he knew that Gilmartin did not expect—or more important, did not want—any reply.

He rose from his chair, collected his set of papers, and said to Jennings, 'Richard, this is very useful material. As you well know there are never guarantees in front of a jury, but at least we have something to work with. I appreciate you have had help in getting the material, and Detective McGeough has obviously proved very helpful thus far.'

Before Jennings could reply, Gilmartin continued. 'Just remember that his methods are sometimes not what you would expect of a Gard, and it would be advisable for you to keep your own counsel and distance from anything he may suggest getting involved in that you have any concerns about. He is not one to be shy of going places he should not, and it may not be in your interest as a practitioner to follow. I will say no more on that subject. I am sure you understand what I am saying.'

Gilmartin and Grant departed, leaving Jennings on his own. Gilmartin's last comments had the effect he'd intended.

Jennings recalled his earlier advice to Moyo in Cloverhill that he would not get involved in anything illegal, no matter what the consequences. Now he was about to engage with a kidnapper, and more like as not a killer, to secure the release of a man he had never met. The existence of a diamond of considerable value and of dubious providence was now an established fact, and yet he had done nothing to alert the proper authorities as to its existence and the apparent plight of his client's son.

What Gilmartin had said was true. He should not be going down the road he was. But what choice did he have. The only thing Gilmartin had said that he did not agree with was that if he was to travel this road with anyone, he was glad it was with McGeough.

Once Jennings left the Four Courts, he called McGeough and arranged to meet at a coffee shop on the quays. Having Mick available as both a driver and companion was proving very useful. Jennings had taken to keeping a lookout to see if he was being followed, and after having told Mick of his concerns, he was satisfied that he was not the focus of any unwanted attention. He chose a table with a pair of seats which were empty and faced the road. McGeough must have been in the area because Jennings had only been in the coffee shop for ten minutes when McGeough came in and sat beside him.

McGeough ordered his coffee, and the two men went through Jennings' meeting with his barristers. McGeough seemed content with what he heard and said, 'Well, at least that is moving in the right direction. You are to talk to Kaseke and hopefully the son tonight at eight?'

'I am,' Jennings replied. 'I was hoping you could be with me for that discussion. This sort of thing is out of my comfort zone, and I would not know what to do or say so that nothing could backfire.'

'I will be there, but what phone are you going to be using?'

Jennings had not even thought about that. 'I was going to call from the office. What difference does it make what phone I use?'

McGeough pulled a mobile phone from his coat pocket and laid it on the table in front of Jennings. 'You have definitely been away from working in crime for too long, Richard. This is a prepaid phone that will not be traceable to either you or me. From here on, any calls to Kaseke must be made on this phone and this phone only. Any calls made or received should not be from your office, home, or any place you would usually frequent. Hopefully in a few days, this will all be over, and we can get rid of the phone. We will need to agree to a time and place to meet for the exchange, and this phone will be the contact for whoever is going to be our man at the meeting.'

Jennings realised as McGeough was talking just how far he was out of his normal working environment. Whatever his intentions, what he was doing was clearly illegal, and the use of a hopefully untraceable phone brought that fact home to him. As he picked up the phone, he asked, 'But I thought you were going to be that man?'

'I may or may not be. There are a few loose ends that need to be taken care of up North, and so it all depends on where people will be at the time of the exchange. Don't worry, though. Whoever is at the exchange will know what he is doing.'

'I hope so, for all our sakes,' Jennings replied.

The two men finished their coffees and left separately. At McGeough's suggestion, they agreed to meet in a pub they both knew just off Temple Bar before eight that evening, to make the call to Kaseke.

Jennings had told McGeough about his insisting on Kaseke having a copy of that day's *Belfast Telegraph* with him and McGeough told him to make sure he had a copy with him and explained what he wanted Jennings to do with the paper later that evening and Jennings set off for the nearest newsagent to make the purchase.

CHAPTER THIRTY-NINE

The pub chosen by McGeough was just off the main Temple Bar hub and was renowned for its late-night hours and live traditional music. It was a magnet for the thousands of tourists that were drawn to the area by its own self-proclaimed Irish authenticity, but it was also a pub that saw little local traffic. At eight o'clock in the evening, it was far too early for even the tourists to have arrived.

Jennings arrived with Mick just as McGeough was going into the pub. As they entered, Jennings could see they were the only people in the pub apart from the barman, who was reading a newspaper behind the bar.

The barman looked up and clearly recognised McGeough with a curt nod of the head. McGeough walked straight past him and made his way to a cubicle from where they could see anyone coming into the pub. He indicated to Jennings to sit next to him, and Mick sat opposite them.

McGeough said, 'I spoke to Mick earlier. He will be involved in the exchange in some form or another, so it's just as well that he be here to know precisely what is involved.'

Given what Jennings knew of Mick and his employer, his concerns about what McGeough was intending to do in the North were immediately heightened. Despite that, and despite the reminder he'd had from Gilmartin to be careful of McGeough's methods, he realised he had no option at this stage but to go along with what McGeough had in mind. Whatever input he had would be purely peripheral to whatever went on in Newry or Belfast, and in many ways, he was happy for that to be the case.

The barman had paid no heed to them since their arrival; in fact, he had left the bar and was making a perfunctory effort at cleaning tables near the entrance to the bar. Jennings got the impression that neither Mick nor McGeough were strangers to the man, and that perhaps his real function was to keep a lookout for any unwanted visitors to the pub whilst they went about their business.

At 8.00 p.m., Jennings dialled Kaseke, who answered after two rings. On this occasion, there was no attempt at any pleasantries, and he got straight to the point.

'Mr Jennings, I understand you want to speak with the gentleman with me. I will give him the phone now.'

Jennings paused for a moment and then said, 'Hello? Whom am I talking to?'

'This is John Moyo, Mr Jennings. Thank you for what you are doing for me and my father.'

'Well, John, there are a lot of things we need to deal with before we can look after the two of you properly. How have you been treated? Are you all right?'

There was a moment's hesitation before the reply. 'I am fine, thank you. I have been treated as well as can be expected by my host.'

'Is he listening to this conversation, John? You are not on speaker, are you?'

'No, he is in the room with me, but he cannot hear what you are saying.'

'Very well. I asked him to have today's copy of the *Belfast Telegraph* available, and for a photo to be taken of you. Has that been done?'

'Yes. Just before your call came in, he took the photo.'

'Very good. What I want you to do now is to is turn to page four of the paper and read the headlines of the article on that page.'

'All right, if you just hold on. I have to ask for the paper.' After a short while, he continued. 'The heading reads, "Local Businessman to Enter Race for Vacant Seat in Stormont."'

Jennings had his copy of the paper open at the appropriate page and was happy to see that the answer given was correct.

'All right, John. Now I have one question for you, and there is only one right answer, so please listen very carefully to what I ask. Stephen has told me that only you and he would know the answer to the question I will put to you.'

There was slight hesitation before the reply. 'Very well. I will do as you ask.'

'If you are John Moyo, only Stephen and you were present when your mother died. Just before she died, she said she had no fear or pain because she knew there was someone waiting for her to look after her in the next world. Tell me who that person was.'

Jennings could almost sense an intake of breath from the man on the other end of the phone. 'John O'Meara,' he said. 'She died at peace knowing she was going to be looked after by him.'

On hearing the reply, Jennings realised he had almost been holding his breath for the past few moments. His relief at hearing the correct answer was almost physical. At least he now knew he was talking to the right man. That meant his doubts about what his client had been telling him were resolved.

'All right, John. Thank you for that. Could you put your host back on the phone, please? We will be talking to each other soon—and more important, you will be talking to your father, who is really looking forward to seeing you again.'

'Thank you, Mr Jennings. I look forward to that day as well.'

Kaseke came back on the phone and was immediately down to business. 'Mr Jennings, now that you are satisfied as to my friend's identity, we can arrange our meeting. I intend to leave Belfast on the second day of your client's trial, and I propose our exchange will take place in the car park of the George Best airport at 10.00 a.m. that day. You will obviously be occupied elsewhere, but I am sure you can make suitable arrangements. I will need to verify the item you hold before any exchange. I trust that will not cause any problems?'

'There will be no problem from my end,' Jennings replied. 'If you have our mutual friend in the car park, we can arrange to have the goods examined. If everyone is happy, the exchange can take place, and we can be on our way.'

McGeough had not said a word whilst they had been on the phone, and Jennings looked at him to enquire if he had any issues to raise. He shook his head, and Jennings said to Kaseke, 'This will be the contact phone that will be used on the day. Whoever answers will be the man you will be dealing with. Is that acceptable?'

'It is,' Kaseke replied. 'Let us hope that once this transaction is complete, we will not have any need to meet or speak again.'

'I agree,' Jennings said. 'One final thing. I assume you took John's photo on your phone. You can send me the photo now. I need to show it to my client, just to be sure we have the right man.'

'I will do that now,' Kaseke replied. 'I trust this concludes our dealings.' Before Jennings could reply, he hung up.

'Right, Richard,' McGeough said. 'The venue could not be better. Mick and I have a bit to discuss, so if you can spare him from driving duties, I suggest we part company. You and I will speak again later. You will obviously be talking to your client before the trial starts, but if I were you, I would not get his hopes up too much. This should go down easy enough, but there are never guarantees. Let's just hope things work out. He will have enough to be worrying about without having to worry about his son as well.'

'I agree,' Jennings replied. 'I will speak to you early next week unless something else comes up.'

CHAPTER FORTY

Despite her best efforts, Grainne had not been able to divert all of Jennings's clients away from him. Jennings spent the week following the meeting with McGeough and Mick dealing with other matters and getting the papers ready for his barristers in preparation for the trial.

Grainne had taken up the jury list for the week of the trial, and Jennings had given it a cursory glance. Normally he would spend a bit of time on this exercise, but in this case, he was relying on other matters falling into place that would make irrelevant the composition of the jury. It was whilst he was going through the jury list that he realised that a lot of things had to come together to get the results they wanted.

Jennings had also had a series of meetings with Gerard Hughes, who had been working on the priest's estate. Although a final death certificate would not issue until after the trial was concluded, and although final probate would not issue for some time it had become apparent that the trust fund which had been set up was of considerable value and properly administered, it could be a valuable tool for the development of the people in Nyanga. Jennings hoped to see the day when that hope would become a reality, and he had already decided that if things worked out, he would look to Stephen and John Moyo to head up the operation on the ground in Zimbabwe.

Despite often thinking of Zimbabwe, Jennings had had no desire to ever return, not even for a visit. That was now changing, particularly given the priest's desire to have his ashes interred above the mission station. Despite their differences, Jennings felt that was one task he could not delegate to anyone else, and he was determined to make the journey with the ashes himself. It was a journey he was not looking forward to, but at least if he had the Moyos with him, it may prove a worthwhile visit.

Jennings had been monitoring various websites that covered news from Zimbabwe. Despite the economy lurching from bad to worse and the political infighting going on, there seemed to be some hope that with Mugabe gone, things may change for the better.

Jennings tasked Grainne with finding out the cost of air fares for the three of them, and he discussed his plans with Hughes, who seemed to think such a visit would be worthwhile for several reasons.

Gerard Hughes had always left Jennings to his own devices and had only had brief discussions with him as to how he was preparing for the trial. Jennings had no doubt that he would have kept up to date through enquiries of Grainne, and he would have access to his files through their case management system, but Hughes should not know anything about the diamond that Jennings had found and what he was up to with McGeough.

Hughes' next question was therefore a bit puzzling. 'Richard, how are you getting on with Ken McGeough?'

'Why do you ask that, Gerard? Has Grainne been talking out of turn?' Jennings enquired, trying as best he could to make it sound as though he found the question amusing.

'Far from it,' Hughes replied. 'Grainne hardly says a word to me and would certainly not divulge any information that she was not supposed to. No, my source is my cousin, former Sergeant Eammon Hughes. One of your potential witnesses, I believe. He suggested to me that you may be getting some help from McGeough.'

'Well, Gerard, given the pressure we have been put under in this case, I will accept whatever help I am given and from whatever source. McGeough has been of help, but I didn't see that as a problem. Do you?'

'Richard, you have been around long enough to know of McGeough's reputation. Let's just say that from my own knowledge, he is a man who likes to get results but is not averse to what you could call unusual methods to achieve them. I would be concerned that if he is involved in any significant way, he does not cause you problems you could do without.'

After the earlier warning Jennings had had from Gilmartin, this piece of advice was not at all welcome. Hughes was no man for gossip or rumour mongering. If he was concerned about McGeough, he would have good reason for that. Jennings was hardly going to tell Hughes the extent of McGeough's involvement at this late stage, and he realised that for better or worse, he was committed to McGeough in a way he had not anticipated he would ever be.

'Gerard, I understand your concerns, but please do not worry about my dealings with McGeough. I will not get involved in anything untoward unless it is a matter of life and death, and right now I do not foresee that arising. This is a murder trial in which the Gardaí have made a series of mistakes for whatever reason, and McGeough has helped uncover those. Your Sergeant Hughes is a good example. Without McGeough, I would never have found out that the blood sample taken from Moyo was not only never lost but also showed he had been heavily drugged. He has done nothing so far to give me any reason to doubt his motives or methods.'

'Very well, Richard,' Hughes replied as he stood. 'You know what you are doing, and what you have to do for your client. I simply want to make sure you do not get sucked into something with McGeough that you can't get out of. If you need me for anything at all in the coming week, just ask.' With that, he left the office.

Jennings once again questioned his reliance on McGeough in seeking the release of John Moyo, as well as the methods they were about to employ to achieve that.

CHAPTER FORTY-ONE

With less than a week to go to the start of the trial, Jennings decided to go to Cloverhill and meet with Moyo to advise him of what he could expect. Very few people had any real idea as to what happened in a criminal trial. Most had as their source of knowledge television series, which left them ill prepared for the reality of what actually happened.

Jennings found Moyo in good spirits when he went into the consultation room. After cursory discussion as to his well-being, they got down to business.

'Stephen, I am going to run you through what is likely to happen next week at the trial. Obviously, there are other things going on with John, but that is something you will have to try to leave to others to deal with. I believe we will have a good chance to persuade the trial Judge on the evidence we have that you have been the victim of a gross miscarriage of justice and should not be put on your defence. Let's concentrate on what we have for the trial.'

Jennings spent the next hour going through the evidence he had put together. He went through the video footage from the apartment again and the report from McGonigle. He went over the medical report on the blood sample and the statement of Eammon Hughes. Although they had gone through this before, Jennings was not prepared to leave anything to chance, and he wanted to ensure Moyo knew what they had. More important, Jennings wanted to know if there was anything Moyo could add. He hoped that Moyo had recovered some memory as to the events on the day the priest had been killed. In that regard, he was to be disappointed.

After going over all the evidence, Jennings turned to the procedures they would have to go through at the start of the trial. 'The first order of business is the selection of the jury. This is a time-consuming business, and there is no magic formula in selecting jurors in this country. To be honest, I am of two minds as to whether to even use the seven challenges we have as the defence, because our best hope here is to make sure the jury never has to decide on your guilt or innocence.'

'What do you mean by challenges, Richard?' Moyo asked. 'Can we object to people being on the jury?'

Jennings explained, 'Potential jurors are chosen by a lottery at random from the jury list. The State and the defence can each challenge up to seven people for no reason whatsoever. If we had the time, I would check the jury list to try to see whom we should exclude if their names came up. The State usually relies on a list from the Gardai of people who are on lists who have previous criminal convictions. They feel anyone with a criminal past is likely to be biased against the prosecution, and they are probably right on that. It's more difficult for us on the defence, and usually the rejection of any juror is purely guesswork based on the look of the person. It's hardly scientific, but it is the system we have.'

'I don't suppose there will be any Zimbabweans on the panel to choose from?' Moyo said with a smile.

'You never know. But as I have said before, in your case it really does not matter who is on the jury if we get the breaks we are hoping for.'

Jennings then went through the procedure to be expected and the role of the prosecution and defence teams. Moyo had still not met his barristers.

'It may seem odd to you, Stephen, but I can assure you that your Counsel know everything they need to know about you for the trial without having met you. We will of course meet on the morning of the trial, but I have them fully briefed on what they need, and they are two very competent men. Don't worry about not having met them yet.'

'Very well, Richard,' Moyo replied. 'I am in your hands, and you know what to do. I suppose we will have to wait and see what happens next week. So long as John is safe, I do not really care what happens to me. I know you will do everything you can for me.'

Jennings collected his paperwork as Moyo left. On his return to his office, Jennings had time to think about what could go wrong in the coming week and how the lives of two men were effectively in his hands. It was a responsibility he had not sought, but it was nevertheless a burden that only he could carry despite the help he was receiving from a variety of sources.

CHAPTER FORTY-TWO

The Trial
Dublin, 9.00 a.m.

The days following Jennings' last meeting with Moyo went by in a blur. Jennings had gone over his paperwork so many times that he felt he could recite every witness statement report and describe every video clip and photo with near total recall.

He had seldom spent so much time on any trial Perhaps the fact that the trial was only a part of what was going on added to his sense of frustration and unease. Despite having had a few phone calls with McGeough, he had not had a face-to-face meeting since their last meeting in Temple Bar. His only refrain was to say that the less contact they had, the better. He tried not to worry about things over which he had no control.

Despite his faith and trust in McGeough, Jennings still felt that he should have done the proper thing and reported what he knew of John Moyo's abduction and Kaseke's involvement to the Gardai, and to Gilmartin. Gilmartin's and Gerard Hughes' warnings as to McGeough's methods weighed heavily on his conscience.

In all his career, he had always believed that despite its flaws, the system generally did protect those who obeyed the law. Now he was working outside the law, betraying everything he felt he had worked for. That was a source of concern given how the investigation into his client had been conducted and the involvement of people he knew had not the slightest respect for the law. He felt he was trapped in a game he had no control over.

On the morning of the trial, Jennings had arranged to meet Gilmartin and Grant at the CCJ. After a brief discussion over coffee, the three went down to meet with Moyo in one of the consultation rooms adjoining the holding cells.

The introductions were brief and to the point, and Gilmartin did his best to put Moyo at his ease. He basically repeated what Jennings had told Moyo as to how things would proceed on the first day of the trial.

After going through the procedures, the time was approaching 11.00 a.m. Gilmartin stood and said, 'Mr Moyo, I appreciate that this is very stressful for you, but I can assure you that Mr Jennings has put together a very substantial defence which we shall use to the best of our ability to secure your discharge. Unfortunately, we cannot show our hand in this matter until the appropriate time, and you will have to trust our judgement in that. On the first day of the trial, not a lot is going to happen. All I can say is that you need to try to remain calm and keep a careful note of the proceedings. If there is anything that concerns you, you will be able to speak with us whenever we adjourn. If there is anything of particular urgency, get Mr Jennings' attention, and he will speak with you.'

Gilmartin and Grant then left, and Jennings had a final word with Moyo before leaving him to the prison warders as he made his way to Court 12, where the trial was to commence.

Colm Murtagh, SC, had been a Judge of the High Court for over fifteen years. For most of that time, he had sat in the Central Criminal Court. He had been a highly successful barrister before being appointed, and he was known as a hard-working and uncompromising Judge. He ran his court with a firm hand.

Jennings had been delighted to learn that Murtagh was to preside given what he knew was to unfold. Of any of the Judges, Murtagh would be the first to take the State to task once the inadequacies were shown in the investigation of the priest's killing.

On entering the courtroom, Jennings could see that the prosecution team were already at their respective positions, and Sergeant McLaughlin was seated in the front row of the gallery with his briefcase under his arm next to him. He looked as though he had not a care in the world, and Jennings could not help but smile to himself because he knew what was coming down the line.

Not surprisingly, there was no discussion of any kind between Gilmartin and O'Halloran. As Jennings took his position in front of Gilmartin, he wondered what it was that had created such animosity between the two men.

At 11.00 a.m., the Judge's tip staff entered the court and announced his arrival. After a perfunctory greeting to all, Judge Murtagh directed the matter to be formally called, and the respective Counsel identified themselves for the record.

The Judge then embarked on a discussion with the jury panel, who were crammed into the courtroom and who for the most part had never had to engage with a court, let alone the peculiarities of jury selection. The Judge explained that under the laws, there would be a lottery. Each potential juror had a number allocated to him or her. If their numbers were called, they should make their way to the front of the court.

He explained that either the State or the defence had up to seven challenges for no reason, and that no one should be offended if either side objected to them. 'The decision to object to a juror is entirely up to the side making the objection, and for the first seven objections they have to give no reason at all for so objecting,' the Judge advised. 'It may be that the colour of a man's tie or the lack of a tie would suffice; if a lady is called, the side objecting may not like the colour of her hair. It is not a system many people are in favour of, but it is what we have, so bear with us as we embark on the selection of the jury panel.'

The registrar began to call out numbers, and potential jurors made their way forward. Some seemed to be genuinely embarrassed to be called, and some seemed to be excited at the prospect of serving in such a high-profile case.

In Jennings' mind, it was irrelevant as to who was to be on the panel. He was confident the matter would not get to the stage where the jury would be called on to decide Moyo's fate. That said, trials could never be predicted, and so he did his best to use his seven objections as carefully as he could. Cathal Murray studied his list of jurists' numbers against previous convictions and objected accordingly.

The process was completed in short order, and the Judge then addressed the panel of jurors who were now seated in the jury box.

'Members of the jury, you have been chosen at random to act as jurors in the trial of Mr Stephen Moyo, who is seated in front of you.' Whilst saying this, he indicated Moyo, who was looking across the court at the jury panel.

'You were asked if each of you had any reason which would disqualify you from acting, and you have each advised that there is no reason and that you will fairly and impartially listen to the evidence to be presented. You will be advised on a number of occasions during this trial that the accused man is innocent until proven to your satisfaction of his guilt beyond reasonable doubt. I make no excuse for saying that you may tire of hearing this, but it is the very essence of our system of justice that the State prove the guilt of the accused. The accused does not have to prove his innocence. Mr O' Halloran will address you shortly as to his role and what it is he will present to you. Mr Gilmartin may or may not address you as well. For the moment, I am going to ask you to leave the court and to decide amongst yourselves to elect a foreman to act on behalf of the jury.'

The Judge went on to explain the functions of the foreman. After allowing them to leave the court, he turned his attention to the barristers in front of him. 'Are there any applications which are to be made before the trial commences?' he asked.

Both Gilmartin and O'Halloran indicated there were not, and Murtagh then inquired as to how O'Halloran intended to present the case.

O'Halloran advised it was his intention to introduce such evidence that was not, as far as he knew, in controversy and could be introduced by way of producing reports and certificates of various witnesses as to technical issues.

'I assume that is in order, Mr Gilmartin?' the Judge inquired.

'It is a matter for Mr O'Halloran to decide how he presents his case, Judge. I cannot give him carte blanche in that regard, and if there are any issues, I shall advise the court as they arise,' Gilmartin said in a tone which left no one in any doubt that Gilmartin did not trust his opposite number at all and would be watching his every move.

The Judge was aware of the animosity between the two barristers in front of him, and he simply nodded. 'Very well. I was hoping that between the two of you, matters not in issue could be resolved, but so be it.' The Judge then leant forward to have a word with his registrar, and after a moment he said, 'I note it is nearly 1.00 p.m., and I propose rising now for lunch. My registrar will advise the jury panel, and we will resume at 2.15 this afternoon.' The Judge stood, bowed briefly to the court as all rose, and left the room.

From the tone of the Judge, it was apparent to Jennings that he was expecting the two sides to speak to see if there were any matters which could be disposed of without having to hear formal evidence. He was not going to impose his will on either side at this early stage, but he was equally aware that the history between the two men did not bode well for an easy trial.

It was not surprising to Jennings that neither Gilmartin nor O'Halloran made any move towards each other. Both simply gathered up their papers and left the room whilst their respective juniors remained behind to see what could and could not be agreed to.

Jennings waited for Gerry Grant to finish his discussion, and then he went across to Moyo to see if he understood what was going on.

'I can see what you meant when you said things will not happen quickly, Mr Jennings,' was Moyo's first observation. 'Are we likely to hear any witnesses this afternoon?'

'It all depends on what Mr Gilmartin decides he will let the State hand in by way of certificate evidence, and what he wants to challenge. There are some matters he cannot object to, but on the whole, I do not think he will let in any evidence without putting the State to the test, so you will have to be patient.'

'I have no issue with that, but my real concern is for John. Have you heard anything more from Kaseke?'

This was not a conversation Jennings wanted to have in the courtroom. He moved in closer to Moyo and said, 'I have not, Stephen, and please do not talk to me about John except when we are alone. When I have something to tell you, I will. But for the moment, you have to accept things are hopefully going to move in the direction we want them to.'

Moyo seemed to accept he had been indiscreet and apologised for raising the issue. He then left with the prison officers for his lunch.

Jennings spoke to Grant and learnt that very little had been agreed between the parties. Jennings did establish that the prosecution were intent on calling the pathologist and were not going to try to rely on submitting the autopsy resort. He could only assume this was to impress on the jury the seriousness of the attack on the priest, but Jennings knew that it could work to their advantage as much as their disadvantage.

After leaving the courtroom, Jennings decided to call McGeough and see if he had any news for him.

As soon as the phone began to ring, Jennings realised McGeough was not in the Republic. After letting the phone ring for some time, McGeough's voicemail came on, and Jennings left a message asking him to call. His request was answered within a few minutes.

'Sorry, Richard. I was not able to answer your call there. I am up North sorting out a few things for tomorrow. How is the trial going?'

'Early days, so nothing really to tell yet,' Jennings replied. 'What are you sorting out? The exchange is tomorrow.'

'Richard, you worry about your end, and let me deal with what I have to. The less you know about what is going on up here, the better for everyone.'

That comment immediately put Jennings on his guard. 'Ken, surely it is not too late to do the right thing, report what we know, and let the PSNI and Gardai deal with this?'

'You know as well as I that is not an option. I understand your concern, but please concentrate on what you have to, and let me deal with matters at this end.'

After a moment's hesitation, Jennings replied, 'All right, but please keep me up to speed. I need to know as soon as the exchange is made because that will affect what I tell Gilmartin and how he deals with the evidence tomorrow.'

'Will do, Richard,' McGeough replied. 'Keep your phone handy.' He rang off.

CHAPTER FORTY-THREE

Newry

1.00 p.m.

McGeough placed his phone on the table in front of him and looked up to see Mick enter the pub. He was concerned at the tone of Jennings' call because the last thing he needed now was for Jennings to get cold feet, go off on his own, and make a formal report of what was in play.

Mick took a seat opposite him, and after looking around to see that no one was in earshot, he leaned in and spoke to McGeough.

'I have been with the lads and gone over everything with them, and everything is in place for tomorrow. How are things your end?'

'The same,' McGeough replied. 'My friend in the PSNI has the house under watch and is ready to move when the time is right. I am worried about Jennings, though. I know he does not like what we are doing. I hope he does not get cold feet and do anything stupid.'

'I agree,' Mick said. 'We have too much invested in this to make any changes now. Surely he realises that this is the only way to go?'

McGeough shrugged his shoulders. Then he nodded his head to the door as a man entered and approached their table. Before the man got too close, McGeough leaned closer to Mick and spoke to him in a quiet whisper.

'Mick, this is my man in the PSNI. I suggest you head off somewhere before he arrives, and I have to introduce you.'

Mick smiled at the thought of that, rose, and made his way past McGeough as though heading to the toilets. He would exit the pub through the kitchen to avoid any unnecessary meeting with McGeough's colleague.

Gary Farrell had been in the PSNI as long as McGeough had been in the Gardai. Although they came from very different backgrounds, their paths had crossed early in their careers, and they had developed a mutual friendship and respect. In many ways, their similarities outweighed their differences, and Farrell shared McGeough's habit of occasionally resorting to unconventional methods to achieve his results.

As Farrell took his seat, he motioned towards the doorway that Mick had taken. 'Anyone I should know about, Ken? You clearly did not want me to meet your friend.'

'No one for you to worry about, Gary,' he replied. 'How are things going with our friend? Are you set for tomorrow?'

'The house is under surveillance, and provided nothing changes, I will have the house turned over at 10.00 a.m., as you have asked. I wish you would tell me why it is important to go at that time and not just move in and lift the bastard now. I have to tell you, though, that if anything happens and it looks as though our man is leaving early, I am going in to lift him regardless of what other balls you have in the air.'

'I can't ask any more of you, Gary. When this is all over, I can tell you what else was going on. For the moment, all you need to know is what I have told you. The man in the house was involved in the murder of Father O'Meara, and I believe he will also provide you with a considerable amount of information as to all sorts of other activities. If I am right, you will have the bust of the year to add to your resume.'

Farrell smiled at that and rose to make his departure. 'Keep in touch, Ken,' he said.

As Farrell left, McGeough saw a call coming through on his phone. He answered without any formality. 'This had better be important.'

'It is,' came the reply. 'Our man has made alternative arrangements for tomorrow, so if this is going to go down, the venue may change.'

'Okay,' McGeough replied. 'I assume you have things covered?'

'We do. I am going to get hold of Mick and brief him. He might have to do a bit of running around tomorrow, but we should still be okay.'

'We'd better be,' McGeough replied, and he hung up

CHAPTER FORTY-FOUR

Dublin
2.00 p.m.

As opposed to other Judges, when Judge Murtagh said his court would commence at a given time, one knew that was precisely when it would start. Several Counsel had learnt to their cost when they first went on the bench that if he said court would start at eleven o'clock, he would be in his chair at eleven regardless of whether Counsel was ready to go.

At two o'clock, everyone was assembled, and Jennings was glad to see the trial finally starting. With what he knew was to happen outside the courtroom, the general nerves he always experienced at the start of a criminal trial were heightened. It would be a relief to see some progress being made.

At exactly 2.15 p.m., Justice Murtagh entered the courtroom, took his seat, acknowledged those present, and called for the jury to be brought in. He waited until they were all seated and then advised them that the first thing to happen would be an address by Mr O'Halloran to outline what it was the State would seek to prove. In finishing his address, he cautioned them that anything the prosecuting team said was never to be taken as evidence. They could only decide the case on what they heard from witnesses, not from what either Counsel wanted them to believe.

After that, he turned to O'Halloran and indicated he could begin.

O'Halloran was a tall man who kept himself in good physical shape. He was always meticulously turned out and spoke with a firm and authoritative voice. As with all good barristers, had he chosen a career on the stage, he would probably have made a success of that as much as he had at the bar. In addressing the jury, he had no need to refer to notes, and he looked at each person in turn as he spoke. It was his way of trying to establish a bond with them and to let them know at an early stage that he was the man in charge to whom they should be listening.

'Ladies and gentlemen of the jury,' he began, 'my name is Sean O'Halloran, and I represent the Director of Public Prosecution in this trial. This is a criminal trial in which you and you alone will decide whether that man'—he pointed with a flourish to Moyo—'is guilty of the most serious crime known to us. That of murder.'

After a short pause for effect, he carried on.

'As I said, I act for the Director of Public Prosecution, and the Director is charged by law to bring to the courts of criminal justice people who she feels are guilty of crimes. She does this based on evidence provided by the Gardai, and it is my job to present the evidence to you.' He raised his voice. 'It is not my function to seek a conviction at all costs, and it is only you as members of the jury who can consider the evidence and convict the accused of such crime as you feel is shown beyond reasonable doubt to have been committed.

'In our system of justice, the State has to make full disclosure of its position and the evidence it will rely on to the defence in advance of the trial. I will very briefly summarise what the State's case is, but at this point in time, and until my friend Mr Gilmartin cross-examines each witness, we will have no real clue as to what the defence is.

'What we do know, however, is that the defence cannot be an alibi because the defence are required to warn us of that, and they have not done so. In other words, the accused is not saying, "I could not have committed the offence because I was not there when it was committed." Maybe he was, and maybe he was not. The evidence we will lead will allow you to answer that question.

'There is also no issue about the state of mind of the accused. It has not been suggested that at the time of the offence, he was under any mental disability so that he could not know what he was doing. You need not worry about that having to be considered. As far as we know, he is also not saying he acted in self-defence or under provocation from the deceased. That is hardly surprising given the deceased was a priest and, as far as we know, a benefactor of the accused.

'It seems a strange way to repay the generosity shown to the accused by Father O'Meara, for him to rob and brutally stab him to death.'

During O'Halloran's opening address, Gilmartin had been staring straight ahead with his hands on the desk in front of him. As the address developed, however, he had begun to tap his fingers on the bench. At the last comment made by O'Halloran, Gilmartin clearly had had enough of the theatrics on display.

In coming out of his seat, he took everyone by surprise, not least O'Halloran, who stared open-mouthed at this intrusion into his opening.

'Judge, I must protest at the way Counsel for the State is opening his case. It is neither the time nor place for him to be making gratuitous and insulting comments about the accused. He knows full well what his function is in opening the trial. His comments about the accused must be disregarded, and the jury advised accordingly.'

Before O'Halloran could reply, Judge Murtagh raised his hand to stop the two from descending into an unedifying slanging match. 'Mr Gilmartin,' he said addressing him with a look that would cause ordinary practitioners to immediately regret their actions, 'you know better than to interrupt Counsel for the prosecution in their opening address.' Then he turned to O'Halloran, took the smile that had begun off his face, and said in a similar tone, 'And you, Mr O'Halloran, know better than to make gratuitous comments about the accused in your address. You are both out of order, and I will not permit such behaviour to continue in my court. Do I make myself clear to both of you?'

As each barrister replied in the affirmative, Jennings stole a quick look at the jury, who were clearly not at all sure what was going on. He got the feeling all of them had felt as though they had been returned to a school room with a very strict teacher putting two unruly children in their place. He could not help but feel that of the two, Gilmartin had scored the first points in their battle. It was clear to anyone that O'Halloran had overstepped the mark, and he would have to be very careful in the future regarding what he said and did.

Given this opening exchange, O'Halloran proceeded to outline the State case in an almost robotic and monosyllabic manner. He finished his address in his usual manner by saying to the jury that with all the evidence before them, they would be able to return only one verdict, and that would be one of guilty of murder. O'Halloran then advised that his first witness would be the State pathologist, Dr Martin Kearney.

After the tense exchange between the barristers and the Judge and the completion of the opening address, there was a general murmuring and movement in the court as people adjusted their seats and composed themselves to get on with the business of the trial.

Dr Kearney was a man in his late sixties who had not aged well. He walked with a pronounced stoop, and his suit looked as though it had not seen a dry cleaner in many years. His hair had seen a comb or brush, but not recently, and he had at least a day's stubble on his chin. Had you not known who he was and saw him in the street, you would have thought of him as a man down on his luck but trying nonetheless to maintain some sense of dignity.

That opinion would change when you had an opportunity to look into his eyes and hear him speak. He had piercing blue eyes and spoke in a deep, measured tone that commanded attention.

After Kearney was sworn in, O'Halloran had him establish his credentials for the jury. Then he took him through the autopsy report carried out on the priest. He had the doctor go through an album of photographs, showing the number of wounds sustained. In respect of the injuries, he asked which, if any, could be described as fatal.

The doctor seemed to ponder his question for a moment before answering to the Judge. 'Judge, as any physician will tell you, a minor cut can become infected and give rise to peritonitis or some other issue which can cause death. On the other hand, a single stab wound in the wrong place can also cause death. In this case, the number of wounds inflicted, and the force used to inflict them means it is impossible to say which specific wound was the fatal one. In the absence of immediate medical attention, death was the only likely result from such an assault. In my opinion, even if a trained physician had been present immediately, I doubt he could have saved the life of a man attacked in this manner.'

O'Halloran paused to let what the doctor said sink in with the jury, and then he indicated to one of the Gardai present in court to hand up a knife to the witness which was in a plastic evidence bag. 'Dr Kearney, could you advise if, in your opinion, the knife now handed to you could have been responsible for the injuries to Father O'Meara?'

The doctor studied the knife before replying, 'Yes, it could.'

'Thank you, Dr Kearney,' O'Halloran replied. As he was about to take his seat, the doctor continued.

'As could any one of hundreds of knives in daily use in this country. There is nothing special about this knife, which could allow anyone to say it was or was not the knife used.'

This last comment was not what O'Halloran had wanted, and it was clear from the way he glared at the witness that he was not impressed by the answer. However, he realised that if he tried to undo the damage done by challenging the last remark, he could be digging himself into a hole he did not want to be in, and so he simply took his seat without further questioning.

Gilmartin rose. Before asking any questions, he flipped through the booklet of photographs that had been produced before the jury. He put down the album and asked the doctor, 'How many stab wounds were there to the deceased?'

'There were sixteen penetrating wounds,' Kearney replied.

'Correct me if I am wrong, but all were to the upper torso of the deceased?'

'Yes, that is so.'

'And given the number and severity of the wounds, would it be fair to assume the attacker must have been close to the deceased?'

'Absolutely,' Kearney replied. 'You cannot inflict such wounds at a distance.'

'And in your experience, Dr Kearney, would you not expect some significant transfer of blood from the deceased to the attacker, given the proximity?'

'That would certainly not be unexpected, Judge,' the doctor replied.

Gilmartin paused to let that answer register with the jury and then said, 'Thank you, Dr Kearney. You have been very helpful.' He sat down.

As the doctor left the witness stand, O'Halloran stood and announced his next witness would be Detective Sergeant McLaughlin.

Jennings had been watching McLaughlin during the doctor's testimony, and with what he knew was coming down the line, in some ways he almost felt sorry for the man who approached the witness stand.

The detective had taken a folder from his briefcase before stepping up to the stand, and after taking the oath, he sat down and rested the file on the witness box in front of him.

O'Halloran introduced him to the jury, took him through his experience, and confirmed for the jury that he was the investigating officer into the crime.

Although the book of evidence that had been provided was very thin the one statement that was detailed was McLaughlin's, and O'Halloran took him through his is statement in such a way it almost appeared McLaughlin had memorised it. It was not unusual for an experienced Gard to stick to the script as set out in his statement, but the way McLaughlin presented his evidence left no room for doubt that he had been told in no uncertain terms to make sure he knew his statement backwards and forwards.

As far as Jennings was concerned. the only relevant material was the assertion that the raid on Moyo's apartment was a result of information received from a confidential source, and the fact that McLaughlin had recovered the knife previously produced in court, which subsequently proved to have blood from the deceased on it.

His evidence at finding the briefcase with cash was also dealt with, as was the evidence as to the missing blood sample taken from the accused. Nothing at all emerged during the hour or so McLaughlin was on the witness stand that was not preordained in his statement. That fact made it even more interesting for Jennings because he knew what was to come in cross-examination.

When the examination was complete, before Gilmartin got to his feet, the Judge advised that as it was approaching four o'clock, and because this had been the first day of the trial, he was going to rise until the next day. That was not unexpected given the time of day, but what he said next was surprising.

'Given we are rising slightly ahead of schedule today, I propose sitting from 10.30 a.m. in the morning unless there are any objections.' Despite the apparent invitation for complaint, it was clear that no objections would be accepted, and Jennings could hardly advise the time did not suit because of what he hoped would be taking place in Belfast. He simply had to bite his tongue and say nothing as the Judge rose and left the courtroom.

Once the Judge left, Gilmartin indicated he wanted a word with Moyo and Jennings, and he went across the courtroom where Moyo stood flanked by two prison officers.

'Well, Stephen, you can see that nothing much has happened today, but that is all to the good in that nothing new has been brought against us,' Gilmartin said. 'I anticipate tomorrow will be a more interesting day, so if you have any questions of me, ask away.'

'I don't think there is anything I can ask now,' Moyo said. 'Perhaps a word with Mr Jennings, though, about a personal issue?'

'By all means. I will leave you two now and see you in the morning,' Gilmartin said, and he left.

'Richard, I know you told me not to speak of my son, but I cannot think of anything else. Please tell me if there is any news.'

Jennings could see the tension on Moyo's face, but he simply could not have this conversation in the courtroom with prison officers in attendance. 'All I can tell you is that as far as I am concerned, we should be hearing from your son before lunch tomorrow. Please try to not dwell on him. Concentrate on what is happening here. Do you understand what has been happening so far?'

'Of course, but they have only heard one version of events. I know things will change tomorrow, but I cannot concentrate for worrying about John.'

'Stephen, I understand, but I must insist we do not discuss this any further now. I will see you tomorrow before the trial continues. I can tell you that I only expect news after ten, and the fact the trial is starting early will make communication difficult. Please trust me. We are doing everything we can for you and John.'

'I understand. I just hope and pray that tomorrow will see the end of this nightmare.'

'So do I, Stephen,' Jennings replied. As Moyo turned and left the room, Jennings realised just how much was at stake in the coming twenty-four hours.

On leaving the courtroom, he tried to contact McGeough, but his call went unanswered. He had no idea what McGeough was up to. He had assumed McGeough would keep in contact, and his inability to reach him was further cause for concern.

CHAPTER FORTY-FIVE

The Trial, Second Day

Jennings had not returned to the office after court and had instead decided
to go home to get some rest and prepare for the morning. Sleep had not
come easily, and by 6.00a.m. he had given up on getting any meaningful rest.
He was in the office by 7.00a.m. He hoped to achieve some distraction by
dealing with what now seemed mundane queries from clients which had
been building up whilst he was preparing for the trial.

He was not supposed to be in the office at all and was confused when
his direct line rang. Only a few people had this number, and he seldom had
cause to use it himself.

On answering the call, he immediately felt a sense of panic. The voice
on the other end was not one he wanted to hear. Jonathan Kaseke spoke in
his usual unhurried tone.

'Mr Jennings, good morning. It is good to see you are conscientious in
your work. I was hoping I could speak to you before you left for court. I
understand you have an early start today. I have to tell you that there has
been a bit of a change to our plans for our exchange.'

'What are you talking about, Kaseke? Everything is arranged as we
discussed.'

'Yes, well, that is where the problem may arise. You see, I would not like
to find that you may have decided to make alternative arrangements for out
meeting today, and so I have decided to change the venue. I am sure you will
be able to accommodate me.'

'Change to where?' Jennings asked.

'Instead of the City Airport, we will meet at the International Airport.
Same time as previously agreed, but we will meet in the short-term car park.

Provided nothing untoward happens, the exchange can proceed I will be on my way home, and you can get on with your trial. I am sure you won't let me down.' Then he hung up.

Jennings stared at the phone, trying to grasp what he had just been told. Why the need to change venue? This whole exercise was beginning to get out of control. What if he could not contact McGeough? His attempts through the night and first thing this morning had been to no avail.

He was on the point of deciding to call the whole thing off and make a call to the Gardaí and the PSNI when his mobile rang. He breathed a sigh of relief to see it was McGeough. When he answered, his tone could hardly be described as friendly. 'Ken, what the hell is going on? I have been trying to contact you since the trial ended yesterday. I have just had Kaseke on the phone, and the bastard has changed the venue for the exchange.'

'Richard, try to calm down. I know I should have called you, but I have not been twiddling my thumbs up here. I know about the change of venue and have been working through the night to deal with that.'

'But Kaseke only just called me. How could you know what he was going to do?'

'He needs to use his diplomatic status to protect him from arrest if anything should go wrong, and I was able to find out that he made an alternative booking out of the country. It has taken some doing, but we are ready to deal with him now. Try to calm down and let me get on with things.'

'I am not even going to ask how you get your information, Ken, but please do not go silent on me again. I need to know what is happening.'

'All right, Richard. I will do the best I can to keep in touch, but with these sorts of deals, that is not always possible. I will speak to you later.'

Jennings was about to reply when he realised McGeough had hung up, and he stared at his phone for a long minute. The day had barely started, and already he felt things were getting out of control.

CHAPTER FORTY-SIX

Newry, 9.30 a.m.

DI Farrell and his team had had the house McGeough had told him about under surveillance ever since McGeough had first spoken to him. Farrell had personally been in a control van directing observations since the previous evening, and as with all surveillance operations, the boredom was the worst part of the job. He had been able to allocate a sizable team to the operation to come, and a tactical armed unit was moving into position to move in at 10.00 a.m. as he had arranged with McGeough.

As he adjusted himself in his chair, one of his officers observing the house from a house opposite came on the radio.

'Sir, just to let you know our guest has a visitor.'

Farrell spun in his chair and asked for a video link on the property to be brought up so that he could see what was going on.

He immediately saw that the visitor was Padraig Hennessey, the former doctor who McGeough had told him had been attending on the house from time to time in the past but had not been there since Farrell's surveillance had started. Farrell was concerned why he should be there now. Hopefully their guest had not taken a turn for the worse.

As Farrell watched the man approach the front door, the door opened, and two men appeared who obviously knew Hennessy and spoke with him briefly in the doorway. Farrell knew from previous observation that there were always at least two men in the house with their guest, and it was obvious this was as much to keep him in as to keep anyone else out. As Hennessy made his way into the house, they in turn left carrying sizable holdalls, which they threw in the back of a car parked outside the house.

They climbed into the car and made to drive away as Farrell's man came back on the radio.

'Sir, looks like our friends are on the move. Should we not lift them now?'

Farrell could see what was happening, and he was immediately concerned at this development, but he told them to stay where they were until further instructions. The two men were local thugs and could always be picked up later, if need be. He decided to contact McGeough and share what he had seen.

McGeough answered his phone on the first ring, and Farrell brought him up to speed in a few words. McGeough's reaction was immediate. 'Gary, this is not good. Forget about waiting till ten. I really think you should get in there now and get the two of them in custody.'

'Right, Ken. I agree.' Farrell hung up and gave the order for his support team to move in.

He watched the screen in the control van as two unmarked vans sped up the road and came to a halt outside the house. A team of uniformed and armed police ran to the front door and smashed their way in. He could hear what was happening through a live audio feed from officers on the ground, and he soon heard the officer in charge confirm both suspects were in custody and the house was secured.

He removed his headset and made his way out of the van to go up to the house and interview his suspects. Maybe now he would find out what was really going on.

CHAPTER FORTY-SEVEN

Dublin, 10.00 a.m.

The trial of Stephen Moyo had naturally caught the attention of the press and the public. As Jennings arrived at the court complex, he had to take his place in a substantial queue of people trying to get in. Upon reaching the courtroom, he pushed his way through a scrum of reporters and others who had not made it inside. Once inside the court, which was relatively calm compared to what was going on outside, he prepared his papers and waited the arrival of his barristers and his client.

All were assembled by 10.30 a.m., and as was his way, without any preliminary enquiry, the Judge's clerk entered the courtroom and escorted the Judge into his seat.

After formal introductions, Sergeant McLaughlin was called to the witness stand and was formally reminded by the court registrar that he was still under oath.

Gilmartin rose from his seat and placed a number of documents on the lectern in front of him before turning to McLaughlin. 'Sergeant, you have been a Gard for many years, and you understand your duties as an investigator, do you not?'

'I do, Judge,' he replied.

'Very well. Yesterday in your evidence, you told the jury what you did do in this investigation. This morning I am going to ask you about things you did *not* do. Perhaps we shall start with one of the more basic matters that should have caught your attention.'

McLaughlin had what gamblers would call a 'tell' when nervous, which consisted of him pulling on the cuffs of his jacket. From the tone of

Gilmartin's opening remarks, the officer knew he was in for a hard time, and he immediately gave his cuffs attention.

'Sergeant, the State introduced into evidence a document which they say was used by the accused to withdraw a sum of cash from an account of the deceased. You of course recall that, but my question is whether you had the document examined by a handwriting expert to ascertain whether it was in fact written by the deceased.'

'No, I did not,' was the reply. 'With the other evidence available, there was no need to carry out such an examination. The document was not the most important piece of evidence available.'

'Would it be of interest to you, Sergeant, to hear that there is in court a handwriting expert who has examined the note and compared the writing of the accused and the deceased—and that he has concluded that neither were the author of this document?' Whilst asking this question Gilmartin, turned and indicated Harry McGonigle, who was seated in the front row of the gallery. McLaughlin should have known he was in for this line of questioning because McGonigle was well-known to Gardai and was used by them and the defence in many trials.

'Sergeant, Mr McGonigle will give evidence that this document was written by someone who was left-handed, and the accused and the deceased were both right-handed.'

As Gilmartin finished this statement, O'Halloran was up from his chair and said, 'I must object to his line of questioning, Judge. Mr Gilmartin knows well that there is no scientific basis on what any expert can state whether a document was written by a person who was left-handed or right-handed. He is deliberately trying to mislead the witness and the jury.'

Gilmartin paused briefly and replied, 'An interesting objection, Judge, from Counsel who in fact relied on the testimony of this very expert to assist obtaining the conviction of a man in this court barely a year ago. He can hardly complain now about the expert on which he himself relied.'

Judge Murtagh had no hesitation in replying, 'I agree, Mr Gilmartin. Mr O' Halloran, if you want to object further, perhaps you will pause to reflect on the objection before interrupting cross-examination. Carry on, Mr Gilmartin.'

Jennings had been watching this exchange, and though he had his back to the Judge and could not see his expression, he detected from the tone that the Judge was laying down an early marker that he was not going to tolerate any gamesmanship between the two barristers. He also detected the barest hint of a smile from Gilmartin as he looked to the jury before continuing.

'Sergeant, if neither the accused nor the deceased wrote this letter, who do you think did?'

'I have no idea, Judge.'

'So here we are with the first thing you did not do. You did not consider there may be another party involved in the commission of this crime. Is that not so?'

'From the evidence, I was satisfied the accused was solely responsible for the murder of Father O'Meara,' McLaughlin said, but with hardly the same level of conviction as he had when giving his evidence in chief.

'We will hear from Mr McGonigle later if necessary, Sergeant. Let me now ask about something else you did not do. Did you ever review any CCTV footage which may have been of assistance in your investigation?'

'I did not, Judge.'

'Did you attend at the apartment occupied by the accused, and did you interview the manager of the apartment?'

'Yes.'

'And did you ask him if there was any CCTV footage available?'

'No, Judge, I did not. I told him the nature of my enquiry and asked if he had anything of use to tell me. He said he did not, and so I left it at that after we found the murder weapon and the cash in the accused's room.'

Gilmartin paused whilst he opened a file in front of him, removed a folder of documents, and opened it in front of him. He did this in a slow and deliberate manner, making a point of turning each document over individually before continuing. Jennings knew this was pure theatre for the benefit of the jury. Having gone through the photographs, Gilmartin motioned to Jennings, who handed in a folder for the Judge and gave two to Cathal Murphy for the witness and O'Halloran.

Gilmartin allowed the Judge to look through the folder before continuing. 'Judge, I have copies for the jury, if I may hand them in subject to formally proving their origin, should that be necessary at a later stage.'

Murtagh looked down to O'Halloran, who after the last skirmish with the Judge was in no mood to object to the photos going before the jury at this stage. 'Carry on, Mr Gilmartin. There seems to be no objection from the State.'

Jennings stood and passed twelve folders to the jury foreman, who distributed them. Once all members had a set, Gilmartin continued.

'Sergeant, these are stills taken from CCTV footage from outside the apartment of the accused on two different days. One was before the killing of the deceased, and one was on the day of the killing. You will see the date and time of each photograph is recorded on the photograph, as is common for this type of system. I have statements from the manager of the apartment and the man responsible for the maintenance of the system, who will testify as to the accuracy of the recordings as to time and date, if necessary. Do you have any comment on that?'

McLaughlin had been going through the folder whilst the other folders had been distributed, and his unease as to what was coming was clear.

'Now, Sergeant, for the purposes of the record, you will see that the first photographs show a group of three men approaching the apartment several days before the killing. There are then several close-up stills of each man in turn. There are two white men and one black. Is that not so?'

'It is, Judge.'

'And of the three men, can you identify any of them?'

McLaughlin was clearly uncomfortable at where this was going, and before answering, he looked towards O'Halloran in the false hope that the barrister might be of some help to him in getting out of the obvious trap into which he was about to fall. No help was to be had from that quarter, however.

'Sergeant, I am asking you the question. Mr O'Halloran cannot help you. Do you recognise any of the men in these photographs?'

'I do, Judge,' McLaughlin replied in a subdued tone. 'The man in the photograph marked G is known to me.'

'How is he known to you?' Sergeant Gilmartin asked in a tone that brought silence to the court as the reply was awaited.

'This man was arrested at the home of Grainne Kellet and is in custody, charged with her assault and attempted false imprisonment.'

'And for the benefit of the jury, who is Grainne Kellet, and when did this incident occur?'

'Ms Kellet is, I believe, Mr Jennings' secretary. This incident took place several weeks after the murder of Father O'Meara.'

Gilmartin paused before continuing. 'Please look at the photographs beginning with the letter 'M'. Can you see the date on the photograph? What date is shown there?'

'The date is the day Father O'Meara was killed.'

'And you can see in photograph G that the man you identify as being in custody for an attack on my solicitor's secretary sometime after these events is carrying a briefcase. You can see that, can't you?' Although the question was for the witness, Gilmartin turned to the jury and held the photograph up so that their attention was focused on the right photograph.

'Yes, I can see that, Judge,' McLaughlin replied. 'But I do not believe that the briefcase is the one that was found in the apartment of the accused.'

'Gilmartin turned to McLaughlin and said, 'I did not ask you if you thought it was the same, but perhaps you will look at the photographs later in the folder, which show the same men leaving. Are any of them carrying a briefcase?'

McLaughlin again realised he had walked into a trap, and he replied in a subdued tone, 'No, Judge.'

'Well, then, we will just have to leave it to the jury to decide whether that is the briefcase in question, won't we?' Gilmartin moved his papers around on the lectern and continued. 'Sergeant, at this early stage, we know of a number of things you did not do. I suggest that if you had any intention of properly investigating the matter, these were things you should have done. You failed to have the note examined, and you failed in recovering relevant evidence that shows there are perhaps other people involved in this matter who should have been pursued.'

'Judge, I had taken the advice of my superior officers at all times in the investigation of this matter, and we are satisfied that there was sufficient evidence available to charge the accused and bring him to trial.'

'So, Sergeant, what you are saying in simple terms is that you were following orders rather than doing your duty in properly investigating the murder of Father O'Meara.'

O'Halloran could not control himself and leapt to his feet to object. Before he could say a word, Judge Murtagh raised his hand and stopped him in his tracks. O'Halloran resumed his seat with a scowl, clearly not wanting a further rebuke by the Judge in front of the jury.

Jennings could see Gilmartin was only getting into his stride and waited for the reply.

'As I have already said, Judge, I was acting on the directions of my superior officers.'

Gilmartin appeared to be intent on papers in front of him, but the reality was he was allowing this exchange to firmly register in the minds of the jury. After a suitable pause, he turned to the witness and continued. 'Sergeant, you are intent on blaming your superiors for not doing what you are supposed to do, so perhaps it is now time to return to an issue for which you yourself are solely responsible.'

Jennings knew what was coming, and he knew the effect it would have on McLaughlin and his career, but he felt nothing for the man who had already put himself in a position from which he would not be able to escape.

CHAPTER FORTY-EIGHT

Newry, 10.30 a.m.

Gary Farrell had been in the house with his two suspects for just over half an hour. Whilst Dr Hennessy was refusing to answer any questions, the other man, who had identified himself as Andrei Kolynov, was giving so much information it was hard to take it all in. From one thing he had said, Farrell knew he had to get hold of McGeough as a matter of urgency.

McGeough answered Farrell's call on the first ring. 'Gary, tell me what you have found.'

'It is a good job we went in when we did. When the team got into the house, they found our foreign friend trussed up like a turkey on the sofa in the front room, and the good doctor was preparing something he was clearly about to inject into him. We don't know what it is yet, but you can guarantee it was not intended to do any good.'

'I am sure you are right, but have you got anything from either of them that is of interest?'

'Hennessy has shut up like a clam, but the other fellow can hardly stop talking. The one thing he has said that you need to know is that the man on trial in Dublin for the murder of the priest is the wrong man.'

'Well, that is one of the things I have been working on, and I believe he is right. But how can he say for certain that the accused is not the right man?'

'He says he was there when the killing took place, and it was one of the two black men who killed the priest. The fellow in Dublin had apparently left the scene before they went into the priest's rooms.'

'He says there were two black men there?'

'That's right, and he said both were in the house here in Newry just the

251

other day. He could not hear what they were saying, but he thinks they were planning on getting out of the country as soon as possible.'

'Gary, I am going to send you two photos. Can you show them to our friend and ask if either or both are involved? If so, get him to point to the one he says killed the priest.'

'No problem. I will get back to you ASAP.'

McGeough scrolled through photos on his phone and sent them on to Farrell. Within minutes, he received a reply. As he stared at the text message, he knew he had to act without delay.

CHAPTER FORTY-NINE

Belfast International Airport, 10.45 a.m.

Mick and a friend had been waiting in their car in the short-term car park for over half an hour. Mick was beginning to believe the deal was not going to go down and was about to call McGeough when the phone he had been given rang. He answered straight away and was told to look for a Ford Galaxy People Carrier. He was given the registration number of the car and was told it would be close to the pay stations. After getting out of his car, he was soon able to identify the vehicle.

'I believe you may have something to show me. Is that so?'

Mick was in no mood for games and replied, 'I am not here for my fucking health. Let's get on with this.'

'There is no need for rudeness, young man. I will be sending over a colleague to inspect the merchandise, and I assume you can see that I have a mutual friend with me here.'

Mick was able to make out four people in the Galaxy, and when he confirmed he was ready to proceed, one of the men emerged from the car and made his way over to him.

There was no need for discussion as the man arrived, and Mick indicated for him to get into the back seat of his car, where his associate was seated. Mick got in the car, leaned over, and handed the visitor a padded envelope, which the man opened with some care.

Mick had no idea what he was carrying. When the envelope was opened, and he saw it was a stone, he wondered what all the trouble they had gone to was for. He was sufficiently street smart to know that this was clearly no ordinary stone; for all the trouble everyone was going through, it had to be worth a lot of money.

The man turned over the stone and brought out a photograph from his pocket, a set of callipers, and a loupe. He examined what he was holding. After a short while, he put the stone back in the envelope, took a mobile from his jacket pocket, and dialled a number.

'It is the stone,' he said. These were the first words he had spoken, and Mick could tell he was certainly not a local.

A moment later, Mick's phone rang, and Kaseke spoke.

'We can proceed with the exchange. Our friend will come across to you with another man, and if you would be so kind as to escort my colleague with the package, we can exchange in the open with minimal fuss.'

'You're the boss,' Mick replied, and he got out of the car and indicated to the man to do likewise.

As he approached the Galaxy, a heavily built man got out of the front of the car and opened one of the back doors. Mick was able to recognise John Moyo from a photograph McGeough had given him.

The two groups approached each other, stopped, and faced each other midway between the cars.

Mick had taken a firm grip of the man's arm as they walked across the car park, and the man had realised it would make no sense to resist. When they came to a stop, Mick let him go and gave him a gentle shove forward. The man wasted no time in walking towards the Galaxy. John Moyo, who was similarly retrained by his minder, was also released and moved towards Mick in a hesitant manner.

'It's okay, John. I am a friend. It's time to say goodbye to these nice people and go see your father.'

The man who had been holding Moyo had not said a word, but on hearing what Mick said, he smiled, turned on his heel, and returned to the Galaxy with the man who had examined the stone.

Mick and Moyo made their way to their car. After putting Moyo in the back seat with his colleague, Mick took out his phone to call McGeough and tell him the exchange was complete.

McGeough told him where he wanted Moyo taken and then hung up.

As he was about to start his car, Mick saw Kaseke get out of his car and walk towards the terminal building. The Galaxy and its occupants moved off towards the car park entrance with no sign of any urgency.

What neither Kaseke nor any of the people with him knew was that the exchange was being carefully watched by several people. One person was apparently an airport maintenance man of some kind, and he fell in behind Kaseke as he entered the terminal building.

CHAPTER FIFTY

Dublin,
11.00 a.m.

Gilmartin turned to another set of papers on his lectern and held them up as he asked his question.

'Sergeant, this is a copy of the custody record relating to the accused on his initial arrest and detention. I assume you are familiar with this?'

'Of course.'

'And you were in the barracks when his detention was being processed?'

'I was.'

'And I note that the custody sergeant made an observation to the effect that the accused seemed "intoxicated and disorientated". Is that your recollection?'

'It is not. As far as I was concerned, there was nothing wrong with the man.'

'Yet I see a doctor was called and a blood sample was taken. Why was that done?'

'It was the decision of the custody sergeant. You would need to ask him.'

Gilmartin knew the answer to the next question, but before he asked, he made the pretence of studying the record. 'Yes, I see it was a Sergeant Hughes. I assume he would be available if needed?'

'Sergeant Hughes has retired, and I believe he is no longer in the jurisdiction, Judge.'

This was going better than Gilmartin could have hoped, and he nodded to Jennings, who stood and made his way out of the courtroom.

'What became of the blood sample, Sergeant?'

'Judge, the sample was one of a number of samples stolen from the Garda Medical Bureau. The incident in question received some publicity at the time in the national press.'

'Yes, it did, and it is most unfortunate that the sample taken from the accused is not available.'

'We can't say one way or the other, Judge,' McLaughlin replied with a shrug.

During this exchange, Jennings had returned to his seat. When Gilmartin looked down to him, he simply nodded his head. Gilmartin continued.

'Sergeant, you have already said you know the importance of telling the truth on oath. I rarely make this accusation, but in this case, I can say without any fear of contradiction that you are a liar.' Gilmartin's voice rose so that by the end of the sentence, he was almost shouting at the now visibly nervous witness.

Gilmartin turned to look into the well of the courtroom and saw the man he was looking for near the door of the court. He indicated to him to come forward, and the members of the jury turned to see who this person may be.

'Sergeant, is this the former Sergeant Hughes who you advised was in retirement and out of the jurisdiction?'

As McLaughlin looked towards Hughes, the colour drained from his cheeks. He now knew what was coming. 'That is Sergeant Hughes, Judge.'

'Indeed it is. And what would you say if I told you that the sergeant has deposed on affidavit that the sample we have just spoken of was not in fact sent to the bureau at all due to a mistake on his part? What do you say to that?'

McLaughlin paused for a moment to decide which road to take: own up and face the consequences, or try to get out of the hole he was in. 'I can't comment on that, Judge.'

'He also deposed in his affidavit to the fact that he specifically told you of this, and you advised him to destroy the sample. What do you say about that?'

'I deny that, Judge.'

'He will also say that the sample that was given to another member of the Garda Siochana was in fact dealt with in the Garda Laboratory, and I have the test result here.' This last statement said, Gilmartin flourished a document in his hand. 'What do you say to that?'

McLoughlin was now clearly uncomfortable and said in a rush, 'Who is this other Gard? I oversaw the investigation. No other Gard had any right to interfere with evidence!'

Gilmartin paused before saying, 'The only interference, Sergeant, was done by you. You have deliberately attempted to subvert the course of justice by directing a fellow officer to dispose of material evidence.'

'I deny that, Judge. I had clear evidence against the accused and would have no need to try to prevent relevant material being made available.'

Gilmartin continued. 'I suppose you would consider it relevant if the sample of blood taken from the accused showed a significant presence of the drug Rohypnol?'

'I have already said that the sample taken from the accused was, as far as I was aware, destroyed. I cannot comment on whatever report you have. This is purely hypothetical as far as I am concerned.

Gilmartin stared at McLaughlin for a moment before stating, 'This is going to be a very simple question, Sergeant. Is Sergeant Hughes telling the truth when he says you told him to destroy material evidence?'

Even McLaughlin realised whichever answer he gave, the damage done to the prosecution's case was going to be enormous. True to form, though, he gave the answer that would do the most damage to the State case. 'He is not, Judge. I do not know why he should say such a thing. I can only assume he has been put under pressure by somebody who wants to harm this prosecution.'

'Very well, Sergeant. The jury will hear from Sergeant Hughes in due course, and it will be up to them to decide whom to believe.'

Justice Murtagh had been watching this exchange with growing interest, as had every member of the jury. In the meantime, O'Halloran had been leaning towards his solicitor, trying to find out what was going on as he saw his case falling apart in front of him. The deliberate concealing of evidence was potentially fatal to any prosecution.

Before Gilmartin could continue, O'Halloran was on his feet. Justice Murtagh said, 'Mr O'Halloran, before you say anything, I am going to ask the jury to leave the courtroom for a moment.' The Judge advised them that because there was undoubtedly going to be a legal issue he had to deal with between the two barristers, the jury would have to step out of the court for a short while.

The jury duly left the courtroom, and the door closed behind them. Before O'Halloran could say anything, Murtagh said, 'I am going to rise and leave the two of you to sort out what is going on in this trial. I am not going to allow my court to degenerate into a circus. Whatever differences there may be between the two of you, get this mess sorted. Don't call me back until it is resolved.' Before he stood, he turned to McLaughlin in the witness box and said, 'And you, Sergeant, are to remain in the witness box until your evidence is complete. You are not to speak to anyone, either in person or on the phone. Do you understand?'

McLaughlin had never been spoken to by any Judge in such a manner, and he was now clearly unnerved. 'I understand, Judge,' he said in a subdued voice as Murtagh stood and left the court.

Once the door closed behind the Judge, O'Halloran was on his feet and came towards Gilmartin in a decidedly hostile manner. 'What sort of stunt are you trying to pull, Gilmartin? If this is legitimate, you should have brought it to the attention of the Gardai or DPP as soon as you knew about it!'

Gilmartin had remained seated and looked up before calmly saying, 'And give your sergeant a chance to get around whatever he has done? I think not. In any event, I have no obligation to disclose anything to you—or have you forgotten the basics of criminal defence?'

Jennings could sense that things were rapidly getting out of control between the two barristers, but it was not his place to interfere, and so he sat back to watch the exchange.

'I have not forgotten anything, Gilmartin, but maybe you have forgotten your duty as officer of the court to bring to the attention of the authorities evidence of a crime. If this so-called evidence is any way credible, it should have been disclosed to the authorities for investigation instead of being hauled out of the hat like some cheap party trick.'

This last comment was the final straw for Gilmartin, and he stood and glared at O'Halloran. 'There is only one trickster here, O'Halloran, and he is sitting in the witness box—with you pulling the strings like the puppet master you are. Your witness has created this mess, and so it's up to you to sort it out.' With that, he turned to Jennings and said, 'I suggest we leave Mr O'Halloran to review his position, Richard. Perhaps a breath of clean air would be beneficial. The stink in here is overpowering.'

CHAPTER FIFTY-ONE

Belfast International Airport, 11.30 a.m.

Kaseke made his way into the terminal building. He had no luggage with him and so made his way through the departure hall clearly intent on going to the departure area.

He passed through security without incident, and the display of his diplomatic passport was obviously of use in preventing him from being subject to the usual searches carried out on ordinary passengers. After making his way into the departure lounge, he went into one of the food outlets and purchased a coffee. Then he returned to look at the departure time displayed on a screen in the concourse.

He checked his watch and moved to take a seat and drink his coffee. To the world at large, he was a businessman going about a routine flight.

The man who had originally followed Kaseke into the terminal building had remained behind him up until he went through the security checkpoint. At that point, another man took up the surveillance and followed Kaseke into the departure area.

This man was in a dark suit with an identification tag around his neck which, if briefly inspected, would have shown him to be a member of airport security staff. A more careful inspection of the ID card would later show that the photograph of the man wearing the tag had been superimposed over the photo that had originally been embossed on the card. The fact that this man was not recognised by any of the other security staff raised no concern, however, because the staff rotated between the two airports in the city, and no one could possibly know who was legitimately employed at any one time.

After watching Kaseke for some time, the man seemed to receive a call over a radio attached to his belt. He answered the call, replaced the radio, and moved towards Kaseke.

As he approached, Kaseke happened to look up and realised the man was making his way to him. Comfortable in the knowledge that he had his diplomatic passport on him, Kaseke was not in the least concerned about the approach of an airport security man.

'Excuse me, sir, but would you be Mr Kaseke of the Zimbabwe Embassy?' the man enquired.

'I am. What is it to you?' Kaseke replied.

The man bent down towards Kaseke and said in a lowered voice, 'I need you to come with me, please, sir. There has been a security alert, and we are about to make a public announcement to evacuate the building. We always try to alert VIP travellers in advance. If you come with me, I can make suitable arrangements for you to be taken to a place of safety.'

Kaseke was obviously not pleased with this news. Just as he was about to protest, the public-address system announced there was indeed a security alert and that all travellers and other persons in the departure lounge area were asked to vacate the building as calmly and quickly as possible under the direction of airport security.

On hearing this, Kaseke needed no further invitation and stood to follow the man who was apparently going to look after him. Diplomatic status does indeed have its advantages, he thought.

The security man led Kaseke through a door he had to access with a security card, and they proceeded to walk down a passage way which had several doors leading off it on either side. As the man opened one of the doors, he said, 'These are secure rooms we keep for things like this, Mr Kaseke. I am sure this will be over shortly. In the meantime, you will be safe and comfortable in here.'

On entering the room, Kaseke did not detect there was another man standing behind the door. What he did feel though was a sharp stinging sensation in his neck. He lifted his hand to his neck as a sudden and excruciating pain gripped his chest. The last thing he would have remembered before he died was the security man catching him by the arm as his legs gave way under him.

CHAPTER FIFTY-TWO

Dublin, 2.00 p.m.

A short while after the Judge had left the court, his registrar appeared and advised the legal teams that the Judge had decided he would not resume hearing until later in the day. Murtagh had directed that the court would resume at 2.00 p.m.

Jennings was not at all unhappy with that news, and as soon as he had heard that, he was on the phone to McGeough to find out what had happened in Belfast.

McGeough had advised that the exchange had been made and that Mick was on his way back to Dublin with John Moyo. Jennings was relieved to hear that and said he would pass on the news to his client as soon as he hung up.

McGeough's request in the circumstances struck Jennings as particularly odd. 'Richard, I would rather you say nothing until we get John Moyo in the courthouse and let Stephen see him for himself. I don't have to tell you that what has been going on today is not strictly by the book, so perhaps we should not do anything which might cause upset in the immediate future. There will be plenty of time for them to celebrate his release once we are sure he is going to be free.'

Jennings could not understand what McGeough was saying, but he could not disagree that what they had done that morning was fraught with potential problems. Perhaps it would be better to say nothing and let Stephen enjoy the moment when John was brought to him face to face.

Before the court resumed, Jennings had had a brief word with Moyo. He told him that things had gone well in Belfast and that Moyo had to be patient, but there was almost certainly going to be good news before the end of the day.

As Jennings made his way in to the court, he noticed O'Halloran and Gilmartin were standing shoulder to shoulder, obviously engaged in some discussion that was not for a general audience. As he moved to take his seat, Gilmartin indicated to him that he wanted a word in private, and they left the courtroom and moved away from the entrance to the court, where they could not be overheard.

'Richard, I have just been told by O'Halloran that he will be asking for the trial to be adjourned in light of new evidence that has come to the attention of the DPP. Apparently, there has been an arrest of a man in the North who claims to have direct knowledge of the killing of Father O'Meara. The State needs time to interview this man and assess his evidence. You would not know anything about what is going on here, would you?'

Jennings paused before he replied, 'I have reason to believe that McGeough was following up a lead in the North. That may account for what has happened, but I certainly know no details of what may have happened up there. You know McGeough as well as I do. He is not the sort of man to tell people what he is up to unless it's absolutely necessary.'

'Very well,' Gilmartin replied. 'I detest working in the dark, but if this new development is going to help our client, I am not going to object to their request. I believe you should explain to Mr Moyo as best you can what is going on. Hopefully in the morning, we will know more.'

Gilmartin and Jennings returned to the courtroom, and Jennings had a brief word with his client before the Judge came into the court and was advised by O'Halloran that he needed to ask for an adjournment.

Justice Murtagh was known for his insistence that once trials commenced, they proceed without interruption. This sort of application was bound to earn a sharp rebuke. Today, however, no rebuke was forthcoming. 'Given the nature of the evidence heard today, I would have thought an adjournment by the State to consider its position would be appropriate. I will advise the registrar to inform the foreman of the jury that we shall not be sitting again today, and we will resume at 11.00 a.m. tomorrow. Lest there be any doubt, I will not tolerate any more delay, and this trial is going to move ahead regardless of what the State does or does not do. Is that understood?'

The Judge rose and left the court, and the parties began to collect their papers. In the process of doing this, Jennings's phone rang, and he saw it was McGeough.

'Ken, the State has asked for an adjournment because they say some man has been arrested in the North, and they have information about the killing. What is going on?'

'Richard, I will be in the CCJ with John Moyo within the hour. I think it is time we reunite son and father, and everything will be explained. Organise a room, and don't let them take Stephen back to Cloverhill. It is important he hears what John has to tell him.'

Before he could reply, McGeough hung up. Jennings was left wondering what was coming now. From McGeough's tone, he could tell he was agitated, and for McGeough that was very unusual.

At 3.00 p.m., Jennings had arranged a consultation room, and he and Stephen were waiting in the room when McGeough walked in. He closed the door behind him and sat opposite Jennings and Moyo.

'Richard, Stephen, good to see you. It has been an interesting day, but before I get John in, I need to bring you up to speed with what has been happening.'

He then described events in Newry earlier in the day leading to the arrest of Kolynov, and he explained that he was rescued just before it appeared Hennessy was to inject him with what had been found to be a lethal dose of morphine.

Kolynov had been more than cooperative with DI Farrell, and the information he had already given would keep police forces across Europe busy for months. The man had an encyclopaedic memory for names, account details, and events. There was no doubt organised crime in Ireland and elsewhere was about to suffer a serious setback.

'Stephen, this Kolynov was also at the priest's rooms when he was killed. He knows who killed Father O'Meara, and from other evidence we have been able to put together, it seems what he is saying is correct. I am afraid it is not going to be the news you wanted, but there is no easy way of doing this.' McGeough stood and opened the door. He gave a nod of his head, and Jennings and Moyo were taken by surprise to see John being brought into the room by a uniformed Gard in handcuffs. McGeough told the Gard to wait outside, and the four men were left alone in the room.

Before Stephen could say a word, Jennings said, 'Ken, what is going on here? John is a victim in this. Surely you do not think he had anything to do with the murder of O'Meara.'

Before McGeough could reply, John Moyo spoke in a defiant and aggressive tone that clearly shocked his father to the core. 'He does not have to think anything. I have told him I killed the priest, and I am glad of it. The man was a hypocrite. He was about to destroy my chance of making a fortune and getting away from Zimbabwe forever. All he had to do was hand over the diamond, but he was too pig-headed and full of his own importance to do that. Father, you always said the man had blood on his hands. It was time he paid the price!'

Jennings and Moyo looked on in stunned silence at the man before them, and McGeough filled in the details as best he could.

'Stephen, your son was not the victim of an abduction by Kaseke. He was a willing accomplice. He has admitted to working for Kaseke for years, and his membership of the MDC was a way of providing information to Kaseke on you and anyone else involved in the campaign against Mugabe.

'Before the diamond went missing, one of the local MDC men saw Kaseke and John together. His cover was about to be blown, and so they had to get rid of the man. The only way they could protect John was to come up with the story that he had been abducted. When the diamond went missing, Kaseke knew you were here with Father O'Meara. It was a simple decision to use you as the tool to get back the diamond.

'Unfortunately, things did not go to plan, and when the priest refused to hand over the diamond, he took John to task for siding with Kaseke and the CIO, and he told him you would be ashamed of having a son who could be so dishonest. John apparently flew into a rage, and before Kaseke or either of the two Latvians could stop him, he launched into an attack on the priest and killed him.

'Everything since then has been a cover-up to get to you and get the diamond. Cian O'Meara was in a serious hole with his paymaster, and he paid the price for that. Then it was up to Kaseke and John to get things over the line and recover the diamond.'

Jennings was trying to take in what he was hearing. He said, 'But John was always going to be brought back to us here. Was he also being sold down the river by Kaseke?'

'Hardly,' McGeough replied. 'When I got information from my PSNI contact that it was John who was the killer, I had him searched. We found a substantial sum of cash, a false passport, and a credit card sewn into the lining of his coat. He was obviously going to make a run for it at the first opportunity, but fortunately that did not arise.'

'And what of Kaseke in all this? Where is he now?'

'That is not something I will discuss now, Richard, but I can tell you that all his plans have come to nothing. As for John, I have arrested him for the murder of Father O'Meara, and he will be taken to Bridewell, charged, and brought before the District Court tomorrow. I should imagine when the DPP hears what has happened, the trial of Stephen will be brought to an end. By lunchtime tomorrow, Stephen, you will be a free man. That can't be said for John here.'

At that, John Moyo snorted and said, 'I will never be prosecuted! Kaseke will see to that. He is not the only person with diplomatic status. In any case, the man who took me from Northern Ireland was not a policeman. I have been unlawfully detained in another country. I will never stand trial here.'

McGeough smiled as he replied, 'You have been taking advice from the wrong people for too long, John. Kaseke will not be there to help you, and I can assure you that with the evidence I have, and now with your confession in front of Mr Jennings and your father, there is only one sure thing in your future: a life sentence.'

Before John Moyo could reply, McGeough opened the door and called the uniformed Gard back into the room, telling him to remove Moyo and wait for him in the holding cells.

When the three men were left on their own, there was silence between them. McGeough could see that Stephen Moyo was having difficulty taking in what he had heard.

McGeough broke the silence and spoke in as reassuring a tone as he could. 'Stephen, I know that this has been hard to hear, but you have to look forward now. This nightmare is all over for you, and you can think about getting on with your life again. It will be necessary for you to stay here until after your son's trial, and I am sure Richard can help you with that. You are going to have to come to terms with what has happened and make the most of what life brings you.'

Stephen looked from McGeough to Jennings before replying. 'In just a few minutes, everything I have believed in and thought I knew has been destroyed. It is going to take some time to deal with what has happened in this country. But you are right. If for no other reason than to honour the memory of Father O'Meara and his nephew John, I will not let what my son, Kaseke, and Cian O'Meara have done ruin my life. Thank you both for what you have done.'

McGeough stood up to leave and said, 'Stephen, I am afraid you will have to return to Cloverhill tonight, but rest assured you will be looked after. Tomorrow when court resumes, you will be a free man. Richard, I suggest you say nothing to your Counsel of this. Let things take their course tomorrow. At least you can rest easy tonight.' With that, he left the room.

When left on their own, a silence descended on the two men, and words were not easy to find to describe their emotions. Jennings decided it was probably for the best to say nothing and let Stephen deal with what had happened in his own way. He simply stood, squeezed his shoulder, opened the door, and called for a prison officer to escort Stephen away.

As Moyo left the room, he turned to Jennings and simply said, 'Thank you.' Jennings could see the tears forming in his eyes.

Jennings stood in the corridor, left with his own thoughts. Despite what McGeough had said, he had every intention of disclosing what had just happened to Gilmartin and Grant, and he took out his phone to call them.

CHAPTER FIFTY-THREE

The Trial, Day Three
10.30 a.m.

The courtroom was already filled by 10. 00a.m, and when the Judge came into the court there was an air of expectation in the room from those who were expecting to see further drama following on from the previous day's events. Although there would be dramatic developments in the courtroom, only the legal personnel knew what was coming.

O'Halloran had spoken to Gilmartin in a subdued tone as soon as he came in. It was apparent that he was delighted to see the discomfort O'Halloran was in after being told his case was fatally flawed and the man on trial was clearly innocent of the charges against him. This was not a situation any prosecuting barrister wanted to be in, and Gilmartin could think of no good reason to make his discomfort any easier.

Once the Judge took his seat and the jury were called in, O'Halloran rose and addressed the court.

'Judge, I have to inform the court that there have been developments in this matter, and I am under instructions to offer no further evidence.' He looked across to Gilmartin and sat down as Gilmartin rose to his feet to make a formal application for the Judge to direct the jury to find the accused not guilty.

For his part, Murtagh took in the latest development without any outward signs of what he was obviously thinking. He addressed the jury and advised them that in the circumstances, it was his duty to direct the jury that as the state had failed to provide sufficient evidence to allow any jury to convict the accused, he was instructing them to find Stephen Moyo not guilty. He directed the court registrar to hand up the issue paper, and he instructed the foreman to enter the words 'Not Guilty' and return it to him.

The formalities duly completed, the Judge then addressed the court generally, in a tone which betrayed his anger and frustration.

'I would like to thank the jury for their attention, and although it has not been necessary for them to come to any decision of their own at this stage, I have no doubt that if called to do so, they would have discharged their duty honestly and to the best of their ability. Having said that, a jury can only work efficiently if all the relevant and material evidence has been put in front of them.'

He paused before continuing. 'In this case, from the evidence heard yesterday, it seems to me that the jury were not going to be provided with all relevant and material evidence. If the case had proceeded, there is the chance a miscarriage of justice would have occurred. It is fortunate indeed that the defence team was able to provide evidence that any competent investigation should have revealed from the start, and this case falls far short of what is expected in this court. I intend to file a report on this matter with the Director of Public Prosecutions, and I have no doubt that this will result in an enquiry as to precisely what has been going on in the investigation into the murder of an innocent man.'

Murtagh turned to Stephen Moyo. 'Mr Moyo, having been found not guilty of the charge against you, your innocence has been confirmed and you are now free to leave. This court will now adjourn.' He stood and left with a perfunctory bow to the room at large.

As soon as he left the room, there was an outburst of noise, and the members of the press were frantically on their phones to get the developments to their news desks. Gilmartin and Grant stood and shook hands with Jennings, and the three then went to Stephen Moyo, who was standing with a bewildered expression on his face.

'Well, Stephen,' Gilmartin said, extending his hand. 'Justice has prevailed, and you are a free man. It has been a pleasure to meet you, and I hope things work out for you in the future.' Stephen took his hand, thanked him, and did the same with Gerry Grant. The two barristers went to collect their papers and leave the courtroom.

Jennings did not bother taking anything out of his briefcase, knowing what was coming. He said to his client, 'Right, are you ready to go?'

Moyo looked uncertainly towards the prison officers, and Jennings said as gently as he could, 'Not that way, Stephen. You are coming with me out the front door. Your days in custody are over.' He took Moyo's arm and escorted him towards the door of the court.

CHAPTER FIFTY-FOUR

Three Weeks Later

Jennings sat at his desk and waited to see Stephen Moyo, who was scheduled to meet with him that morning. As he did so, he recalled the events of the last three weeks.

The departure from the court when the trial had so dramatically collapsed had been frantic, and it was a job to get away from the scrum of reporters anxious for a comment from either Jennings or Moyo.

Fortunately, their attention was diverted by the arrival of a convoy of Garda vehicles and the sight of a man being taken from the complex in handcuffs and in the company of Detective Garda McGeough. A well-placed leak had tipped the press off as to what was coming, and the scent of a new story was sufficient to distract them from what was soon to be old news.

Jennings had offered to take Moyo home with him for the night, but Moyo had asked instead to be allowed to be on his own. Jennings had booked him into a quiet bed and breakfast run by a client of his who he knew could be trusted to keep the identity of his latest guest quiet.

On his way home, Jennings had turned on the local news on the radio. When he'd learned of the death of a Zimbabwe national believed to be a diplomat in Belfast Airport the previous day, Jennings nearly caused an accident because his attention was diverted from driving the car to giving his attention to the news report.

He listened in disbelief as he heard that a man had apparently taken ill in Belfast International Airport the previous day and was pronounced dead at the scene when emergency personnel arrived. The identity of the man had to be confirmed before news of the incident could be made public, and the PSNI could now advise it appeared the deceased was a Zimbabwe national and a diplomat. They had been unable to advise on the matter earlier because they had to first confirm the identity of the deceased.

That had now been done, and the Zimbabwe embassy in London had requested the man's identity not be disclosed, pending notification of his family in Zimbabwe. The report went on to say that it was believed that the man had been in Northern Ireland for a personal visit and that the death was not being considered suspicious. Further details would be provided later.

Jennings immediately got on his phone to McGeough. As soon as McGeough answered, Jennings could barely contain his anger. 'I have just heard about Kaseke. What the hell is going on here, Ken? No one was supposed to be killed over this!'

'Calm down, Richard. I don't know what you are talking about. As far as I heard, the man's death is not considered suspicious. He obviously got what he deserved. Maybe there is karma after all.'

'Don't try to be smart with me,' Jennings replied. 'I don't believe in coincidences, and I know you don't either. It can't be right that the man responsible for so much misery just happens to drop dead just after he is given a diamond worth tens of millions of euros. In any event, what the hell happened to the diamond?'

'Richard, don't get yourself involved in matters that don't concern you. I was not even in Belfast at the time, and you certainly were not, so neither of us are responsible for whatever may or may not have happened. Unless and until you can tell me his death was not through natural causes, I am not going to give the bastard another thought. I suggest you do the same.'

'You know I feel nothing for the man, but I don't want his blood on my hands either. If I had gone to the authorities in the first place, he would still be alive. Can you tell me otherwise?'

There was a pause before McGeough answered. 'What you do or do not know or believe is irrelevant. You are the lawyer. Whatever you may think, if you were to go off to the PSNI or the Gards and tell them what had really been going on with John Moyo and Kaseke, do you honestly believe you would not be pulled into the frame? Obviously, I had to get help in putting the exercise together up in the North, and nobody does that type of work for nothing. If the diamond fell into somebody else's hands, I know nothing about that, and neither do you, so just let it go. Justice has been done, and the right man is walking free. The guilty have paid for their crimes. Leave this alone and move on.'

Jennings realised then that his concerns about McGeough were well founded all along. The man was moved by his own sense of what was right and wrong, and the end would always justify the means. He was also right that if Jennings raised anything relating to events in Northern Ireland, he would be putting himself in line to be charged as an accessory to whatever crimes had been committed.

Two weeks after Stephen's release, Jennings decided to contact McGeough to enquire as to John Moyo's position.

The two men were guarded in their conversation.

'Hello, Ken. Any word on what is to happen to John Moyo? I am going to be talking to Stephen later, and I know he would want an update.'

'There have been some developments, all right,' McGeough replied. 'We have been able to persuade John that it would be in his best interest to enter a plea to the charge of murder and take his chances in the Irish prison system, rather than be deported to Zimbabwe post-conviction. He is under no illusion that if he were to be sent back anytime soon, his life expectancy would be dramatically reduced.'

'Well, that is something, I suppose. How are you going to deal with events up in Belfast?'

'A fairly sanitised version will be provided, but he is still looking at the mandatory life sentence for the priest's killing. There are some things we are working on with him, and if he comes up with what we are hoping for, he will be looking at the possibility of an early parole. He has something to look forward to. In ten or twelve years, he should be able to go back to Zimbabwe, or even stay here if what he claims he can give us proves correct.'

'What has brought on his sudden desire to be helpful?' Jennings asked. 'The last time I saw him, he seemed fairly belligerent.'

'The word on the street was that he was a marked man for what happened up in Belfast. We had credible intelligence that a contract had been put out on him on, and that focused his attention. He at least has some chance of survival in prison if he cooperates with us, but without our backing, he would be a dead man walking.'

'And what about Stephen? Is he under threat?'

'There is nothing to suggest that, Richard. I understand he is planning on going back to Zimbabwe. It might be safer for him to stay here, but he does not strike me as a man who would scare easily.'

'You are right there,' Jennings agreed. 'There is one other thing I need to ask you about, though. Eammon Hughes had been working on the late priest's estate and a very substantial anonymous donation was made to the trust days after the trial of Moyo had collapsed. You would not know anything about that, I suppose?'

'I know nothing about any donation, Richard,' McGeough replied. 'If it is going to be used for a good cause, just take it for what it is.'

It was clear Jennings was going to get nothing more from McGeough, and their conversation ended with a promise from McGeough to keep him up to date with any developments on Moyo's trial.

Jennings had arranged for Stephen's flight to Zimbabwe, and his appointment was to discuss his return to Zimbabwe. Jennings intended to go out to Zimbabwe to assist in interring the ashes of Father O'Meara, but Stephen was anxious to return as soon as possible.

Moyo had come into the office, and after a brief discussion about what Jennings had been told by McGeough regarding John, the pair shook hands and Moyo made his way out of the office. It was only after he had gone, and Jennings returned to his desk that Jennings realised he had not given Moyo his copy of the probate papers. He decided he had better chase after him to pass these on, so that Moyo could study them on his journey home.

As he entered onto Abbey Street, Jennings saw Moyo walking away from him in the direction of O'Connell Street. In view of the LUAS tracks, the road was closed to general traffic. Apart from delivery vehicles, there was usually no other traffic on this section of the road. Jennings was surprised to see a black BMW approaching from O'Connell Street, and he was even more surprised when he saw it swerve across the street and stop opposite Moyo.

Surprise turned to shock as Jennings saw the barrel of an automatic rifle appear from the rear window of the car. As Jennings heard the sharp crack of gunfire, he saw Moyo stagger backward under the impact of a number of shots. Moyo sank to his knees and collapsed as the BMW accelerated away amidst the sound of screams from nearby pedestrians.

Jennings sprinted to Moyo, fell to his side on the pavement, and turned him over. He could see that Moyo was badly wounded, and as he tried to raise his shoulders, the wounded man coughed up blood, which covered Jennings's hands.

Moyo looked into Jennings' eyes and tried to speak. Jennings held him close to his chest and said, 'Hang on, Stephen. We will have help soon. Don't try to talk.' He frantically looked round to see if in fact any help was on its way.

Even though he had to be in pain, Stephen Moyo smiled and said, 'It is all right, Richard. I have friends here with me now. It is time for me to join them.'

Moyo coughed again and then said in a clear voice as his eyes began to glaze over, 'Richard, I can smell the rain again. I am going home now, aren't I?'

Jennings could barely speak as the tears ran down his cheeks. He held Moyo as he heard sirens approach. 'You are, Stephen. You are going home.'

The End

ABOUT THE AUTHOR

Born and raised in what was then Rhodesia, Tony qualified as a Barrister in 1978. He was a public prosecutor and prosecuted crimes in the lower courts before being promoted to the Office of the Director of Public Prosecution, where he prosecuted more serious crimes such as murder, rape, and security-related crimes.

He was an in house legal Counsel and subsequently returned to practise as a barrister for several years. He appeared in a number of high-profile criminal trials

He then practised as a solicitor from 1986 in the capital Harare, and from 1989 in the city of Mutare in Zimbabwe, before leaving Zimbabwe and coming to Ireland in 2001

Tony worked in the newly formed Office of the Chief Prosecution Solicitor in Dublin and was engaged in prosecutions in the Dublin Circuit and Central Criminal Court before leaving to go back to private practice. He is the principal of his firm, Tony Donagher, Solicitor, based in Carrickmacross County, Monaghan, where he lives with his wife, Cheryl. His son, Ryan, is also a resident of Carrickmacross and is the Director of Golf at Castleknock Golf Club in Dublin.

Lightning Source UK Ltd.
Milton Keynes UK
UKHW01f1935180518
322855UK00001B/62/P